Sophie Draper won the Bath Novel Award 2017 with this novel. She also won the Friday Night Live competition at the York Festival of Writing 2017. She lives in Derbyshire, where the story is set, and under the name Sophie Snell works as a traditional oral storyteller.

The Stranger in our Home

Sophie Draper

Published by AVON
A division of HarperCollins*Publishers* Ltd
1 London Bridge Street
London SE1 9GF

www.harpercollins.co.uk

A Paperback Original 2019

First published as *Cuckoo* in Great Britain by HarperCollins*Publishers* 2018

Copyright © Sophie Draper 2018

Sophie Draper asserts the moral right to
be identified as the author of this work.

A catalogue copy of this book is available from the British Library.

ISBN: 978-0-00-832045-4

Typeset in Minion by
Palimpsest Book Production Limited, Falkirk, Stirlingshire

Printed and bound in the United States of America
by LSC Communications

For more information visit: www.harpercollins.co.uk/green

19 20 21 22 LSC 10 9 8 7 6 5 4 3 2 1

For my parents.

PROLOGUE

I am floating between two worlds, the living and the dead. As I lie here in my hospital bed, the faces shimmer above, voices distant and unfamiliar.

Slowly I return. I cannot move. I am a doll, placed exactly as they choose. They're quite unaware that I'm awake, that I can see and hear – the machines, the trolleys on their wheels, the tubes wriggling from body to bed, the clicks and beeps that mark each breath, each beat a ticking clock, each sigh discharged as if my last.

Today I can see the table. Someone places a small painting beside me. It shows a boy. He sits on a grave under a tree, ivy coiled around his feet. He holds a pear drum.

I know this object. Not a *drum*, but something else. The shape appals me, a large pear-shaped box, too big for the boy's lap. The strings that stretch across, the handle at one end, the strange creatures painted on the side. An instrument. It plays the devil's music. My heart jolts, leaping against my ribs, hammering like a condemned man. The machines fill my lungs with air. I feel my chest expand, stretching until it is so taut I think my body will burst. But no, the machines deflate. Once more I hear their steady beat. I watch the drip, drip of the feed that punctures my arm and my consciousness fades away.

When I wake, I hear hushed tones, regret. They're talking about me. My mind is surging, willing myself to move, to make one small sign that I'm alive. But the feeling dissipates like smoke in a chimney. I watch the boy. He winds the handle on the pear drum, round and round . . .

The hours turn into days, then weeks, time sliding between each heartbeat. Slowly memory returns. When I see the sky, it's white or grey, reflections of the room bouncing off the window glass. And black. Sometimes against the grey is the tiniest streak of black, one small bird buffeted by an invisible wind.

As I lie in this bed, they all think I am as good as dead.

Except I am not dead – not yet. How disappointed they must be.

CHAPTER 1

She was watching me, my golden sister. Her eyes were dark; her hair long. She stood opposite me on the far side of the grave.

The black earth stained my fingers. I folded them in as if to hide the weight of the clump of soil sitting in my hand, damp and clammy against my skin.

My sister had come, despite all expectation.

She held her head upright and her gaze was unwavering. The flaps of her calf-length coat were caught by the wind, revealing a flash of red, her dress, her perfect legs sliding down into perfect shoes, heels sinking into the thick grass. I pressed my lips together and lowered my head. She was like a designer handbag lit up in a shop window on the King's Road, glossy and beautiful and out of reach.

My stepmother's funeral was a quiet affair. The small churchyard clung to a slope on the edge of Larkstone village, gravestones like broken teeth, the surrounding hills of Derbyshire cloaked in a fine drizzle that seeped through the thin cloth of my coat. There were a few neighbours, a bearded man standing on his own and an older woman dressed in black silk. I felt as though I should know her. I tilted my head. Her husband stood behind with an umbrella slick with rain and she turned away from me.

And there was my sister, Steph, in her red dress. She had bowed her head too and I could no longer see her face. The wind blew my hair over my eyes, tangling against the wet on my cheek. I let my eyelids close.

I flinched as that first clump of earth hit the coffin below.

I tried to concentrate on the vicar's words, his voice. I took a peek. He held his prayer book with hands that were open and expressive. His skin was smooth and brown and he spoke with a clear, cultured accent. Not a local. I wondered then what the village thought of him. I wanted to smile at him, but he was too engrossed in the service. As I should have been.

'Let us commend Elizabeth Crowther to the mercy of God, our maker and . . .'

Crowther. It still hurt. My stepmother had taken my father's name, my mother's name, along with everything else.

'. . . we now commit her body to the ground: earth to earth . . .'

Another clod of black sodden earth hit the coffin. I reached forward and opened my hand.

'. . . in sure and certain hope . . .'

What hope? My lips tightened. I was not, had never been, a believer.

'. . . To him be glory for ever.'

4

More earth tumbled down into the grave. The vicar lowered his head again, we all did, as he intoned a prayer. I kept my eyes open. It was cold, the air spiced with rotting leaves and autumn smoke. A single bee struggled against the wind to land on the cellophaned flowers at our feet. It looked so out of place, late in the year. I watched it hover, a dust of yellow pollen clustered under its belly, tiny feet dangling beneath, oblivious to the drama playing out above.

I risked another look at my sister. I felt a kindling of old fear. She lifted her head and our eyes met and I drew a staggered breath.

Steph.

The back room of the pub was half empty, the walls a dank musty brown, the ceilings punctuated by low beams riddled with defunct woodworm holes. Decorative tankards hung like dead starlings from their hooks and beneath, a cold buffet was laid out on white linen with the usual egg mayonnaise sandwiches and hollowed-out vol-au-vents. An elderly neighbour cruised down the table with its foil trays, prodding this and that as she loaded up her plate.

My sister kept her distance, nibbling on a sandwich, talking to the vicar. A stack of blackened logs in the grate behind them spat and hissed without any sign of a flame. Her blue eyes fluttered across me as I stood on the other side of the room. She was waiting, I realised. Waiting to see what I would do.

I felt my chest tighten, the hands at my side clench. I thought perhaps I should forgive her, that I should be the one to go over and talk to *her*. Beyond the function room, I could hear the bellow of a man at the bar, the recurrent beeps of a slot machine by the entrance and the slash of rain battering the front door as it juddered open and closed again.

'Hello,' I said as I approached. My voice was husky and unsure.

'Caro.'

Her voice surprised me. It had a distinctive New York drawl. The tone was gentle. If it was meant to encourage me, it had the opposite effect. I didn't reply. I could hardly bear to meet her eyes. The vicar moved on, scarcely acknowledging me.

Then Steph put her glass down. Her body relaxed, her arms opened. I wanted to step closer, but my feet refused to move. We hugged, a loose, cautious kind of hug, her pale, flawless cheek brushing cool against my skin.

'I didn't think you'd come,' I said.

'I almost didn't, but then I thought, why should I let *her* stop me? She's gone.' Those long vowels again, so alien to me. But then it had been many years since I'd last heard her voice. 'And I wanted to see you. You're my sister.' Steph's expression was cautious, assessing my response.

'I . . . I . . .' *Now* I was her sister?

'I've seen your website, your illustrations. They look amazing!'

'Really?' I said. I pulled myself up, keeping my tone light and neutral.

'Yes, really. I love *The Little Urchin*, with her spiky hair, her nose pressed up against the window.'

My latest book. It was a compliment. I hadn't remembered her ever giving me a compliment, not when I was little. But Steph's face was open and sincere. She was different to how I remembered. I wanted to believe.

'You're very talented, you know, I always knew you would be creative,' she said.

'Oh, well, um . . .' Praise indeed, to hear that from my big sister.

'I mean it. I could never do something like that.' She smiled. Her arms waved expansively and her coat parted, another glimpse of red.

I shrugged. 'Thank you.'

She'd cared enough to look me up, when had she done that? It was unexpected. I was suddenly conscious that I knew very little about her, what she did for a living. Was she married? Did she have children? I didn't even know that. She was seven years older than me and it was quite possible that she had a family of her own by now. I eyed her flat stomach, the clothes. No, I thought, no children. Somehow, I couldn't see her with children.

A movement caught at the corner of my eye, the curtains at one of the windows flapping in a draught from a broken pane.

'Can we go somewhere else?' Steph's voice dropped. 'Anywhere you like, but not here.'

I swallowed. It made sense to refuse, my head screaming at me to walk away. It was almost twenty years since she'd left home, when I was nine. She'd been sixteen. We'd had no contact at all since then, despite all my attempts to stay in touch. Christmas, birthdays, they'd meant nothing. Perhaps my early cards had ended up at the wrong address.

But I wanted to. I really did.

'Yes,' I said.

* * *

7

'I got a job at a hotel in London, manning reception.'

My sister's voice was measured and quiet. I could imagine her smart and sleek behind a desk.

We'd found a café in the small town of Ashbourne a few miles away. The smell of freshly ground coffee beans and vanilla seedpods cut across the muted chatter in the room and I lifted my cup to hold its warmth against my fingers.

'Then they offered me a job in the marketing department.'

She flicked her hair across her shoulders. Blonde, but no roots – it had been brown when we were young. She must have dyed it, I thought.

'I moved to Head Office and worked my way up. Then I joined the US team. I've been based in New York now for six years.'

There was a pause. Her eyes travelled across my thin, gawky frame. Six years. In New York. Yet there had been so many more years when she'd been in London, in the UK. Close enough and yet so far. I didn't reply, struggling to find a common ground.

We both took another sip from our respective drinks. The traffic beeped through the glass window, a sludge of rainwater washing onto the pavement, green and red traffic lights reflected in the puddles. Colours, I saw everything in colours.

'And you? Where did you study?' Steph leaned in over her cup.

'Manchester. Art and Creative Design.' I tucked my fingers into the palms of my hands, feeling my short nails scratch against my skin.

'Really? I somehow thought you'd have gone as far as possible from Derbyshire.'

I bristled. Manchester was only an hour and a half from the village by car, but by bus and coach it was much longer, and you still had to get from the house at Larkstone Farm to the village bus stop. Manchester had seemed a million miles away. The bustling big city, new people, a whole new life.

'Did you enjoy it?' she asked.

'Yes, I did. The course was brilliant.'

I side-stepped the truth: my self-imposed isolation; my lack of confidence; my distant manner.

'I'm glad.' Steph stretched out the fingers of her hand, wriggling each one before folding them back into her palm.

There was another silence.

'And now you're in London. Bet it's nice being self-employed, working whenever you want.' She smiled encouragingly.

'Hmmm, depends how you look at it. There are so many other illustrators out there, vying for the same jobs for not much pay. It's not an easy way to make a living.'

Already I was saying too much, filling the space with words, justifying my own ineptitude. Why should I feel defensive?

'I can imagine.' My sister nodded, sipping her coffee again. There was a soft chink as she placed the cup carefully back on its saucer. A waft of perfume made me lift my head up. I wasn't a fan of any kind of perfume.

'How did it happen?' Steph's voice broke.

I flashed a look of surprise at her. Did she even care? I scanned her face, the perfect arch of her eyebrows, the smooth forehead, no lines, as if she never frowned, or even smiled. Like a Greek statue, head turned away, poised in her indifference. Except . . . the voice was at odds with her face.

'They didn't tell me anything,' she said.

It had been the family lawyer who'd made the call to her. I felt a pang of guilt.

'I'm sorry I didn't ring. But I didn't have your address or a telephone number. It was the lawyers that tracked you down.'

They'd organised the whole thing, the funeral, the reception, much to my relief. They'd rung me too.

'That's alright, I understand.' Steph watched me still, ignoring the implied criticism, waiting for an answer.

I threw a glance at the neighbouring tables, but the occupants were all too engrossed in their conversations to pay any attention to ours. I drew a breath, bringing my hand up to my head, thrusting my fingers into my hair.

'I . . . that is, she . . . she fell,' I said. 'Over the banisters from the first floor. Some time during the morning, they said, though apparently she was still in her dressing gown.'

'How could she fall over the banisters?' Steph asked.

'I don't know. Some kind of accident, I was told. She was found face down on the rug in the hall below. Broken neck. Bit of a mess.'

I thought it best to stop there.

'Ah.' Steph hesitated. She cast her eyes to her lap, folding her napkin.

Then she reached out a hand, covering my own. 'So, it's only us now.'

I nodded. My eyes searched the fine cracks on the back of her hand. Expert make-up could disguise an older face, but not the hands.

'Yes,' I mumbled. 'It is.'

'I'm in London after this, for a few weeks at least, in a hotel near Tottenham Court Road.' She drew a breath. 'Can we start again?'

I looked up.

'It's been too long, I know.' Her hand was cool over mine, her face earnest.

I held my hand still, resisting the urge to move it. I really did want to believe this different Steph. What had happened to her? I'd never understood whatever it was that had gone on between us. Or between her and Elizabeth.

Her eyes held mine. They were blue. Mine were brown. The street lights wobbled in the wet glass of the café windows, amber yellow.

Steph's lips parted.

I nodded again. 'Yes.'

I thought of my stepmother. I tried to picture her body lying on the hall floor. The blood smeared on her lips, pooling on the rug, her red-painted face still smiling, as if to say, as she'd often said:

'*Shall we start again, Caroline?*'

CHAPTER 2

The phone rang.

'Caro?' It was Steph. She'd promised to ring before she left the UK. I was back home in London and hadn't heard a thing for days and now suddenly there she was.

'Hi.' I could hear crackling over the phone line.

'Fancy a curry? My treat.'

I caught my breath. 'That sounds great. When?'

'Tonight? We need to talk.' She named a restaurant.

'Sure, what time?'

'Seven.'

'Okay.'

I put the phone down slowly. It felt strange talking to my sister like that, as if we were friends.

* * *

We met up, Steph and I, in a curry house behind Leicester Square. We chatted about not very much, avoiding anything to do with the funeral or our childhood.

'My office is amazing, in one of those skyscrapers overlooking Central Park. I thought I'd faint when I first looked out of the window and realised how high we were!'

I found myself following each word, each lift of an eyebrow, each smile, wondering what Steph was really saying as she talked about her work, her apartment in New York, the glamour of Fifth Avenue boutiques and constant traffic, flashing advertising boards leaching light into a sleepless city sky. Look at me, she was saying, how fabulous my life is, how lucky I am – unlike you, my *little* sister. That's what she was really saying, wasn't she? I caught my bottom lip between my teeth. I didn't want to feel like this. I wanted Steph to be my friend, to be my sister.

It was the end of the meal when Steph finally brought it up.

'What about the house?' she said.

'Larkstone Farm?'

The house where we grew up. I couldn't call it home. The waiter was hovering, leaning in to whisk away a plate, his eyes sliding down towards Steph's long legs.

'Yes. It's sitting there empty. It's not good for the place. And someone's going to have to go through all that stuff, sort out the paperwork, ready the house for sale. Unless you want to move back up there?'

'I don't understand.'

'It's ours. Except I don't want it. Why would I ever want to go back to that place!' She sounded bitter. 'Besides, my home is in the States now. I'm seeing this guy . . . But you

– you could go back and live there.' She hesitated. 'If you wanted.'

'Ours? I don't get it. I mean, Elizabeth had a cousin, didn't she? It wouldn't come to us, surely? We were only her step-daughters.'

'No, that's not how Dad arranged it. I went to see the lawyer. When Dad married Elizabeth, he set up a trust. Elizabeth didn't own the house after he died. She had use of it whilst she was alive, but it reverts to us on her death.'

My sister's words sank in. And then the thought flashed into my head: she'd been to see the lawyer, on her own? But then hadn't I been avoiding it myself? I hadn't wanted to think about the house, all that stuff that had once been Elizabeth's, that had once been my dad's.

'We'll inherit the house?' I said. *The two of us?*

I sat up. I couldn't quite believe what she was saying.

'Yes. Except, like I said, I don't want any of it. It's been on my mind a lot ever since I found out, I didn't know what to say to you. But I realise now that I really don't need it. My life's in New York and I have more than enough money. It's the least I can do. Besides, the funeral was bad enough, I couldn't bear to go back to the house itself, even for a short while.'

She fell silent. There was a moment when I thought she was going to say something else.

'I don't know what to say.' My eyes searched hers.

She shrugged and then smiled.

'It's not much of a place, as I recall – probably in desperate need of attention, in the middle of nowhere. I don't have time for a project like that. It's yours, honestly. Sell it, keep it, rent it out, move in. I don't mind. Whatever you want to do with it.'

Larkstone Farm. Compared to London, it *was* the middle

of nowhere. In the wilds of Derbyshire. It wasn't a working farm, not any more; I couldn't remember whether it still had any land. Steph leaned across the table and topped up my glass of wine.

But *live* at Larkstone Farm? It seemed incredible that this should happen right now. I was effectively homeless, bunking down with my friend Harriet, except she'd already left for her new job in Berlin. I had a few more weeks till the notice on her flat ran out. She'd done me a favour, but I was still struggling to find somewhere else affordable.

'I . . .' I tried to gather my thoughts. 'What did the lawyer say, did you tell him?'

'I did. It's entirely up to us what we do with the place. But whether you move in or sell up, it has to be cleared of all her stuff. And someone really should be there whilst that is happening, if only to keep an eye on things. If you want it, it's yours, that's all I'm saying. And I'd be glad not to worry about it.'

My mind leapt ahead. I could sell it, buy something smaller, closer to London, giving me some cash to fall back on when the commissions slowed down. Or I could live there whilst I decided what I wanted to do. Now that Elizabeth was gone, why shouldn't I stay there? It was just a house. To live rent-free would be a huge relief. Did Steph really want to waive her inheritance?

And besides . . . Maybe I needed to go back, to see the place just one more time, to put the past behind me once and for all. Elizabeth was dead. I was never going back to Paul and I'd had more than enough of London with its sky-high rents and unaffordable houses. I could work wherever I was, couldn't I?

The thought was exciting, the timing perfect.

'Why don't you think about it?' said Steph.

Elizabeth had married my father when I was a baby, not long after my real mother died. I should have been young enough to think of her as my mother, but somehow I never did. She used to say how I screamed and screamed in her arms, wriggling to get out. Perhaps it was my fault. I had rejected Elizabeth before she'd ever rejected me. Then my father had died too, barely four years later, leaving Steph and me with Elizabeth, growing up at Larkstone Farm. Just the three of us.

As I sat at my painting table, back in Harriet's basement flat, I could hardly bear to dwell on it. The house, my childhood, my old life in Derbyshire.

I looked up through the window, the one that faced the street. I could see the feet of the passers-by, boots and shoes slapping against the pavement, buggies rolling in the wet, listening to the steady swish of cars cruising down the road. The temperature had dropped since the funeral at the beginning of the month, the first bite of winter in November – so early.

Derbyshire was something I'd pushed to the back of my mind. There, where the rain fell straight and sharp, like needles on your back, punishing. In London it ran along the paving slabs, splashing into gullies, a smooth plane of water brimming with dirt, lapping at your feet. I'd never gone back, not after that first day I went to university. I'd never wanted to go back.

The laptop to my side chimed. I couldn't resist a quick check. London, it was the life I'd chosen to lead, but it was hard being on my own, here in the midst of all these people.

It was an email from David, my agent.

Dear Caro. Great news, you've had an enquiry for a commission to illustrate for Cuillin Books. It's a collection of fairy tales. Now that should be right up your street. The brief and the text are attached. You've got about three months to do it. Let me know what you think? D.

I wriggled in my seat and tapped a reply.

Dear David, that sounds promising. I'll take a look and let you know.

I liked to play it cool, but the truth was it was unlikely I'd have turned it down, whatever it was. Fairy tales, though. He was right about that; I had a soft spot for fairy tales. I clicked on the file. Then I saw the title.

The Pear Drum and Other Dark Tales from the Nursery.

The Pear Drum.

My fingers halted in mid-air. I felt my stomach heave. It filled my head; the words, each letter a different colour like bulbs around a make-up mirror. And the thing itself, as vivid as the day I first saw it, my stepmother's pear drum.

I snapped the laptop lid down onto its keyboard, stood up and walked away.

Later, I tried to view it dispassionately. *The Pear Drum and Other Dark Tales from the Nursery.* It was an odd title for a book of fairy tales. A bit of a mouthful and not the kind of thing you'd give to a young child. It seemed strange that it should appear in my inbox now, after Elizabeth's funeral, prodding my memories of the past.

I closed my eyes, the words leaping out at me despite my attempts to distance myself. *Pear Drum.*

The pear drum was something I had deliberately buried in the past. But it was always there, a part of me I could not shift, hidden in a corner of my consciousness. Perhaps that was why I'd ended up in London – as far away from Derbyshire as possible. I was beyond that now. Time had passed.

I would have been about six years old when I first saw the pear drum. I wasn't sure. The memories of my childhood had always been patchy, especially those first years. But this was perhaps my earliest memory. It was like a black curtain – before the pear drum, after the pear drum. I tried not to think about it too much.

We'd just come home, after some kind of family gathering. Elizabeth was dressed in black linen, pearls about her neck. Elegant – she'd always been elegant. She'd dropped her handbag onto the hall table and grabbed my tiny hand. She pulled me into my father's old study, long painted fingernails overlapping about my wrist. The room was at the back of the house, behind the stairs. I knew it had been my father's room from the pictures on the wall, the bookcase and the desk by the window. An armchair was positioned beside the fireplace, the stove blackened with age, the iron griddle top layered with dust. My stepmother didn't normally use this room.

In the corner furthest away from the window stood a crate, large enough to hide a child in. I pulled back, reluctant to let myself be dragged any further.

'Stop that caterwauling, Caroline!' I must have been crying already. 'It's time I showed you something!'

Elizabeth let go of my wrist and I stood there shivering, the scent of her perfume conflicting with the lingering smell of old leather and damp unloved books. She was already dragging the lid of the crate open, fingers pulling at the double catch, resting the weight of the lid against the wall. Her arms reached inside and I swear I thought there was a dead body within.

But what she brought out from the crate was the pear drum.

It wasn't a drum at all. It was like a mechanical violin, or 'hurdy-gurdy'. Its real name, as I discovered later, was 'organistrum', but Elizabeth had always called it her pear drum.

It had a pear-shaped body with strings and a broad, over-sized decorative arm. At the wide end was an S-shaped handle which turned a wheel against the strings. But the arm was actually a box into which the strings disappeared. It could be opened to reveal the workings inside, the keys, the 'little people', my stepmother had called them. Pressing down on the pegs alongside the box made them dance, creating the notes.

She adjusted the shape of the thing onto her lap as she sat down on my father's old chair. It was so big each end rested on the chair arms on either side of her. She began turning the handle and the thing fired up. I almost jumped at the sound. It was a drone, hesitant at first. It got louder, a vile, screeching sound that filled the room, forcing me to step back and clasp my hands against my ears. But as I listened, the sound consumed me; loud as it was, it was seductive too, a slow lingering melody filling the room.

It was the weirdest kind of musical instrument you could ever have thought of. But the pear drum wasn't the problem. It was the story that went with it.

CHAPTER 3

The M1 stretched out in front of me – endless tarmac, sweeping clouds, the trees bordering the roadside skeletal black. London was behind me. It hadn't taken so long to leave.

It should have surprised me, the ease with which I'd turned my back on so many years in London. Except it did not. Never mind Paul, it was as if I'd been waiting for an excuse, my sudden inheritance prodding my inertia. I'd been in London seven years – didn't they say that life moves in cycles of seven years?

It wasn't like anyone was going to miss me. Not Paul at any rate. He and I were done and I certainly wasn't going to miss him. I missed Harriet, though – I'd just started to get to know her. We'd met at my first public exhibition. She'd been loud and brash and I'd been quiet and shy. She'd made me laugh and she'd said my paintings made her cry. She'd been the voice of reason telling me to get out of there when things had gone so badly with Paul. Her generosity and kindness when I'd needed somewhere to go wasn't something I was used to. I'd never told her about Larkstone.

She'd been full of remorse over her job in Germany.

'I can't leave you like this,' she'd said.

'Yes, you can,' I replied. 'Absolutely, you can. I got out of there and I have a new life. You've been amazing, but now it's your turn to follow your dreams.'

Harriet had been offered a job in a gallery in Berlin, a chance to experience a new country, to take her own work in a different direction – how could she turn that down? Perhaps that was why the time was right. I had a few friends, work contacts, fellow artists I'd met like Harriet, but no one close. I liked it like that. In an odd sort of way, I was glad she was gone. It was easier keeping people at a distance. I completely understood why Steph had ended up in New York and had never wanted to go back to Derbyshire.

But meeting and getting to know Harriet had made me think. She wasn't afraid to start again. To brave a new life, to put the past behind her. Leaving the noise and traffic of London felt to me like a snake shedding its old dead skin. I'd packed up everything I had, handed in Harriet's keys, and here I was, on my way to Derbyshire. I had a new commission to work on as well as the house clearance and, for the moment at least, it was to be my new home.

I lifted my back, flicking on the windscreen wipers as sleet began to slap against the car windows.

Eventually, I turned onto the dual carriageway that led into Derby. The sleet and rain had stopped and there was a break in the clouds through which the sun shone, lighting up the roofs of the houses. The city was a tangle of incomprehensible ring roads and roadworks, but twenty minutes later I was free of it, heading down country lanes, chasing the shadows of the growing dusk.

The village of Larkstone was quiet, a few rainbow Christmas lights blinking on the street. I drove slowly, looking for the right turning back into the countryside. A couple of pedestrians dived across the road, heads bowed against the wind. It was even colder now that the brief sun was lower in the sky.

Someone beeped from behind. A man in a muddy jeep. He was far too close. He beeped again. I touched the brake pedal, enough to trigger the lights. It had the desired effect. In the mirror, I saw his hands gripping the steering wheel, his face scowling. A woman on the street stopped as our two cars drove past. Her expression was fierce, it took me aback, until she broke into a smile, waving at the man in the jeep. I carried on. I felt a surge of satisfaction as the jeep was forced to follow me out of the village, tailing me for a couple of miles until I slowed for the house. The jeep growled up a gear, swerving around me as it accelerated away and down the lane.

The house was at the end of a track, on a hill overlooking the valley. Tall chimneys stood proud against an unexpected blazing sunset sky. I peered through the windscreen, my teeth catching on my lower lip.

It was a tall building, hewn from thick Derbyshire stone, part farmhouse, part fortified manor house. The second-floor windows were tucked in under the eaves and one small attic window peeped out from the tiles above. All the windows were an empty black, save for a glint of red at the top where the last rays of the sun reflected off the glass. A low wall enclosed the front courtyard and two semi-derelict outbuildings sheltered behind. I drove the car forward the last few metres, its wheels skidding over the gravel, spitting stones as it came to a halt.

I sat in my seat, watching the last of the daylight playing on the colours in the stone. Already a picture was forming in my head: the house inked out in black lines on its hill, angry colours exploding in the background, windows like bullet holes peppering the walls. My fingers itched to draw. I felt a strange kind of lift. The house, its history, its memories, it was like I needed this. Elizabeth's death was a fresh start, for me and Steph, and the house.

I slammed the car door shut and searched in my handbag for the key the lawyers had sent.

Something soft touched my ankles. I yelped in surprise. It was a cat, her head rubbing against my legs. I reached down and she seemed content to let me draw my fingers through her fur.

'Hello there, Puss.'

She was small and black, save for a single white sock on her front paw. Half-starved by the look of her. I made to pick her up but that was too much. She skittered away, jumping onto the wall to look at me reproachfully.

'Okay, fair enough,' I said, fingers finding the keys.

I swung round towards the house. Water stained the front step and dripped from the leaves of the shrubbery around me. A security light bounced on as I stepped up to the door and the key turned smoothly in the lock. The house, it seemed, didn't know whether I was friend or foe.

It smelt stale as I entered. I snapped the switch on the wall. The hallway was instantly familiar, the smell, the clock, the objects around me. The walls were lined with paintings, scenes of rural Derbyshire, the crags at Mam Tor, a pheasant stalking a field; it was all as I remembered, except somehow different. There was a space on the wall marked by a dirty grey outline where a picture had once hung and the hall table with its two drawers was thick with dust – even the cut-glass bowl that sat on top was grimy with dirt. How long had it been like that? Longer than the six or seven weeks since Elizabeth's death in the middle of October. The house mouldered in genteel neglect and I felt a prickle of unease; my stepmother had been fastidious in her housekeeping when I was younger.

Two rooms led from each side of the hall and a wide staircase hugged the back elevation. A tall window overlooked the stairwell and my eyes were drawn to the banister above. Its richly polished wood curved up to the first and second floors. A patterned rug sprawled on the stone floor beneath, a rust-red stain at its centre. I felt my chest contract. Why hadn't someone taken it away? It was a stark reminder of the manner of my stepmother's death.

I wondered how she'd fallen. With a piercing scream, or a silent thud? They'd said it had been an accident. Had it been a sleepless night blundering in the dark? No, hadn't they said morning? I couldn't imagine how someone could fall over a banister. They'd also said there'd been signs of excess alcohol in her system. When had Elizabeth started to drink? I tried to feel sympathy for her, gawping at the stain, fascination and horror holding me still, the rug a simple testament to Elizabeth's death.

I moved forwards, snapping on all the switches I could find, flooding the house with light, determined to chase away the ghosts.

* * *

An hour later the Aga in the kitchen creaked as heat seeped into its old bones. A table dominated the room, perfect for painting. I slung my last box onto the wooden worktop. Fishing out the contents – tubes, brushes, small tins and cloths – I lined them up like precious toys, spacing out each item. Next came the laptop, phone, dongle and printer, juggling cables until they trailed across to the sockets and my emails filled the screen. A welcome connection to the outside world. Not quite so alone.

I returned to the hall. All my possessions stood in pathetic isolation, dwarfed by the grandeur of the house and the triple-height ceiling over the stairs.

In the sitting room I found Laura Ashley florals, scented candles and a TV. This was where my stepmother sat, on the big sofa, her favourite blanket neatly folded on its arm. I snatched it up, striding from the house to dump it in the bin. Adrenalin fired in my veins. I swept through the entire ground floor, harvesting photos, magazines and papers, soap and towels, even a stray cardigan from the kitchen, still smelling of *her* – I held it between my fingers and dropped it into a black bin bag as if it were contaminated.

I had to drag the rug from the hall out the front door. It was a heavy wool and felt as if a body were rolled up inside. The thought was almost comical, except it made me nauseous. I felt guilty, as if it were my fault, as if I'd killed Elizabeth myself and was now removing the evidence. It made no sense, but the feeling was there, with every item that I found, soiled by her touch, her scent, her sweat, her very blood.

The purge had only started, but it was enough for now. The rest, including upstairs, would have to wait. I scrubbed my hands, ate the remains of a pot of salad, fetched my duvet and climbed onto the sofa. I tried to sleep, lying there too aware of the size of the house, the emptiness of the rooms above my head, the wind whistling at the windows outside and the clock ticking in the hall.

The cat was there again in the morning, sitting on the window sill outside. Behind her hung a pall of winter mist. She watched me through the glass. I pretended not to notice. Her head turned as she tracked my movements, her eyes blinking with curiosity. I scrounged a cup of coffee from a jar in the kitchen, standing in the midst of more of Elizabeth's stuff, things I'd missed the night before – a basket of unwashed clothes, newspapers, scribbled Post-it notes stuck to the fridge – the kind of clutter that fills every house. I sighed. I'd had no actual plan for the day, but now I set to work, once more focusing on the ground floor.

I couldn't face upstairs, the bedrooms on the first floor – Elizabeth's, Steph's – and my old room on the top floor. Not yet. As I worked, I didn't want to think of Elizabeth, so I tried to remember Steph instead. In the hall, I paused to look up the stairs.

She'd been a girly girl. Not like me. Her dressing table with its big mirror had been her pride and joy, crammed with make-up and brushes, hair tongs and all the paraphernalia of beauty. I might have been younger than her but even when I was older I never knew what to do with all that stuff. I wanted to paint real pictures, not myself.

'Caroline!'

A voice fired across my thoughts. A memory of *her* voice. Elizabeth. Sharp and cultured and authoritative. I was standing at the bottom of the stairs, dithering about going up. My hand was on the polished balustrade, and I could clearly remember that voice, calling me from the bottom of the stairs.

'*Come here!*'

I'd been in my room, right at the top. Maybe seven or eight years old? I'd put my book back onto the bed and slid reluctantly from the covers.

'Caroline!'

I was wearing only knickers and a vest as I stood at the top of the stairs, my short bare legs pale white against the shadows of the upper floor. Elizabeth was on the landing below, outside her bedroom door, silhouetted against a blaze of yellow sunshine. Steph was in her bedroom, opposite Elizabeth's, sitting at her dressing table. She was applying eye shadow and the door was open so she could hear every word.

'Come here, Caroline!' Elizabeth again.

I descended the stairs until I was standing right in front of her, rubbing the sweat on the palms of my small hands against my thighs, as I always did when she called me to her.

'Look at you. Can't you even be bothered to get dressed?' Elizabeth snorted.

She seemed so tall and elegant and I stood there not daring to look up.

The slap whipped against my face, throwing my head backwards. It brought tears to my eyes, the sting of it burning on my skin. Elizabeth bent down to look at me, her face within inches of my own. She spoke loud and slow, as if I was particularly dim.

'Get . . . dressed . . .' She turned away. 'You disgust me, Caroline.'

My hand had reached out for the banister, my fingers too small to meet around the wood. I glanced up and Steph caught my eye. I could feel my cheek stinging. Elizabeth was still within earshot and Steph hadn't said a word, her blue eyes watching me as I climbed the stairs again.

My stomach growled. I'd scarcely brought any provisions from London. I needed food, so I decided to check out the village shops. Perhaps it was also an excuse to get out. The car bumped along the lanes and I parked alongside the village green, sandwiched between an old Ford Escort and a gleaming black and silver motorbike.

Larkstone wasn't exactly a thriving commercial centre. Eight miles north of Ashbourne, it was too off the beaten track to be particularly touristy, but it had a pub, a Co-op and a butcher's. I wondered if I would recognise anyone, or more likely if anyone would recognise me. It had been ten years since I'd left for uni. As I walked along the street, I saw roads and terraced cottages juxtaposed by uneven pavements. An old-fashioned but familiar lamppost stood on the corner by the Co-op, black paint peeling from its length. Still lit, a flare of white highlighted the mist that floated around it. That lamp had obsessed me; I'd sketched it over and over again when I was at school. Even later, when I was at uni, I would draw it from memory; there was something about the shape of it, the repeated glass, the cracks in the panes, the state of decay. I dragged my eyes away from it. Villages had a way of holding onto the past in this part of Derbyshire.

I went to the butcher's first. The shop had the dull metallic stench of animal flesh, the counter laid out with neat folds of fat sausages, blood pooling beneath the steaks, bacon piled high.

'Hello!' I said.

28

The assistant looked only a little younger than me.

'Can I help you?' she said, smiling.

'Er . . .' I stood there mulling over what to get. Even the bacon rinds were perfectly aligned to show the stamp printed on the skin.

'I'm sorry,' the assistant said, 'but do I know you?'

I looked up. Perhaps she knew me from school but I didn't know her. I struggled to picture faces from the playground.

'Maybe,' I replied. 'I used to live here years ago. Up at Larkstone Farm when I was a kid.' I didn't know why but the words came reluctantly to my lips.

'Oh.' She fell quiet. Then, 'I'll be right back.' And she disappeared through a door to the rear of the shop.

I lifted my head, annoyance prickling. A man appeared, a large stained apron covering the expanse of his belly. He was followed by the assistant and the two exchanged glances as they entered the room. *Did* they know me? They must have known Elizabeth. Had they seen me at the funeral? The other faces there had been a blur, my thoughts mostly concentrated on Elizabeth and Steph. The woman stepped back to allow the man to take over.

'We're closed,' he said.

'Oh?'

I was taken aback. It seemed unlikely that the butcher's would be closed at this time of day, with the door open and inviting.

'Phone order,' the man said. 'We've got a large phone order. You'll have to come back later or go to the supermarket.' He nodded towards over the road.

He was clearly lying. What on earth? I stood there, dumbfounded.

'Um, sure.'

I left the shop and turned back to look through the window. The butcher and his assistant were talking. The woman lifted her head towards me and there was something about her expression. I felt a flush of embarrassment, like I'd been caught stealing. Anger swept over me. Closed, really? What was their problem?

I crossed the road to the Co-op. A small queue gathered at the desk. I lowered my head, flipping up my hood, still aware of the heat on my cheeks. So much for company, now I felt the need to hide. I picked up a basket and headed down the aisle; it didn't take long to choose what I wanted. As a last thought, I grabbed a couple of tins of cat food and made for the till.

'Hello, Sheila, two packets of your usual?'

The assistant was addressing a middle-aged woman in front of me. She turned to pluck two cigarette boxes from the shelf behind her.

'Thanks, Em,' said the customer. 'And a book of stamps.'

'First or second?'

'Oh, second will do. Have you heard? We think we've found it.'

I wondered what *it* was.

'Yes, Pete was in a minute ago. Crying shame.' The assistant opened the till, fishing for the stamps.

'The sheep must have got run over last night. Some idiot driving too fast.'

I winced. A sheep hitting a car would have been nasty, for both parties.

'Pete's really angry, he loves his animals.' The woman opened her purse.

'Where did he find it?' The assistant seemed to have forgotten about payment. There was a shuffling of feet behind me.

'Outside Elizabeth's house.'

The hairs on the back of my neck pricked up.

'Well I suppose that makes sense, he's got the field opposite, hasn't he?'

'Yes.' The woman sighed, clutching her purse. 'But the body was hidden in the verge – took a while to find it. Not much left of it either – the foxes had already had a go. Pete's gone to fetch the trailer to shift it and ask his brother to help. But he's annoyed with himself. It must have escaped the night before. Normally Elizabeth would have spotted it and given him a call.'

'Well, she couldn't have done that no more,' said the assistant. 'Twenty-one pounds seventy, love. Isn't the house still empty?'

There was the chink of money and a rattle as it was stashed away in the till.

'Pete said there was a car outside first thing this morning. Reckon one of the daughters has finally turned up.'

'Really? Which one? The flashy one or the nutcase?'

I felt my ears burn, humiliation flooding my body. I lowered my head, fingers pushed deep into my jacket pockets. What was wrong with these people?

'Don't know, the car's a bit crap, Pete said. Perhaps it was that car which hit our sheep?'

I ground my teeth. What right had they to make that assumption?

'Oh, well, tell that lovely husband of yours how sorry I am when you see him.'

'Sure. Thank you. See you tomorrow.'

The woman lifted a hand and left. I presented my basket and waited patiently. The assistant ignored me as she scanned the items but threw me a look when she got to the tins of cat food. My eyes dropped and I paid the bill as quickly as I could.

Back in the car, I pulled over when I got to the bottom of the drive to the house. On the roadside, they'd said. I told myself I needed to see what I'd been accused of, but perhaps the truth was that I'd always been drawn to the macabre, the visual trickery of the surreal, an artist's fascination for the biological structures behind our physical façade. My car eased onto the verge and I stepped out.

The wind had picked up, with a bitter edge, bending the trees on either side of the road, already twisted and contorted from years of exposure on the hill. My hood whipped down and my hair caught in my eyes. One of the poppers on my coat was broken and I had to grasp the folds of it over my chest to keep the flaps from bursting open.

There it was. The feet were visible through the long grass and a tangle of briers growing in the hedge. It was just about recognisable as a sheep. The head was intact, but the body had been badly damaged, not just by a car. Entrails splayed across its woolly coat and something had tugged and pulled at the flaps of skin. The eyes were wide open, bulging from the skull, and its tongue lolled uselessly between its teeth. I couldn't help but think of my stepmother, how her body must have looked lying on the floor at the foot of the stairs. I tried to push the image from my mind, gazing at the animal. Judging by the state of it, that hadn't happened today.

I thought – what if it *had* been me? Yesterday, as I'd arrived? I'd been tired those last few miles, not particularly alert. What if I'd hit the sheep myself? No, I didn't believe that. I would have felt the impact. And there was that car behind me. The driver would have noticed too. Surely, he'd have reacted if either one of us had hit an animal that big.

I reached out with my foot, giving the carcass a nudge. A bevy of flies rose up from the body, flying in ever decreasing circles before settling down to their business again. I felt my stomach flip. It was disgusting. But a sheep was just a sheep, wasn't it? Another animal bred for consumption, its death inevitable one way or another. Like all of us, I thought.

I looked around me. I saw the last few leaves hanging on the trees, great piles of damp and blackened vegetation heaped on the verge below. I saw the remains of a pheasant cleaved to the tarmac further down the road, berries that clung shrivelled and inedible, rejected even by the birds. Already I'd alienated my neighbours without doing anything wrong at all. The strange looks at the butcher's, the assumption of my guilt over this sheep, made without a shred of proof, and the vague gossip about Elizabeth's two daughters.

'The flashy one or the nutcase,' they'd said – I certainly wouldn't describe myself as 'flashy'.

I'd only just arrived, after an absence of ten years. Why would they say that about me? I felt a sense of helplessness. Already it was as if I'd never left. This was meant to be a fresh start, wasn't it?

CHAPTER 4

'Caro? Is that you?' It was Steph's voice on the phone, distant and contorted.

'Hi Steph, how are you?'

'Oh, I'm fine, fed up with this weather, that's all.'

It had been raining in New York, apparently.

'But at least I've got a trip to Miami coming up – for work,' she continued.

'When do you go?'

'Day after tomorrow.' Steph sounded harassed. 'Early flight. Which means an even earlier cab to the airport. It's only for a few days though.'

'Oh.'

Miami sounded very glamorous. You didn't get business trips like that with book illustration.

'Everything okay with the house? You got in alright?'

'Sure, yes. It's a bit cold and damp, you know.'

'Well, yes, I s'pose. Been empty for a while.'

Steph paused. Somewhere in the background I could hear movement. Then she spoke again.

'Listen, I've spoken to the lawyer. I've told him I don't want any of it.'

'Are you sure about that?' I felt a stab of guilt. Steph had said she was well off, but still . . . 'I mean, the house must be worth a fair bit of money and some of the things here are antiques. There's all Dad's old stuff too, you know, books and pictures – from when we were little. Don't you want some of that? It's your inheritance as well.'

'No. No, thanks. I've moved on and I don't want anything that reminds me of those days. Anyway, how would I get all that stuff over to the States? It's like I said, Sis, I don't need the money. Really.'

Sis. It felt good hearing her use that word, after so many years of silence.

'Well, it's very generous of you.'

In truth, I was delighted. I'd been penniless for years, scarcely managing on the fees from my work. It had been a mistake moving to London. Whether I stayed or sold up, to have a home, rent-free, even the prospect of a modest independent income, was amazing. Life-changing stuff. I hadn't thought Steph really meant it, but now it was clear that she did.

I didn't linger on the guilt. She didn't need the money, she'd said. You could see it in her clothes, the make-up, no cheap brands there. And the house hadn't been her home for almost twenty years, had it? It was her choice. Still, I asked one more time.

'Are you really sure, Steph?'

'Yes. Caro, if I could undo the past, to make it up to you that I never got in touch, I would. We're family. I shouldn't have let my feelings about Elizabeth and the whole situation get between you and me. Can you ever forgive me?'

Forgive her? I didn't know about that. I chewed my lip; I hadn't tried that hard to contact her either.

'Do we need to think like that?' I said. 'Forgive each other? What's important is now. Only I wish you didn't live so far away.'

'Well, this time I promise I will keep in touch. I get over to the UK quite a bit these days. I'll let you know when I'll be around next and we can meet up. We'll hit the shops, eh? Get you some nice clothes, a haircut.'

I flinched at that, remembering her quiet look at my wild hair. Paul had sneered at my hair, even when things had still been good between us.

'. . . and go to a show. I'd like that, Sis.'

That word again.

'Sure, I'd like that too.' I smiled down the phone.

'Right – gotta go. Oh, and calls are stupidly expensive from New York. You got Skype?'

'Yeah.'

'Great.'

Steph reeled off a Skype address and I noted it down.

'Add me and I'll Skype you every now and again. It'll be nice to see your face. You take care, Caro. I'll be thinking of you!' Steph called off.

The house was too quiet after she'd gone. Steph had never really been a sister to me. But now? I scanned the kitchen, my painting gear laid out on the table, my laptop, the emails filling up the screen with rubbish. I clicked delete and stood up. Time to check out the upstairs.

I was reluctant to use the bedrooms on the first floor. No way was I going to sleep in Elizabeth's room and, though I couldn't explain it, I didn't fancy the other ones either. But I needed a proper bed, I didn't want another night on the sofa. I hung back, feet on the first step, then curiosity got the better of me and I climbed the stairs to the top floor.

My old bedroom was right under the eaves. It was the most neglected of all the rooms and hadn't changed much. It didn't surprise me, I could just picture my stepmother shutting the door after I'd gone and forgetting all about it. There was a single bed under the window overlooking the back of the house, a desk against the wall and a lamp tinged with yellow. A bookcase stood between a wardrobe built into the eaves and a small Victorian fireplace. The ceiling was low and, in the middle, a large spider dangled from a web strung out across a hatch into the roof. A fly was caught in its strands, still moving as the spider wrapped it with thread. I wanted to pull out my sketchbook, to record the shape of it suspended like it was, pencil lines capturing the spider's legs, the way they tapered and moved, weaving silk with the delicacy of a pâtissier making spun sugar. I lowered my head. The room had seemed bigger when I was little.

I opened the wardrobe. The doors stuck; the wood had swollen and loose flakes of paint fell onto my fingers. Inside smelt of charity shop clothes, damp cardboard boxes and old bedding. I fished out a soft toy, a felt penguin. Its beak was bent and worn, its once white breast grey from a thousand childish cuddles. I'd had it for as long as I could remember. It was missing when I'd looked for it when packing to go to uni. I hadn't realised then that I wouldn't be back, even once; that I'd have to find jobs in the holidays to support myself. I held it for a moment, stroking its beak, then placed it gently on the floor.

I reached further into the cupboard. More stuff. A wooden doll, her clothes worn ragged, and a Monopoly set. I grimaced at the board game – I'd been thrilled to get it all those years ago, but I'd never had anyone to play it with, neither Steph nor Elizabeth had ever been interested. I would set up the bank, line up the penguin and doll and we'd play like that, the three of us. Sometimes I won, sometimes they won, that in itself had been the game, which toy would win. Sad, I thought. What a sad little girl I'd been.

I shut the wardrobe door and turned to the bookcase. Books had been my escape. *Peter Pan, Five Go to Smuggler's Top, Black Beauty*, all classics. *The Little Mermaid* caught my eye, a picture book, its glossy pages smooth beneath my fingers. It had arrived in the post one year. I'd been first to the door that day. I wasn't sure about the name on the card, some relative on my mother's side, Elizabeth said. Whoever it was had never come to visit, at least as far as I knew. It had been a fantasy of mine, my mother's relatives hammering at the door demanding to see me, but that had never happened. I pulled the book from the shelf. There was something about the story of *The Little Mermaid*. The sea princess who has to lose her place in the family and give up her beautiful voice, whose every step with her new feet felt like walking on a thousand shards of glass. Even then, she still didn't get her prince. I'd read that story again and again.

The bed was by the window. My refuge, there where the light was best, where I could look out over the hills and immerse myself in stories of another time, another place, away from my existence at home. Something caught my eye, the corner of a book peeping out from under the bed. I reached down to pull it out. A collection of fairy tales. It had been one of my favourites. How could I have left it behind? Had that too been missing? I frowned.

I brought the book to my nose, drinking in the old-book scent, a mixture of woody glue and grass cuttings, old paint and vanilla candles. The pages fell open in my hands. It was as if the black ink already stained my fingers, my hands tracing the beautiful line drawings – princesses with long rope-like hair; trees gnarled like old man's hands; lilies, roses and wild garlic blossoming around the words, winding about the letters. It was the book that had inspired me to paint, the fine detail, the insects under the leaves, the sense of a hidden, lush world of fantasy.

I'd first met Paul at the British Library, at an exhibition on fairy tales. There'd been old woodcut prints and illustrations from all the books I remembered from my childhood. H.J. Ford's illustrations from *The Fairy Books* of Andrew Lang, Arthur Rackham's prints for the collections of the Brothers Grimm, I'd been in heaven moving slowly from one display to the next. I was standing in front of a book, the pages open at the full-page picture of a cat perched like an owl upon a branch. *By day she made herself into a cat.* Its expression scowled at me, teeth and claws etched angrily onto the print, the dark shape of the animal like a black cloud bursting onto the sky. I'd scarcely noticed Paul at first, as I peered down at the book.

'Not exactly the cute, cuddly kittens you see on Facebook,' he'd said.

I'd swung round to look at him. He was tall and slim, dark-haired with a neatly trimmed beard and high pale cheekbones that made his eyes leap out from his face. He looked like he must be a writer or a poet, someone who spent his time in the proverbial garret, too intensely absorbed in his work to spend time outside in the sunlight. It turned out he was an accountant, working for the one of the firms that had sponsored the exhibition.

'I don't like cute, cuddly kittens,' I said, only half a truth. I stood up and made to move on.

'She was a witch,' he said. 'She turned women into birds, and men into statues.'

'I don't like stories about witches,' I said. 'It's misogynism, pure and simple.'

He nodded in agreement. 'Not helping the reputation of black cats, either. But look at the fur on her haunches, the way it echoes the lines of the storm clouds behind, and the tint of orange in her eyes. It's not the cat that was being drawn but the repressed anger within.'

His hands were slender, pointing at the image, and a smile illuminated his face. As we talked, I imagined him standing trapped within the stained-glass window of a Victorian church like one of those translucent tortured saints. I found myself wanting to paint his face, to capture the angles of his features, the long line of his neck. One of my favourite artists had been Modigliani, known for the exaggerated necks and seductive features of his subjects. I felt the warm heat of a blush seeping across my face. *Paul* – even the letters of his name sparked that image in my head, long and lean, his legs white against the covers of my bed. Paul had been the man from my teenage fantasies, intelligent, courteous, patient. By the time we first slept together all my nervous reservations had gone.

I let the book drop from my fingers onto the floor of my old bedroom. I thought about the commission. *The Pear Drum and Other Dark Tales from the Nursery*. I hadn't even started it and already two weeks had gone by. Too busy packing up to leave London. Or had I been avoiding it?

It was there on my phone, an attachment to David's email. I reached into the wardrobe, pulled out a musty eiderdown, and dragged it over to the bed by the window. I propped up the pillows, arranged the eiderdown about my body and curled up with my phone, swiping through the emails to download the manuscript, then pausing to look out of the window. The sky was pastel pink, white mist shrouding the valley, trees fanning out against the horizon. The height of the window made me feel distant and alone, safe. The file loaded up and I scrolled through the contents, quickly passing over *The Pear Drum* to stop at a story I recognised, *The Wild Swans*. I settled down to read.

There were eleven brothers spurned by their new mother; their father, the king, under her spell. They'd been trans-formed into eleven black swans, their long bodies drooping as they flew low over the valley. Their sister, the youngest, mourned their loss and swore to turn them back. She spun and she sewed, weaving nettles into flax, blisters bubbling on her skin. Each night she crept out into the graveyard where the nettles grew, gathering what she needed. Each day she sewed the shirts. Ten she made, one after the other, glad to start the last.

But by then her stepmother had discovered her plan.

'She's a witch!' she cried, persuading the king to have his daughter burnt at the stake.

One final shirt the sister had to make, sewing as quickly as she could, as the cart dragged her towards the fire, as the guards pulled her against the stake, one last shirt floating up into the air, not quite finished, as they bound her hands behind her . . .

The swans appeared, darkening the sky, their cries drowning out the crowd as they swooped down. Scooping up the shirts, they slipped them over their feathers, transforming back into men. The truth was out, the princess was saved, the stepmother put to death, the brothers restored to their family. Except the youngest, number eleven. He was fine, almost. Apart from his arm. It was still a feathered wing, you see, where his sister hadn't quite finished his shirt.

I looked out of the window, the late sun burning up the hillside, streaks of mist streaming out across the valley like a line of swan brothers. I could see them as clear as day, the swans, pink eyes blinking, red beaks snapping, hissing, crowding round their sister, beating their wings, pushing her, almost crushing her in their eagerness for freedom.

I closed my eyes. I could feel her hands fighting back, the panic rising in her chest. This time it was me. Boys, girls too, crowding round me, pulling at my hair, kicking at my feet. Voices shouting, laughing, their hands reaching out to tug the feathered wings from my back . . .

I shook my head, as if to loosen the image from its grip. It was just my imagination, too vivid. It was how I experienced stories, as if I were there, the action a tangible thing, reaching out to touch the shapes and colours as they formulated in my head, buzzing around me like a swarm of bees. Crazy girl, that was what Paul had used to say, laughing, when I tried to explain to him how I felt about stories, about painting.

But this was different, this time it was more. My heart was racing, my knees trembling, my lips moving as if to scream. It felt real. A memory – but of what? My feet had gone numb. I unfolded my legs from under my body and swung them out onto the floor. Perhaps it was something at school? It felt that way with all those children. I wriggled my toes. I tried to picture the classroom in the village school, a building not far from the church. But it was too vague.

It was freezing up here, no heating in the room. I wasn't going to sleep here, I decided. I levered myself from the bed, left the room and shut the door behind me.

CHAPTER 5

It was the next day, after another night on the sofa. I was perched on a stool in the kitchen, my hand sweeping across the paper, sketching with a light, confident motion the wings of a black swan. I'd been fired up by that first story, eager to get started on the commission in between clearing the house. As the image grew, my heart warmed to him, my swan prince, his eyes soft and human.

There followed a series of pictures, paper floating frantically to the ground as one sheet after another was rejected. I couldn't capture him properly. The feathers were too bold, the angle of his wing too taut. I couldn't fathom his expression. Was it fear? Was it joy? Was he wilful, wild and free? The lines had to be perfect, so pleasing to the eye that I couldn't stop looking at it. I wasn't there yet. Then at last, I had it. This, the youngest prince, *my* prince, was sweet and innocent, untouched by the human world, the purity of his black feathers a mirror to his sinless soul. Now I was happy, I stopped. The secret to a good picture is to know when to stop.

My fingers ached. I tipped off the stool and pulled on a coat, deciding to head down to the village. Or maybe I would go into Ashbourne. There were tea shops there and more people. I craved human contact, albeit the impersonal kind.

As my car swung out from the bottom of the drive, another car appeared behind me. It was the jeep again, I recognised the driver, the same impatient craggy-faced thirty-something who'd beeped at me before. He seemed content enough this time, driving behind me, a large dog hanging out of the front passenger window despite the cold. When we got to the village, the road widened and he accelerated past.

Larkstone was quiet. The cottages that lined the road were built with solid stone, curtains drawn, blinds lowered, as if the whole village was closed to me. The Co-op shop window was full of local adverts and Christmas-cracker boxes piled high in a stack, but the doors were locked, the lights were out and no one stirred on the street. Only the butcher's lights were on. Tinsel was strung across the window and a pheasant, hanging from its neck, bumped against the glass. A figure moved away from the door and a blind dropped into place.

I decided Ashbourne was definitely a better bet.

I managed to nab a space in the market square car park and ambled down the hill to the main street. It had a pleasant buzz to it, fairy lights in every shop, traffic passing slowly under the street decorations. I didn't really have a purpose. I wanted to soak in the atmosphere and the voices around me.

There were various gift shops. I thought, why not buy something for Steph for Christmas this year? But what did you buy for someone who could afford to waive a substantial inheritance? Perfume? A silk scarf? Those seemed eminently suitable for Steph, but a little boring. I wanted to give something more personal, something that I'd taken my time over, that spoke to us both, even after all these years of silence between us. One of my pictures, I thought. She'd said how much she liked them. I'd give her one of my pictures, something I'd painted especially for her.

There was an artists' supply shop on St John Street and I went inside. I wanted paper the right size to fit into a table-top picture frame. The shop was a tiny space, pungent with the smell of oil paint and varnish. I lingered awhile, appalled at the prices – I usually bought my supplies on the internet. I selected a pad of thick watercolour paper, adding a pack of pencils, paid for them and left. Back out into the cold air and the damp.

I couldn't have been looking where I was going. I ricocheted off a passing man.

'I . . . I'm so sorry!' I cried. My pad had landed on the pavement and the pencils were rolling out of their box. 'Damn!'

'Fucking bitch, don't you look where you're going?'

I recoiled from the man's language, the aggression in his face. He stepped towards me, a huge athletic man with thick blond hair, his face right against mine. His hands were grasping my shoulders as if he were about to shake me. I felt fear ripple down my spine.

'I . . . that is . . .'

'Leave the lady alone, Angus!'

Another man appeared, forcing his way in front of me,

knocking back the ugly hands from where they gripped my shoulders.

'You don't want to get physical now, do you?' he said.

He had his back to me, this new man. He was tall too, and brown-haired. At his feet was a large dog. I stared in dismay; it was the one from the jeep. It sat on the pavement, tongue hanging out, panting, quite relaxed. It was more than how I felt. The dog watched its master and I watched the two men. I was shaking, desperate to rub off the feel of those hands on my shoulders.

The animal rose up onto its feet, a low growl in its throat. The blond man's posture shifted, aggression distorting his face.

'She's a fucking stupid—' said Angus.

I backed up, ready to run.

'Well that may be,' interrupted my rescuer, 'but not worth getting an assault charge for, eh?'

How dare he, I thought. What was the point of coming to my aid if he then colluded with this oaf to insult me? I felt my anger rise, my courage re-grouping. I bristled behind him.

Angus, whoever he was, took a moment to think about it. There was an uncomfortable standoff. Then he seemed to concede, nodding to the stranger, kicking my block of paper as he marched off. The dog sat on its haunches and cocked its head to look at me.

I reached down for my things, even more annoyed when I considered how much they'd cost. The paper was marked, the pencil leads broken; I wished I'd never come out. The man looked at me from on high. Was that pity or exasperation on his face? It didn't help.

47

'What are you staring at?' I said ungraciously.

'Nothing at all,' he said. 'Here, let me.'

He bent down to pick up a stray pencil.

'I've got it . . . thanks . . .'

No thanks. I tucked the pad under my arm, snatching the pencil from his hand and turning aside, refusing to look at him. I walked away, side-stepping the dog, picking up speed with the urgency of embarrassment.

But the man followed me. He caught up, walking alongside without a word. I tried to walk faster, but he kept pace. I stopped.

'What do you want?' I said.

'I want to know that you're okay.'

'I'm okay, now go away.' I bit my lip at my rudeness.

'You're staying at Elizabeth Crowther's old house, aren't you?'

'What's that got to do with you? You know her?' That second sentence was a mistake, an invitation for him to engage.

'*Knew* her, yes.'

I nodded, acknowledging the correction. But you weren't at the funeral, I thought. At least, I didn't remember seeing him there.

'We were neighbours. Let me introduce myself. I'm Craig. And you must be Elizabeth's daughter, Caroline?' He held out a hand.

I ignored it.

'I was her *step*daughter, and it's Caro, actually.'

I'd always hated *Caroline*, Elizabeth had called me that. I started walking again.

'I live at Lavender Cottage, it's further up the lane, past your drive.'

So that explained why he'd appeared to follow me the first night. I didn't reply.

'Look, that guy was pretty nasty, back there—'

'Who was he?' I saw his flash of irritation at my interruption.

'Angus McCready.' He gave a sigh. 'Let me make it up to you. Let me buy you a cup of coffee. There,' he pointed to a coffee shop on the other side of the road, all big chunky wooden tables and artsy ironwork chairs.

'Thanks, I appreciate your help, really, but my parking's about to run out.'

A white lie.

He looked taken aback. Maybe he wasn't used to being blown off by a girl. He was, after all, quite good-looking.

'No problem,' he said. He stopped walking. 'Drive carefully!'

His words were softly ironic. But I wasn't listening, I was already heading back up the hill to my car.

The drive home seemed painfully long, though in reality, speeding, it must have been no more than fifteen minutes. The lane was overhung with trees, the headlamps of my car picking up the droplets of water clinging to the roadside grass. I kept looking in the rear-view mirror, expecting to see the jeep with its dog hanging out of the window. But the road was empty and I noticed the remains of the dead sheep near the house had gone.

I couldn't wait to get inside. I shoved the key in the lock, leaning against the door as it clicked shut. I turned around holding out one hand, fingers straight but trembling. I snapped the chain into place on the door, reaching up to bolt it top and bottom. Only then did I draw breath.

Okay, there were plenty of men like Angus, bullying creeps who couldn't even show a bit of respect for a stranger, let alone offer up some sympathy for a brief moment of clumsiness. But since I'd dumped Paul, I'd been reluctant to admit even to myself how I felt about men.

Paul had been a nice guy, too nice. At the beginning. Not that nice wasn't good – I really wasn't into the exciting, dangerous type – safe was good, safe was *safe*. I'd barely dated anyone for longer than a week until Paul. As time went by, I was drawn into his friendship. We met for dinner, we went to the theatre, we headed out of London for day trips to Brighton and the seaside town of Southwold. Then he asked me to spend the weekend with him in Bath. I knew what that meant. Here was someone that wanted me, we had a future, didn't we? I'd never thought that might happen, I wasn't the glamorous type, the kind of woman most men went for. I didn't see what was coming.

'*Limpy, lumpy Caroline!*'

The words punched into my brain from nowhere and I sucked in my breath. A little boy voice – another memory from school? Where had that come from? I leaned my head against the front door of the house, feeling the wind outside battering against the wood, roaring through the gap at my feet, the iron bolt cold beneath my fingers.

I made for the kitchen. With unsteady hands I reached for a bottle of wine skulking in a corner of the worktop. I poured it out into a mug and sat down.

I didn't normally drink, perhaps the odd glass in front of the TV once I'd finished work. The liquid seemed to move in the middle, a regular ripple, circling out from the centre of the mug. It shone under the bright kitchen lights, my heartbeat reflected in the liquid, the beat transferring from hand to drink.

I lifted the mug to my lips and drank it down in one swift, grateful, needy gulp.

CHAPTER 6

I had to choose a bedroom – I couldn't carry on like this, what was wrong with me? The sofa, which on my first night had seemed so inviting, was now excruciating, the cushions hard and lumpy, the ridges of the seams digging into my hips. I tucked the blankets under me and rolled over, one hand flung out, feet hitting the armrest. I resolved to sort out a proper bed in the morning.

The house was quiet, except for the tick of the clock in the hallway and the wind rattling down the chimney and buffeting the windows. I'd left the curtains open and snowflakes lightly touched the glass, slipping down as they melted. I lay on my side and drifted off, only to wake again some time later in a pleasantly floating state, aware, yet limbs hypnotically frozen in sleep.

Clack, clack, clack. The noise pierced my slumberous state. The wind had died down and it was a sharp, staccato sound, at odds with the peacefulness of the house.

Clack, clack, clack.

I moaned, unwilling to relinquish my warm, now comfortable position. But the noise penetrated, demanding a response. I'd had some kind of dream, something to do with a bird stuck in the chimney of my old bedroom, black feathers covered in soot clouding my vision, choking in my throat. It had left me on edge and in my sleepy daze the clacking sound momentarily sent shivers down my back.

I rolled onto my feet, dragging the blanket about my body. It was cold, far colder than normal, even in this house. I reached for the lamp, but it didn't come on. A power cut? I looked towards the window. The air was thick with wide, slow-falling snowflakes, this time the kind that really settles. Snow was rapidly building up on the ground, the front drive white, the low walls too, and an eerie blue light filled the room. I knew what was coming, it had happened so many times before, when I was a child. I made a mental check of the fridge. There was enough food for a few days and for a moment I quite liked the idea of being snowed in, up here on the hill, cut off from the world in my snowy kingdom. Except it hadn't been like that before, with Elizabeth.

But where was that noise coming from? I wondered if it was the boiler, something that had worked itself loose, or pipes contracting in the cold. Had the boiler broken down too? I pushed on my slippers and padded through to the kitchen.

I started to fill the kettle. Then I berated myself – no electricity, remember? I turned to the Aga; it was oil-fired and still warm, thank God for that – heat and something to cook by. I filled a saucepan and set it down on a hotplate.

A flurry of wind caught the side of the house, whipping

the branches of a tree, clattering against the window frame. Was *that* the noise? By now I was too awake to sleep again. It was relatively pleasant in the kitchen and the sitting room felt uninviting. I rifled in a drawer where I thought I'd seen a hot water bottle and pulled it out. I fished out a candle too, jamming it into the empty wine bottle from the day before. I sat down on a chair to wait for the water to boil.

My thoughts turned to the man in the jeep. My rescuer, Craig. There was something about him. Maybe it was his height, or the way his hair grew, unkempt, curling at the back. Why was I even thinking about him? Just because he'd taken an interest in me. The cottage had always been empty in my childhood. I bit my lip; I hadn't banked on a neighbour that close, I'd been looking forward to the isolation. I stood up to peer out of the hall window. I could see the cottage he lived in, further up the road, its roof snuggled close to the ground where the road climbed and fell away.

I returned to the kitchen. My phone was still on the table, where I'd left it after drawing the swan prince. Reading from my phone wasn't quite the same as reading a physical book. I thought of all those stories where the moonlight on a particular night could make the letters of a book come alive, or reveal the secret opening of a door cut into rock, shimmering, brightening, an arc of light bursting into life as the door magically opened onto a world of princesses and fairies, goblins and monsters, promises broken and resolved.

I'd stolen a book once – why had I only just remembered that? – from the mobile library van, in the days when they still had such things. I'd loved it so much I couldn't bring myself to return it. *Thief.* I rolled the word around in my head. That was me. The sense of guilt gave me a brief shiver.

I picked up the phone, swiping the screen until the file jumped into life. I looked down the list of stories in the commission:

The Foundling.

King Rat. I knew that one – wasn't that about a boy who liked to play jokes? He got turned into a rat at the end of the story.

The Stubborn Child.

I almost laughed when I read this one – with satisfaction, not humour. A snippet of a tale in the way that some folk tales were – short and ambiguous. Perfect for me to put my own stamp on. The water was boiling, I filled my hot water bottle and made myself a cup of tea. Hugging both, I sat at the table, pulling the candle closer. Reaching for a pencil and paper, I began to draw. The old house empty around me, the wind struggling at its walls, the snow like cold fingers clawing at the windows, the clacking in the distance, it all merged within my head. And I was there, an uneven sequence of sketches sprawling across the page.

In a graveyard, a woman dressed in black stood watching. She was standing beside a mound of newly dug earth, her head bowed, her hair caught beneath a long black veil. The grave was small, a scaled-down stone at its head. In the fading light, the letters were unclear.

The ground was moving at the woman's feet, the earth breaking, cracking. Something thrust out from beneath. A hand, a small white arm, the black soil clinging to its skin. The fist was closed tight, the whole thing stiff with rage.

The mother stepped backwards in alarm, her feet neatly

booted. The child's arm stretched out, the fingers uncurled, feeling for her legs. But the mother wasn't having it and she kicked the hand away.

The hand reached out again, scrabbling for a hold in the dirt. This time, the mother bent, batting it down and stamping on it. She picked up a branch fallen from the trees. The child's hand moved once more, persistent and imploring, stubborn. Now the mother lifted up her branch and brought it whipping down upon the arm.

The arm shot back into the ground, shrivelling from sight. The soil folded into place and the grave fell quiet.

What kind of story was that? These stories were intriguing, like little windows into human weakness – mothers don't always love their children, I knew that. What made a mother anyway? An accident of birth, marriage or an inner instinct to love and care? And who knew what was behind this story? Perhaps the boy deserved his fate? Perhaps he was a fairy child, a changeling, substituted into the mother's family to torment her? As the thoughts passed through my mind I picked up a stick of charcoal and began to draw again.

The last picture lay before me, the lines so heavily smudged that my fingers were ingrained with black. It was a grave. But this grave was ripped apart, the soil piled high on either side. A tall yew hedge stood behind, each branch, each twig bending in the same direction. Line after line, twig after twig. So close together, it seemed as dense as the earth beneath. At the bottom of the hole was a child, a boy, his eyes wide open. The hole was too deep for his escape. He was sitting, his knees pulled tight under his chin, his arms wrapped around his legs. It was a young boy, maybe nine years old? Defiance etched onto his face. Then he moved, one arm reaching out. Upwards. Towards his mother. Towards me.

I let the stick of charcoal drop to the table as if it stung. It broke in two. I had become completely immersed in my drawing, my interpretation of the story, and the image was so austere, so . . . disturbing . . . moving. Why did I think that?

CHAPTER 7

Clack, clack, clack.

The noise broke into my thoughts. Where was that stupid sound coming from? I leapt to my feet. It wasn't the Aga, or the trees outside. It was coming from somewhere else in the house – upstairs. I thought maybe one of the bedrooms on the first floor.

I turned towards the stairs. I didn't want to go up there. I was okay down here, where the rooms were familiar, where the outside was easily accessed. But at night, upstairs was something else. Even my old room. Unexplored rooms that hadn't been used for all those years, their memories struggling under a thick layer of dust.

There it went again, louder and more persistent. The noise. I couldn't ignore it.

I climbed the stairs, one step at a time, one hand sliding on the banister. It was a long way down, the grand height of the building soaring over my head and beneath too. The wood was smooth beneath my touch and as I reached the first floor, the point where my stepmother had fallen, I gave a small cry and snatched my hand away. A large splinter stuck out from the fleshy part of my palm. I stared down at the banister. I hadn't noticed before that it was scratched. I pulled the splinter out and sucked my hand. But now the bare wood jarred against the finely polished surface. Had that been something to do with Elizabeth's accident?

My other hand reached for the wall switch, flicking it on/off, on/off . . . the electricity still wasn't working. It seemed deliberate, vengeful – why would I think that?

Clack, clack. Don't be ridiculous, I thought. It's only a noise, a branch against a window, a pipe knocking in the wall. Suddenly, the hall flooded with light, the power back on, and I blinked. I looked down. Even from the first-floor landing, the drop to the hall below seemed dizzying. There was the front door, the table by the wall, the space on the floor where the rug had been, the ground still bearing a faint tell-tale stain of red.

Then I heard a different sound. The familiar ping of an incoming Skype call, my laptop in the kitchen. I almost skipped down the stairs, dashing into the kitchen, grabbing for the mouse to answer the call, cursing as my mug of tea crashed to the ground.

'Hi, Sis.' It was Steph. 'Sorry it's so early.' Her face quivered into focus on the screen.

I didn't reply. I looked at the clock. It was almost seven in the morning. Dawn wasn't far off. It would be two am in New York.

'Caro? Are you there? I saw you were online – I've just got

in from a night out. Thought I'd see if the connection worked. Are you okay?'

'Yes . . . no, really I'm fine.'

I spoke too quickly, actually not sure that I was. But I was pleased to hear her voice. The electricity coming back on must have triggered a reconnection to Skype. Blood welled slowly from my palm and I was unsettled.

'How's it going?' she said.

'Okay – well sort of. There was this guy in Ashbourne who was a bit nasty.'

'Nasty? Oh Caro, what happened?'

I gave her a potted history of the incident outside of the artists' shop.

'That's horrible, some people are prats. Don't let it get to you. But this man who tried to help, he sounds nice – what did you say his name was?'

'Craig something. He said he's my neighbour, the cottage down the road.'

'Oh, I think I know that name.'

'You know him?'

'Sort of. That sounds like Craig Atherton.'

I waited, expecting to hear more. 'And?'

'Well, there's not much to say. I remember him from school. He was cool. You won't have known him, he'd have been in the older class. I heard he's a carpenter now, he's on Facebook.'

The village school had been tiny, only two classes, that much I did remember. And Steph was right, I had no memory of a Craig Atherton. I tried to picture the man as a boy, kicking a ball around in the playground with his mates . . . No, it didn't gel – I couldn't remember him at all. But that didn't surprise me, most of the kids had kept their distance, I'd always been the outsider.

I opened my mouth to speak, but Steph was before me.

'Look Caro, I've gotta go, it's really late over here. I just rang to check in with you. I wanted to know that you're alright.'

I felt the warmth of her voice enclose me. Only Steph could have understood how I must be feeling, back here in this house.

'I'll call again, if you like, tomorrow evening, your time. Take care of yourself. Bye!'

'Bye!' I said.

I felt unexpectedly bereft. But Steph had already signed off.

As the morning progressed, the weather didn't improve. The sky was heavy and grey and whirling with large snowflakes. The house was like a fridge and I went to find another jumper. When I got back to the kitchen my mobile rang.

'Hello?'

'Miss Crowther? Is that Miss Caroline Crowther?'

'Yes.'

'Hello, Gareth Briscoe here, from Briscoe, Williams and Patterson.'

'Oh, hi.'

I gripped the phone and sat down. It was the lawyers, the ones who were handling probate. They were Elizabeth's lawyers really and it had been Briscoe who'd organised everything. His voice was low and deep. I imagined a portly fellow, propping up the bar at his gentleman's club, cracking open another bottle of Châteauneuf-du-Pape.

'I understand you're now at the house.'

'Yes.'

'And all is well, you have what you need to settle in?'

'Oh, yes, thank you. Everything's fine.' Sort of.

'Wonderful.'

Briscoe sounded uncomfortable, I wasn't sure why.

'I'm glad you felt able to move in for a while,' he carried on. 'And deal with the contents, it's not an easy job after losing a loved one.'

Loved one – didn't he realise? Probably not and why would he? I'd never met him, and it didn't seem likely that Elizabeth would have ever discussed with him the exact nature of our relationship.

'It's a big old house and not in the best of condition. It's been a bit neglected over the years too. And I don't know to what extent the funeral directors . . .' he gave a cough '. . . cleaned up.'

After Elizabeth's fall – that's what he meant, didn't he?

'I'm sorry, I've no wish to distress you,' he said.

I began to warm to the man; did he have a family, grand-children? He sounded genuinely concerned.

'No, it's okay – I'm fine.'

I thought of the rug that had been in the hallway, the stain underneath. Briscoe, with the best of intentions, was serving only to remind me of what had taken place. Elizabeth lying dead in the house. I suddenly wondered who had found her. How long had her body been lying there? A few hours, a day, longer? Slowly decomposing in this house? No one had said. Had that been the reason for the musty smell? It hadn't occurred to me when I'd agreed to come that I would be living in an isolated empty house where someone had recently died. Or that there would be visible evidence of her death. I shifted on my feet, straightening my back. I wasn't superstitious about that, was I?

Briscoe coughed again.

'Good. Don't worry about the bills, heating, et cetera, they'll be charged to the estate whilst probate is still pending. Just send me any invoices and statements that you find, or anything that comes through the post, and I'll deal with them. It's all in hand, but I have to warn you, in a case like this, probate can take a while.'

'A case like this?' I asked. 'What do you mean?'

'Oh well, only that the property in the estate can take time to value and unravel. Everything has to be totted up, for inheritance tax purposes, you understand. We've had an estate agent visit the house already, but the investments may take a little longer, and the trust is quite complicated.'

The trust – Steph had already explained about the trust.

'Hang on, did you say investments?'

'Yes.'

'I didn't know anything about any investments.'

'Ah, well, it's mainly stocks and shares that are bound into the trust, and the estate includes a small cottage.'

'A cottage?'

I heard a murmur of voices in the background. Was that the rattle of a tray being placed on a desk?

'Yes, Lavender Cottage. I believe it was rented out. The tenant is still there, a Mr Atherton.'

'Oh.'

I felt my heart sink. Craig, the man in Ashbourne, had been Elizabeth's tenant. And was presumably now my and Steph's tenant.

63

'So it might take us a while to settle things and resolve probate, but I promise you that everything's in hand.'

'Thank you, Mr Briscoe. I appreciate the call.'

After he rang off, I sat there looking through the kitchen doorway, into the hall with its pool of light from the window on the stairwell. I felt the blood rushing to my head. The rug might be gone, but there was still that stain, a disturbing reminder of what happened. I'd never been one to get superstitious, but now all those films and stories about restless spirits and ghouls lurking in abandoned houses came rushing into my head.

The last thing I wanted to do was to get down on my hands and knees and scrub Elizabeth's blood from the stone floor.

I decided to distract myself. I turned out the drawers of the hall table, emptying leaflets, maps and business cards onto the floor, kneeling to rifle through them. The business cards were illuminating: Dave's TV aerials, Ashbourne Window Cleaners, Larkstone Butcher's. So, Elizabeth had been a regular at the butcher's? Not really a surprise, but did that have something to do with their apparent snub to me? I shook my head. I pushed the papers and cards into a pile to throw away.

There was a knock on the door. I started, not expecting visitors in this weather, well, in any weather for that matter. I clambered to my feet, scooping the papers into my arms. I unbolted the front door and opened it cautiously.

My eyes widened. It was Craig. I kept the door half shut in front of me.

'Hello?'

His jeep was parked on the drive behind him, with a trailer full of logs, huge tyre marks in the fresh snow.

'Log delivery,' he said cheerfully.

'I didn't order any logs.'

'No, but your mum did. Before she died.'

'She wasn't my mum.' It was all I could think of to say.

'Oh, yes, right, sorry.'

I couldn't take my eyes off him. His weather-worn face was framed by a thick grey scarf and the upturned collar of his jacket.

'Well, she ordered and paid for them in October and I never got the chance to deliver them, given what happened. So, I thought I might as well deliver them now that you're here. You'll be in need of them in this weather. We're about to get snowed in. Have you had a power cut?'

'Yes.'

I supposed it must have happened to him too if both houses were on the same line.

'Hmm, thought so. It's back on now, but it'll go again, always does. I'm guessing these logs will come in handy.'

I stood there, papers from the clutch in my arms drifting to the floor.

'Well, come on, I can't stay here too long or my car will get stuck on your drive.' He lifted his hands, catching snow-flakes floating in the sky. 'And then you'll have to invite me in! Do you want them or not?'

'Paid for, did you say?'

'Yup.'

'Okay.' I gestured to the wall to the far side of the driveway. 'Can you pile them up under there, please.'

'Sure thing, ma'am!'

I grimaced as he turned back to the trailer.

I disposed of my papers and watched him from the safety

65

of the sitting room window. It felt mean not helping him, but for the life of me I couldn't bring myself to join him, to talk to him. It had only been a couple of months since . . . I hadn't spoken to Paul and the thought of interacting with any man after . . . Craig wore a path across the snow, to-ing and fro-ing, neatly stacking logs. He moved with a sure-footed smoothness, bending, lifting, reaching. My eyes couldn't resist following the lean line of his body. He was a strong man, practical, you could see it in the way he moved.

But I'd always felt uneasy with the physical, outdoors type of man. Those like Angus, the man I'd crashed into. I winced at the memory. He'd been the epitome of everything I disliked, brawny, aggressive. I was more attracted to the intellectual, creative type, wasn't I? Like Paul. But look where that had got me.

I had moved in with him after about a year. He'd seemed impatient by then, anticipating the closeness our relationship had brought. I was intoxicated, eager for the next stage in my life. Here was someone who wanted me, loved me. He hadn't said those words, not quite yet, but I wasn't mistaken by the way his eyes followed me, the pressure of his hands upon my arm in the street, the way he rang me every day. It was like it was a relief to him when I moved in. He'd driven to fetch me from my old digs. He looked surprised at the amount of stuff I had – there were a few suitcases with clothes and shoes and the like, but mainly it was boxes filled with painting gear, paints and brushes and folders overflowing with my work. He'd scowled when he saw all that piled up in his flat; his place was always neat and strictly ordered. But he knew I worked from home, he'd been to visit me many times, so he must have known what to expect, surely? I had my eye on a corner of his dining room, by the window that faced north. The light was bright but unheated, perfect for what I needed. I'd mentioned it and he'd nodded absent-mindedly. I'd got it so wrong. As I was to discover.

So why did I now find myself watching Craig?

No, this man was different, I realised, from both Angus and Paul. I didn't know what to make of his kindness, not just the logs but the stacking of them too. I resisted the urge to offer him a mug of tea, to be grateful, friendly. What was he after? Was he checking me out? Or had he decided to keep his new landlady sweet? The thought hovered in my mind.

A little while later, he knocked on the door.

'All done. There's enough there to see you through a good few weeks. It's well-seasoned wood, so you can use it straight away.'

He'd put some plastic sheeting over the top. He followed my eyes and nodded.

'That'll keep it dry. By the looks of things, we'll be snowed in for several days. They never clear this road, it only comes to you and me, then loops round the hill to the other side of the village. It's not worth their time. Have you got plenty of food?'

I dipped my head. We'd been snowed in so many times – Elizabeth and Steph and I, and later just Elizabeth and I. It came with living in this house. To most kids it would have been exciting, the thought of all that snow and no school. But it had filled me with dread, the long days with nowhere to go, hiding in my bedroom, trying not to be noticed, to not get into trouble. To avoid Elizabeth.

The winter when I turned eleven had been particularly bad. The snow blew in great drifts through the hedges and filled up the lane. Out the back of the house the entire garden had been buried under four feet of snow – reaching half way up the back door to the kitchen. At the front it was even worse – the car had been buried completely and the wind blasted a layer of snow against the windows so that you could scarcely see through the glass. There was no way I was getting into school, even on foot.

Steph had left two years earlier and it was just me and Elizabeth in the house. She'd sat in the sitting room by the fire most of the day and I'd kept to myself upstairs on the top floor. After Steph had gone, Elizabeth had stopped cooking a sit-down family meal. She'd eat on her own on a tray in the sitting room, leaving a meal for me to eat in my room. Now, with the snow, it was like someone had flipped a switch. For the first time she told me to cook for myself. I was old enough now, she'd said. All day, every day, and I didn't speak to a single person, living off baked beans and cereal until the milk ran out, then it was cheese and biscuits and anything I could scrounge from the fridge. There was no radiator in my room and it was so cold that I wore fingerless gloves and a triple layer of jumpers, sitting under the blankets in my bed by the window, tracing the myriad star shapes of the frost flakes that grew on the inside of the glass.

It was then that I'd got frightened. What if the snow never melted? What if the snow queen flew down from the North Pole and breathed ice on the whole house, turning it into a giant iceberg marooned in a sea of white? What if the noisy geese that migrated in autumn returned early to break chattering and gobbling through the windows to steal all the rest of our food? What if I awoke to hear the wolves howling hungry in the distance and came down to find my stepmother frozen solid to the sofa, a human block of ice? How would I get out, how would I eat? Who would ever come looking for me?

But it wasn't like that now. I wasn't a frightened, over-imaginative child. And the house was mine, I could roam each room to my heart's content, enjoy my solitude and the time to paint. Thanks to Craig I had a huge pile of winter fuel and could sit in front of a roasting fire, and I'd seen plenty of tins in the cupboards.

'Caro?' he said quizzically.

'Yes,' I said, coming back to reality. 'Oh, I'll be fine.'

'I'm that way,' he pointed north. 'About five minutes on foot. You have any problems, you call me, okay?'

He pushed a business card into my hand. *Atherton Woodcrafts and Log Supplies*. There was a picture of a log fire, a kitchen and a web address.

'Thank you,' I said.

'No problem,' he replied.

I clutched the card in my fingers. He was smiling and the warmth of his expression made me feel ungracious. I knew I'd been rude before. All he'd done was honour a purchase Elizabeth had made before her death – what was wrong with me? I tried to think of something to say, something more friendly.

'How's your dog?' I said.

'Patsy? She's at home, having a snooze. Well, bye then.'

He loped back to his jeep, turning towards me before climbing in.

'And she's not my dog,' he said. 'She was Elizabeth's.'

Before I could respond, he'd got into his car. As he drove away, the swirling snow dropped like a curtain behind him.

CHAPTER 8

Later that evening, I sat by the fire enjoying my new logs. The flames spat and crackled and I watched them dancing green and yellow as sparks disappeared into the chimney. The soot clinging to the stack glowed, colours flaring and fading like shooting stars in the night. As the heat began to build, I couldn't help but feel encouraged. It was more than the heat, it was the sense of home a fire brought to a room, even here in this house, where I'd been so unhappy as a child. It wasn't the house, I reasoned, it was the people who lived in it.

I felt Craig's card in my pocket. I pulled it out. *Atherton Woodcrafts and Log Supplies.* I decided to look it up on my phone.

There was a picture of Craig, sleeves rolled up, presumably in his workshop. Beside him was an old-fashioned wood-turning lathe. It looked a bit like a trestle table but with an upstand and wooden arms that held the piece being worked on. A large wheel led via a drum belt to a long pedal beneath. I could imagine it turning as the pedal thumped. For a moment it reminded me of the pear drum. On the wall behind were shelves laid out with a host of tools and a large lavender bush nudged up against the window.

'*Kitchens, furniture and joinery. Logs supplied by arrangement,*' said the strap line, '*Specialist in hand-crafted oak.*'

I almost envied him. I worked with paper and paint, pictures from my head. He worked with solid wood, creating tangible, functional objects. From the photo galleries that followed, some of the furniture looked very beautiful. I felt a softening in my attitude; he was someone who worked with his hands, who created things like I did. And he'd taken in my stepmother's dog, how many neighbours would do that? I chewed the inside of my cheek. It hadn't seemed to occur to him to offer to give it to me, but then what would I do with a dog? I'd never had any pets, had never wanted one. I wasn't good with animals.

I realised then that I was avoiding the real tasks, faffing about with hall table drawers and distracting myself with speculation about the house and Elizabeth. This wasn't a holiday, I had a job to do. In fact, two. I set the printer going, churning out a full copy of the commission text. Tomorrow, I would do some sorting in the house first, then later I'd paint. Painting had always been my reward.

When I was thirteen, the school took us to the art gallery in Derby. We were deemed old enough to explore the different floors of the gallery on our own without the teachers, as long as we stayed in groups of at least three or four. I hung around with a group of girls whilst the teachers were in sight, but once the staff had wandered off, the girls turned on me and shooed me away.

'Can't you find your own friends?' said Kathy Taylor.

'Why don't you go to the prehistoric room on the first floor – you'll be amongst your own kind there!' Paula March and Susan Pritchard sniggered behind my back.

I was more than happy to abandon them. I climbed the stairs to the first floor, meandering through the galleries till I came to a room marked *The Joseph Wright Gallery*. Here the walls were painted a dramatic dark grey. Huge paintings in heavy gilt frames hung all around me and the lighting was dim to protect the artwork. I felt enclosed, as if I'd walked behind a curtain to a hidden space, a sequence of scenes in a theatre, each picture peopled with actors playing out a story. In one, a woman in eighteenth-century dress leaned over a man prostrate on the ground. She was partly turned away, one hand held up as if to ward off an assailant. In another, a seascape showed black cliffs towering to left and right, the centre lit up like a scene viewed through a telescope, the oppressive walls of rock giving way to pale silver water and a tiny boat, miniscule figures clinging to the deck.

On the furthest wall was the biggest painting, a blurring of russet browns and red. As my eyes adjusted to the light, I saw the scene of a family gathered round a kitchen table, several adults of different ages and two girls. The elder held her sister as if to comfort her, the younger child's head turned away in shock. The table was filled with scientific instruments, poles and jars and rubber tubes, their purpose unclear. The faces of the onlookers were lit from beneath and the candle-light flickered in their eyes, throwing shadows on their skin. It took me a while to figure out what was going on.

I read the label. *An Experiment on a Bird in the Air Pump.* Now I understood. The bird was trapped in a bell jar and a wild man with long hair gesticulated to his audience. His other hand wound a handle on the box beneath the jar and the bird had its wings splayed and beak open as if it were gasping for air. No wonder the two sisters – I assumed they were sisters – looked so distressed. The scientist was demonstrating a vacuum. With each turn of the handle he was starving the bird of oxygen.

I stood mesmerised. Each detail was painstakingly accurate. But the story was told by the contrasting light. Colour, shade, light and dark playing out the drama. I wanted to reach out and touch the painting, to feel the brush strokes that had created such a work. My eyes darted from one face to another, reading their reactions, each character, each object, each shade of colour contributing their own notes, like a symphonic piece of music.

I knew then what I wanted to do. I was going to paint. I wanted to tell a story with the same skill and flair. To channel the emotions that I felt, to observe and interpret and shock and please. I felt the buzz of it fill me with hope.

I drew, I read and learnt and practised and painted in every moment of the day. At the house, Elizabeth had no idea. She had no interest in whatever it was that preoccupied me. She never came into my room. I smuggled the materials back from school and the art teacher turned a blind eye to my thefts. I think she'd guessed what it was like for me at home. Slowly my efforts improved and I developed my own particular darkly curious style.

* * *

I rose early, the next day. It was still snowing. Outside was pristine white, thick snow covering every surface. The road, hedges and fields were indeterminable, rising up to meet a similarly white sky across a non-existent horizon. The trees hung out their arms in petrified silence, white giants riveted to the hillside like they'd been caught out in some fantasy game of Freeze Tag. There was a childish joy in seeing all that virgin snow; even the sheep in the field opposite the drive were just frozen white blobs huddled near the gate close to the feeding rack. I lingered at the window.

It was time to tackle the bedrooms. It wasn't something I looked forward to. Elizabeth's room was the largest, with a window overlooking the front of the house and its own bathroom. The bed had an expensive-looking quilt and a set of six pillows. Six, for goodness sake, three on each side, one in front of another. On the bedside table were a pair of glasses and two books. Agatha Christie's *And Then There Were None* and a collection of short stories. Beside them was a small china box painted with blue flowers. Inside were yellow pills. I had no clue as to what they were for.

I gripped the black bin bag in my hand and swept up the glasses, the box and a nightdress I'd found neatly folded under the pillows. The books I couldn't bear to throw away. The next hour went quickly. I dived into the wardrobes and drawers, dragging out every item of clothing, every dress, jacket and blouse, even the underwear – *urgh* – pants, bras, tights and petticoats; no one wore petticoats any more, did they? Everything I could find I stashed in plastic bags ready for the charity shops of Ashbourne. Her clothes were expensive, formal suits, dresses and matching shoes, respectable and impressive. I could imagine Elizabeth wanting to make an impression, appearances had always been important to her. She hadn't been short of money then, despite the state of the other rooms in the house.

There were a few more practical countryside clothes too, the kind you might see the Queen wearing as she strode along the Scottish hills followed by a flotilla of corgis. I thought of the dog, Patsy. I'd never seen Elizabeth with a dog. When I'd known her she'd always been a stiff, clean-loving type, not one for mud in her kitchen and a slobbering dog leaping in her face or lolling out of the window of her car.

Her car – there was no sign of it outside. She must have had one, I thought vaguely.

Had she been lonely? After Steph and I had gone? I didn't believe that. The few times I'd rung up, to check that Elizabeth was okay, she'd never been interested in talking to me. A short exchange and a cold, sharp tone had been more than enough to tell me that she really didn't want to hear from me. Had it been the same with Steph? And yet, there had been a dog, a warm, living, breathing animal that didn't talk back, that learned to do what it was told, but thrived on love and atten-tion. It made me think: the dog had been well cared for, you could see that, Elizabeth must have treated her well. Had the dog been her weak spot, her one little indulgence? Had she mellowed in those intervening years?

And what about Craig? Why had he ended up with her dog? Elizabeth's neighbour stepping in to care for it. Had they gone for walks together? Had she visited his workshop, talking about his craft, or the weather, or the people in the village? Had he fixed her kitchen, arriving each day with a toolbox in his hand to build the cupboards and worktops? Had she watched, as I had earlier, whilst he worked away at them, sanding them down, smoothing the wood, oiling the grain and polishing them?

It made me laugh, Elizabeth admiring her younger neighbour. She'd been sixty-one when she died. Women that age didn't have lovers, did they? Of course, they did, but Elizabeth and Craig? No, not lovers, I decided. But he'd been kind enough to take in her dog.

The make-up was the worst thing. It was stuffed into a single box on a shelf in the en suite, a room that looked like it had been newly renovated. The shower gleamed with that brand new, never-been-used look, and a strong vinegary smell of freshly applied mastic clung to the surfaces. In the corner by the floor, someone had missed out the grouting between the last few tiles. Elizabeth, it seemed, had died before she could enjoy her new bathroom. It repulsed me, touching such personal things, the eye shadows, the powder compact, the little brushes and sponges she'd used to apply it all.

Then I found the medicines. There was a whole load of them, in one of those posh hatbox kind of bags, designer crocodile plastic, in bright lipstick red. There were pills and creams and tubes of this and that, with various painkillers tucked into the pockets, some of which looked pretty lethal. You could have poisoned a battalion with all that stuff, a much kinder way to go than pitching over a banister. She must have been ill, suffering pain. I didn't know how I felt about that. I put the medicines in a separate bag for the pharmacist. It wasn't the kind of stuff you wanted to put in the bin.

I stripped the bed, cramming the bedding into more bags, unwilling to sleep on them, *her* sheets, *her* pillows, the very thought made me sick. I was soaked with sweat by the time

I'd lugged all those bags down the stairs, piling them up in the dining room.

Already the day was fading. I still couldn't decide where to sleep. Elizabeth's room was the biggest, the smartest, with that view over the front and its own bathroom. But it was the last place I wanted to be. Perhaps if it were redecorated? I tried to imagine it art-gallery white, *my* paintings on the wall and a simple contemporary bed. No chintz, no fuss, no heavy curtains blocking out the light, not one whiff of my step-mother or anyone else.

A crash reverberated through the house. My head swung upwards.

I was standing at the bottom of the stairs, one hand clutching a bin bag. Had it come from the top floor? Or was that the attic? I wasn't sure. I was reluctant to go up there. Was it an intruder? In this weather? Who'd want to break into the house in the middle of a snow storm, the road was surely impassable by now.

There it came again, another crash and a blood-curdling yowl. I started, unable to prevent the hairs rising on the back of my neck. It sounded exactly like the tom cat that used to pick fights with my neighbour's cat in London. In this house?

I took the stairs two at a time, following the yowls. They were louder and more intense with each step. Up to the second floor, past my old bedroom, to a door on the right. The attic. I thrust the door open. Something shot past my legs, racing across the landing. I caught sight of a black animal as it leapt down the stairs. I spun on my heels and ran after it. Down both floors. It belted across the hall floor and skidded to a halt at the front door where it crouched low, glaring at me, hissing. I stayed on the last step.

A cat. It was the same cat as before, but not as friendly. The fur down its spine was all fluffed up. It bared its teeth, whiskers lifting, gums whitening as it hissed again. Something had spooked it good and proper. I was spooked too.

I looked behind me but there was nothing, no reason apparent for the animal's distress. How had it got trapped in the attic? I took a pace forward and it – she? – ran again, scooting through the gap of the sitting room door. I followed just in time to see her dive under the sofa.

I stood for a moment, chewing my lip. Did I really want a cat in the house? To make friends with it? It wasn't as if I was staying long. I thought of the cat food I'd bought at the Co-op – why had I done that? I walked out of the room and shut the door.

I climbed the stairs, right to the top, till I was standing in the entrance to the attic. The door was open, exactly as I'd left it. There were a few narrow treads, boxed in, leading up to the attic itself. Where the main stairs were carpeted, these were bare and wooden, the walls likewise. It was much darker than the rest of the house. I reached for the light. It wavered, buzzing, struggling to stay on as I took the steps, one by one, my shoes overly loud against the wood.

The attic was right under the eaves. As I emerged into the space I shivered, hugging my arms, a blistering draught tugging at my hair. I peered through the dim electric light which pooled on the floor between the roof beams. A single small window had been cut into the sloping wall, the highest window visible from the drive. It was totally inaccessible from the outside. The window was wide open, snowflakes blustering in.

How had it got open? I looked around, but there was nothing, no one as far as I could see. Just vague shapes, old bits of furniture and tea chests covered in blankets and dust sheets so that they loomed out of the shadows like trolls and goblins lurking in the woods. A gust of wind caught at the window and it slammed shut. The draught pulled it open again. Clack, clack, it went as the casement shuddered. Finally, I had the source of that noise from yesterday. It must have been the attic window all along, slamming in the intermittent wind.

I reached for the handle, relief making me bold. It was real, not some imagined bogeyman. The handle was ice cold, grasping at my skin, burning it, unwilling to release me as I struggled to close it. Looking at the frame, it seemed to me to have been forced. Perhaps a crowbar, or some other tool, bashed or levered against the fitment from the inside till it had twisted and no longer fit. How had that happened?

The window wouldn't shut completely. Even when I got it to hold firm, the outside air blew through the gap, sucking at my hand. It must have been like that for days, even weeks: everything near the window was wet, or frozen, white as if Jack Frost himself had cast his spell. My fingers trailed along the roof struts, leaving a wet line in the ice.

Day had almost gone. More snow was already smothering the window frame, blotches of white slapping against the glass, too fast for it to melt, too thick for it to slide down. The electric bulb fizzed overhead, blinking on and off like an angry fly attacking a lamp, useless but persistent. I surveyed the space.

I moved forward, avoiding the beams as I edged along the narrow height of the room. Dust flew up from under my feet, sparkling in the bleary light. I coughed, then stopped. What was that? A scratching noise?

I scanned the lumps and bumps on the floor. A few items, too big to be covered, rose from the ground. A tailor's dummy, a spindle-back chair, newspapers tied up with string. Ice clung to the print and I rubbed it clear, the paper damp beneath my touch. I could make out the headlines. February, 1953: *East coast floods cause devastation. Lives lost in bleak winter disaster.* The blades of a broken fan moved slowly round, clicking as they did. Had I nudged it by accident? I didn't think so. What had scared the cat so much it had shot out of the attic like that?

I slid my eyes back across the room. There was a definite movement, a small lump beneath one of the sheets. It twitched and jumped, stopped and jumped again, wriggling towards me.

I reached for a cricket bat propped up against a chair. My fingers tightened around the handle. The lump disappeared, the fabric sinking to a loose fold on the ground. It was quiet, the single bulb flickered on then off, on then off . . . I was plunged into a fusty gloom.

Something scuttled over my foot.

I yelped.

It stopped, mid-run, right in front of me. A rat, black and greasy, beady eyes glinting in the twilight. It was huge, its fat body bulging over in the middle as it sat back on its haunches, fixing me with its glare. I felt fear sweep over me. I absolutely loathed rats. It was so close, so revolting, so big . . . I lashed out with the cricket bat, screaming at the thing. It fled across the dust towards the stairs.

'No! Don't you go into the house!' It was a useless cry.

Both hands gripping the bat, I swung it wildly. Thunk! It hit the stairwell, wood splintering beneath. The rat darted out through the doorway, onto the landing. It streaked across the carpet towards my old bedroom. I leapt forward, pulling the bedroom door shut just in time, holding the handle as if the little bugger could have reached up and opened the door. It stared at me, surprised at my audacity. My heart was racing, my breath came in short, staggered puffs and I stood there watching, the skin on my back, my neck, my arms crawling, cricket bat still in hand.

Then the rat moved, turning tail to scamper down the stairs. One floor, two floors, just like the cat, only this time it bounded into the kitchen. I ran after it. The rat skittered alongside the cupboard kickboards, searching for an opening. I slung my bat onto the table and threw open the back door as the rat approached. It sniffed the cold air, gave me one last beady glance and bounced through the gap. I slammed the door shut and stood there, catching my breath.

That was what had scared the cat. A rat, a lone rat trying to live its life, seeking the warmth of the house – all farms had rats. That was why they had cats too. What was wrong with me?

I had a fleeting image of another rat, its yellow teeth chattering in my face. A nightmare from when I was little? I felt my fingers itching for the cricket bat.

I resolved to let the cat stay.

CHAPTER 9

'Hi, Steph.'

I was in the kitchen, the cool blue light of my laptop shining out across the table. Even a few hours later, I was still shaken after dealing with the rat. I'd lit a candle to cheer myself. The tiny flame danced in the corner of my eye as Steph's face wobbled and blinked and came into focus.

'You okay? You sound a bit down.' Steph's voice was a surprising beacon of familiarity.

'Oh. I'm fine, but it's horrible going through all her stuff.'

Steph nodded. 'I can imagine. Rather you than me. How's the weather? We've had a great blizzard here in New York. All flights are cancelled. I didn't get to Miami. The whole place is under wraps, state of emergency and all that. We're not supposed to leave our homes even to go to the shops whilst it's like this.'

I nodded. I'd watched the news whilst eating my tea, seeing the reports of a sequence of east coast blizzards in America and how they'd reached us from across the Atlantic.

'Yeah, it's a whiteout here too, I won't be able to drive anywhere for a few days in this, but I'm well stocked up. Craig, my neighbour, has been round with a load of logs.'

'Has he?' Steph was smiling, reaching out for a mug of coffee. 'And?'

'Oh, he didn't stay long.'

There was a pause. Maybe Steph was hoping I might fill the silence with more details.

'I've got a cat in the sitting room,' I said.

It was still there, supplied with a plate of cat food and a bowl of water. I'd have to let it out in a bit.

'Really?' Steph sounded distracted, disappointed perhaps that I wasn't giving up more information about my kind neighbour.

'Yeah, the cat turned up in the attic. God knows how it got up there.'

I decided not to say anything about the rat.

'And how are things with your work, are you managing to do some painting too?'

'Oh, it's good. My agent's sent me a new commission for fairy tales and some of the stories are . . .' I brought my hand up to cough. I wasn't sure exactly what word to use, but I didn't want to admit the effect they were having on me. 'I've got loads of ideas.'

I didn't mention the book included the story of *The Pear Drum*.

'That's nice.'

My sister sipped at her mug, hands curled around it, clothed in a casually elegant mohair sloppy jumper. There was an awkward silence.

'Which one are you working on at the moment?' she asked.

'*The Juniper Tree.*'

'Oh?'

'It's about a young boy and his stepsister. His father has remarried and the stepmother hates him, wanting his inheritance for her daughter.'

'Oh right, that sounds familiar. Why are there so many evil stepmothers in those stories?' Steph leaned back in her seat.

I laughed. 'This one's particularly gruesome. The stepmother kills the boy and feeds him to his father.'

'Yuk! Murder and cannibalism, what happened to happy ever after?'

'Fairy tales aren't always what Disney would have us believe. It's not like my usual commissions, this one's not really for children.' I grinned.

Steph laughed. 'I should think not, from what you're telling me!'

Later, after the call ended, I started to paint.

The house was quiet, the cat asleep on the sofa, apparently no longer distressed. I glanced outside. The night was arctic clear, the snow sparkling. As I stood in front of the kitchen table, brush in hand, I felt calmer, happier, I was in control with a paintbrush. Time didn't matter, here on my own, surrounded by nature's very own blank canvas.

Already I was filling in the purple blue berries and evergreen needles of a juniper tree. The story had so many starkly visual elements. It began with a young woman, desperate for a child, praying at the base of a juniper tree.

She cuts an apple, but the knife slips, slicing into her thumb, blood staining the snow on the ground.

'I wish,' she says. 'I wish for a child, as blood is red and the sun hangs in the sky.'

A child arrives, a little boy, exactly as the mother wanted, except she does not live to see him beyond a few hours. The juniper tree is her grave.

I sketched out the tree, its branches close and dense. I could feel its empathy for the mother, her love for the baby to come, its grief at the mother's death.

A new mother arrives, with a daughter of her own. Though the woman hates the boy, her daughter loves him.

The stepmother scowls with distaste. 'Would you like an apple?' she says to the boy.

'Yes,' he says, surprised that she has offered.

She points. 'Look inside the chest.'

The boy moves across the room. There's a wooden crate on the floor, the wood heavy and rough. He struggles to lift the lid and looks inside. But as he leans in, the stepmother slams the lid shut and the boy's head is cut right off.

I painted an open crate, the boy's bloodied head staring back at me. I spent time on his face, I couldn't let it go, his cheeks, his mouth contorted by death. It was as if I'd seen that face. I painted a green apple rolling beside his cheek, his stepsister looking down in horror.

Now the stepmother cooks a meal, a stew for the father home from work.

'Mmmm, this is very tasty, my dear. But where's my son? Why isn't he here to eat?'

'Oh, he's gone to visit his uncle, my love. He'll be back within a week.'

I painted the stepmother smiling at her husband, her lips twisted with delight, and the little girl, too small for the dinner table, perched on her chair. She was staring at the stew, a finger rolling to the surface.

'I don't think I've ever tasted a meal as good as this!' says the father, stripping the bones with his teeth, throwing them over his shoulder onto the kitchen floor.

I drew the little girl on her hands and knees, gathering up the bones, placing them inside a folded handkerchief. I painted miniature bees and butterflies embroidered on the silk.

The girl carries the bones to the juniper tree, arranging them on the grave like flowers. They move, scuttling across the stone, nudging each other, jostling for place, shaping the figure of a bird.

I painted the bird as it sprang to life, its wings a shimmering kingfisher blue, flying over the girl's head, its beak open as it sang.

'My mother, she killed me,
My father, he ate me,
My sister, she gathered my bones . . .'

I painted the bones again, re-creating the shape of a bird. Except it wasn't the same bird. Not even a living bird. This time the image was that of a bird like the one in the butcher's shop, its head hanging down, its feathers limp and wet, its beak breathless and hanging open. I stared at it, my mind struggling to move on. My fingers plucked a fine-tipped pen from the stash of pens and I added more detail, lines and dots and strokes of ink, hunched over with an intensity I couldn't relinquish, until it was no longer identifiable as a dead bird, but a solid block of black.

Later, I climbed the stairs, looking for somewhere to sleep. I was Goldilocks searching in a strange house. I didn't want to use my old bedroom – it was small and depressing. The room next to Elizabeth's was too close to hers and I didn't want to use Steph's old room. On the far side of the hall was a fourth room, directly over the kitchen. It had been the guest bedroom, not that we'd had many guests. It had a side window, through which reared the black shapes of the derelict barns and a second window overlooking the garden. I felt my body relax.

I hadn't really paid much attention to the garden since I'd got there. I stood at the window looking out over the lawn with its flower beds draped in white. The moon shone directly down onto a wrought-iron bench on the patio where a bird had left delicate marks in the snow. Trees dominated the far end of the garden, their thick limbs piercing the sky. Beyond was a snowy hexagonal roof, a summerhouse. My eyes slid across to the fields and the spectral hills gleaming in the distance.

This last room had been stripped of everything. The bed was unmade, the shelves bare. Good, I thought, this would do fine.

But sleep evaded me, my head still creating pictures.

Clack, clack, the noise echoed through the house. And when I closed my eyes I saw the attic, with its blanket-covered bumps and frozen window.

Clack, clack, the window was opening, slowly spilling moonlight onto the floor.

Clack, clack and a long finger of silver white reached out, stretching across the room, pointing towards one lump in particular. It moved, the covers lifting, two beady eyes peering from beneath. The covers dropped and the eyes disappeared. But the larger shape remained. Ominous but familiar. In the furthest, blackest corner of the eaves.

The morning was bright, light reflecting back off the snow. The attic was at the forefront of my mind. I'd chucked the cat out the back door and she kicked a leg in protest as she stalked off, waving the tip of her tail, shaking her paws in the snow. I climbed the stairs, this time prepared with a torch.

The attic smelt of mushroom damp, cold air still blowing through the gap in the window. A pile of snow clung to the inner window sill and I brushed it away in a useless gesture of distaste. The bulb popped, finally giving up, but there was enough early morning sunlight to shine across the room. I didn't need my torch. The sheets that covered the floor looked a whole lot less sinister by day as I pulled them off, one by one, like a waiter in a Michelin-starred restaurant.

There were toys I didn't remember, boxes of Lego and farmyard figures, adventure books and tennis racquets. Surely, if we'd had these, I would have known? I felt a surge of frustration, I had remembered the books in my room, the Monopoly game and soft toys, but these things felt alien to my hands. They must have been Steph's. It was normal, wasn't it, to not remember stuff from when I'd been so young? I searched my mind, but it was obstinately unresponsive.

My hand reached out again, then stopped, dropping to my lap.

There was another shape, much bigger. I felt a twinge of recognition, the images from the night before hovering, like the fingers of a hand too close to the nape of my neck, enough to make the hairs stand upright and crackle with electricity.

It was a crate. But different. This was the one I'd been looking for. The one that had been obsessing me.

It was large and wooden, rectangular and deep, with a brass lock. The timber, the rough, heavy wood, the way the lock levered up, unhooking itself from a double catch, it was exactly as I'd drawn it the day before for the story of the juniper tree. The realisation startled me. I had recreated it with such accurate detail, the image must have been buried in my head.

I dragged it towards me, hands reaching for the catch. It wasn't locked. Perhaps Elizabeth had known that it was safe from prying eyes up here in the attic. My fingers pushed the lever and the lid flipped open like a toy nutcracker's head.

I'd known what was inside, despite my reluctance to name it. With its life-sized wooden belly, a handle at one end and that long arm with its own secret box, reaching into the full length of the crate.

I'd found it.

The pear drum.

CHAPTER 10

Painted figures danced across the side of the pear drum. Birds and animals and humans too, limbs and faces blurring one into another. They frolicked and laughed, leering like drunken revellers with expressions of twisted joy. Was it some kind of pagan ritual, a circle of villagers driven into a frenzy by the heavy rhythmic thrum of a pear drum?

My fingers clutched the edges of the crate, my knuckles bent white. For a moment I was drowning in remembered fear. But my stepmother was dead, wasn't she? And I was an adult, a rational, intelligent adult. She had no power over me any more.

I made myself lift it out, struggling to fit it on my knees as I pushed the crate away. I was a child again, sitting with my legs tucked in, staring at the pear drum, overwhelmed by the size of it, the weight of it.

I'd seen pictures of one once, on the internet. It cropped

up when I was researching early musical instruments for a project. For the rest of that day it possessed me despite all attempts to put it from my mind. I'd found videos demonstrating how it worked. It was so big that normally it was balanced on the knees of two people, one of them winding the handle at the far end, the other pressing the keys on the side of the box. There was a stone carving of something similar, held by two medieval minstrels, side by side, high on the wall of a cathedral in Barcelona, their bare heads baking in the Spanish sun.

I remembered my stepmother, that day in my father's study when I was six, when she was dressed in black, her face narrowed in concentration, the wild, raucous, hideous notes, their screaming tearing at my ears.

It felt illicit, just holding the thing.

I'd no idea where she'd got it from, she'd never said. She'd brought it with her, the day she arrived, or so I assumed. But it was a part of her taunting of me, asking me to explain how it worked, knowing that I had no idea.

Then she would tell me the story.

This was the memory of Elizabeth that haunted me the most. That story. And those words, with which the story always ended.

I thought of the commission. *The Pear Drum and Other Dark Tales from the Nursery.* I supposed it was inevitable I would come across the story again at some point, with my interest in fairy tales and my job. Or was it the other way round? Had my interest come from an obsession with a story I couldn't quite let go? It had given me such a jolt seeing it there in the title of my latest project. I didn't need to read it, I knew the story off by heart.

I closed my eyes, picturing Elizabeth in her coffin, newly placed in her grave in her best suit, her face made up. The lid had been removed and she was sitting upright, the wild autumnal winds snatching at her hair. She glared at me as if to tell me the story again.

I opened my eyes, staring into space.

It was Elizabeth's voice that I heard in my head.

Two children, sisters – Turkey and Blue-eyes . . .

Who would call a girl 'Turkey'?

Don't interrupt!

They had wandered off one day, out of their mother's sight, when they met a ragamuffin girl. The girl had a pear drum and she was playing it by the side of a stream. The sisters were intrigued.

'What's inside the box?' they asked. They meant the pear drum itself, the box built over its arm into which the strings disappeared, not the crate discarded to one side.

'Little people,' came the reply.

'Can we see?'

'Maybe. If you've been bad enough.'

The sisters were confused but went home. In the kitchen, they kicked over their mother's basket of laundry.

'Ohh, you mischievous little girls, whatever made you do that?'

The sisters ran away giggling, back to the stream, and demanded to see inside the box.

'Have you been bad enough?' asked the ragamuffin girl.

Turkey and Blue-eyes told her what they'd done.

'But that's not very bad, kicking over the laundry. I meant something proper bad!' said the ragamuffin girl.

The sisters thought about it this time and stole into the kitchen whilst their mother was outside. The elder rummaged in the cupboards whilst the younger stirred the stew.

'Salt! That'll do it!'

They laughed as Turkey shook the salt, showering it into the pan.

'More! More!' cried out Blue-eyes, till the stew was quite ruined.

Elizabeth told the story to me, not to my sister. This one thing I knew for sure with a certainty that gripped me like a hand around my throat. How come I remembered that and not other things? Why was that? And why would Elizabeth have told the story only to me?

Steph had known about the pear drum though. I'd seen her sneaking into our father's study, opening the crate. She'd wanted to know, when Elizabeth wasn't around, demanding I tell her the story Elizabeth had denied her, then gazing at my terrified face.

Turkey was smiling, thinking about their mother, her face as she tasted the stew. But the ragamuffin girl was still not impressed.

'That's better, I suppose. But you'll have to do much worse than that if you want to see inside my box!'

This time the sisters went wild, upending every piece of furniture in the house, even the beds. They broke the windows, lifting chairs and smashing them through the glass. It surprised them both, how good it felt, letting rip. They ran all the way to the stream and boasted about what they'd done. The ragamuffin girl just smiled, winding the handle on her pear drum, the music screeching in their ears.

When she stopped, she said:

'Are you sure that you really want to see inside my drum? Because do you know what will happen if you do? If the little people aren't satisfied, they'll hide from you and when you go home, your mother will be gone. In her place will be a new mother, with black glass eyes and a wooden tail!'

Of course, in the story, eventually Blue-eyes and Turkey did look, how could they resist? They'd gone home, one last time, bursting with so much curiosity, it overcame all their inhibitions.

Turkey spotted their mother's favourite hen. Blue-eyes fished out one of the kittens hiding under the table, the little tabby that their mother was so fond of. They both put their hands around the creatures' necks and squeezed. At first, not very hard, as the animals wriggled in protest. The hen squawked, the kitten's eyes widened, so the girls squeezed again. Harder and harder still.

By the time their mother came home and found the little bodies lying on a stone outside the house, feathers scattered all around, fur matted with sweat, it was too late. To undo what had been done. To think again.

Their mother sat upon the ground and cried.

The sisters ran, with all the eagerness of children at

94

Christmas, jostling the ragamuffin girl this time.

'You have to! Now you have to let us look!' cried out Turkey, pulling at the pear drum.

The ragamuffin girl let go and they opened the box, but there was nothing inside.

Had they not been bad enough? Had it all been a trick?

They walked home without talking. When they got back, the house had been put to rights, the glass in the windows was brand new, the furniture back on its feet. The hen and the kitten were still dead, but the bodies had been removed and the feathers swept away. Inside the house, there was no sign of their mother.

Then they heard it.

A thwack, thwack, coming up the path.

It was the new mother. She was beautiful, with smooth, jet black hair and skin as soft as snow. And eyes as black as glass.

Behind her, slithering out from underneath her full-length silken skirt, was a long wooden tail.

That wooden tail had put the fear of God in me – glass eyes and a wooden tail, that's what she'd said, whenever Elizabeth had showed me the pear drum.

Have you been bad enough, Caroline?

CHAPTER 11

I'd never opened the pear drum. The box where the little people lived. In all those years, Elizabeth had never let me.

I suppose I could have sneaked in and opened it anyway, but I'd never dared. Perhaps I'd been too afraid of what I might find. It was only a story, but even now, as I sat there with it on my lap, I still couldn't bring myself to open it. Even holding it made me feel sick, stomach acid burning up my throat.

As a child of barely six, curious, needy, and desperate to please, not long after Elizabeth had started telling me the story of the pear drum, I'd tried to think of all the things that I could do. To be naughty, to be wicked and evil, a monster in my stepmother's eyes.

But why? Why did the box – or was it the little people? – demand such a price? Where had the story come from – had Elizabeth made it up? I didn't think so. Truth be told, I had no idea. My memories of those early days were confusing. And before? It was so frustrating – I'd never really thought about it much, why my memories stopped before the pear drum.

I felt its smooth wooden curves beneath my fingers. Every day after that first day when she showed me the pear drum, she would taunt me, when other people were out of sight. She'd even make suggestions.

'Tip the table over, go on – that little one, the coffee table, you can manage that. Watch the mugs go flying to the floor!'

I'd scream as the burning hot coffee scalded my arm.

'Pull your sister's hair. Give it a good tug. Stronger. Look how it makes her yell!'

It did, but it made her kick me too, till we were rolling on the ground, biting, fighting each other, my tiny fists punching as my big sister tried to pin me down.

'Take it, Caroline, take the book, tear the pages out. Isn't it fun? Look at the mess it'll make! You can write on it too, spit on it, anything you want!'

It was a book a friend from the village had lent her, an expensive 'coffee-table' type book, all glossy photographs and artistic prints. When her friend came back into the room, Elizabeth would show her.

'Look what that horrible child has done. She hates me. She hates everyone! What am I supposed to do with her?'

And her friend would stare at me as if I had sprouted from Mars.

I'd been so naïve, not understanding. The gossip spread. Elizabeth's devil of a child, always causing trouble.

Until one day, Steph had gone. And I was alone. With my stepmother. And her pear drum.

* * *

I put the pear drum back in its crate. I closed the lid and fastened the catch. Then I pulled the blankets and sheets back over every object in the attic exactly as they'd been before, leaving the crate where it was, a shrouded shape amongst many shapes in the middle of the floor in the attic.

I had an early lunch that day, balanced on a kitchen stool, staring out of the window into the garden. I'm not sure I was even aware of the wetness on my cheeks until I reached up with my hand. The clouds were hanging low over the fields with that pregnant grey colour that promised more snow. I felt an overwhelming need to get out of the house, so I pulled on some boots, grabbed a coat and headed outside.

The snow was deep, piled up against the back door, and my feet sank unexpectedly far as I waded out across the lawn. I relished the cold on my hands, my face, numbing my feet. After a few moments, I stopped, looking back at the house. All the windows were lifeless, save for the kitchen where an orange light burned with an unexpected warmth. I could see the table, my artist equipment sprawled out across its width, my laptop, the lid open, the kitchen sink, crockery, one plate, one saucepan, one mug, stacked up on the draining board. My life. In the other rooms there was nothing, the blank glass reflecting only the grey clouds and the white laden trees outside.

I walked on, to the bottom of the garden, the summerhouse to my left surrounded by trees. The brick walls had crumbled with age, the windows partially shattered and overgrown with ivy. The wind blew inside, spiralling leaves and screaming through the glass. It was straight out of Shelley or Byron. But it was too real, too broken. It was like seeing a homeless person lying in a shop doorway. I felt pity and shame, a sense of helplessness and guilt, as if I was somehow responsible for its neglect, something I did not want to face. I turned away, heading down the slope and across the fields, head bowed against the cold.

Elizabeth had hated me, I knew that. She hadn't told me the story of the pear drum to amuse me, this was no sweet bedtime tale. Her eyes had glittered when she spoke the words. There was an energy in the telling of it, a chanting under-beat in the rhythm of her voice, the repetition of familiar words, vowels and consonants raining down on me like hailstones pelting from above.

How long had it been since I'd thought about all this? I'd consciously put it behind me when I'd left home . . . *home*, the word had a hollow ring. It was being here again, in the house and garden, dredging things up, the familiar, hate-filled words seeping back into my head like some foul poison bubbling up from the ground beneath.

After Steph had left, Elizabeth was less restrained. Or maybe as I grew older, I became more aware. Of the vicious tone in her voice, the coldness of her manner, the way her eyes followed me, watching my reaction, waiting for my shoulders to sag, my eyes to drop, my skin to flinch, with each word that fell from her lips. She enjoyed every moment. I came to fear that small room that had once been my father's study. The leather chair where he'd sat, the paintings on the wall, that monstrous shape festering in the corner of the room. She'd drag me through the door and the whole routine would start again.

'Stand up straight!'

Drilling every syllable.

'Don't you move!'

Every word punching the air.

'Lift your head, girl!'

As I stood there, frozen to the spot.

Even as she left the room, leaving the door open so she could watch, she'd make me stay, facing the crate, standing for an hour or more, until my knees began to shake, and my legs began to buckle. A punishment. For what?

At the bottom of the field was a set of footprints – a man and a dog, following the line of the hedgerow. I lifted my head, looking further down the field, half expecting to see Craig and his dog. Elizabeth's dog. Or someone else. I shrugged, I didn't care, or so I told myself. The field was empty, clumps of snow clinging to the twigs and branches of the hedges, here and there slipping down to the ground beneath.

I walked for an hour, until my breath was rasping, my trouser legs wet through and my feet sodden in their boots. Only then did I turn towards the house, climbing up the field, following my own footprints. I clambered over a stile, almost falling onto the snow on the other side, and there he was. Craig.

The dog barked the moment she saw me, bounding up with her tail waving, jaws open, tongue flopping out and a cloud of warm breath lighting up the air. I drew back, I wasn't used to dogs.

'Good afternoon!' Craig's voice was warm too.

'Hi.'

Even to my own ears, I sounded awkward. I stumbled, my foot slipping sideways over a buried rock. I struggled to right myself, cringing at my own clumsiness.

'She won't hurt you,' he said.

Craig reached out to Patsy, hanging onto her collar, dropping to his knees to make a fuss of her.

'I hadn't realised Elizabeth had a dog,' I said.

Patsy sat in the snow obligingly as Craig rubbed behind her ears.

'You didn't know her so well.'

It was more of a statement than a question.

But wasn't it true? I hadn't really known Elizabeth. Thinking of her with a dog and a pile of pills by her bed gave me a different picture of the woman than the one I'd carried around in my head all these years, and I wasn't comfortable with it.

'No, I didn't,' I said.

It was too late now, anyway. I was relieved.

'How come the dog ended up with you?'

'Patsy? There was no one to look after her after Elizabeth died. Someone had to take her in.' He looked at me then and I dropped my gaze. 'She's a lovely dog; I don't mind. And she knew me. I wouldn't be without her now.'

I licked my lips, they were dry and chapped from the cold.

'How's the house?' His tone softened. 'You settling in okay?'

'It's fine.' I almost snapped the words. Then, after a pause, 'Thank you for the logs.'

He looked at me, his eyes travelling across my face. I blushed, to my intense embarrassment.

'You're welcome. If there's anything you need, don't hesitate to let me know. Neighbours have to look out for each other in weather like this.'

'Sure,' I mumbled.

I stepped back. I didn't want this – for him to be nice, reasonable, attractive. I didn't want to feel like this. Not after

Paul, not here, not anywhere. Paul had taught me that *nice* was just a front.

Patsy leapt to her feet, tail brushing the snow behind her, eager to set off. Her eyes looked as if she expected us to all walk together. Craig gave her another pat.

'Right,' I said. 'Enjoy your walk.'

And with that I launched into the snow, taking a direct line towards the house and not looking back.

CHAPTER 12

'Briscoe, Williams and Patterson. Can I help you?'

'Hi there, can I speak to Gareth Briscoe?'

It was two days after my walk across the fields. I hadn't ventured out since then, nor even done much painting. The commission was something I'd been avoiding, snatches of the story of the pear drum drifting through my head. Instead, I'd concentrated on clearing the house. But each object, each corner of the house seemed to only reinforce the details of the story, a set of pans in the kitchen, an apron in the laundry, a dog-eared Victorian postcard of two children.

I was in my new bedroom, a headache building behind my eyes, my fingers clutching the phone. I was cold, despite just having had a warm bath.

'Hold on, please.'

The woman sounded breathy and eager to please. There

was a click and the line switched over to Vivaldi's *Four Seasons* blasting optimistically down the phone. The music was interrupted by a deep, slow voice.

'Hello, Gareth Briscoe speaking.'

'Hi, it's Caro Crowther. I'm the stepdaughter of Elizabeth Crowther.'

'Yes, Miss Crowther, I remember. How are you? How can I help you?'

'Has there been any progress?'

I bit my tongue, I was prevaricating, and I must have sounded desperate, as if I couldn't wait for this whole probate thing to be dealt with. I knew it would take time, but the truth was one particular question had been weighing on my mind.

'Well, it's only been a few days, Miss Crowther. Papers are being drawn up and I'm in correspondence with the investment funds. At the moment, I have no further news for you. But I can promise you that I'll be in touch as soon as I hear anything.'

He sounded impatient. My teeth had begun to chatter, the cold once more overwhelming me – why was the house always so cold?

'I understand.' I knew I must have sounded a bit frantic but I couldn't help myself. 'But what if this goes on for months? I'm not sure I can stay here that long.'

I reached out to drag a blanket from the bed and wrap it around me.

'You don't have to stay there, Miss Crowther. We can employ a clearance company. It's common practice with deaths where there's no close family. Ultimately, the estate *will* get distributed. It's my job to make sure that everything is properly accounted for, that your full inheritance is gathered together. We don't want to rush into things, do we?'

Rush into things? Didn't sound like there was much chance of that. But leave the house and its contents for someone else to sort through? And the pear drum? I was sure I didn't want that. Why was that? Besides, where was I going to go? I had no home anywhere else. Having taken the decision to come here, I was stuck, wasn't I? At least until the estate was settled.

'I've started to go through stuff, collecting things for charity. That *is* okay, isn't it?'

My real question – it had come to me as I was sorting – what if I got rid of it, the pear drum? Would that somehow transgress the terms of probate? Could I legally destroy it, dump it, right now?

'That's fine, Miss Crowther, quite acceptable. As long as it's only clothes and personal items that have no worth. You can't arrange to sell anything yet, or otherwise dispose of anything of value. Furniture, antiques and the like must remain in the house until we get the go-ahead. I already have a rough list.'

My heart sank. His estate agent, or valuer, had already done their job. Did Briscoe know about the pear drum? I had a hunch it was very old and probably very valuable. My sister knew about it. What would she say? I didn't want to ask.

'However,' Briscoe continued, 'whilst the estate is unresolved you're free to live there, as I told your sister. I understand you've given up your lease in London?' He didn't wait for my reply. 'And if you're struggling for money, I might be able to arrange for a small allowance. Technically it would be a loan, but we would simply repay it from your inheritance when probate is given. Have a think about that.'

'I will. Thank you. But surely there's something we can do to speed things up?'

How long did I have to live with that awful thing in the house?

'Not at the moment, we just have to wait.' He coughed, a rough, nervous kind of cough. 'Miss Crowther . . .' for the first time, Briscoe seemed unsure of himself '. . . is everything okay?'

'What?'

'Are you alright, Miss Crowther? You sound . . . I'm sorry, I don't want to speak out of place, this must be a very difficult time for you.'

'I'm fine,' I mumbled.

How could I tell him? That until matters were resolved, it was like living with a malevolent ghost. I didn't know what I wanted to do – to live in the house or sell up. It was hard to picture myself living here with the whole house infused with Elizabeth's existence and the pear drum still sitting in the attic. I swallowed. My emotions were all over the place.

'I see. Good. Is there anything else, Miss Crowther?'

'No, that's it, thank you Mr Briscoe.'

That evening it snowed again and the lights went out. There was another power cut and the boiler was on the blink again. I found the torch, some candles and matches. It soon looked quite festive downstairs with a few small flames dancing on the shelves, but it was too dim to continue clearing the house.

I went through all the rooms checking the radiators but they were ice cold, including the one in my bedroom. I returned to the sitting room and lit the fire, resigned to another night on the sofa and no TV. Even my laptop and phone were useless after a couple of hours, with nothing to charge them up by.

I propped myself up on the floor in front of the fireplace, leaning against the sofa. I'd found a bottle of whisky in one of the cupboards – I contemplated it, whisky was a bit out of my league. But it was there and, hey, why not? A bit of Dutch courage, I thought – I knew I had to get on with the commission too and I thought it would take my mind off the pear drum.

I poured myself a glass, my hands fingering the printed pages of the fairy tales, neatly stacked in a pile by my side, leafing through until I found a story that caught my eye. I started to read.

A sister and brother are in a garden. They must be rich because the garden is full of fruit trees, apple, pear and cherry, green leaves filtering the sun. As the sister reaches up to pick some cherries, the brother watches. His eyes follow her soft white hands curved around the fruit. He steps up behind her, slipping his arm about her waist, pressing into her body.

'Sleep with me, Sister.'

I took a slug of the whisky. The taste of it made me almost choke but its heat curled in my belly.

'No!' she says, her head twisting away from him.
The young man is furious. 'Why not?'
'Why do you think, Brother!'
She pulls free, spilling the cherries onto the grass at her feet. They scatter like drops of blood from a wounded animal.

I poured myself another glass of whisky. The amber liquid clung to the sides of the glass, glowing in the candlelight as I gave it a thoughtful swirl.

The next day the brother tries again, spinning his sister around, pushing her against a tree. He catches hold of one of her hands, holding it against his cheek.

'You are so good, so sweet. So perfect!'

He nuzzles her neck, holding her hand.

'Sleep with me,' he whispers in her ear.

'No. No! I will not, Brother!'

'Then I will ask our father that we should marry!'

And he does. The father is horrified, but the son is persistent and persuasive.

'Think, Father, if we marry, if we have a child between us, will he or she not be the most perfect of children, a pure-bred, with no risk of some disease brought in by an outsider?'

My glass was already empty, so I poured another one, my head pleasantly muzzy as I sank down onto the rug.

The father agrees. When the daughter hears the decree, she is distraught, begging her father, her brother to reconsider, but to no avail. She descends into the kitchens, seeking out the cook, holding out her hands.

'Take them,' she says. 'Cut them off, my hands. Then I will no longer be perfect and they will think me mad and they will not marry me to my brother.'

The cook wields the knife and her hands fall to the ground, two perfect silk white flowers.

I looked up from the page, reaching out for the bottle, tipping it to see how much was left.

I thought of Paul, the way he'd changed after I moved in with him, his ugly attempts to control me, my daily routine, my food, my clothes. I'd thought it was concern for me at first, but it turned into something else. Was that my fault? I thought of the other men that I'd met – not many – who had touched or approached me. Steve, a co-worker from the days when I was a student in Manchester, working in a bar.

He hadn't liked it when I'd said no, when he'd whispered rude suggestions in my ear and I'd slapped his hands away and ignored him. I'd felt sick. What right had he to assume I wanted his hands on me, or to hear those words? He'd got worse, cornering me in the back room. He'd pressed his body against mine, one hand on the wall by my head, the other sliding over my breast. I'd felt revulsion like a physical wave sweeping through my body, tarnished by his touch. I'd knocked his hand away and kicked his shins, but he just reached back, pressing closer, grinding into me, smiling.

'You little flirt!' he'd said, his foul breath hot against my ear.

He only let go of me when one of the other women came into the room.

Now I was 'irresistible'. He groped me whenever he could, even with the other staff watching, like he had the right. Everyone knew. I'd swear at him and push him away, always looking over my shoulder before going into the stock room or out the back on my own. Then I was a 'cold bitch', unnatural and unwomanly. Even the manager seemed to collude with him, winking when he saw us fight.

I lost my job in the end. I was getting desperate. The

manager said we had a 'personality clash', that he had to choose between us. He needed staff who could get on, who were friendly with the customers, smiley, happy, whatever it took to sell drinks and give the bar the right atmosphere, not cold like me.

Maybe I *was* cold, trapped inside my own inadequacy, incapable of intimacy. Maybe that was why I always made the wrong choices, why I always ended up alone. My own pathetic fault.

I found my work as an artist absorbed me. And I'd thought London would be good for me too. All those people, so many things to do, a buzzing world of art and culture. At first, when I got there, I hid from them all, hardly ever went out or connected, apart from what was necessary for work. I painted at home; I couldn't afford a studio or even to join a collective. It was much easier that way, not to take a risk, not to let people judge me the way they had here at Larkstone. I felt ashamed of my own cowardice – was this how I wanted to live? I'd been such a fool, playing it safe for too long. You couldn't live like that. Not *live*. When was I going to wake up? To get brave? To live the way my pictures were? Vibrant, sensual, exciting – unapologetic!

So then I started to reach out. I plucked up the courage to go to exhibitions, to force myself to meet people. My new-found confidence was fragile when I met Paul. He knew that, he liked it. It meant I was more focused on him.

I craved his company at first. Happy to abandon all my plans to meet with my new friends after I moved in with him. I was so pathetically grateful for his attention, and he was so charming, so *nice*.

But Paul didn't stay like that. He became more forceful,

frustrated as he put it, wanting more than I was willing to give. Maybe after that first anniversary after I'd moved in he relaxed, stopped being on his best behaviour. Maybe he got fed up with the way I had taken over his flat. My drawings, my clothes, my stuff. He started shouting at me, undermining me in front of others, treating me like another thing that hc owned.

'You've never been one for studying, have you, Caro? But she's a lovely artist, I think it's wonderful to have a hobby like that. Especially for a woman.'

By then I was too caught up to walk away. You have to love someone warts and all, don't you? But he knew how to press my buttons, to get a reaction.

We rowed once about my going to an event without him. It was a British Council presentation for artists thinking about participating in an international exchange. Harriet was bursting with enthusiasm and had asked me to go along. I told her I wasn't interested for me, but I'd go to keep her company.

When Paul found out, he wasn't happy. He was used to me always being there at his beck and call, doing what *he* wanted to do. Perhaps he thought since I worked from home, that that was my role. He slammed the door shut before I could pass through, grabbing my elbow, pushing my head sideways against the wall. My face was crushed, my eyes wide open and I felt pain shooting up my arm.

'You take one step through that door,' he said. 'And we're through.'

He leant against my body, his breath hot against my skin, spittle slapping against my cheek.

I don't know why I didn't stop it then. Walk away. It was

like I expected it, deserved it. I wasn't good at friendships, I'd barely dated anyone for longer than a week until Paul. Here was someone who wanted me, we had a future, didn't we? I'd never thought that might happen; I wasn't the glamorous type, the kind of woman most men went for. This was just Paul in a particularly bad mood, he hadn't been like this before.

But Paul was openly aggressive after that and my trust in him evaporated. The sex was rough and humiliating. I'd wake in the morning with bruises on my body and tears on my face. I thought he loved me, but then how could he want to hurt me? Passion wasn't meant to be like this.

When Harriet guessed she was furious. She was leaving for Berlin and that was when she offered me her flat.

'There's only a few weeks left on the lease, but it will buy you some time to find another place.'

'Stupid cow!' Paul said after I left. He'd rung me a few days later, still not believing I had gone. 'I'd like to wish you good luck, Caro. But what man is going to want someone like you? You have to work at a relationship. It's give and take! Can't you stand up for yourself?'

The derision in his voice was like a knife flung directly at my heart, twisting the truth so that it was all my fault. But I had, hadn't I? Stood up for myself.

I'd hung up. Whatever he'd said next, I didn't hear it. I didn't want to hear it.

So much for *nice*.

What the heck! I raised the bottle of whisky to my lips. The liquid seared down my throat to my stomach and my head spun. The bottle upright again, I raised a hand to wipe my mouth and stared at the fire.

I thought back to the story of *The Handless Girl*. I thought I could see the cook's blade flashing within the flames of the fire. Like watching clouds in the sky. I could see the woman holding up her handless arms, the two stumps gushing with blood. The severed hands were twitching on the slab floor, more blood running along the cracks, wriggling between the stones, one line of blood joining up with another.

The image made me gasp, it seemed so real, though I knew that it was not. What a painting it would be, I thought. It felt familiar, so strong was the image in my head. Perhaps I should read stories like this more often, with a glass of whisky to stoke the flames of my imagination.

Another slug of my drink and the red blood was flowing, spilling out through the kitchen door, flooding the hallway. There was another trail of liquid, was it the whisky? Amber gold, snaking across the stones from the opposite direction. The red and the gold met, rising up, spiralling like a great roaring dragon. I wanted to touch it, to capture the whisky blood dragon in my hand, to let it pour through my fingers.

I closed my eyes, imagining my hand reaching into the fire, fingers splayed. Now my hand was blistering, the skin turning brown, smoking, but I couldn't scream. The sound was trapped within my throat. I tried to visualise how I could paint that – a silent scream, or the smell, the horrendous smell of burning human flesh. The very idea consumed me, an almost hypnotic fascination with the skin, burning, bubbling, crackling, shrivelling before my eyes, long shreds falling off until the bones were revealed, skeletal fingers clasping and unclasping, tiny, flying, singing bones, rattling in the firelight.

I opened my eyes. In the flames of the fire, I thought I saw another face. The man from the story? Or Paul. But he was changing, morphing into a small boy, blood pouring from *his* hands, the golden flames rising up around him, smothering him, until I could no longer see anything but fire and smoke and a burning stump of black.

I reached out for the glass. The skin pulled tight over my bones. It was the whisky. Just the whisky, wasn't it? I wasn't used to drinking spirits. And my too-vivid imagination, trying to conjure up the story. My hand was shaking. My eyes had closed again. And all the while the screeching music of the pear drum was echoing in my ears. Where had that come from? The whining, droning low-pitched notes throbbing behind my eyes, drowning out the sound of the flames, exploding in my head.

The snow-bright sun was shining in my eyes and I rolled over to one side to escape it. The duvet was trapped around my fully clothed body, the cold floor of the sitting room hard and unforgiving. I must have fallen asleep by the fire last night, despite my plan to sleep upstairs. The logs had reduced to grey crumbling ash and my hands were soft and cool beneath my cheek.

The clock in the hall chimed three times and I groaned. Three in the afternoon? I'd slept all day in my drunken stupor.

I reached out to pull the duvet closer, moaning in my reluctance to wake up and the headache hammering at the front of my forehead. I wasn't used to hangovers. Something was next to me, resting against my arm.

I opened my eyes. It was the pear drum.

CHAPTER 13

I scuttled back across the rug. The pear drum toppled over with a thud, now inches from my feet.

How had it got there? I knew I'd left it in the attic. Had someone come into the house? Walked past me sleeping in the sitting room, climbed the stairs, entered the attic and opened the crate, then left it right next to my arm? I felt a shiver of horror ripple across my skin. That was ludicrous, wasn't it? Who would do that? And in this snow. Who would even know or care how I felt about the pear drum? But it hadn't moved itself, had it. Had it? I closed my eyes and opened them again. It was still there.

My brain was befuddled from sleep, and from the whisky the night before – it must have been me. Had I fetched it down earlier and forgotten? So drunk, so intoxicated, I'd overcome my own fear? Without its wooden crate it seemed bigger, more dynamic and more threatening. Now I was more than just alarmed. I felt my head burst with denial. No, this time someone must have come into the house.

I leapt to my feet, picking up a poker from the fireplace. The weight of it was almost pleasant in my hand. Energised by my anger, I searched every room, opening cupboards, banging doors, making sure I could be heard. I swapped the poker between my hands as I stormed from one room to the next, dragging open the curtains, looking under the beds, shifting any piece of furniture a person could be hiding behind. In the hall I flung open the front door, checking the drive for footprints but there were none.

I stood there, the wind biting at my face, poker raised in one hand. My car was a blur of white, almost completely submerged under a drift of snow. On the far side of the road a man was tipping food out for the sheep. He looked up at me. I sucked in my breath, but it was only a farmer. The one who had lost his sheep the day I arrived? I lowered my hand feeling foolish. What was he thinking now? I dithered over whether to call out to him, to ask for help. But no, I couldn't, what would I say? It must have been me. I must have moved the pear drum myself. The farmer scowled from across the road, snatched up his sack and waded back across the fields.

I closed the door. It *was* me, it had to be me. Nothing else made sense. Except I hadn't checked the attic yet. I spun around, my heart slamming against my chest. The farmer was already out of earshot and I was going to have to go up into the attic.

I climbed the stairs. The door was ajar. I could hear the same clacking as before, it had started up again. Each bang sent a jolt shooting down my back. A blast of cold air roared from above. My head emerged over the top of the wooden steps, poker held in front. The window was open, swinging in the breeze. I looked along the length of the attic, with its sheets and boxes and dust. It all looked exactly as it had before, even the wooden crate. It was there, as it had been, the lid shut.

I stabbed at every bit of cloth with the poker, hitting and banging each hidden object. I even opened the crate, fingers shaking, but it was empty. The pear drum was still downstairs. I was so angry now, fear pushed to the back of my mind as I slammed the little window shut. It stuck! I snapped the window bolt home. Amazing what a bit of aggression could do. I threw myself down the wooden stairs, fetched the pear drum and raced up again, placing it in its crate. I shut the attic door firmly behind me. There was a key, why hadn't I noticed that before? I turned it in the lock.

I ran down the stairs and tried the lights. The electricity was back on. I checked the front door. I checked the back door. Both were firmly locked and my keys were in my coat pocket. I checked that too. It was me, I was sure, I must have fetched the pear drum down myself in my drunken state. I was obsessed with it, always had been. It was being here again in this house, remembering Elizabeth and her story, haunted by those words. The same old fear stalking my subconscious. Had I walked in my sleep to fetch it? I took a deep breath, trying to calm myself.

I looked down at my hands. My fingers were black where they'd gripped the wrong end of the poker. It made me think of my visions the night before. I stared at the thing and almost laughed. I suddenly saw myself as I must have been, running around the house like a mad thing, waving a poker in my hand. Pokers, cricket bats, Jesus, what was I doing? Of course there was no one in the house. All those rooms harbouring shadows from the far corners of my imagination. *I* must have moved the pear drum. It *must* have been me. I felt the agitation in me bursting for release. Already I was dreading the coming sunset, the long night, noises in the attic. It was seeing the things I grew up with, facing up to my past, that bloody story . . . always that bloody story haunting me. I didn't want to remember anything, I'd moved away to forget.

Why had I come back?

The garden was exactly as before, only now it was criss-crossed with tiny footprints, birds and animals that had made the most of the faltering sun. I stood in my boots and coat, my heart still thudding in my ribs. Out, I had to go out. Anywhere but inside the house.

The light was fading, the whole day almost gone without me scarcely being aware of it. I ploughed into the snow, heading for the circle of trees at the far end of the garden, a hint of the summerhouse shimmering within. I felt a chill beyond the temperature outside, my hands pushing through the shrubs, sweeping aside the branches until there it was, its snowy roof lit by a last flare of sunlight, the unexpected glare hurting my eyes.

The summerhouse was the shape of a hexagon, the lower half brick, the upper half glazed all the way round. Except much of the glass was broken, missing or on the floor. A few panes remained, half slipping out of position, jagged and cruel, and the door hung from its hinges like an old coat flung against the wall. Inside was overgrown with ivy, moss and liverwort bonded to the metal frames. Piles of leaves had blown up against one corner, each leaf traced with ice, frozen in position, peeping from the drifting snow like bookmarks.

The sun slid from sight behind the clouds rolling in over the horizon and I felt the deepening chill enfold me. I stepped inside, reaching out to clasp the edge of a window. A sheet of glass dropped from above, crashing to the ground. I snatched my hand away, a line of blood welling on my palm. My anger, my bravery had gone. In its place was something else, a bitter taste upon my tongue, a prickling of my skin, a damp trickle of sweat rolling down my back despite the cold. I lifted my hand, sucking the blood gushing from my skin. It was warm and sweet. I moved forward.

My feet sank into the snow, crunching on the hidden bits of glass beneath. I stopped. I turned my head. My reflection flickered in the partial remnants of the windows. My hair was wild about my head, my skin pale and shining. As I moved, the profile of my face was distorted and repeating, each image leaping in its frame like a dark animation trapped within a spinning lantern. Perhaps it was adrenalin. Perhaps it was the effect of my hangover from the night before starting to fade. My brain was alert, recognition piercing the foggy clouds.

Was that another face in the windows, not mine? The head small and round, like a child's, the only feature a pair of eyes blazing from each wall.

I squeezed my eyes shut. When I opened them, the face was gone. It was only my face staring back. I closed my eyes again and there he was, imprinted on my eyelids. A boy. Here, in the summerhouse. Revelling in the broken glass.

I felt faint. My head swayed. There was that sound again, clack clacking. Like the attic window, except it couldn't be. Not now, not here, outside, on the wrong side of the house. I shook my head. It was still there, always a clack clacking, like wheels revolving inside my body, teeth grinding one into another, churning, driving a shaft that pierced the length of my spine, twisting my veins, spiralling into my heart.

I spun on my heels, skidding as I did. My head crashed against the side of the doorway, more glass dropping to the ground. The pain didn't register. I stumbled from the summerhouse, running across the snow, racing away from the house, the garden and its buildings. But it was like running in a nightmare, each step heavier than the last, cold icy snow filling up my boots, weighing down my feet. It had begun to snow again, the wind whipping up great flakes that filled the sky, blinding me, freezing me, enveloping me in ice. I kept on running, breath stabbing in my chest, burning as I clambered over gates, forcing my way across the field as far away from the summerhouse as I could go, all the time hearing that clack clacking, clack clacking, getting louder and louder and . . .

I stopped. There was the lane, winding and empty, devoid of all colour like a black and white photograph. Huge drifts of white snow had blown through the hedges, blocking the way. In front of me was a cottage with snow-capped lavender bushes pressing up against the wall.

The noise of the clacking was even louder, a rhythmic crash, like a wooden plank slapping against the floor. It came from a large outhouse straddling the cottage garden and the field. There were more bushes by the windows and a spill of electric light from under the door. I limped forwards across the snow, drawn to the sound, until my bloodied hand pushed at the door.

Craig was standing inside, his body facing away from me. His hands were outstretched, holding a tool against a lump of wood gripped within the lathe. His foot rested on a pedal thumping down again and again as the machine spun, the wood trapped at its heart, like a fly pinned to a spider's web. A pile of shavings had accumulated on the floor. They shifted in the breeze as I walked unseen into the shed.

I stood watching him. He was dressed in jeans and a T-shirt, despite the weather, a stove in one corner belting out heat. I was mesmerised, by the noise, the movement of the lathe, his hands. Beads of sweat clung to his skin, shining on the fine hairs of his arm, muscles flexing as they followed the rhythm of the lathe, his foot pounding on the pedal. Up and down, up and down, clack clacking.

I balanced precariously on the doorstep, my hand reaching up to my head. The skin at my hairline was wet. My fingers touched my cheek with red-stained tips. My ears rang and the noise of the stamping of the pedal slammed in my head.

Then Craig turned around to face me and I caught my breath. His eyes were black like an animal's. I swayed on my feet. Black and sharp and shining like glass.

Like the new mother in the story of the pear drum.

CHAPTER 14

'Caro?'

Craig's voice seemed to come at me from a long distance. A dog barked right behind me and the wind ricocheted off the door, slamming it into my hand. Fear, pure unadulterated fear swept over me.

I spun on my heels and ran back out into the night.

The front door key fell to the ground, the ice cold of the metal still stinging my fingers. The rest of me was oblivious to the cold, the pain in my chest, the rise and fall of my lungs as they pumped up and down. I reached down for the key, jamming it into the lock again. The door thrust open under my hands and I pushed it shut behind my back, jumping round to lock it from the inside. Once more the key tumbled to my feet, this time skidding across the floor towards the table. I staggered backwards.

I lurched towards the sitting room. Reaching to the windows, I dragged the old farmhouse shutters from each side. I slammed them across and bolted them in place. Next, I ran from room to room, bolting each pair of shutters until the ground floor felt like a fortress. Upstairs, I did the same, each bedroom and the floor above, double-checking the attic door was still secure. I ran back downstairs, peering through the small window high in the front door to look across the driveway. It was empty. No footprints. Except my own across the snow, already disappearing.

I darted into the kitchen, snatching up the phone. I fumbled to find the number for my sister. The tone rang out but there was no reply. The battery indicator blinked. I cast about for the charger. There it was. I struggled to push it in, but it didn't connect. I checked the ceiling lights, tapping the switch on and off and on again – another bloody power cut. I thought of my laptop, there'd be some juice left in that, but as I looked across the kitchen table, it wasn't there. What? It had been there earlier. What had I done with it?

I tried to think. Sitting room? Bedroom? I ran up and down the stairs until my legs were shaking, but there was still no sign of it. I collapsed on the wide bottom step, almost in tears.

What was wrong with me? Where was it?

How could I have mislaid my laptop?

I sprang to my feet again – it must be upstairs. Under the bed?

I took the stairs more slowly, pausing in the hall. One of the bedroom doors was open. Not the one I was using. The little one next to Elizabeth's. I'd left the door shut, I knew I had. I'd been in there only moments before in my scramble to close all the shutters.

But the door was swinging, the hinge smoothly quiet. Too

quiet, it had creaked before. The new white mark left by the splinter breaking off on the banister caught my eye and I heard a sigh.

It was coming from inside the room. The shutter swinging open perhaps, not quite properly fixed. I pushed the door and stopped in the threshold, my body refusing to move.

The room was dark. In my head, it seemed familiar. The same room but different. A memory of another time. The shutters were fully closed exactly as I'd left them, a faint gleam of winter white sneaking through the hinges. The light crept across the floor interrupted only by a small shape. There was something in the middle of the room. About the size of a crate. My eyes adjusted and I felt my chest heave.

It was a child. Sitting on the floor.

Maybe eight or nine years old. A boy. His hair was unkempt, curling at his shoulders, his face hidden as he looked down, his arms spread wide across his lap.

He was holding the pear drum.

Caroline? he said. *Is that you?*

His little voice was thin and reedy. Gratingly childlike.

I didn't reply. My eyes were fixed upon the pear drum on his lap. It swamped him. One hand was clasped around the handle. He started to wind it slowly. As it moved so did the wheel beneath the strings. At the other end of the pear drum his fingers pressed upon the keys, his arm impossibly long, fingernails overgrown and peeling. The keys hit the side of the box, clacking as the whole thing began to drone. The air hissed around him, the handle rhythmically rotating as the drone slowly took over, the notes long and low, rising in tempo, a thrumming that filled my ears and wrapped around my throat, squeezing the air from my lungs.

There was a hammering at the front door.

'Caro! Where are you? Are you alright?'

Was that Craig, his voice hollow in the distance? My mind was buzzing, my chest tightly constrained, the blood roaring in my ears.

Caroline – is that you?

My head swung back to the boy. He was speaking to me, and he knew my name.

'*What?*' I croaked.

He looked at me, his head tipped to one side like a bird, his eyes wild and vacant.

I couldn't see his face. Yet I knew him. The memory was getting clearer. It felt as if I was playing out an old, favourite script.

Caroline . . . He spoke again.

I couldn't drag my eyes away. No one called me Caroline. Only Elizabeth. My mouth moved but the whisper was voiceless in my head.

'*No!*'

The drone got louder, almost drowning out his quiet little boy voice.

Caroline . . .

The boy moved his head. The shutters and the window gave a shake, the light flashing across the room. His face blurred in and out of focus and the ground seemed to leap up towards me then rear back. I thought he had pale lips and white cheeks, or was it pink and grey? Grey like a pair of old net curtains draped across his face, torn and shredded to bits. No, that was his skin. I gasped.

Have you been bad enough?

CHAPTER 15

'Caro! *Caro!*'

Someone stormed up the stairs.

I ignored the words, staring at the empty space in front of me, the drone of the pear drum still filling my head.

He'd gone. How could he just disappear? I took an unsteady step. The door behind me crashed against the wall and a blast of cold air shuddered up my back. A pair of hands pushed down upon my shoulders, spinning me around.

'Caro!'

It was Craig, his voice louder.

The drone dissipated, like a tight cloud of brown butterflies bursting apart in my head, flying in all directions, fluttering across the shafts of winter sun until they were gone. I felt weightless. It was Craig that stopped me from falling.

'For God's sake, Caro, what's wrong with you?'

I didn't answer. The boy had gone, not even a mark upon

the floor in the dust where he'd been sitting. And no sign or sound of the pear drum. I couldn't drag my eyes away from the thin lines of silver moonlight streaking out across the room from the cracks between the shutters. It was moonlight, not sunlight. I threw a confused look at Craig. The cut on my head was throbbing, the skin swollen, more blood trickling over my eyes. What had happened? What had I seen? Had I been hallucinating? The pain in my head was getting worse.

'Come away, Caro. What's got into you? Why did you run off?'

Craig's voice, coming at me from a distance.

I felt his breath upon my skin. I almost flinched. But the spell had broken. I let him draw me from the room. He shut the door behind us, leading me down the stairs into the kitchen. He pushed me onto the hard, wooden seat of a chair and I heard the banging of kitchen cupboards. A minute later, he was thrusting a mug into my hand.

'Here, drink this!'

I took the mug, expecting scalding coffee, but no, it was cold and the liquid burning my throat was whisky, more of Elizabeth's whisky. I spluttered, pushing the mug away, but Craig forced it back, holding my hands around the mug, lifting it to my lips.

'Drink it. Just a little. It'll do you good.'

I wasn't sure I wanted to drink alcohol. I remembered what had happened the last time I drank. By now, though, I hadn't the energy to say no. I let him pour the liquid into my mouth and it scorched a trail into my stomach, leaving me unable to speak.

Craig watched me, the beam from a single torch lying on

the table splayed across its surface. It was unnerving now that I was back inside myself, those eyes of his holding mine, probing. They were no longer black. Why on earth had I thought they were black? I pulled away, looking at the mug instead.

Craig sat beside me. As the whisky warmed my belly, I realised I hadn't been afraid of *him*. My response to the pear drum, the summerhouse, had overwhelmed everything else. What had I been thinking of? What was wrong with me?

'What's going on, Caro?' Craig's voice was softer.

I coughed, pushing away the whisky-tightness gripping my throat. What should I tell him? That something was haunting this house? That I was having hallucinations? That *I* was haunting this house? Or that memories were returning I couldn't bear to face. Pour out the entire sorry tale of my childhood.

Tell him, a voice was whispering in my ear, *just tell him.*

'Nothing,' I said. 'It's nothing.'

'No, it's not. Something's wrong. You come bursting into my workshop in a right state. Having run, it seems, all the way from your house to mine.'

'It's not that far!'

I nodded towards the back door. It was far enough in this weather. My eyes drifted towards the windows, the shutters firmly bolted from the inside. Craig followed my gaze.

'And what's going on with the shutters?' Craig seemed too close. 'Why have you bolted them all?'

'I thought it would help, you know, keep the house warm. There's another power cut.'

All these power cuts. Was that normal? How could I

possibly explain what I'd just seen? Or heard? What I'd thought. And everything else that had been going on since I'd got here.

I sipped the alcohol. It kicked in a little more, relaxing my limbs. Had it all been in my head? Was I going mad? Or were memories that had always been elusive, inhabiting the unused rooms of the house, re-emerging in fits and starts now that I was back in the place where I grew up?

No, it was concussion from the knock to my head in the summerhouse, or shock, or something like that, a physical thing manifesting as visions and hallucinations. And my over-active imagination reacting to the stories of the commission. It seemed downright daft now, thinking about it, things being moved around by some unknown force, noises in the attic and a broken window. I didn't believe in ghosts and all that stuff.

Stupid lone female too scared by her own imaginings to cope without a man in the house, that's what Craig was thinking, wasn't he?

But what about the boy? He'd been so . . .

'And that's why you came all the way to my cottage? Because of a power cut? Through that weather?' Craig asked.

I dragged my eyes back to him. Was he like Paul? Not all men were like Paul. One minute I was running to Craig for help, the next minute I was running away – what must he think of me? The whisky must be doing its job: I felt the fog clear, the life slowly seeping into my body, my brain kicking back into focus. I took another gulp.

'Slowly, Caro, not too much.' Craig tapped the mug away from my lips, looking amused.

'I'm sorry. I only went for a walk, to the bottom of the

garden. I went inside the summerhouse, it's a wreck. I think I bashed into one of the panes of glass. They're broken. Cut my hand. Must have been what cut my head too.'

My lips were struggling to form the words. I'd begun to shiver.

'Then I was running across the field until I found your workshop. I wasn't looking for your house, you know.'

I was keen for him to understand that. I hadn't been searching him out. I wasn't interested in him. Like hell.

'Hmmm.'

There he was again, watching me.

'So, you were in a panic?' he said.

That made me sound like a foolish idiot.

'Yes, I suppose so.'

Even to me, my explanation sounded pathetic. Why had I run from the summerhouse? Why had I run from Craig? I knew why. My eyes were caught up by his. Rabbits and car headlights, I was thinking now. Perhaps if he thought I was stupid . . .

'And you came looking for me?'

'No.'

I tried a smile. I barely noticed him taking my hand, the fog was there again. I shook my head.

'It's alright, Caro, I don't mind,' he said.

His thumb was rubbing the inside of my wrist as if to warm me. I watched it circling my skin, sending trails of fire along my arm, like the whisky down my throat.

'Can you stop that, please?' I said.

'What?' he said.

'That thing you're doing with your thumb.' I nodded towards his hand.

'I'm sorry,' he said. He looked at his hand as if he hadn't realised what he was doing and let it drop.

He stepped away from me and for a moment I felt bereft, as if I really wished I hadn't said that.

CHAPTER 16

I awoke on the sofa. Someone was moving about the kitchen. My body tensed. I could hear music, the radio, a song playing out against the sizzle of breakfast, a buzzer jarring into life as the timer went off. Nothing unusual about that. Except it wasn't me. Then I remembered – Craig had said he would stay the night, to keep an eye on me. I wasn't sure how I felt about that.

I stood up, heading for the cloakroom. My head hurt, pain stabbing behind my forehead, but the cut had dried up. Craig had washed it the night before and found a plaster. Gingerly I peeled it off. I peered in the mirror. My face was pale, my hair tangled from the night, my eyes staring back at myself like an animal seeing its reflection for the first time.

I could remember Craig leading me into the sitting room, pushing me down onto the sofa and pulling a blanket over my shoulders.

'Sleep,' he'd said. Like a parent to a child. 'You'll feel better in the morning.'

But I didn't. I felt awful, not my head or the cut, but the embarrassment of my behaviour, bursting into his workshop, running off, drinking myself into a state whilst he watched me. What must he be thinking?

Craig was still here. Why?

'Caro!'

He must have heard me. He called again and I walked into the warmth of the kitchen.

'Good morning,' Craig said, smiling as the fridge door swung shut with a clunk.

The room was toasty from the Aga and Craig was in corduroys and a well-fitting T-shirt, a jumper thrown onto the seat of one of the chairs, his feet bare against the stone floor. I swallowed.

'Morning,' I replied, unwilling to commit my emotions one way or another.

'How's your head?'

Was he asking about the cut? Or my state of mind?

Or do you mean after all that whisky you poured down me? I thought. But I'd chosen to drink it, hadn't I? Why did I do this with people, think the worst? Push them away in my head. He was trying to look after me, wasn't he?

'Oh, I'll live,' I said. I gave a watery smile and my hand reached up into my hair, fingers pulling on the strands in a useless attempt to pat them in place. 'Electricity's back on, then?'

'Yes,' he replied. 'Come on, I'm guessing you haven't eaten properly for a while.'

He slapped a plate of eggs, bacon and fried bread onto the table, pushing a knife and fork into my hands. Where had all that come from? He must have gone home to change and brought the food back. We sat on either side of the table and ate.

After a few moments, I saw his eyes drift across to my artist equipment, the paint brushes propped up in a jar, bristles neatly smoothed, the lines of coloured tubes perfectly placed in order of shade in their box.

'You paint?'

'Yes. I'm an illustrator.'

'Really?'

'Yes, children's books mostly, you know.'

'Of course, the art shop.'

The one in Ashbourne, he meant, where he'd rescued me from Angus McCready. I nodded. I eyed the empty whisky bottle on the floor by the kitchen bin.

'Do you have children?' I asked.

I bit my lip. He smiled and shook his head.

'God, no – I'm not currently attached, if that's what you wanted to know.'

'Did you know Elizabeth well?' I rushed the words. 'I mean . . .'

Oh, Lord, what did I mean? My mind was drifting to the night before . . . My eyes flashed up at Craig and my teeth caught on my lower lip.

'Not really, I'd see her every now and again. You know, when I was driving by or in town. She used to walk Patsy past my house most days. I'll need to go home soon and take her out.'

I nodded, pushing the food around my plate.

'Where did you sleep?' The words burst from my lips.

'Hmmm?' He popped a chunk of bread into his mouth.

'Last night, where did you sleep?'

His growing smile broadened.

'Upstairs, in the big bedroom at the front.'

Elizabeth's room.

'Oh.'

'And you slept downstairs on the sofa.' He was laughing at me now, wasn't he?

'Oh.' I busied myself cutting a piece of bacon.

We both ate in silence. I could feel him observing me though. I felt warm and shuffled in my seat, reaching out for a glass.

'Want some water?' I said, standing up to fill my glass at the sink.

'No thank you,' he said.

'Thanks for cooking breakfast.'

'You're welcome.'

'You should know that Elizabeth and I didn't exactly get on.' I pulled my eyes up to his face.

'I know that. It's not for me to judge your relationship with your mother . . .'

'Stepmother.'

'Families are complicated, I know that.'

He stabbed a piece of bacon, not looking at me.

You're telling me.

The bacon gone, he stood up, gathering his plate and then mine, carrying them over to the sink where he left them on the side. Not a washer-upper then.

'Caro, you were frightened last night.' He swung towards me. 'Properly frightened, up there in that bedroom. What was it? What did you see? What did you hear?' He leaned against the table, his face close.

Hear? What did he mean by hear? Had he heard it too? The boy? Now my heart was hammering in my chest.

'I don't know what you mean,' I said. 'It was nothing. There was a broken window in the attic and it's been banging on and off since I got here. I thought I'd fixed it, only then it started up again. It gave me the creeps, that's all, you know, big house, on my own. It was just my imagination. And . . . Elizabeth, she . . . she died here, in the hallway. There was a splinter on the banister, I didn't see it at first and then it came away in my hand, exactly where she must have fallen, and you can still see the blood on the floor underneath. I can't help thinking about it. How she . . .'

My voice tailed off. I was annoyed with myself. I sounded like a complete wimp. That wasn't me, was it?

'I can fix the banisters for you, if you'd like?' Craig obligingly picked up on the hint. 'It won't take much. A bit of wood filler and polish and that mark will be gone. But I can't change what happened, Caro. You can't undo what's been done.'

What on earth did he mean by that?

'What—?'

I didn't get to finish my sentence. He'd reached out and taken my hand and I was caught unawares by his touch.

'Show me, Caro. I'll see what I can do.'

He'd left. I stood at the front door watching as he strode down the drive and onto the road towards his cottage. At least that damn scratch on the banisters was gone. He'd returned home and found what he'd needed, coming back to spend more than half an hour sanding and polishing it away.

I looked out at the snow. It was even deeper than before,

136

totally impassable by car. I was stuck, when all I wanted to do was jump in the car and drive back to London. Away from . . . what? I flung the door shut, bolting it top and bottom. I turned around to face the hall, stairs and landing, and the banisters.

It was just me now, alone in the house.

CHAPTER 17

The sound of my mobile made me jump.

'Hiya, Caro!'

It was Steph, her voice smooth and round with that now familiar nasal New York twang. I wanted to paint her voice, like steam rising from the vents in the pavement, and the gentle shuddering of subway trains beneath your feet.

'What is it?' I snapped the question, rubbing my hand across my eyes. Why hadn't she Skyped? Then I remembered, my laptop was still missing. I groaned.

'Caro? I can't hear you right – hold on, I'll try again.'

The phone went dead. Then it rang.

'That's better. I was hoping I would catch you. Got some news.'

'Oh, what's that, then?' I took a breath, willing myself to sound cheerful.

'It's the lawyer, he rang me late yesterday.'

Briscoe? Hadn't I spoken to him only two days before?

'He wants to meet with both of us. Says it's important.'

'I don't understand. I spoke to him myself and he said we just have to wait for probate. Why does he want to meet with us?'

'There are papers we have to sign, he said your call reminded him. So it's got to be in person.'

'Oh. But you're in the States and I'm snowed in here in Derbyshire and it's Christmas soon.'

Fortunately, my sister either didn't hear my irritation, or was too distracted. I realised my 'best behaviour' manner, since we'd been reconciled, was starting to slip.

'No, I think he understood that. We've arranged a meeting in a few weeks' time, after Christmas, on the twenty-fourth of January at his office in Derby. Can you make it?'

'I suppose so.'

'Great. I'm going to book a flight. We can do the sales. The shops are pretty good in Derby, or there's Nottingham. We can have some fun, like we said we would!' Steph sounded happy.

'Sure,' I said, wondering why I felt less than enthusiastic.

It was mid-morning. I wanted to draw, to immerse myself in a story, someone else's story, images running in my head, clashing one with another, bursting like fireworks across my thoughts.

I'd always been obsessed, notebooks stuffed in my handbag, my phone full of photos. It was the small details that caught my eye, the cracks on a window pane, dirt clinging to the glass of a lamp, the ambiguous reflections in a murky puddle of rain. I had a particular thing about insects, dead insects, the articulated segments of a woodlouse lying on its back, the long legs of a spider tangled in the dust, the ladybirds that clung to the window frames in winter, a narrow line of red and black climbing up the hinge, their colours fading and dry.

I sketched angrily, exploring ideas for the book. Wide sweeping black charcoal strokes, monsters, dragons and gothic arches rising from the mist, morphing into writhing lizards. I'd get it out of my system if it killed me, my fingers black from the dust, a pile of broken charcoal sticks accumulating beside me. Perhaps it was the concussion from yesterday, or the cumulative effect of being here in this house, seeing and touching familiar things. Perhaps it was the shock of seeing the boy with the pear drum. In London my paintings had been brighter and more childlike, colours splashed on the page like exotic fruit spilling on the ground, but here, in Derbyshire, everything was darker, denser. Pandora's box was open, the one in my head, and with each sketch, scenes from my childhood were peeling their fingers around the gap.

Like the day my sister left home, when I was nine. It wasn't a memory I cherished, but now it slid into my thoughts.

Elizabeth had been wearing one of those retro sixties-style dresses, a high scooped neckline and bare arms. Steph was standing on the doorstep, a beat-up old Ford Focus running its engine on the drive, a young man slouched behind the steering wheel. Already, at sixteen, Steph was leggy and chic, in a way that made heads turn. I admired her cool beauty. She was arguing with Elizabeth. They seemed to argue a lot.

I couldn't hear all the words, but the gist of it was Steph was leaving.

My sister thrust a small package into my hands.

'I'm sorry,' she said. 'It's a leaving present, Caro.'

'Sorry' seemed an odd thing to say as you gave someone a present. But I knew what she meant. We'd never been close, but now it felt like she was abandoning me.

'Thanks, Steph,' I said.

The package rustled beneath my fingers, there was tissue underneath the wrapping paper. Something girly? My nine-year-old self was curious.

'Don't let her get to you,' she said. 'Stick up for yourself.'

There was something about the urgency of her tone, but an underlying excitement too. She cast her eyes towards the car and the lanky teenager at the wheel. I felt a pang of jealousy. She had a chance to get away, to start afresh, what wouldn't I have given to do that? I took a step forward towards Steph.

'Take me with you!' I said.

Steph stared at me as if taken aback, and with an expression I didn't quite recognise.

'I can't,' she said. 'I'm not allowed to.'

At nine, I didn't understand what she meant by that.

'But you're my sister!'

'I'm sorry.' Her eyes flickered across my face.

There it was again, those words, a phrase that could mean so much, or so little.

Then she raised her voice so Elizabeth could hear.

'Goodbye.'

Steph hesitated, waiting for Elizabeth's reply, but there was none.

Her lips tightened and she stepped towards the car and climbed inside. The car door slammed after her and the car rolled away.

My stepmother didn't wait to watch it go. Her face was a

closed book, the kind with no real content, like lists or time-tables or scientific reference charts. She turned on her heels and went back into the house.

I stood for longer, gazing across to the road at the bottom of the track, a black line winding down between the green fields. A breeze caught my skirt, cool around my legs, and there was a whiff of wood smoke drifting from the chimney at the top of our house. I'd been too young to go with her, I understood that now – but then, it had felt as if I'd been left behind deliberately: the sacrifice that allowed Steph to escape.

Later, in my bedroom, I'd torn open the paper and looked at Steph's gift. It was a small mirror framed in cheap plastic. The kind you put in your handbag. A freebie from a Christmas cracker. My face scowled back at me in the glass. I hadn't realised then that I wouldn't see Steph for nearly twenty years. She really had abandoned me. And as the years passed, I had felt more and more bitter, as if I'd somehow believed she would come back for me. But then, I acknowledged, as time went by, had I even cared? Had anyone ever cared?

I painted the lane in front of the house, a girl standing bold against the wind. In her hand was the mirror, in the mirror was the face of the girl, in her eyes was the reflection of a bird, its talons outstretched, its beak wide open, its tongue flickering like a snake's.

I went to bed early that night, my head throbbing. It was so cold and I planned to snuggle up in a proper bed with a book. My laptop hadn't turned up, I'd searched and searched, but hadn't been able to find it. It made me feel even more isolated than before. What was wrong with me? I'd look again in the morning. I filled a hot water bottle and placed it in the bed not far from the pillow, under the covers to warm the sheets. I stripped off, throwing my clothes onto the floor and padding my way to the bathroom. I stepped into the shower and pulled on the taps to release the water. It sprayed down over my head as I tilted it to avoid the cut, warm water rolling over my shoulder, steam rapidly fogging up the screen. I leant against the tiles, letting the heat slowly bring my body back to life.

Tomorrow I'd clear the attic. Tomorrow I'd do at least one more painting. Maybe I'd work on that picture for Steph, the one I thought I'd do for her for Christmas. I was still struggling for ideas. I reached for the soap, vaguely aware of the bathroom door nudging open from a draught.

A few minutes later I stepped out of the shower. My hair was slicked back against my neck, dripping down my spine. I pulled a towel around my chest, tucking it in under my arms. I felt warm and clean, the blood coursing through my veins. I stepped over to the sink to brush my teeth. Tomorrow I should go through my father's old study. I'd avoided it so far, because of its associations. I coughed, filling a glass with water and swilling it round my mouth. I wasn't taking enough care of myself. I closed my eyes and gargled. A breeze lifted the corner of the net curtains at the window.

When I was done, I walked over to the window. I hadn't closed the main curtains, there was no point here in the middle of nowhere, out in the Derbyshire wilds. I pushed the nets to one side, wiping the condensation from the glass, staring at the blue night outside, the garden with its white covering, the contrasting shapes of the trees and hedges beyond. Something moved beneath the branches of the trees in front of the summerhouse. A fall of snow, slip-sliding onto the ground beneath. I was warm enough now and I let the towel drop to the bathroom floor.

I made my way back to the bedroom, bending down to snatch up my clothes. I stood up and made to chuck them on the bed. My hand froze in mid-air.

The covers had been pulled down. I hadn't done that. And the hot water bottle was on the floor. On the sheet below the pillow, exactly where my shoulders would lie, was a black and bloodied shape. A rat. A dead rat.

Its tail had been cut off. It lay against the sheet, a long tapering tallow-coloured tail lined up against the body. The greasy fur was matted and wet, crimson red staining the sheet, and the mouth was fixed apart, the two incisors top and bottom meeting in the middle. Yellow and bloodied and brown.

I clutched my mouth, the rank stench of the creature's flesh making me gag. I ran to the bathroom and only just reached the sink in time. But I couldn't bear to face the wall, my naked back open and vulnerable. I snatched up a T-shirt, pulling it over my head. When I turned around, the cat was sitting in the bathroom doorway, looking smug and well-fed. I hadn't seen her in a while and now she was here – with a gift.

I screeched at her, shooing her down the stairs and out the kitchen door. Then I grabbed a hand towel from the laundry basket, running into the bedroom to the bed. The rat was still there, its eyes open but clouded over, claws pulled in, pathetic in its solitude, lying there frigid on the sheets.

There had been another rat. It came to me now, a memory so strong I wanted to be sick again. I wasn't sure when. It was in the exact same spot, well almost, in my bed, a different bed. I could hear my little girl screams. Someone was looking in from the outside. Someone was watching me, tracking my movements across the room, laughing at me. He had a crown upon his head, his two hands drawn together like an animal's front paws, his jaw thrust forward and teeth chattering.

For a moment I rocked on my feet. Was this really a memory? It felt more like a flashback to a scene in a horror movie. Was my imagination confusing me? Playing back some film clip that had scared me when I was small? Like hiding from the Daleks in *Dr Who*. Was this a genuine memory from when I was little? Before Steph had left? Before even the pear drum?

I dragged my eyes down to the creature on my bed. The rat in my head had been disembowelled, this one was still intact. But both of them had their tails cut off in exactly the same way – did cats do that? I didn't think so. The sense of déjà vu was overwhelming and I stumbled backwards, my hand flying once more to my mouth. I spun on my heels and made another dash to the bathroom.

I couldn't sleep in the bed that night. I couldn't sleep in any of the beds that night. I sat in the kitchen for a while nursing a hot drink. I thought about why I was here, the inheritance, was it really worth all this? Wouldn't it be easier just to let someone else deal with the house, pick up my old life and forget about Larkstone Farm? And everything that came with it.

But I realised I didn't want my old life. There was no way I'd go back to Paul or London, and where else would I go? I could land on Harriet's doorstep in Berlin, I supposed, but I didn't want to impose on her again. It wasn't like she was family. But then, I thought, a wave of bitterness washing over me, what did *family* mean? This house was mine now, almost. I was entitled to be here, wasn't I? Why should I let the old feelings of alienation and fear take over me? Besides, I was stuck, at least for a while, snow or no snow, trust or no trust. I couldn't justify moving into a hotel even if Briscoe lent me the money. My emotions were all over the place. There was the commission too – I'd lose so much time if I upped sticks and had to search for a new place to live. I needed to figure out what I really wanted to do, where I really wanted to be.

And there was the pear drum. It was still skulking at the back of my mind. I didn't want to leave it unopened. But I didn't want to open it myself. Wasn't that the truth of it?

I stood up and moved into the sitting room, curling up on the settee with the television on full blast. Anything to break the silence in the house. When I got bored of that, I left the room, leaving the TV on and the door wide open for company. I perched on my stool at the kitchen table, the one I used for painting, and I drew. This was a drawing for me, anything I liked. Not the commission, not work, nor even the picture for Steph, not yet. But a way to get things out of my head, whatever they may be.

I drew an ugly sabre-toothed beast, hiding in the bushes beside the front door of the house. Its yellow eyes were burning from the paper. Was that Elizabeth? Steph? Or was it me? I drew a field full of indifferent cows. They were munching on grass, scattered in twos and threes across the turf. In the middle was a single tree, rising up towards the sky, its long branches coiled and bare, as naked as I had been. Hanging down was a body. A woman. Her hair was tipped to one side, trailing down her back, her feet pointing down. Her face was turned away, gazing in another direction, but I could tell it was me that I'd drawn. It was as if I could feel the rope taut like wire around her neck.

I kept on drawing all night. Until the paper lay in swathes about the table and the day dawned crisp and bright. I got up and stood at the kitchen window, shrugging and rubbing my neck, looking out over the lawn towards the trees that shaded the summerhouse. There had been a swing there once, underneath the biggest tree. I could remember using it, hour after hour, rain or sun, feeling the wind on my face, my hair whipping back and forth, my legs swinging forward and behind, my body thrown each way with the movement of the swing. The rhythmic sway soothed me, the blood pumping in my veins till it made my feet tingle and my hands glow warm.

I sat down again. This time I drew myself as I might have been then, sitting on the swing, in mid-backwards flight, hair damp and swept against my cheeks, eyes huge and bleeding.

The images frightened me. Why was there so much pain in these drawings? What was wrong with me? Or was I this pathetic twisted thing, channelling malevolent thoughts into my paintings like some psychotic patient playing at art therapy? It was still there, that blank wall, like a giant black speaker box, thundering out a heavy beat. Impenetrable, inescapable. The more I tried to remember, the more images and snatches of memory broke through then faded from sight, the more it felt like I was a wild animal scratching and clawing at a wound I could not reach.

CHAPTER 18

I was brain dead from lack of sleep. The idea of clearing the attic wasn't very appealing, but it had to be done sooner or later. The house was getting to me; being here was more disturbing than I liked to admit. Sorting the rooms weighed heavily on my thoughts and the sooner I got it done, the better.

It was bright daylight, the snow reflecting back the sun. Perhaps by facing my demons head on, I would feel better by evening. I climbed the wooden steps from the top landing into the little room. The window was still jammed shut and stripes of dust-sparkled light illuminated the space between the rafters. Now that the window was shut, it smelt of dank, neglected fabrics and prickling overtones of rat urine.

I started by dragging the blankets off, pulling each item down the steps, piling them up in the hall beneath. There were suitcases, cardboard boxes, the old fan and the mannequin.

But there was no way I was going to touch the pear drum. So it stayed there in the attic, alone in the middle of the floor-boards, as I scooted down the steps, dragged the attic door shut and locked it securely.

The hall was a mess, most of the stuff destined for the tip. The suitcases were mainly empty, but there was a hatbox too. I opened it to find a vintage black pillbox hat. I lifted it out. It looked scarcely used, with a short black veil. I held it with one hand, twirling it around. My forehead creased, I'd seen this before, I knew I had. I closed my eyes. A faint hint of perfume clung to the hat. *Her* perfume, and flowers too, the delicate scent of roses, too many roses all in the same place at the same time. What made me think that? And something else, another smell, strong and sweet and cloying.

It came to me, the black dress. This was the hat to match the dress. Elizabeth often went to church wearing a hat. I remembered seeing her in that dress wearing that hat, her fingers clasping a black and silver bag. She was staring out in front of her towards the altar, not even blinking. There was a coffin laid out between the choir stalls. It was a funeral – my father's funeral? Roses lay all around. They were on the coffin lid, on the floor, in baskets on the steps. People were carrying them too – the church was filled with people. The smell of incense mingled with the roses. I was right at the back, my hand held tight by another woman, for the life of me I couldn't say who she was. My fingers were crushed, the woman's face fiercely stern. She didn't speak or even look at me.

The members of the congregation seemed restless, many of them twisting around to look – at me in the back, and then my stepmother at the front. I heard one of them whispering.

'Such a wicked child. An ungrateful, dreadful, wicked child.'

'How does she put up with it?'

'I couldn't bear it if it were me. So brave.'

This last woman had lowered her head, her eyes sliding to glare at me, like the woman in the butcher's shop, their words sinking into the flesh of my chest with the swift accuracy of a sharpened filleting knife.

I went into my father's old study. For so many years, the room had been a place of dread, the only memory I associated with it being that of the pear drum and my stepmother's punishments. I stood in the middle of the room contemplating the corner where the crate had been all the time I had lived there. There was still an imprint on the carpet where its weight had crushed the pile. At what point had she moved it to the attic?

I couldn't picture my father. I'd been too young, somehow that had left me feeling even more bereft. And yet there must be a picture of him somewhere – surely my stepmother would have had photos of him? A wedding photo, holiday snaps, the kind of pictures any wife would have held onto, especially after the death of her husband. In all this time, it hadn't occurred to me that such things were missing from the house.

I let my hands trail upon the furniture – my father's chair, the bookcase, the desk. I opened the drawers and pulled out the books from their shelves, searching for anything, papers, files, boxes that might contain any clue as to what he'd been like. But there was nothing. Just dust and cobwebs and the dead remains of insects and mites that thrived upon old paper. I turned back towards the corner, to the rectangular shape on the carpet. I dropped to my knees. The edge had lifted away, blackened with dust that had never been hoovered so close to the wall. Perhaps it had been disturbed by the dragging of the crate. I pulled the carpet up. My fingers caught upon the gripper rod and I gave a sharp cry, pulling my hand away to rub finger against thumb. Something caught my eye. An envelope, crushed from long years under the carpet trapped beneath the crate.

I pulled it out, giving a sigh as I withdrew the contents. Hidden – they'd been hidden. All this time. By whom, my father?

A few minutes later, coffee mug beside me, I spread the contents over the kitchen table, a cluster of old photographs.

I sifted through the black and white images first. A woman sat formally on a chair, in a long plain skirt with a high-necked cotton blouse. Her head was stiff and uncompromising. Behind her stood a man in a bowler hat. They weren't smiling, in the way that people didn't smile in photographs in those days. I turned it over, 'Great Uncle George and Aunt Annabeth Lumley, 1910'.

There were more stiff, grainy photographs, startled babies in christening gowns like fishtails, repressed children in sailor dresses and miniature suits. There was a family group clustered around a small table. The men were standing, the women seated on wooden chairs. The table was bedecked with a lace tablecloth and flowers. One picture, its corners peeling, showed a grand-looking farmhouse: from the windows, the arrangement of the front door, I could see it was this house in better days. I pressed the photograph flat, smoothing away the years, trying to feel the shrubs growing under the windows, to stroke the cat sitting on the stone wall – it was a black cat with a smidgeon of white on one paw, exactly like my cat. I smiled. Of course, there had always been cats on the farm, in the barns in particular. Cats with a white sock. It must run in the cat family, that sock. I liked the idea that generations of cats had lived on the farm. Their house, not ours.

I reached in the envelope again. There was another envelope, '1989' written in faded blue ink. I slipped my hand inside and drew out a cluster of more recent photographs.

They were pictures of the seaside, the bright colours in contrast to the last ones, like stripy jumpers hanging from a washing line. There was a man and a younger woman laughing at the camera, carefree, feet splashing at the water's edge, shoes clutched in one hand, fingers entwined with one another. I could smell the salt sea air, hear seagulls screeching overhead, dive-bombing for ice-cream cornets and crisp packet crumbs. *His* face had that long nose, *her* face had my wild hair. My parents. I held the picture in my hands for a long time. Eventually, I set it down to one side on the table.

I searched through the rest of the contents. There were more like that, happy pictures. I felt a stab of envy. There was one of her on her own, in profile, gazing out to sea. Her flapping skirt was as joyous as the bunting on a fairground roundabout. A picnic, a boat on a lake, the pile on my side grew. A bedroom – she, my mother, was lying back against the covers of a bed, fully clothed, her arms stretched out, relaxed and happy, looking right at the camera. She looked so young, much younger than I was now.

These photographs had been my father's or even my mother's. He must have kept them, here in the study, hidden under the crate where Elizabeth wouldn't have thought to look. His previous life, before *her*. I'd hit upon a treasure trove of memories. Good memories. I thought of Steph and how she would feel when I told her. I ransacked the envelope with the same feverish clumsiness of a fox raiding bins in the street.

The last picture pulled me back. It didn't look like it belonged with the others, the paper was different and it was torn in two, the other half missing. It was me, in the garden. The summerhouse was in the background, sleek and shiny and new. I hadn't seen many pictures of me as a child, so at first, I wasn't quite sure. It was confusing because there were other children in the shot, a birthday party perhaps? But I thought it *was* me judging from the hair, standing in the foreground, not quite smiling.

I looked about six years old, in a brown and white print dress smudged with grass stains, grey socks wrinkled about my ankles. Steph was behind me, taller, looking past me to the other half of the picture. I knew it was her, not yet grown up, her floral sprigged dress smooth and clean, her hair hanging straight down her back. Her eyebrows were knitted together, her lips clenched. She looked furious. What was making her so cross? The ragged edge of the photograph teased me. What was in the rest of that photo?

I tipped the remaining contents of the envelope onto the table. There wasn't much left, no more photos, and my fingers shook as I sifted through scraps of paper, bent paperclips and old photograph mounts. A hint of colour peeped from underneath, the colours of a garden, green lawn and blue sky. My fingers tugged more urgently.

I laid the two segments side by side, sliding them into position. The torn edges were a perfect fit. Why had it been ripped up and not thrown away? Had somebody changed their mind? We, Steph and I, were looking at Elizabeth, a younger Elizabeth, smiling the first genuine smile I'd ever seen on her. She wasn't looking at us though. She was looking down at a small boy, maybe two or three years older than me,

153

his hand tightly enclosed in hers. A long-haired boy in a bright red Power Rangers costume.

The clothes were different, he was not so pale and this time he was grinning, but he was the same. The same little boy I'd seen only two days ago, sitting in the middle of the bedroom floor, playing the pear drum.

CHAPTER 19

I couldn't take my eyes off him.

'Have you been bad enough, Caroline?'

That thin, reedy little boy voice grated in my ears. A parody of my stepmother's.

My hands were shaking as I reached for the phone. I didn't care if she was in New York, or Timbuktu, I needed to speak to Steph right now. It was almost four pm here, so it would be, what, eleven in the morning over there? I still had no laptop so Skype wasn't an option. She'd be at work, I reckoned, but could answer her mobile.

The tone rang out, tortuously long in the wait.

'Hello?' Her voice quivered over the phone line.

'Steph? Is that you?' I was so relieved to speak to her.

'Caro?'

'Yes, yes it's me.'

'You alright? You don't sound okay.'

'No. I mean, yes, I'm fine.'

Like hell I was. I closed my eyes, trying to picture Steph's face, her cool classical features, her frizz-free golden hair, perfectly swept back from her head.

'Listen, I've been sorting through the house and I found a load of photographs, you know, from when we were young.'

'Oh, Lord, really? I looked dreadful when I was young,' she said.

Actually, Steph had always looked stunning in photos, a child beauty. But then one's sense of self is always relative and it occurred to me that even Steph must have her insecurities.

'You look fine,' I said, a little impatiently. 'There's pictures of Mum and Dad! You know – before *her*.' I waited for Steph to respond but she didn't speak. 'And there's this photograph I've found. We're at some kind of party, outside. Maybe it's a child's birthday party. I look about six years old and you're standing behind me.' I left out the bit about Steph looking cross. 'Elizabeth is there and we're both looking over towards her.'

'Really?' Steph didn't sound too enthralled. 'Where was this?'

I thought about it for a moment. 'It's here. I'm sure. In the garden.'

I looked at the photograph on the table. Yes, of course it was here, the trees, they were younger, smaller, but they were the same trees, in the same configuration.

'She's holding the hand of another child, a boy a little bit older than me. And . . . she obviously loves him!'

It was in her eyes, the slant of her head, her whole-body demeanour. I could see Elizabeth really loved that boy. Then it struck me, that look of fury on Steph's face was jealousy.

She'd gone quiet. I thought I knew the answer before I asked the question.

'Who is he, Steph? The little boy, who is he?'

I could hear the rustling of papers over the phone, footsteps and a door slam, as if Steph had stood up and closed her office door. Her voice was quieter but clearer when she replied.

'What's he wearing?'

Was she playing for time?

'A red Power Rangers costume.'

'Oh.' There was a pause. Then Steph spoke slowly, as if each word was cautiously pushed through her lips. 'He loved dressing up. That was his favourite costume.'

Another pause. The silence screamed in my ears.

'That would be Danny,' she said.

'Danny?' I jumped on the word. 'Who's Danny?'

'You don't remember?' Steph didn't sound surprised. Yet there was something about her voice. Frustration? Pain?

'No, I don't remember! I wouldn't be asking otherwise, would I!'

'It was *his* birthday . . .'

The line crackled, then it went dead.

I punched the number into the phone again, scratching the kitchen table with my nails as I waited for Steph to pick up.

'Caro . . . ? Is that you?' Her voice sounded different, distant.

'Steph? Yes.'

'I'm sorry, Caro. I . . . I don't think I can do this right now. I can't talk about Danny.'

I felt shock shooting through me. The name, her voice.

'I'll ring you again. Soon,' she said. The line went dead.

This time, when I rang back, all I got was an engaged tone.

I flung the phone on the table in disgust and it skidded to a halt against the butter dish.

Who the hell was Danny?

I paced the kitchen, holding the photograph in my hand, staring at it with the intensity of a stalking predator. Danny, Danny, Danny. The name meant nothing to me. And yet . . . the boy's face, his hair . . . it was almost there, hovering at the back of my head, a lurking monster of a memory. But whatever it was, was dangerous, like a shark circling under a boat, its body disappearing beneath the shadow of the hull and back again. I thought of the image I'd painted of the girl on the lane and the bird in her mirror. I pressed the photograph down against the table.

I wanted to remember more. If this house, the bedrooms, were bringing back the past, I thought maybe if I went outside into the garden, where the party in the photograph had taken place, I would remember.

I dragged my arms into a coat and pulled on my boots, unlocking the back door in the kitchen. It was almost dusk, streaks of blue gold lingering on the horizon, the colours sucking me out into the falling night, feet sinking into the snow. I ploughed my way across the middle of the lawn, swinging round to look at the house and then surveying the garden; the shrubs by the kitchen window, the stone patio with its ironwork bench, a table and chairs and various tubs, all darkening silhouettes capped with snow.

I tried to picture the scene in the photograph. The lawn in summer, green and lush, dotted with children like grazing sheep. A gazebo stood underneath the trees, dappled sunlight backlighting the canvas, balloons bobbing at the corners, shading a table heaving with food. Adults clustered together in small groups, wind chimes tinkling, laughter and screeches rising up with the heat.

The snow was up to my knees, spilling in over the top of my boots. I struggled to cross the lawn and my feet stumbled. I felt myself tip forward onto my knees, the breath knocked from my lungs. My hand swept down and I touched something. Wet and sticky, snow, but stained with red. A half-buried lump. I swore, my hand snatching back. It was the rat. The same rat? Surely, not, I'd put it in the bin. How . . . ?

I looked at it, memory edging into my head. He'd done it: the boy. The boy with a paper crown on his head. Dropping it onto my bed – not a proper bed but a sleeping bag, in a tent? – and laughed. He'd watched from the doorway of the tent as I discovered it, me screaming so loud that all the other kids could hear, and he'd laughed again.

Suddenly the memory of the party in the photograph grew. The black and white of the snowy garden around me melted away and lucidity swung like a beacon into my head.

'Caroline! Limpy, lumpy Caroline!'

How that reedy voice had rattled on my nerves, even then.

I'd spun around. He had a stick and was prodding it at the backs of my legs. A boy with overly long hair and a malicious glint.

'Happy birthday to you, squashed tomatoes and poo!' he sang.

It wasn't my birthday party in the garden, it was his, yet he was singing that song, mocking me. I stuck out my tongue and made a grab for the stick. He swung it up and out of my reach, laughing at me.

159

'Made you look, made you shit, made you fuck the juicy bit!'

I had no idea what he meant, but I knew it was rude, that it was naughty. He'd always swear when he wanted to wind me up. He knew it was rude too, of course he did, but I bet he didn't know exactly what it meant either. He sure liked the sound the words made though, and the reaction they got.

His head bobbed up and down as he whacked the stick against the grass at my bare feet, taking a swipe at my legs whenever an adult wasn't looking. He was clever that way.

'Give us a kiss, Caroline!'

This time he threw the stick to the ground and lunged at me. I ducked my head away and lifted up an arm. One small pint-sized punch landed him on the nose.

'Waargh!' He was running away. Finally. 'Waaaargh!!'

Right into the arms of Elizabeth. She swept him up off the ground, the blood gushing from his snotty nose staining her lovely linen dress.

'Caroline Lucy Crowther! You nasty little girl!' Her eyes pinned me to the lawn. 'Get inside, right now!'

The boy was crying, piteous tears rolling down his ruddy cheeks, one eye slanted towards me as he buried his head in her dress. All I could feel was righteous indignation and a burning rage. Somebody, another woman, the one from the church perhaps, had caught up with me. She grabbed my arm. I felt my shoulder hoisted out of position as I was dragged into the house, out of the sunlight. Through the hallway and up the stairs, round and up the next lot of stairs, to my bedroom on the top floor.

The room was on the north-west side of the house, hidden from the sun. It smelt stale and damp, a pair of curtains at the window left over from the 1970s, bright orange and white interlocking circles. The curtains were partly closed as if to reflect my shame. I refused to look at the woman who'd dragged me there, but already she was gone. The door slammed shut behind me and the key turned in the lock.

My phone rang, breaking the cold silence of my snowy kingdom. I clumsily pushed at the glass screen, walking towards the house.

'Steph? Steph, is that you?'

I tripped over my boots, fumbling to take them off one-handed, leaning against the stone wall by the back door.

'Hello Caro.' There was a coolness to her voice, her old British accent briefly slipping through.

I blundered into the kitchen with its warm orange glow and smell of freshly ground coffee grains.

'Thanks for calling me back . . .' The words were queuing up to spill from my lips – *who was he, this Danny?* But already Steph was interrupting.

'Look, Caro, I really think you should get some help. You look drained when I see you on Skype and you sound so stressed. What's going on? Maybe it wasn't such a good idea you staying in the house, sorting through all that stuff. Old memories and all that. I know it's an awful job. I didn't think, you know, with everything that's happened. It's been years. Leave it, Caro, leave it all and get out of there.'

'But I can't,' I said, stunned.

How could I leave now? Being here was bringing it all back – things I had buried in my brain. I didn't want to leave, not now. Despite everything. I needed to know.

'It's like I said, I'm snowed in. No one can come in or out.'

She knew that, didn't she? I pushed the phone under my chin, slapping one glove after another onto the kitchen table.

Steph had gone quiet. I could hear whirrs and clicks in the background to the call. We were going to get cut off again, any minute now.

'Who is he? Who's Danny?' I cried. 'That's what I was trying to ask you!'

More silence, except I could hear Steph's breathing on the phone. It came in short anxious rasps. Another quick change of manner. Or was that me? I picked up a stray pencil rolling on the table, pressing its newly sharpened point into the soft pad of my thumb.

'Steph?'

'Yeah, I'm sorry. I thought you knew. That you would remember. But I guess you were too young.' Steph's voice was normal again, slow and measured.

'Danny, that little boy in the photograph,' she said. 'He was hers. Elizabeth's. He was our brother.'

CHAPTER 20

'I don't understand. Our brother? Our . . . stepbrother?'

My voice was quiet, I was surprised that Steph could even hear me.

'Sort of. He was three years older than you. From before they got married, Dad and Elizabeth.'

'What, Elizabeth was married before? I didn't realise.'

'No. You don't understand, do you? He was theirs – Elizabeth and Dad's. They had an affair before they were married and she got pregnant. I was only about three at the time, so I don't remember anything about it, but Elizabeth took great delight in telling me later. She couldn't wait to marry Dad, once, well you know . . .'

Once our mum had died, she meant.

'. . . Danny was our half-brother.'

I glanced at the stairs. The lamp was on in the hall, on the table near the door, a circular pool of yellow fanning out across the floor. The stairs wound up to the levels above, plumes of dust gathering in the corners of each step. I'd had no idea. But it made sense, the memories of that long-haired boy, Elizabeth's evident fondness for him, *her* child. The boy I'd seen, imagined, in the bedroom next to hers – a memory of Danny.

'He had an affair – our father – before Mum died? Whilst he was still married to Mum? With *her*!'

'Yes.' Steph sounded defeated, ashamed even.

'Jesus! Is that why he married her? So soon after Mum died?'

'Who knows? Perhaps he wanted to be a father to his son. Perhaps he wanted a mother for us?' I almost spluttered. 'Perhaps . . .' and now she spoke softly, 'perhaps he loved her, Caro.'

'Where is he? Where is Danny now?' The words hissed from my lips. 'And why didn't he come to the funeral?'

'He's dead, Caro. He died when he was nine. Don't you remember that either?' Steph's voice crackled and broke.

'No, I don't remember.' My own voice was rising.

I didn't remember. Why couldn't I remember? My head felt like it was splitting in two. I felt overwhelmed with a sense of urgency and failure.

I'd had a brother. How could I not remember I had a brother? But he was dead. Pain exploded in my head and the words formed like barbed wire on my lips.

'How, Steph? *How?*'

'It was an accident.'

I opened my mouth to speak again, but Steph was talking over me.

'I don't want to talk about it any more. I'm sorry, it's too awful. I *do* remember it!'

And she put the phone down.

I stood there, holding the phone, dumbfounded. I'd had a brother? Could I believe that? Steph had said so. The memory of the garden party, the boy with a rat, the little boy I'd conjured up in the bedroom – that had been his old bedroom, hadn't it? The coffin at the funeral, the one with all those roses . . . The dismay ripped through me. How could I have forgotten that I'd had a brother and he'd died? And why had Steph never mentioned him before?

It's too awful. What did she mean by that?

I had a dread feeling of unease. I remembered the laughter of the boy I now knew was Danny. The taunts, the bullying, snatches of his voice, words and phrases I couldn't remember, that voice, its sneering tone and spite.

I had no memory of Steph or Elizabeth ever talking about him when I was little. Nine, Steph had said – he died when he was nine, when I was six. Had I been too young to remember? I'd always tried to think about my childhood as little as possible. A great curtain of pain descended on me whenever I thought of those years. I'd blamed it on Elizabeth, her twisted punishments, the tormented story of the pear drum that she – no, I? – had been obsessed with.

But was there something else? I thought of all those photographs I'd swept up that first night of my arrival, mainly of Elizabeth herself, or with a friend. But not us; Steph and me. That hadn't surprised me. And no son. Whatever happened, had it left her unable to bear looking at her own son?

I took a staggered breath. Why should I waste any time on it? He was *her* son. He wasn't even my full brother. What good was it to dredge things up? I'd had no family for so long. I'd lost my parents forever. I'd almost lost my sister too. What did losing a half-brother matter to me? I didn't want to

165

remember him, not now. I had this conviction that I should leave well alone.

Steph was right. I should never have come here. Being at Larkstone Farm had unleashed something, unlocking my brain to reveal a great yawning hole. Grief. Was it grief? I felt my stomach heave. Had he died in the house? Was that a ghost that I'd seen sitting on the bedroom floor? A flush of cold air swept down my back. No way did I believe in ghosts.

But memories and hallucinations, yes, and they were bad enough.

CHAPTER 21

The next morning, I couldn't bear to think about the day before. I determined to crack on and find anything that the solicitors needed to finalise probate. This new urgency, I told myself, had nothing to do with *all that*.

There was a bureau in the sitting room, one of those elegant perpendicular antique desks that folds down, revealing miniature shelves and drawers. As a girl I'd been fascinated by them. I opened it and papers came tumbling down to the floor.

There it was, my missing laptop. I lifted it out. I felt relief. But I couldn't recall putting it there. I chewed my lip, wondering if my pathetic memory was symptomatic of something else. I shook my head.

The bureau was stuffed full of bills from right up to the day Elizabeth had died. I began sorting them into piles, glad of the distraction – credit card receipts, household bills, paid, unpaid. There wasn't much unpaid, Elizabeth had been a conscientious accountant, if a little haphazard.

But it wasn't my favourite job, sorting through bills. Sunshine streamed through the sitting room windows giving an illusion of heat on an otherwise freezing day. The hills on the far side of the valley were long shadows of pastel blue and pink, shimmering with white as the sun rose in the sky, bathing the trees and hedges in a pale, sepia-like colour. There was a stillness, as if nothing was moving in weather like this, no cars, no tractors, not even the odd bird or two. Everything hunkered down for the duration.

The doorbell rang.

I peered through the window in the sitting room. It was Craig. His hands were tucked into his pockets, his legs planted in the snow, waiting for me to answer the door. Patsy was with him, her tail wagging enthusiastically. I felt an unwilling lift at the sight of them.

I closed my eyes and opened them again. He was still there and he'd seen me. He waved and smiled at me through the window.

I took a breath and went to the door.

'Hello?'

Patsy was up at the door immediately, excited by familiar smells, or maybe simply keen to see another human being. I opened the door wider and her big lolloping body made to launch itself at me but was caught short by a quick tug on her lead from Craig.

'I'm so sorry, she doesn't see a reason to wait.'

Why would she, I thought. It had been her home until Elizabeth had died.

'I can see that.'

I was being rude again. I tried to soften the words with a mock scowl of disapproval at the dog. Craig already had her sitting nicely on the doorstep, tongue hanging out, big eyes looking up at me, tail brushing the snow on the ground behind her.

Craig grinned.

'We've come to check on you,' he said.

'Oh?' I was embarrassed at my own lack of vocabulary.

He looked at me, his head tipped slightly to one side. His expression mirroring Patsy's, except his eyes were sharper.

'How's your head?'

I didn't reply and he carried on.

'I've brought you some lunch, see? Thought you might like some company.' He swung his shoulders around to reveal a backpack. 'And a bottle.'

He grinned and patted his chest, then unzipped his jacket to pull out a bottle of wine with a suitable flourish.

'Don't have to drive, do I? I'll cook.'

I hesitated and then stepped aside to let him pass. Craig reached down to unleash the dog. She shook her body free of the snow and pattered across the hallway towards the kitchen, sniffing hopefully.

Craig strode into the kitchen after Patsy. He tossed his jacket onto a chair and began unpacking his bag. There was steak, green beans, a plastic box of what looked like ready-cooked mashed potatoes and a smaller tub of sauce. I felt bemused, where had he got all this? The freezer? Expensive packets? It was another kindness from him – and wasn't this exactly what I needed right now, a bit of a lift?

I was feeling hungry already.

* * *

I sat at the table watching Craig at the Aga, my hands reaching down to tickle Patsy's head. She was sitting on her haunches to my right, looking from one to the other of us with excited canine interest.

Craig and I had been talking about nothing very important for a while, skirting round anything personal as he cooked the food. I'd opened the bottle of wine and was happily sipping a glass. I watched his back as he worked at the stove, noting the movement of his shoulders, his arm. His hair teased into curls at the base of his neck and he moved with a simple ease that held me transfixed. Patsy watched him too. I felt the tension slip out of me and finally succumbed to my curiosity.

'How did you get into carpentry?' I asked.

He turned to face me, as if deciding how much to say.

'I mucked about for several years after school. I never liked studying much and I'd messed up my exams. I messed up with a few friends too – and my family.' He shrugged. 'My dad told me to sort myself out. He was right of course, but I wasn't listening then. I wanted to make things, to do something tangible with my hands. I took a job in a factory that manufactured excavators for the construction industry and forklift trucks, but the pay was crap and the corporate management style wasn't for me.'

The steaks were sizzling. Craig turned back to fork them out one after the other onto a plate. He tipped the sauce into the pan and it jumped and jittered, the microwave pinged and Craig reached up to pull out the potatoes.

'For a while I couldn't find a job I liked at all. Then I got offered a place as a mature student at Buckinghamshire College studying Furniture Design and Fine Craftsmanship. I think by then I was ready to get more serious about my life.'

He lifted one hand to rub at his forehead.

'It was a revelation, crafting beautiful, practical things and learning how to work for myself. After I graduated I set up business, here at home in Derbyshire. My parents had both died by then. Cancer, one after the other . . .'

His hand moved to the meat on its plate and he prodded it without much purpose.

'But people knew me, and with a small inheritance to get me started, it didn't take very long for the business to develop.'

'I'm sorry about your parents,' I said.

'Yeah, me too.' It seemed a statement loaded with regret, and he quickly moved on. 'My bread-and-butter work is kitchens and built-in cupboards, but what I love best is making bespoke furniture and practical objects.'

He paused, looking down at his hands as if surprised at the skilled work they could do. 'I like to think my mum and dad would both be proud of me now.'

He frowned, memory taking him somewhere else.

The fat in the frying pan sizzled loudly and I heard him swear as it spat onto the back of his hand. He brought his hand up to his mouth to suck his burnt skin and grimaced at me sheepishly. I smiled and blinked sympathetically.

His hand reached out to hover over the meat with a grinder.

'Do you like pepper?' he asked, changing the subject.

I nodded. I watched his other hand grasping the pepper pot, the knuckles rolling under his skin emphasising the breadth of his palm.

He served up the food. I let Patsy go, standing up to wash my hands. I had to squeeze by Craig between the stove and the table, holding my breath until I was past. It was a relief to sit down opposite him and start to eat.

'What about you? How did you get into book illustration?'

I contemplated Craig's face, trying to assess whether he was genuinely interested. Paul had never been. Yes, I thought with a jolt of surprise, Craig really wanted to know.

'I've always loved painting. I see things in colours – numbers, letters, emotions, all of it. Show me a piece of writing and I see a kaleidoscope of colour, but it's not a jumbled crazy mess, they're sweeping lines, waves if you like, leading me down a path.'

I lowered my eyes, feeling an idiot for trying to explain it to him.

'Go on,' he said. His voice was low with interest.

'I . . . I don't know how else to describe it. Colour is story to me, the building blocks of mood and emotion, like words are to a writer. It's not only about drawing a line in the right place or getting a particular shape, it's about how you put it together, how the whole image *feels*. That comes from perspective and colour and texture and technique . . .'

I moved my hands as if to replicate the pictures that I saw.

'. . . it's about what I *see*. Inside.'

I drew a deep breath.

'I read loads when I was a kid, anything I could get my hands on. I'd see the stories in my head, the setting, the characters – sometimes they were dancing and I'd make them leap and spin, colours spiralling from their bodies, bursting into the air . . .'

My voice trailed away, until my face turned again and I saw that he was listening still. I felt a surge of confidence, he understood!

'I have to go beyond the writer's words, to find the personality in every character, even the minor ones, to root out the detail that will take the story further. It's a bit of a compulsion. I couldn't do anything else.'

I stopped. I'd said enough and was slightly out of breath.

'Sounds like you're in the right job,' Craig said. His eyes were shuttered. And then he seemed to relax again: 'You're lucky. It took me a while to figure out what I wanted to do. I got there in the end, but some people take a lifetime to work it out.'

I nodded. He was right about that. I was still watching his hands, imagining them at work, smoothing over the wood, grasping the tools, shaping, kneading. He wasn't so different from me, making things, creating sense and beauty out of raw materials and imagination. I looked up. He was smiling again.

'How long have you lived in London?'

For a moment I wondered how he knew where I'd lived before. Had Elizabeth talked about me? More likely it had been the village grapevine. I gritted my teeth.

'Since I left uni in Manchester – about seven years.'

'Do you like it?'

Did I? Had I? Maybe at first. I pushed my hand through my mussed-up hair.

'Not really, but I thought that was where I needed to be, close to the publishers and galleries.'

'And do you have someone waiting for you there?'

The question threw me off guard.

'I . . . that is, no. I did, for a while, but it didn't work out.'

I was fudging over the truth there somewhat. I dropped my eyes, unaccountably wanting to be honest with him.

'He turned out not to be very nice,' I added.

'Ah.' His hand slid across the table, flat against the wood. But he didn't touch me.

I held my breath.

'I'm sorry. Not all men are like that,' he said. I felt a small leap in my heart. 'If you told him where to get off, then good for you!'

I almost laughed at that, lifting my head.

'How's the steak?' he said, levering himself onto his feet.

'It's good.' Our eyes met. 'It's really good!'

Later, we washed up in silence, the easy silence of friends. I felt buoyed up, surprised at my own enjoyment. When the last plate was in its cupboard, Craig put his tea towel on the counter.

'Right, I'm going to let you be now, so you can get on with your work. I enjoyed our lunch, Caro.'

He clicked his fingers to Patsy and she jumped to her feet. I had a fleeting sense that Craig liked to be in control, that maybe he had felt as unsure as I had. But I felt more relaxed than I had before, more confident. And he was going to leave. I didn't want him to leave.

'Craig?'

'Yes?'

'I . . .'

I gulped. I wasn't used to this. His eyes observed me, a teasing smile spreading over his face. But he didn't move. Patsy sat down again.

'I . . . That is . . .'

'Yes?' He was smiling fully now.

'Thank you. For staying and looking out for me, you know, when . . .'

I stepped a little closer.

'That's okay, Caro. What are neighbours for?'

'And for the lunch.'

He moved towards me just a little. I felt the warmth of his body, even with the distance still between us. His eyes had caught mine and I was transfixed. There was an expression on his face, part amusement, part hunger and . . . what, self-restraint? Maybe that was it. He was a good man, I thought. Look at the way Patsy adored him. Dogs had always run a mile from Paul. Why was I wasting time thinking about Paul?

'I . . .'

I felt the need to say something, to fill the space between us, but what could I say? What had happened to me? Perhaps it was facing up to my past, finding out I'd had a brother, albeit one who'd died many years ago. My world was changing, it was changing me. And this man was different, I was sure of that.

My eyes slid over his shoulder and saw the empty wine bottle on the table. My feet shifted nervously as I tried to figure out what to do with my body. I rocked back on my heels as if to step away.

He lifted a hand and caught my fingers. He started that thing that he did with his thumb against my wrist, still holding my gaze.

Then he lowered his head and kissed me.

CHAPTER 22

Craig's lips passed across my own with the softest pressure. This wasn't Paul asserting his will. This wasn't anything like how Paul had been. Craig was teasing me, his touch smooth and tantalising. My head was dizzy. It was as if the whisky from the other night still smouldered in my belly. I felt my body lift towards him and I kissed him back tentatively.

'Caro,' he said.

His voice was guttural. He kissed me more firmly, pressing into my body, fingers pushing gently through my hair. Then he pulled away and took my hand, holding me with his eyes. We walked across the hall to the sitting room. I wanted this to be different, to erase the memory of Paul, of Elizabeth, of everyone who had ever despised me, even Danny. The flames of the fire I'd set earlier that day were still glowing in the grate and, with my hand in his, Craig rummaged in the basket to add kindling. He leaned down to blow upon the logs and I watched his lips as a small flame jumped into life.

His thumb moved slowly against my skin. He drew me close and we kissed again. I let him lower me to the sofa and I reached up with explorative fingers, watching his eyes as they closed in pleasure.

I awoke on the sitting room rug in a state of sated warmth. Somehow, we had progressed from the sofa to the rug and Craig's body was tucked around mine, his nakedness like a welcome hot water bottle, drawing me to hug his back, stroking my fingers across his skin. I lay like that for a while, enjoying the tingle in my toes – no more frozen feet.

I felt the slow movement of his breath, heard the steady rhythm of his heart. How long had it been since I'd been close enough to hear someone's heart? The house was quiet, the wind outside was still and I lay there listening, feeling, indulging myself, drifting back to sleep.

When next I woke it was daylight. The room was cold, the fire a blackened pile of charred strips of wood and white ash. I was alone on the rug. Someone, Craig, must have pulled an old-fashioned woollen blanket over my body, tucking it around my legs, my arms. I rolled over, staring at the pattern of light and shadows playing on the ceiling plasterwork; filtered by the wooden shutters at the window, they reminded me of ripples dancing on the water, fluid and repeating, soothing. I imagined a paintbrush in my hand, sweeping water across the page, colour blotting the paper one shade after another, each subtle hue merging with the next until I was appeased.

I could smell coffee and toast. I felt hunger drive me into

wakefulness. I rolled onto my stomach, the strands of the rug tickling my skin. I stretched out my legs and arms as if I were swimming, wriggling back down into the blanket, relishing in its rough comfort. Then I sat up, eager to get dressed, to follow the smell of breakfast across the hall. I felt a small tug of pleasure to think that we had just violated the sanctity of Elizabeth's pristine floral Laura Ashley sitting room.

I felt this was how the house should be lived in. By the two of us, Craig and me. I wondered if I was foolish to feel like that, but I couldn't help myself. As the day wore on, it was strange how easily I abandoned my work and daily routine to be with Craig. Patsy sat in a corner on her doggy bed, content to lay her head upon her paws and snooze as Craig and I chatted and kissed, lying close, reluctant to be apart for even a few moments. Time became meaningless and we ate and made love when we were hungry.

Over the next few days, I couldn't get enough of him. Craig did eventually go back to his cottage, but he came and went as if the house had become his second home. It was like I'd never been in love before, had never felt loved, full stop. I was excited, bewitched, every inch of my skin singing for his touch, eager – like an eager puppy. Was that pathetic? No, it was amazing.

It had never felt like this with Paul, even at the beginning. All thoughts of my troubles, Danny and my memories of the house had gone, supplanted by the sheer joy of being with Craig. Even the house seemed more at ease – gone were the creaks and groans and there were no more power cuts or disturbing noises in the night. Or perhaps I was just too distracted and happy to notice.

I hadn't heard from Steph for over a week. I swallowed my sense of guilt. Had I stirred up her own bad memories? I didn't want to think about Steph, or Danny or Elizabeth or Paul. About anyone else for that matter. Why should I think about any of them? I was defiant. Funny how with the presence of someone else, someone meaningful, all those ghosts and ghouls in the corner of the attic and the back of my mind were chased away.

So the days went by quickly, a second week, it was a blur. I couldn't stop thinking about Craig. Eventually I did have to work. I got an email from David, my agent, reminding me of the deadline.

In fact, David wrote, *the client is saying if you could possibly complete by the end of January they would be really pleased.*

It brought me up – I'd been expecting to submit mid to late February. A deadline always focuses the mind.

'It's alright,' said Craig. 'We've both got work and clients.'

He pulled me close and kissed me a little more forcefully than normal, as if the threat of work intruding on our fragile bubble of new love made him angry.

So now Craig went home to his workshop and I returned to my painting. But when he wasn't at the house, I was waiting for him to arrive. If I was lying in my bed alone, or sitting at the kitchen table working, I was waiting for him to ring. He didn't use Skype. My feet jumped the moment the mobile beeped and my eyes were drawn constantly to the front windows, watching to see if a figure was coming up the drive.

It was intoxicating. I felt liberated, free to be myself, to express myself in a way I'd never done before. I put music on and the paintings for the commission flowed. Each image was filled with colour and movement, each scene enhanced with mischievous detail. A forest where the trees were all entangled lovers. A pair of frantic snails etched into a stained-glass window. Two serpents, each consuming the other, wound in a translucent figure of eight.

But somewhere in my brain, it nagged at me, buried deep, as if I were avoiding it. The boy in the garden, Danny, my brother, and that blank wall. Why couldn't I see beyond it? Did I want to see beyond it?

CHAPTER 23

'Happy Christmas!'

'Happy Christmas, Steph!' I sat down in front of the computer.

I couldn't resist grinning at Steph's face on the screen as I waved a Christmas cracker in one hand and a glass of Elizabeth's sherry in the other. I'd been impressed that Craig had managed to rustle up a pair of Christmas crackers, given there was still so much snow. They were left over from last year, he'd said. The whole country had ground to a halt for its first proper white Christmas in years. Craig leaned in over me, his image alongside mine suddenly in view.

'You look happy, Caro!' Steph's face was pinched and she didn't seem very pleased. Was she thinking of something else?

'Oh, I am! Steph, meet Craig; Craig, meet Steph, my sister!'

Craig was bare-chested, his jeans respectably held up by a leather belt, except the buckle was still undone. He peered over my shoulder at the screen unabashed, his face in the camera looming large with an apparently squished nose.

'Hello, Steph, Caro's sister!' he said, waving his hand cheerfully. 'Happy Christmas!'

'You remember Craig,' I said.

As if Steph hadn't remembered Craig, my neighbour from the cottage. Funny, I thought, she really doesn't look too thrilled, you'd think she'd be pleased for me. I remembered our last conversation, but in my semi-alcoholic loved-up daze, I really didn't care. I didn't want to think about the past or the future. Only now. And she was in New York and I bet she had some athletic Wall Street banker tucked under her blankets. Hadn't she mentioned someone back in November, after the funeral?

'Hello, Craig.' Steph pushed her laptop further away and her face veered almost out of screenshot.

'You still got snow?' I asked, raising my voice.

'Yes, but it's under control and they've got the transport system working again.'

'Well, that's good then?'

It was a question, warning Steph that I'd picked up on her mood. She ignored me.

'I haven't posted you a gift, Caro, since we're meeting up soon. I thought you might let me take you shopping like we said, and you could choose something.'

'That sounds lovely, thank you. I'll have something for you too. I'll bring it with me when we meet up.'

My painting for Steph – I still hadn't decided what to paint for her, and what with Craig and my new deadline, it hadn't been at the forefront of my mind. I bit my lip. It was important, this gift – our first exchange of presents for many years. Far too long.

Steph nodded and I took a slug of sherry. Offscreen, Craig was doing his best to distract me with his toes and I struggled to keep a straight face.

'Okay, then,' she said. 'Look, I can see you've got company. I wanted to wish you a Happy Christmas and all that. Enjoy the rest of your day!'

Steph gave a wave and the screen shrank with a soft pop and she was gone.

Not a very successful Christmas call, I thought with a stab of guilt. I gave Craig a friendly shove.

'That wasn't very tactful, you know!'

'What, letting your sister know you'd got company?'

'You know what I mean – half naked, all over me. It's a bit much, isn't it?'

'Depends; most sisters would be pleased for you, wouldn't they? If they knew you had a "friend".' He gave the word 'friend' a little emphasis.

I lowered my eyes. Why would he want to have a little dig at my sister? But now he was reaching out and pulling me into his arms and it was a while before we spoke again.

Boxing Day came and went, and the day after. The temperature outside was rising and the snow had begun to melt. The farmer's tractor had been up the lane and Craig had made it through the road on foot down to the village. He'd left Patsy with a friend. He didn't say who and I didn't ask – all I wanted to know was that he was free to stay with me uninterrupted.

183

He'd come back with a top-up of food supplies, and at night the house glowed with candles on every surface, the kitchen littered with our coffee cups, wine glasses and plates. Craig and I spent our time together feeding each other titbits, snoozing in between sex and cooking in the kitchen. Work on the house clearance and commission had stopped and with it all thoughts of the past. I couldn't stop smiling.

The next day, I woke alone in my bed. Craig had left a note – *Had to go and fetch Patsy.*

I dragged myself from the bed to stand at the window. The sun was bright outside, warm enough to create small pits in the snow. I could hear the chink, chink of water flowing from the drainpipes around the house. I was reminded of my deadline for the commission. I got dressed, skipped downstairs and brewed myself a cup of tea. Sitting at the kitchen table, I thumbed through the pages to a story headed *Eostre*.

Eostre was the daughter of the Sun and the Moon . . .

A footnote announced that this was a Romany tale.

A goddess, her parents said, does not fall in love with the wrong type.

But unfortunately for Eostre, she did. She was so in love, poor thing, her eyes shining, her face beaming, her feet dancing across the floor.

'Who is it?' her mother asked. But Eostre was too excited to say.

'You must tell us,' said her father. 'We want to welcome this new god!'

Eostre calmed herself. Rubbing her palms against her dress, she took a deep breath. 'I have fallen in love with Earth!'

There was silence. The Sun looked at the Moon and the Moon looked back. The Earth was not a god. They spoke in unison, 'We forbid it!'

Eostre was in shock. The Earth was so warm and loving, so vibrant with colour and life. How could her parents not approve? But all the pleading and persuasion would not win them round. She fled the hall, seeking the one god she thought might be sympathetic, the one who had created the animals of the world.

'Can you help me?' she said.

'Yes, I can change you so that your wishes will be so, but once it is done, there will be no changing back.'

'I don't care. I want to lie in my lover's arms. I want to sleep against his body, to feel his breath upon my skin.'

Her friend smiled. He changed her there and then. Eostre looked down upon soft brown fur and a body that crouched low. Her nose twitched and her ears reached up. She sat on her haunches and smelt her lover's scent.

'Thank you,' she whispered.

She went a little mad with the joy of it, Eostre the hare. Leaping and bounding across the fields, pausing to listen for her lover. That night she slept in his arms, as her friend had promised. She hid amongst the tall grasses and laid her cheeks against the rich black soil. And when she listened with her long ears, she heard the rumble of his voice, the moans and groans of a thousand voices, the tiny creatures that lived within his flesh, the red rivers that pumped

185

through his veins, the deep, dark core of him beating out
a rhythm.

I put the papers down, unwilling to read any more. It was a story of love and happiness, but somehow tinged with regret. Love, it seemed, came at a price.

CHAPTER 24

Overnight, the snow had reduced considerably, though the great drifts that had blown down from the fields still clung to the hedges like a giant had strode across the hillside and spat on them. Water bounced and tumbled down the road, draining off the fields, and birds cheeped. The world outside was slowly coming back to life; there was even the distant growl of a car going by on the road, signalling our return to normality.

Now that Patsy was back with him, Craig seemed reluctant to be around more than a few hours at a time. He would stay late, sure enough, long into the night, but by the early hours he'd say he had to go home, that he didn't want to leave Patsy too long. It didn't make sense, he'd brought her with him before and it annoyed me, waking up on my own. I said we could go to his, but he just shrugged and laughed.

'It's a tip at my place, all dirty laundry and smelly socks. It's much nicer at yours.'

I wasn't sure about that. But perhaps it was too soon for him, to show me his home. I had to be patient. But I wanted to see more of him, not less, to hold onto that feeling of being cuddled up to, to wake in his arms with no rush to get dressed, no obligation to do anything at all, all day.

'What about tomorrow?' I said. 'It's New Year's Eve. Surely you can bring Patsy here for that?'

It was mid-morning. I still hadn't got up. I rolled onto my front on the bed, talking into the phone, remembering how the moonlight looked on Craig's neck.

'Oh no, I don't think she'd like that.'

'But that's nonsense. She lived here when Elizabeth was alive.'

'Of course, but that's exactly it – Elizabeth's not here any more and Patsy's been missing her. It'll be even worse with all the fireworks in the village for New Year, she'll be even more jittery.'

I didn't get it – Patsy adored Craig, and she'd been fine before. Could she still be pining for Elizabeth after all this time? But then I realised, Craig needed his own space, of course he did. The dog was an excuse to have a bit of a break.

'Okay,' I said, trying not to dwell on it.

Craig hung up, promising to come in time for dinner the next day.

I couldn't face the commission that afternoon. I couldn't concentrate. I decided to finish going through the bills from the bureau.

It was illuminating, looking through Elizabeth's credit card receipts, seeing how she'd spent her money. She had a fondness for farm-shop home delivery and a weekly flower display

188

from a florist in Ashbourne. She'd had expensive tastes. I scanned the statements. There was at least a year's worth. Last December's bill was high. Several department store charges, a wine merchant and two Ashbourne boutiques. Was that all for herself? The most recent statement didn't appear to have been paid and I placed it on the 'For Briscoe' pile. There were more prosaic bills, a delivery of domestic oil, household insurance, a car service . . . the papers fluttered to the ground one after the other, her life laid bare for me. I was sure she'd have hated the idea of me going through her stuff.

The service bill was interesting. She'd had a BMW X5, smart and eminently practical for the countryside, but where was it? There'd been no sign of a car outside. I could have done with one of those in this weather. I placed it in a new pile, before picking up the next bill.

'Hulland Ward Log Supplies'.

It was an invoice for firewood, dated 4th October, two weeks before Elizabeth's death. £150. It wasn't marked as paid as most of the others were. I fingered the paper thoughtfully, then reached for my phone and tapped out the numbers from the header. It was a long shot but they might be open.

'Ian Stokes here. At Hulland Ward Log Supplies. I'm sorry, but we're closed for the Christmas holidays, please leave a message after the tone.'

Not a very helpful answer machine message since it didn't bother to say when they were re-opening. I left a reply.

'Hi, this is Elizabeth Crowther's stepdaughter.' There wasn't much point in giving my own name. 'Could someone please ring me when you're back in?'

I gave my number and hung up. I tucked the bill into my

pocket and made a mental note to try them again later next week. I looked at the logs piled up beside the fire. Why would Elizabeth have ordered wood for delivery so close to another order of logs from Craig?

The next day, I was working when Craig arrived earlier than expected. The afternoon sun was shining across the kitchen table and I'd had to pull one of the shutters over the window. He came through the back door and slid his arms around me, pressing his lips to the side of my neck.

'Your nose is freezing!' I said.

'You'd better warm me up, then,' he said.

After a moment, I pushed gently away.

'I need to do some shopping. I thought you were coming later,' I said. 'I promised you something nice to eat for tonight and the snow's almost gone.'

Craig laughed. 'Shopping is not what I had in mind!'

I felt myself lean in towards him, one hand reaching for his chest. But I shook my head. I really did need to get some supplies. If we didn't go soon the shops would be closing early for the New Year.

'Later,' I said warmly. 'Come shopping with me.'

Craig's fingers tangled in mine, but I could hear it in his voice, the hesitation.

'Sure,' he said.

We drove in my car and I parked by the green. The butcher's shop was still open. As we walked past, the assistant and her customer looked up. I took a sharp intake of breath. The customer was Angus McCready, the man who'd been so unpleasant to me in Ashbourne. He was wearing a leather jacket, his yellow hair brushed back. He grinned in a nasty, derisive kind of way and I glared back. Craig hadn't seemed to notice.

I was jittery inside the Co-op, convinced that Angus was going to come in too, that I would have to face another confrontation. The look he'd flashed towards me was definitely indicative of his recognition and scorn. Horrible man, I thought, trying to dismiss it. I filled a small trolley as fast as I could and Craig followed me, picking out a bottle of wine.

'Morning, Craig!' A middle-aged woman stopped next to us. 'Did you have a good Christmas?'

'Yes, indeed, Miriam. And you?'

'Oh, pretty hectic, you know – the boys are all home and we've got my sister and her husband here as well.'

Miriam cast a brief glance at me but carried on addressing Craig. I tried to catch her eye, to include myself, but she kept her head focused on Craig. After a few more pleasantries, she walked to the till. I watched Craig's face but it was expressionless. My fingers clenched around my handbag and I reached out for a loaf of bread.

It was the same at the till. The assistant was all smiles with Craig as he bought his wine, but when it came to me she fell silent. As we left, I looked over my shoulder. The assistant was watching me. There was no aggression but I felt uncomfortable. I shot a look towards the butcher's but the closed sign had gone up and the blind on the door had been drawn down. There was no sign of Angus McCready.

'How long have you lived here?'

My question seemed to take Craig by surprise. His stride slowed a pace.

'Here in Derbyshire?' I added. I opened the car door and placed my shopping on the back seat.

'We've talked about this already. I don't know, a few years, I guess.' Craig rested his arms on the car roof, bottle still in one hand, looking across at me.

'But you were brought up here, you said, before you moved into Lavender Cottage.' I lowered myself onto the seat behind the wheel.

'Yes, here, then Ashbourne. I left for a while, like I told you. I haven't always lived in Derbyshire.'

He'd opened the door and laid the bottle on the floor. I waited as he climbed into the passenger seat.

'Oh. How old are you?' I knew he was older than me, but I wasn't sure by how much.

'Hmmm?' Craig had picked up his phone and was idly tapping on the screen.

'How old are you?'

'I'm thirty-four. What is this Caro, worried I'm too old for you?'

I felt heat rising up my face. I chewed the side of my lip.

'I'm sorry, I didn't mean to pry.'

'That's okay.' Craig was peering at his messages, clearly not that concerned. 'Do you fancy going to the Wassail?'

I was distracted by the about-turn. 'The Wassail?'

'The village Wassail – on Twelfth Night. It's a tradition, you remember, don't you?'

I did. On the 6th of January, they held a parade through the orchards and gardens of the village. The aim was to anoint the fruit trees with cider and make as much noise as you could to chase away the evil spirits. Though most of the cider got drunk instead. It was a noisy affair in more ways than one. It hadn't been Elizabeth's kind of thing and I couldn't remember ever having been. If I had, I had no desire to go again.

'Oh, I don't know about that – I'm not sure . . .'

'I think it would be a great idea, meet the locals, get to know a few people. Break the ice.'

Break the ice? Had he noticed too? The chilly reception I seemed to be getting in the village. The knuckles of my other hand clenched on the steering wheel and I felt my body tense.

'Maybe.'

He nodded, apparently satisfied with my answer. I pushed the handbrake down, released the clutch and the car slid onto the road.

It was only later that I noticed. After Craig had gone, a quick check on Patsy he'd said.

I'd gone back to the car to fetch that bottle of wine. Craig had sent me a text to say he'd forgotten it. The late afternoon sun was poking through the clouds, shining on the bonnet when I saw it. A continuous thin scratch, right along the passenger side of the car, from the rear wheel arch to the front bumper. Like a key held against the car, except there on the door the line morphed into letters.

BITCH.

The word leapt out at me. Someone had deliberately vandalised the side of my car. I'd have noticed it yesterday or this morning – it must have happened in the village, whilst we were in the shop.

Oh God, had it been Angus? Or someone else? The locals hated me, I was sure of it now. It wasn't just the butcher's or the women in the Co-op, the gossips resenting a newcomer. I wasn't a newcomer, this had been my childhood home.

It was all of them, wasn't it?

CHAPTER 25

When Craig returned an hour later, I didn't say anything about the scratch. I didn't want to ruin our evening and the celebrations for the New Year. I'd briefly considered calling the police, but what would they do? They wouldn't be interested, especially on New Year's Eve. There was no way of knowing who'd vandalised my car and I couldn't face the fuss. But I did talk Craig out of a trip to the village pub for midnight. He seemed happy to agree. We raided Elizabeth's drinks supply instead and drank the bottle of wine too, lying later in my new bedroom, bodies warm and tangled, only half aware of the sound of fireworks exploding in the sky above us.

The next morning, I couldn't get the damage to my car out of my head. After Craig left I went to look at it again, running my fingers along the scratch. It wasn't deep but effective for all that. I felt shame, for no good reason. I couldn't drive around in a car with that word. Could it really have been Angus? Revenge for his confrontation with Craig? Or sheer nastiness? Or was I jumping to conclusions? It could have been anyone, after all – someone who'd already been drinking perhaps, having a laugh. At my expense.

It was Wednesday morning, the 2nd of January. Craig had rung to say he couldn't see me for a couple of days. It came as a shock after such intensity. He had a project to finish. I said I quite understood, I had my own work to do. I held it in. It didn't mean he'd lost interest, I told myself. We couldn't carry on like this forever. There was a real world out there, life had to get back to normal sooner or later.

The shops were open again and I drove to Matlock Bath to get my car fixed. I couldn't bear to drive around with that scratch for all to see and I was lucky enough to find a garage actually open. It wasn't a proper fix, a full re-spray was beyond my budget, and I was still agitated about it when I got back. I threw my keys on the kitchen table just as the phone rang. It jangled in my head and I went to pick it up.

'Caro Crowther,' I said, wariness vibrating in my voice.

'Oh hello, is that Mrs Crowther's daughter?'

'Her stepdaughter, yes.'

'Hi, it's Hulland Ward Log Supplies. Happy New Year!' It was a woman. Her voice sounded reassuringly normal and cheering.

'Oh, hi.' I stood up in an attempt to make myself sound more positive on the phone.

'You rang.'

'Yes, yes I did. Thank you. Elizabeth died a few months ago and I'm up at her house going through her papers. I found a bill for logs from your company. It's dated the fourth of October. I wanted to know if it's been paid?'

'That's very kind of you to check. Let me take a look.'

There was a pause. I could hear voices distant in the background and the tapping of fingers on a PC.

'Oh yes, here it is. The invoice was cancelled.'

'Really?'

'Yes, someone rang to tell us she'd passed away. I'm so sorry for your loss.' She paused but I didn't reply. 'The logs hadn't actually been delivered yet, so it was a simple thing to cancel the order and reverse the charge. Please don't worry yourself, it's all sorted.'

Now I was confused. The order had been cancelled after Elizabeth's death and the logs had never arrived.

'Please, can you tell me who rang you?' I asked.

'Oh well, I'm not sure I can. I can ask around, but I don't think anyone in the office here would be able to remember.'

'Don't bother. It's okay. Thank you.'

I put the phone down slowly. Someone had been through Elizabeth's things, had rung to cancel the log order after her death. Who? Who would have had access to her papers, to the house? One of Briscoe's agents? I still didn't understand about the second log order from Craig. Why would Elizabeth have done that?

That afternoon, the doubts crept back. I was missing Craig already. Had it been too much, too soon? Had I been too enthusiastic, too eager, had it put him off? More doubts filled the void where Craig had been – about the people in the village, the rat, my car, the pear drum moving from the attic to my side that night. Danny. I didn't want to think about Danny.

To make matters worse, the clacking sound started up again. I checked the attic but the window was still fixed, so it wasn't that. It seemed to be coming from everywhere this time, in the wall, under the stairs, and I couldn't figure it out. I searched but found nothing to explain it. Was I going mad? Was the house really haunted? Of course it wasn't. But when I looked at the flagstones in the hall, at the bottom of the stairs where the rug had been, was I imagining that dull red stain growing? Maybe Elizabeth *was* haunting me. No, when I took a closer look it was nothing, just an old stain of who knew what and probably the reason why the rug had been placed there in the first place, to cover it up.

But with the house to myself these thoughts tormented me. Memories flashed up in my head as I touched the banisters, or sat in the sitting room, or opened a door.

'Look at you, Caroline,' Elizabeth had once said. 'What on earth have you done with that belt?'

I'd used one of my dad's old belts to pull a skirt tight around my waist. Trying to give my teenage self a figure. To be attractive to the boys at school, I suppose.

'Really, Caroline, you're ridiculous!'

Elizabeth mocking my appearance, as she often did.

Or another time when I'd come running in from the garden.

'Caroline! *Caroline!*'

I'd fallen in my rush to climb down from a tree. My hands were covered in mud and my hair hadn't been brushed for a week, my trousers had been rolled up to my thighs and my knees were black and bleeding.

'Look at the state of you! Do you expect to eat tea like that? You can go to bed early tonight with no supper!'

I was already close to tears from the pain of the fall. I'd

stared at her like Orphan Annie. She'd cuffed me round the ear then and my head rang as I stumbled up to my bedroom.

My memories of Steph were more confusing. There had been too much of an age gap for us to play together, and she was gone by the time I was nine. Mostly she ignored me, but we did occasionally fight, much to Elizabeth's satisfaction – it gave her an excuse to punish me again. Me – always me. If there was a choice between us, it was Steph who got away with it. Her own arguments with Elizabeth, however, were different. There was a bitterness I didn't understand.

One day, in the summer when I was seven, I was reading a book in the garden. Elizabeth had given it to both Steph and me, a shared gift at Christmas.

'You know how to share, don't you both?' Elizabeth had said. I could see Steph frowning.

Steph commandeered it, but months later, I'd found it in the sitting room and thought I'd take a look. It was an illustrated copy of *The Lord of the Rings*. I was struggling with most of the words but loving the pictures: dragons and hobbits and all those elvish runes lining the edges of each page.

A shadow fell over me.

'That's mine!' Steph's hand whipped the book from my lap.

'No, it's not! It belongs to us both!' I had the strident voice of a child for whom right and wrong is black and white.

'It's mine now!' Steph held the book high above my head.

I stood up and tried to snatch it back. When she laughed, I grabbed the sleeve of her dress. The fabric tore and she gave a shriek of distress. Her arm lowered and the book dropped to the ground.

'You little . . . !'

I dived for the book, but already Steph was there. We each

held one half, pulling with all our might. I could hear the spine of the book rip.

'Please, Steph!'

A book was such a precious thing to me, even then. It would split down the middle if one of us didn't let go. Steph wasn't letting go. My fingers opened and I fell back on the grass with a sob.

'Cry baby!' screeched Steph, waving the book in my face. 'Nothing in this house is yours!' she hissed. 'You don't belong!'

It was the law of possession, and who was biggest. I knew that.

She came to me the next day. I'd heard voices, moments before, Elizabeth and Steph shouting, Steph's voice shrill and fierce. I didn't know what it was about.

Steph came to my bedroom – she never did that. She walked into the room without knocking and closed the door, holding something behind her.

I was sitting on my bed by the window, leafing through a picture book from school. I pushed the book under the pillow behind me. She didn't react.

'Hi Caro.' She seemed oddly not herself.

'Hi, Steph.' I didn't know what to say.

She sat on the edge of my bed, her face turned away from the window, so I couldn't see her expression. Her long hair fell over one shoulder and with her free hand she was fidgeting with the end of it. I wriggled back against my pillow as far from her as I could get.

'You know, you and I shouldn't fight. We're sisters, you know that, don't you?'

What was she trying to say?

She brought her hand from behind her back. It was the

book from yesterday. She dropped it onto my lap. I looked at her in surprise.

'It's you and me, just you and me against Elizabeth and the rest of the world, right?'

I didn't reply. Being sisters didn't make you best friends, at least not in my experience. I looked at the book in my hands, eyes darting back to Steph.

'Do you remember our father?'

I shook my head.

'Nothing? Nothing at all?'

'No.' My voice was just a whisper and my fingers clutched the book.

'What about Mum?' She didn't wait for my reply. 'No, you wouldn't remember her, would you. You were just a baby.'

There was a hint of contempt in the word *baby*. Then her face softened.

'I remember her, though.'

She seemed to think.

'You and me are sisters, Caro. Elizabeth's not our mother. Whatever happens, we should remember that.'

Then she stood up and left the room.

CHAPTER 26

I hadn't forgotten these things, I'd simply chosen not to think about them once I left Derbyshire.

School could have been my escape. I'd loved my studies, curiosity filling me with an eagerness that earned me the name *Swot*. Yet school had been no better than home. The other children had sneered and shouted at me. Me, the pathetic waif in the corner of the playground, the one with no friends. They'd all snubbed me in the end.

There'd been a new girl once, Natalia. I'd been about ten years old. Her dad was a vet, newly moved down from the Lake District. I'd liked her – she was quiet like me. She'd had a recorder and she played it for me on that first day she started at school, a shy rendition of *Greensleeves*. I'd thought it was wonderful, the tune liltingly romantic, like listening to a small bird singing amongst the brown solidity of the playground's drystone walls. I asked her to sit next to me at lunch – and she did. I showed her my sketches, scribbled in pencil on the pages of my English exercise book. We even got into trouble, the two of us, for talking in class – I never got into trouble for talking, but I did that day. I was happy. For the first time in a long while, I had a friend.

But the next day when I'd got to school, several of the other girls had already surrounded Natalia, laughing and smiling, complimenting her hair, inviting her to sit with *them*. She soon realised. If she sat with me, she got ignored, but if she sat with them, she was Miss Popular. Why did they do that? It didn't take long. By the end of the week I was on my own again. That was the way it stayed, throughout my school years.

The one memory I couldn't recover was Danny. When I tried to think of him, my mind veered away, as if this was a place it didn't want to go. I'd been young, and memories were bound to be vague or non-existent, but he was my blank wall – *nothing*. Why? *Why?* How could I possibly have forgotten him so completely? Now I wanted to know what had happened. An accident, Steph had said. What sort of accident? I resolved to ask her again when next we spoke, if only I could find the right way to approach it.

In the evening, I painted, working on the commission. It was an attempt to distract myself, to unravel the terrors of the long night ahead, tossing and turning, listening to every creak and groan of the house, the last remains of the snow slipping from the roof, hidden pipes singing and rattling in the wee small hours, each sound amplified in my head. It fuelled my imagination, the images transferring to paper now that the house and my bed were empty again. More versions of my swan prince burning from his nettle-spun shirt. The handless girl drifting through her orchard, cherry-red spots speckling the grass at her feet. Eostre supplicated against the earth, her face filled with love but disfigured by her downy cheeks and hare lips.

When I did eventually sleep, I was dogged by nightmares, snatches of something I couldn't pin down, waking to the blood surging through my veins, my body slick with sweat and a name hovering on my lips.

Danny.

I put off calling Steph. In the end, it was she who called me just a few days into the new year.

'Hello,' she said, peering down her camera, like a dog, nose down a badger hole.

'Hello, Steph.'

There was a short uncomfortable pause. But my state of mind wasn't her fault. I sat myself up, speaking more cheerily.

'What have you been up to?' I said.

'Me? Oh, not very much. I was back in the office yesterday.' Her voice was bright. 'We went to see a musical, last night.'

'We?'

'Me and my boyfriend.'

'You never said. Well, not much. What's his name?'

'Oh sorry, Scott. He's a financial analyst.'

I was right about the banker bit. Men liked Steph. As a teenager she'd always had some kind of bloke in tow. I remembered a lad she'd sneak off to meet in the hills. She'd take me too, when she was babysitting. I'd have to watch, plucking at the long grass as they sat on a bench in some bleak, windy car park, the two of them groping and kissing, oblivious to my presence. She'd moved up in the world since then.

'Oh, he's gorgeous.' Steph laughed, that last word spoken with particular relish.

I felt a chill. I was reminded of the old Steph. Had she enjoyed that little boast?

I looked outside; the fields were green once more, thin streaks of white marking the hedgerows on the far side of the valley where the slopes faced north.

'Snow's all gone then?' I asked.

'Not quite, but everyone's getting on with life, you know. We're used to it here.'

Her voice had softened. I felt remorse at my ungracious thoughts. She wasn't the same girl as when we were children – we'd both grown up. She'd become elegant and sophisticated. I imagined New York by night, lines of yellow cabs moving slowly down the streets, neon signs blinking from every building, cars honking, colours glinting in the reflections on the wet sidewalk, like a scene from *Blade Runner*.

'Listen, I'm sorry, but I've got to ask. Danny . . . I can't remember him at all. How could I forget him? And I need to know. How did he die? You said it was an accident.'

Steph looked over her shoulder. She was sitting on a sofa. Was there someone else in the room listening in? Scott perhaps?

'Is someone else there, Steph? Is someone with you?'

She faced me again, leaning forward.

'No, it's fine. Scott's out.'

I stared at her, waiting.

'It was all a long time ago, Caro.'

'But an accident – what kind of accident?' Suddenly, I was determined to know.

'I . . .' Steph dropped her eyes.

She brought her hand up to her hair, pushing it through the strands then letting them fall across her face. Was she crying? She was upset. Really upset. Why hadn't I realised?

'It was in the garden. In the . . . I'm sorry, Caro, I just can't talk about it.'

Her voice trembled. But her tone was stern. Was she cross with herself? Her own loss of control, her emotion. Steph had never liked to show weakness.

'It's alright,' I rushed in. 'You don't have to tell me. It doesn't matter, really. Don't worry.' I hadn't the heart to insist.

'I have to go.' And with that she was gone.

The blank screen tormented me. *In the garden*, she'd said. *In the* . . .

My mobile buzzed with an incoming call. It was Craig. He was coming over, he said. I felt a leap of relief.

'Okay,' I replied, my tone deliberately neutral. I didn't want to sound too enthusiastic. I must have sounded childish instead. I bit my lip.

'I'm sorry,' he said. 'I couldn't come over sooner. I wanted to.'

Then why didn't you, I thought.

'My project's all done now,' he added. 'Thought we'd go out for a meal. Tonight?'

I made a pretence of thinking about it.

'Yeah, sure.'

'Great. Pick you up at seven.'

We ate at the Brassington Arms, near Ashbourne. A corner table by the fire. I was hot on one side and cold on the other, but I didn't really notice. Craig's thigh nudged up against mine and it wasn't long before I was tucked into his body, his arm around my waist, my hands resting on his knee. His hand covered mine and he leaned down to kiss me.

We skipped dessert, paid the bill and drove home, down lanes bumpy with the last frozen remains of snow and mud churned up by the 4x4s. So much for playing it cool. We had sex in the sitting room, climbed the stairs to bed and had sex again. This time he stayed the whole night. I slept with his legs wrapped around mine, one arm over my chest, my skin tingling with the afterglow of our loving and the warmth of his body contrasting with the cool air of the night.

After Craig left, I checked my emails. There had been a message from my agent. He said there was a last-minute addition to the text for the commission, a new story. A file was attached. I clicked on the file and read it. It was about a water nixie, a mermaid-like creature that preyed upon lonely, suicidal men. I knew of one such tale in the Peak District, even if it was a land-locked area – Black Mere Pool, supposedly inhabited by a demon mermaid after the death of her beloved sailor.

Craig rang later. A teasing call to remind me I was not neglected. I mentioned the new story.

'A field trip – that's what you need,' he said. 'It'll do you a world of good to get some fresh air.'

He was right – something to inspire my imagination away from the house and all my introspective musings.

'There's Black Mere Pool,' I said. 'But it's a long drive from here, across the border into Staffordshire.'

'Do you have to go that far?' said Craig.

I thought about it. 'There's Carsington Water.'

It was a reservoir on the other side of Ashbourne. In the summer, it was known for its sailing and cycling, buzzing with tourists and families. In the winter, on a day like today, it would be grey and cold, a wide expanse of empty, silent water. Just the thing for a nixie.

'That's a great idea,' said Craig. 'I'm only sorry I can't come with you, but I have to work. I'll speak to you later.'

CHAPTER 27

After lunch, I parked in the main car park at Carsington, lines of unused bays interspersed with litter bins and gritstone boulders. A few lights glistened from the double-height barn tearoom, partly obscured by a thin drifting fog. I bought a parking ticket and slipped it onto the dashboard, fingers already numb with the cold.

There were several tracks that circled the reservoir. It could take more than two hours to walk its full circumference, longer if you took the path that weaved in and out of the woodlands. I chose the shorter one, away from the dam which was prone to gusting winds. The trail followed the water's edge before veering off into the woods that intermittently opened out to long vistas across the lake. I walked for an hour, seeing only a single runner dressed in loose jogging pants and a hoodie pulled low over their face. Him or her, I couldn't tell, the figure briefly visible in the distance, as if following me on a different path. The androgynous clothing and solitary state of the runner seemed to be symptomatic of the bleak land-scape, the story in my head and the growing pools of fog that hugged the trees around me.

I saw a bird hide in the distance. It was right by the shore. Drawn to the water for my story, I followed a stretch of boardwalk to get to it. A brood of geese was feeding on the grass beside me. They gaggled in objection to my presence, shuffling their wings threateningly, stirring the fog as I gingerly stepped around their droppings, piles of green mush dotted on the boards. Reaching the shelter, I gratefully stepped inside.

It took a few seconds for my eyes to adjust. The gloom was generated by brown timber walls and the narrow horizontal slats that served for windows. The wood smell was over-whelming, accentuated by the moisture in the air and the closely growing oak saplings outside. Most of the shutters were closed, but one had been left up. It revealed a reed pool that merged into the lake beyond. I sat on a bench, opening another shutter. I picked up a pair of cheap binoculars chained to the wall, leaning on the wooden shelf to focus on a pair of chaffinches flitting from spot to spot. Their delicate weight bent the strands of grass, their coloured cheeks reflecting in the water beneath.

The cool air pricked my skin. I tracked a new bank of fog rolling across the reservoir, engulfing the distant floating geese. The greyness all around had a dampening effect on my mood. It was exactly as I'd hoped, evocative of the toxic spirit of the nixie, her thirst for the dead and dying. I rooted the imagery in my head, pulling out a notebook to sketch some of the details I would need for my painting, the monochrome colours, the thin, long shapes, the shimmering reflections. Yet the cold, the isolation, the shadows in the hut, the musky, woody scent, it all served to comfort me in a strange kind of way. Time had stopped in this natural space, away from people and cars and busy streets, where nothing mattered to the birds on the lake or the trees that swayed in the breeze, other than food and weather and shelter.

I tried to identify the different birds by reference to a wall chart but I was too immersed in my thoughts. Strands of white reached out towards the hide and dusk began to fall. I put away my sketchbook. Yet still I lingered, unwilling to go home, rooks cawing in the distance.

I thought of Elizabeth, her death. At sixty-one, she'd been too young. I'd seen the array of alcohol in the kitchen, so many bottles for a woman on her own, some of it strong stuff – vodka, whisky. Perhaps Elizabeth had drunk too much, had tripped and crashed into the banister? I'd never seen Elizabeth drinking, not in all those years when I'd lived in the house. Had she grown lonely? I thought of the pills, the painkillers in her bedroom. Had she been ill? Had the alcohol been another form of pain relief? I tried to imagine her, stumbling out of her bedroom, glass in hand, dressing gown half undone, like in a Tennessee Williams play. Maybe the belt had been trailing, tripped her up so that she'd crashed against the banister and tipped over? Was that how it happened? I'd been told that Elizabeth's death was a tragic accident. That it would have been instant, the moment her body impacted on the ground. Even now, the thought of it made me flinch.

My fingers traced the lines of wood on the shelf of the shelter, tentatively touching a splinter poking out at right angles. It was sharp, waiting to draw blood. It reminded me of the one on the banister, except that one hadn't been so obvious – only when my hand slid over the wood had it become apparent. Why did it worry me? Something or someone must have hit the banister unless it had already been damaged. A careless workman perhaps. I held my finger on the point of the splinter. It didn't hurt. I pushed the spike into my flesh. This time it did hurt. Blood, my own, trickled down the wood. I pulled my finger away and sucked it, the taste warm and sweet in my mouth. The pain was strangely comforting.

Beyond the hide was a wall of white. The fog had evolved into a thick blanket, strands swirling through the shutters, curling up against the draught moving within the hide. I had stayed too long, indulging myself. It was colder, damper. Darker.

Time to head home.

I left the wooden shack, intending to follow the boardwalk to the main path. But as I stepped into the fog, I was shocked by how dense it was. I couldn't see beyond the end of my arm. The white swept across my face, tugging at my feet. I'd never experienced fog like this before, not even in London. I was an idiot – why had I stayed so long?

I tried to think which way I'd come. I turned left to retrace my steps, but the fog was so impenetrable and the boardwalk seemed too short. My foot skidded off the edge and I tripped. Landing on my knees, I caught my breath. I stood up, but once off the wooden boards I was disorientated. I spun around searching for the path. My feet slipped in the wet mire. I swung back. The fog caressed my face. Claustrophobia clawed at my chest. Cursing at my own stupidity, I plunged forwards, each step blindly taken, the air ice cold around my body.

Then the white wall drifted apart. A figure emerged in the distance, in a hoodie and tracksuit. Was it the runner on his way back? He seemed to hover ahead, lifting one hand to wave at me.

'Hello!' I called.

The hand lifted again, beckoning, then pointing towards my right. He was too far away to hear me but the signal was reassuring. The fog closed and the figure disappeared. I heaved a sigh of relief, stepping towards the direction he had indicated. Wet branches brushed against my legs, brambles caught against my jeans. Somewhere I heard a pathetic bleating. Sheep loomed in and out of vision, tottering on their short legs, weighed down by their wet coats. I felt heartened. At least they were a sign of land and human habitation.

The day had gone. The fog was now a thick curtain masking the night. It shimmered as if lit from within, swallowing my hands and my feet as I tried to reach out. I cursed myself again for my tardiness at the hide, brooding on a woman who'd always hated me. How would I get home if they'd closed the barrier to the car park? I increased my pace, then spun around to get my bearings, but nothing seemed familiar. I could feel the bogginess of the ground, sucking at my boots, water seeping through inadequate soles. Something brushed past me, I couldn't tell what it was. I stumbled in alarm, throwing out a hand to grab a branch. My aim missed and I tumbled down to my knees again, thick clay clogging my clothes.

'Bloody hell!' I cursed out loud. One of my feet was stuck.

I fought to move it, reaching down with my hands to pull. My leg released with a glug. I took another step but my foot sank even deeper, water flooding the holes left by my feet. The fog swept around me, clearing enough to reveal a great arc of black water ahead. It was the lake – I'd somehow walked straight into the lake. Jesus Christ! I swallowed hard, disbelief washing over me. How had I done that? I must have misunderstood the jogger's signal, still distracted by my thoughts. I felt the water between my toes.

I tried to return the way I'd come but the fog spiralled with me, rolling around my body, another wall of suffocating white. With every step, I waded further into the water. It rose above my knees, lapped against my thighs. Like a sick lover reaching up with cold arms.

Oh God! What a fool I'd been, not taking the fog seriously. I was going to die here, my body floating between the lush green reeds like Ophelia in her pre-Raphaelite grave. No, I told myself. I wasn't going to drown. The water was back down to my knees. I could walk my way out of this! But whichever way I turned was fog, thick, all-encompassing fog. I finally admitted I had no idea which way to go, horror rising in my gut.

Then I remembered, my mobile was in my pocket. It would still be dry. I fumbled with frozen hands, cursing at my own stupidity. I pulled the phone out, stabbing the numbers for emergency services. I knew I was in trouble, this was no time for pride. It began to ring. My breathing slowed, the familiar sound already soothing me. But I was shivering, the mud beneath my boots shifting uneasily. I felt something slither against my calf. I yelped and lashed out, but the fingers of my free hand snatched at nothing. My feet slipped. I tipped forwards into the lake, suddenly out of my depth. The ice-cold water hit me like a slab of rock. My lungs heaved, water filling my mouth. I scrabbled for air, feeling the phone slide between my fingers. I watched in horror as it plunged into the lake.

'Shit!'

The words spluttered from my lips, green stagnant water gagging at my throat.

I thrashed about, coughing and gasping for breath, gulping in the air. I could swim, I was a strong swimmer, or so I thought, but the shock of the cold had thrown me off balance. My head sank again beneath the surface. I kicked with my legs, arms reaching out uselessly until my feet found solid ground. My head emerged into the air and I stood there, heaving and spluttering, half in and out of the water, the soggy weight of my wet clothes threatening to drag me under.

I was stranded. Petrified. The lake stretched out for over a mile. If I took the wrong direction . . . I couldn't move either forward or back.

'Shit, shit, shit!'

I wanted to cry. I was stuck, partially immersed in the lake, in the fog and the night, with no phone and no one to hear me.

'Help!' I screamed.

And again, with all my strength. 'H . . . ELP!'

CHAPTER 28

My world had shrunk to a small cube of air surrounded by pearlescent black fog. I don't know how long I remained there. Ten minutes? Or was it nearer three hours? I crouched in the water shaking, no longer able to stand upright, no longer aware of the cold and the wet.

I felt fear and nausea, sick with my own stupidity. How had I allowed this to happen? My shaking slowed. I was hoarse from shouting, each call quieter than the last, fatigue seducing me. I closed my eyes. I deserved this.

The water slapped around my body, green weeds winding about my legs. I thought of the water nixie then, from the story. She who preyed on foolish humans. In my delirium, it seemed to me the strands of weed parted and I saw a face. Blue eyes shone through the water and the face slid silently out of sight, then back into view. It was as if she was curious, the water nixie, wondering what it was like to die, watching my last throes of life, the light fading from my eyes, my final threads of hope pulled to their very edge, like wet leather drying out.

'*Caroline Crowther!*' The voice was distant but commanding.

The nixie smiled, knowing the voices were too far, that they would never find me.

'Caroline!'

Her green hair wound itself around my legs, tightening their grip.

'Caroline Crowther!'

'Over here!' A man's voice bounced across the water.

Torchlight swept through the fog. A beam caught the nixie's eyes. They glittered with anger. Her face skimmed just below the surface of the lake. I felt her rage, her mouth opening and closing, making me a promise. Then her face sank from view, one long sweep of her slime-green hair gliding out of sight.

'*Miss Crowther!*'

A pair of hands reached about me, taking my weight. There were more voices, shouting.

'She's here!'

I lifted my head. I saw yellow suits, faces peering at me, men and women wading through the lake. I felt myself being lifted up and out of the water. A single line of bubbles wriggled up from beneath and I closed my eyes and let it happen.

I awoke lying on a hospital trolley. Blue plastic curtains swung from a rail to my left and a nurse stepped into view. She began tapping on an iPad. I moaned. She put it down and picked up my hand, holding it firmly as she smiled.

'Caroline? Can you hear me? Squeeze my fingers if you can hear me, my love.'

I squeezed her hand clumsily.

'That's fantastic. Well done. Don't try to speak. You're fine, you're absolutely fine. You're suffering from mild hypothermia, but you're going to be okay. Rest.'

She moved to check the machinery. A drip dangled from my arm and I could hear the competing beeps of a heart monitor and something else. I closed my eyes and slept.

'You've had a very lucky escape, Miss Crowther. This could have been very serious. If that boyfriend of yours hadn't spotted your car and alerted the police, well I dread to think what would have happened. I hope you'll think twice before taking another stroll in thick fog by a lake!'

Stating the bleeding obvious, I thought. I smiled weakly.

'Yes, Doctor.'

The woman nodded, her stethoscope jumping like a snake. A man stood next to her.

'I'm happy for you to take her home now,' she said. 'All the vital signs are good. Lots of rest, some sensible food and if you have any concerns you can phone this number day or night. She might be a bit dozy from the drugs we've given her, but she should be back to her old self by tomorrow. She was found just in time.'

She waggled a sheet of paper at a man. I could make out telephone numbers and a series of paragraphs in black print. The paper blurred in and out of focus along with the man who held it. Craig.

A nurse hovered behind us, keen to clear the bed. I stood up obediently and shuffled into a wheelchair. I was perfectly capable of walking but the staff insisted. My head was pounding, my mouth felt like I'd been eating sawdust and all

I wanted was to get away from the stink of disinfectant and vomit and the threat of more needles puncturing my arm.

Craig wheeled me through the doors and down the corridor. I didn't speak. In the lift, I couldn't even raise my eyes to look at him and he didn't say anything either. A few moments later he was pushing a blanket around my body as I sat in his jeep. I felt the warm doggy breath of Patsy against my neck as she pushed forward from the back seat.

Craig drove. Cars, buildings, street lights whizzed past me, the noise of the car heater hissing in my ears, the radio quietly playing music. Forty-five minutes later, we swung up the drive to Larkstone Farm. Craig held out his hand and I passed him my keys. There was a blast of cold air as the car door opened. Craig had unlocked the front door and he lifted me out, still wrapped in a blanket as if he was worried I might disintegrate without it. I was deposited on the sofa. An electric fan heater belted out hot air at my feet and a cupboard door banged in the distance. Craig reappeared a few minutes later with a hot mug.

'Drink this,' he said.

My hands folded around the mug obediently and I nuzzled the steam rising up from the liquid. No alcohol this time. I gave a sigh of disappointment.

'What happened?' I asked. 'I don't understand what happened.'

'You strayed from the path. In the dark and the fog, you ended up in the lake. If you'd been there much longer you could have died of hypothermia. What on earth possessed you?'

I flinched at the censure in his voice. Why did he have to speak to me like that? I didn't reply.

'You were a heck of a way off the path, they said. They only found you because I raised the alarm. I called round the house and you weren't back. You didn't answer your phone either. I knew you'd gone to Carsington and when I got there your car was still parked up. There was a whole group of us looking for you. That, plus the fact your phone is waterproof; the police were able to trace your call.'

Waterproof? That was news to me. Mind you, the phone had been expensive. It was apparently money well spent. I sat up a little, wondering if it had survived and if so where it was. Somewhere at the bottom of Carsington Water with my fictional water nixie. I shook my head. I could still picture her. I must have been hallucinating from the cold, but even now I could have sworn she was there.

'I followed this guy, a runner. He was in front of me, pointing the way. At least I thought that was what he was doing. I must have been confused, the fog was so dense.'

'No one said anything about a runner.' Craig frowned. 'Whoever it might have been was long gone, there were no other cars in the car park. It was the emergency services that found you.'

'Oh!' I sipped the tea. It was strong and full of sugar, but that was fine. Had it been only yesterday? I still couldn't remember more than the vaguest details of my rescue and the journey to the hospital.

'I'm staying over, Patsy too,' he said. He nodded at Patsy, lounging on the rug near the fireplace.

'I don't understand. You said Patsy couldn't stay here.'

'I know, but let's give it another try.'

'Don't you have work to do?'

'Yes, but it can wait.'

Clearly, he'd decided he had to stay with me. For the moment, I was more important than work.

The cat appeared, jumping up onto my knees, staring at the dog disdainfully as if to rub it in that she was on my lap and Patsy was only on the rug. She lifted up one leg and began to lick her bottom to emphasise the point.

We watched a film that afternoon, eating a slow meal on trays by the fire. I couldn't ever remember having done that with Paul. I snuggled up to Craig and lowered my eyes, revelling in the warmth of his body. When the film was over, Craig talked about his time at college learning his craft. I listened, struck by the earnestness of his joy in carpentry, his description of different trees, how they grew and their relevant properties. The love of his work and his creative instinct shone through. In this respect at least, he was like me.

We slept in the same bed that night, no sex, but side by side. I felt safe. No bad dreams. No strange noises. Just sleep.

CHAPTER 29

'It's Twelfth Night tonight,' said Craig.

It was the next morning, only two days after the events at Carsington. I felt entirely normal, but Craig was still being super attentive. I was quite enjoying that.

We were walking Patsy round the top field, the one that ran alongside the front drive. I was allowed out but not on my own, Craig said. He was wearing an oversized sheepskin jacket, his jaw jutting out from a loose woolly collar in a way that made him look like one of those aftershave ads in *Country Life*, the kind of magazines found piled up at the hospital.

'So?' I pretended not to understand the significance of the date.

'The Wassail, remember?'

'Oh, that.' I'd hoped he'd forgotten about his suggestion we go together. 'You planning on going?' I said, playing innocent.

'*Us* going. Remember?'

'Oh, I don't think so, not after . . . I'll be fine. I'll look after Patsy for you, if you like. There's a good film on tonight and I'll enjoy a night on my own.'

I wanted to let him off the hook, that's what I told myself. How could I explain I didn't want to go, when I didn't fully understand the reasons myself?

'Patsy will be quite happy for an evening. And I did ask the doctors, you'll be okay as long as the weather's not too cold and we don't keep you out too long. I think you should come with me.'

His tone was one of instruction, not invitation.

'I hardly think your friends in the village will appreciate seeing me by your side. They don't seem to like me much.'

'Don't be silly. Why wouldn't they like you?' His tone softened. 'It's up to you, but if you think you might stay here . . .'

Was that a question?

'. . . you're going to have to get to know people sooner or later. And what better way of doing that than coming along with me? I can introduce you to some of your other neighbours.'

If you think you might stay here . . . I didn't know what I wanted to do. I was still here, and that was as far as my thoughts had got. Had meeting Craig changed things? I drew breath, trying to ignore the tentative flutter of excitement in my belly.

Maybe I shouldn't let the hostility of some of the villagers get me down. I thought of the scratch on my car, why should I be intimidated? And he had a point, he must know all of the neighbours. Maybe they would accept me more easily, at least for a while, if I was seen tagging along with Craig.

Sod it. I quashed my misgivings.

'Okay,' I said.

The evening was much milder than previous ones. Just as well since the entire proceedings of the Wassail took place outside. Craig wrapped me up like an Egyptian mummy and I was on a strict curfew at the first sign of any chill. He insisted he drive us in his jeep.

The pub on the High Street was heaving and Craig headed straight for the bar. I skulked in a nearby doorway, snuggling into a deep scarf, already feeling on edge. The entire village had turned out, men, women, old and young, kids squawking in excitement like ducks flapping at their parents' feet. The women had lanterns on sticks, the men brightly coloured rag capes draped across their shoulders, all of them armed with drums and pots and pans, for the moment silent. It could have been a scene from *The Wicker Man*.

A troupe of Morris dancers clustered together, bells jangling restlessly. I felt the tension in me grow. A man began to sing, his voice deep and tuneful. When the song came to an end, the crowd cheered appreciatively, the air blossoming to life with their warm breath, the smoke from their lanterns floating into the night. A fiddle player lifted his bow. As the music rose above the crowd, it seemed familiar. I pulled my coat around me, tucking my chin further into my scarf. The Morris men leapt into action. They kicked out with their bells, flourishing with their hands. The crowd stirred, swaying to the beat of a single drummer. My eyes scanned the street and a movement caught my eye. A small face pushing through the crush – a boy. Was he jumping up to see? No, his expression was derisory and fierce, directed straight at me. I gasped, cold withering down my spine. Was that him? The boy I'd seen at the house?

'Wonderful, isn't it?'

I almost jumped at the voice in my ear.

'I'm not much of a cider drinker,' the woman carried on. 'Give me a beer any day!' She had a distinctive mellow lyrical tone, not American like Steph, Canadian.

My eyes flew back to the boy but already he was gone. Had I imagined him?

'I love orchards,' she carried on. 'The blossom and the colours. Not sure which season I prefer, spring or fall! But I don't understand, what's this all about, this *wassailing*?' Her smile was wide and appealing.

The woman was older than me – forties? Apparently on her own. A vivid purple cap perched on her head and a full-length coat accentuated her short, rounded stature.

'I . . .' I coughed, lifting my chin. I had to jolt myself out of this mood I was in. 'It's a blessing of the trees for the coming year.' I tucked my scarf down.

'Oh, how quaint!' the woman said, her voice full of unabashed warmth. 'Why do they do that?'

'The oldest tree is inhabited by Apple Tree Man – the fertility of the whole orchard relies on him. They pour cider on his roots and he points the way to treasure in return.'

'Oh, wow! Hi, I'm Mary Beth Wheeler.' The woman proffered a hand.

I took it reluctantly.

'Hi, I'm Caro.' My eyes still pulled towards the crowd.

'I moved into a cottage on Flagg Lane a few months ago.' Mary Beth waved an arm in the direction of the village school.

'Saw you arriving with your other half. He's pretty cute, isn't he?'

'Er . . .' Had she said Craig was *cute*? I didn't comment on the 'other half'.

'Where do you live?' she asked.

'I'm a bit out of the village.' I nodded vaguely towards the hills.

I hoped that was enough, stuffing my hands in my pockets and shifting my feet as if I was about to move on, but she continued.

'Whereabouts, exactly?'

I hesitated. 'Larkstone Farm.'

'Oh, you're Elizabeth's daughter!'

My heart sank. She'd obviously known Elizabeth.

'Stepdaughter,' I said, feeling the weight of those words defeat me.

'I'm so sorry for your loss,' the woman replied. 'I haven't lived here long, so I didn't know her well, but I knew of her.'

There was something about her tone, a sympathy. As if she'd known, or guessed, what Elizabeth was like. She didn't seem like the other villagers I'd encountered. She had the manner of an independent-minded soul, who liked to make up her own mind about people. I felt my spirits lift.

'It's beautiful up there,' she said. 'The views are stunning. I'd have loved to have been properly out in the countryside, but the village is more practical for me. I'm an artist too!'

'I . . . I beg your pardon?'

How did she know I was an artist? Did the gossips know that too?

'I'm sorry, hon, word gets around!'

I groaned inwardly, dreading to speculate what people had

said, whatever it was behind their rudeness since I'd got here. Perhaps it was my art? Some people thought my style was strange, dark. That was the worst thing about gossip, trying to second-guess what rubbish people were actually thinking. Mary Beth's hat bobbed up and down, the colour catching in the light of the lanterns about us.

'Ain't it pretty, all this?' Her hand swept around in an expansive loop. 'I love all this folksy stuff!' She beamed at me again.

I pushed my nose back into my scarf, trying not to let her see my conflicting expressions of horror and amusement.

'It's lovely,' I mumbled.

She was looking at my boots. Doc Martens. They were practical. I looked at hers – fur-lined wedges in purple patchwork suede. Not at all practical. Cosy though. We both smiled.

'An artist, you said?'

'Well, I'm a potter in fact,' Mary Beth explained. 'Had to find a cottage with a shack in the garden!'

'I just need a big table.' I relaxed in spite of myself.

Mary Beth took me by the arm and swung me round to face the crowd.

'You see that woman over there?'

I nodded.

'See the ink on her fingers? She's a teacher. And her hair tied back from her face? She's a primary school teacher. They do that to stop themselves from catching nits!'

Her laugh was like nutmeg and ginger sprinkled on a cup of coffee, warm and unexpected, with a hint of mischievous spice. She shook her head.

'They work hard, teachers,' she said, respect in her voice.

She pointed to a middle-aged man in a bottle-green jacket and a flat cap on his head.

'Now he's a car dealer.'

'How do you know that?' I asked.

'He's got a copy of *Auto Trader* in his pocket and he's been eyeing up the parked cars down the lane. His car's the brand-spanking-new Range Rover blocking the vicar's drive. The vicar bought a new second-hand car last week, told me all about it, very proud he was. Thinks he got a good deal. More like our car dealer got a good sale!'

The man did indeed have a smug look about him.

'You get all sorts moving into these villages, ousting the local families with their cash.' She grinned at me sheepishly and shrugged her shoulders. 'What can I say?'

I laughed, enjoying her self-deprecating, acerbic sense of humour. She poked me with her gloved hand.

'How about that fellow talking to your boyfriend?'

'Oh, he's not my . . .' Was Craig my boyfriend? I felt a spread of heat on my face.

I turned to look at Craig, then stopped. He was poised in the door of the pub, two pewter mugs balanced in one hand, his wallet in the other, deep in conversation with a man. I almost choked. It was Angus McCready.

'Your go, Caro; what do you think his job is?' Mary Beth's eyes sparkled with anticipation.

I watched the two men. Craig was engrossed in his conversation, certainly not desperate to drag himself away. My heart leapt against my ribs. I'd never mentioned the damage to my car, my suspicions. But he did know about McCready's behaviour towards me in Ashbourne – so why were they talking like friends?

I decided to play along. Maybe Mary Beth would tell me something useful.

'Er, I reckon . . . he's a dentist.'

'Dentist?' Mary Beth exclaimed, eager to enjoy the joke.

'Yeah, look at his teeth, they're a perfect white, you've got to be a dentist or a film star to have teeth that white.' I pulled a face. 'And he's got a tan, bet he's been to the Bahamas. Only dentists can afford to go on holiday in the Bahamas – pirates, the lot of them!'

Mary Beth gave a tinkle of a laugh. 'Oh, I like that! Ah but no, I think he's a builder. Look at his hands, they're rough. He works outside with those hands and that tan.'

A builder. I supposed that fitted. Did he and Craig work together? Was that how they knew each other?

Angus threw his head back in laughter and I gritted my teeth. Ashbourne – how could Craig even speak to a man who'd treated me like that?

CHAPTER 30

Craig must have looked up and caught the expression on my face. He tucked his wallet into his pocket and extricated himself from the conversation with Angus. The man gave another bellow and pushed towards the bar and Craig weaved through the crowd towards me.

'Mary Beth, this is Craig, a *neighbour* of mine.'

Craig's eyebrows rose as if to question the faint inflexion on 'neighbour'. Mary Beth, fortunately, didn't pick up on my antagonism, or at least was too polite to let it show.

'Hi Craig.' She smiled. 'Now would that be Craig Atherton, the carpenter?'

Craig nodded, flashing me another look as if he were still worried about my wellbeing.

'Oh, well then, you're just the man I could do with talking to. Someone mentioned your name to me the other day. I've got a cottage on Flagg Lane and my kitchen needs . . .'

'Excuse me,' I whispered. I had an urgent desire to get away, to be on my own, to process what I'd just seen.

I ducked past Mary Beth to slide between two women chattering on the side-lines, avoiding Craig's probing glance. He was clearly wondering where I was going. Mary Beth raised her eyebrows as if to ask the same thing, but I was already out of reach. When I looked back, Mary Beth was once more at full throttle, presumably quizzing Craig about his work.

A few moments later, the noise of the crowd erupted, a crashing and banging on all those drums and saucepans and implements. The sound jarred in my ears. I felt a wave of panic, my need to escape intensifying. The man on the fiddle led the way, like the Pied Piper of Hamlyn. I watched the people following, the Morris dancers and the men in capes, the rest of them with their faces flushed with alcohol and the rhythm of the beat. The clashing colours of their clothes, the steam from their breaths, the sway and swagger of their hands and arms as they played their makeshift instruments. The noise increased and the movement of the crowd gained momentum, surging down the road. I felt alienated and alone, the pagan ferocity of their enjoyment engulfing me with ir-rational fear. The smiles that leered and turned away, the jostling of careless bodies, pushing me along. I thought of the boy I'd seen earlier in the crowd and a fleeting memory jogged in my head, a previous time – when I was little. Was this why I hadn't wanted to come?

I swung round, catching sight of a group of children crowded round a house. They were screeching with excite-ment. I pushed out, suddenly even more anxious. Their heads were bent low over a large wooden tub. I saw apples bobbing in the water. One of the girls leaned down, her hands behind her back, teeth snapping as she tried to bite one of the apples. A boy reached out to grab hold of her head. It plunged into the water and I saw the strands of her dark hair drift out like a bloom of ink. She shook her head, hands releasing to grasp the edges of the tub and push back. Bubbles of air exploded up from beneath her face. Shrieks of laughter pierced the fog in my mind and I stepped forward.

'No!' I cried, memory leaping into life.

The same tub of water, the same noise of the Wassail, the same peals of malignant laughter from the crowd of children around me. My lungs bursting for breath, my eyes open and staring beneath the water, my head shaking, shaking as the boy behind me grappled with my hair and held me underneath and the water slipped down my throat.

I forced my way between the children, seized hold of the girl and dragged her from the tub. Her eyes blinked, laughing at me as I held her head. Water from her hair drenched her clothes and mine. The boy hooted with glee and caught her hand and they and the rest of the children scattered down the street.

People were staring at me. Walking past as if I was contam-inated. Did they think I had tried to drown the poor girl in the water? I swung around, stepping away from the tub, shame flooding my face. But I was confused; they weren't staring at me, they were walking after the man with the fiddle and the Morris men, hooting, banging, drinking as they went.

I was right, I shouldn't have come, I wasn't well enough yet. It was like I was back at Carsington stranded in the lake, surrounded by a sea of indifferent people, drowning beneath the weight of the noise filling my head.

I hung back from the crowd, breathing deep to calm myself.

Waiting for the memory to go, retreating again, slipping like sand through my fingers.

Some time later, I wasn't sure how long, I spotted Craig on the far side of the crowd. Mary Beth's purple hat was by his side. Our eyes met and he lifted one hand to wave. He must have been keeping an eye on me, despite being caught up on the wrong side of the street. He was frowning. Had he seen my bizarre reaction to the apple-bobbing?

All I could think of was Craig and Angus talking at the bar. And the words Angus had used in Ashbourne – *fucking bitch*. Craig had agreed with him. *Well that may be, but not worth getting an assault charge for, eh?* It made me curl up inside. Perhaps he still thought that now, after my sorry escapade at Carsington Water and my foolishness tonight.

I was undecided whether to follow or abandon Craig completely. It was a long walk home, but there was no way I wanted to stay. I searched the pub for a sight of Angus. He was at the bar drinking, quite indifferent to the festivities. I didn't want to go back that way. I willed myself to look and feel normal, reluctantly joining the crowd.

The procession reached the next house, the noise bouncing off the stone walls of the village. I had that same sense of being an outsider looking in, but everyone was having too much of a good time to take any notice of me. There was more good-natured jostling and dancing and banging of pans. We passed through a gate into a field. Trees were dotted all around, their myriad branches shaking moonlight patterns at our feet. Paper lanterns marked a path across the orchard to a central tree and candlelit jars swung from its boughs. The Morris dancers took their places in a circle around it. Then one of them stepped forward. He raised a tankard of cider and the crowd fell silent.

'Oh apple tree, we wassail thee, and hope that thou will bear,
For the Lord doth know where we shall be when apples come another year.
So to bear well, and to fruit well, merry let us be,
Let everyone take off their hats and cry health to the old apple tree!'

The crowd cheered, hands raising a sweep of tankards. The man turned with his drink and tipped it onto the roots of the tree.

'Wassail! WASSAIL!'

Another cheer rose from the crowd and the fiddle player struck up. I felt two hands slip around my waist and Craig's warm breath against my cheek.

'There you are,' he said. 'I thought you'd abandoned me.'

The circle of men around the tree began to dance.

'Are you alright? You're not cross with me again, are you?'

I leaned away from him. 'I saw you talking with that man.'

'Ah.' Craig lowered his head to my ear. 'Angus is a customer, Caro. And a bully, I get that. But he won't bother you again, I promise.'

His tone was hard. In that moment, I almost felt sorry for Angus. It was nothing, all of it, just my anxiety and confusion. I was aware that Craig was watching me closely. I shook my head and smiled.

'He's not worth the time thinking about him,' I said.

I let Craig gently pull me down the street.

There were more gardens after that, each rendering of the Wassail more raucous than the last. The music was infectious, the drink flowed, poured from two barrels wheeled behind the crowd. Craig passed me a mug and kept it topped up. My mood lifted. The music and banging got even louder, but now it didn't seem to matter. I danced with Craig and the rest of them and as he'd promised, Craig introduced me to one rosy-cheeked face after the next.

To my surprise, most of them were friendly. Had I got it wrong about the village? Perhaps it was the effect of the cider, or more likely, Craig's choice of friends. I began to realise most of them didn't live in the village but were from further afield: Ashbourne, Derby, the crowd swollen by visitors enjoying the spectacle.

There was just one older couple I didn't like. We almost collided with them under the archway of a barn.

'Elizabeth's stepdaughter?' said the woman, placing a slight stress on the 'step'.

'Yes,' said Craig. 'You'll remember, she left several years ago to study art.'

'I'm sure Elizabeth did mention it.'

Her voice was icy crisp and authoritative. I felt my back stiffen. The woman was tall, make-up carefully applied to her face. One of *her* inner circle. Now I thought about it, I recognised her from Elizabeth's funeral, the woman in black silk. Her husband was still holding an umbrella. She hadn't come up to speak to me then.

'Well, I hope things go well with the sale of the house,' she said. 'It must be so distressing finalising the disposal of family possessions, though it's not like Elizabeth was your *real* mother, or that the house was ever meant to be your home.'

I took a sharp intake of breath. No, Elizabeth hadn't been my mother, but the jibe still hurt. How dared she? It had been my father's house long before he'd met and married Elizabeth.

I saw Craig glaring at the woman but before he could reply on my behalf, I chipped in.

'That's true, a death in the family shakes us all. But it was my father's house, not hers, and I'm looking forward to living in it.'

I don't know what made me say that, announce that I was staying. A perverse desire to upset the woman. I jutted out my chin.

Craig looked pleased, I felt a curious tug of pleasure. The woman looked furious. The husband muttered something about finding some food and the couple melted into the crowd.

'I'm sorry about that.' Craig took the empty mug from my hand. 'I guess you can't win them all.'

'Don't worry, she's not my type anyway,' I said.

'Thank God for that! So, you're planning to stay on at the house?'

'Er, I don't know why I said that. I . . .'

I felt a rush of pleasure. He'd seemed pleased to hear me say I would be living at the house – like it was a permanent arrangement.

A mobile phone rang and Craig reached into his pocket to answer it. I watched the dancers, a genuinely happy smile now on my face as the music and banging started up once more.

CHAPTER 31

My ears were ringing by the time Craig and I arrived at the car. He tucked me into the front seat with a blanket.

'Can you wait here a moment, Caro? There's one thing I have to do.'

I wasn't going anywhere at this stage; my head was hurting again and I was more than ready for bed. I leaned back against the seat and nodded.

Craig sprinted off in the direction of the village hall on the opposite side of the road. I watched the last lantern bobbing up the street, listening to the strains of *The Derby Ram*, another drinking song emanating from the pub.

With Craig gone for a few moments, I found myself pondering his apparent friendship with Angus. Their acquaintance had been obvious that day in Ashbourne, the way Craig had spoken to Angus, talking him around. A client? Even if Craig didn't like the man any more than I did, I rationalised, sometimes you had to pretend, for the sake of professionalism. Craig was self-employed like me. I knew what it was like trying to keep a flow of reliable work and pay the bills. Perhaps he couldn't afford to take offence, even if Angus was an overblown Neanderthal git.

Craig had been gone five, ten minutes. No, longer. I waited and he still hadn't returned. I stirred myself from my snooze, glancing at the clock on the dashboard. He couldn't have gone far. I threw the blanket from my knees and got out.

It was colder than before, or maybe it was just the contrast with Craig's heated car. I shivered, recalling the paralysing chill of the lake. A stab of remembered fear pierced my thoughts. It was quiet, the street empty. I heard a sudden girlish laugh, the slam of a front door, then silence again. I pulled my jacket tighter around me and ran across the road.

The village hall was lit up by two old-fashioned carriage lamps, the light flaring out against the walls. I stepped around the boundary hedge, thinking Craig must be inside the building, but the doors were locked. I peered through the windows. Inside was pitch black apart from the green glow of an emergency exit sign.

I followed the line of the building, rounding the corner where the grass verge ended and the car park started. The white lines of the bays shone in the night and I could just make out the shape of a van parked in the far corner.

The driver's door was open. There was a light in the cab. Leaning against it was a man, heavyweight, his stance overly casual, deliberately contemptuous. Angus. In front of him was Craig.

I felt myself stiffen. Craig was animated, waving a hand. I could hear his voice, angry and accusing. I hugged the brick wall. The men were too far for me to make out their exact words, but the body language said it all, hands jabbing, faces contorted. I hung back, unwilling to interrupt such a heated discussion. Then Angus pulled away from the van towards Craig.

I couldn't breathe. Angus's face was furious. He threw out a fist. Craig swung his body aside only just avoiding the blow. He closed his own fist and raised his arm. It hovered in the air, but his fingers unclenched and he stepped back.

Shock held me frozen. Angus swiftly closed the gap. He thrust his head forward, butting Craig. I heard the crack of their skulls. Jesus! Craig staggered backwards clutching his nose. He dodged as Angus took aim again. Craig found his balance and punched. I stood there, hand on my mouth. Angus reeled back against the van and Craig stood, legs apart, fist ready to fly, watching his opponent.

I tried to think what I should do – they'd both be in trouble for this, let alone the damage they were doing each other. Should I run over? Should I call the police?

A sudden gust of wind rattled a cluster of bins by the hedge. The Wassail, I thought of the Wassail, the sound of the pans being clashed together. I kicked with my leg. The first bin teetered, then crashed to the ground, spilling out its contents. The noise reverberated across the car park. I pulled out of sight, inching forwards again to watch.

Their heads had both swung towards the sound. Angus shouted something at Craig, but Craig ignored him, striding across the car park. Angus climbed into his van, slammed the door and fired up the engine.

I scooted back across the hedge, for some reason unwilling to let Craig see that I'd been watching. Black puddles shimmered on the road where a barrel of cider had fallen over. I could smell the sweet stench of alcohol. I threw my head around to check if I'd been seen. Craig was by the village hall, his tall frame silhouetted against the wall. He'd stopped, lowering his face, a handkerchief held to his nose. He lifted his head, looking towards the van as it drove out of the car park far too fast, heading in the opposite direction.

Craig fished out his phone. Still holding the cloth to his nose, he tapped on the screen one-handed and started to talk.

I ran, clambering into the car. I scrambled to tuck the blanket around my legs, my heart hammering as I saw Craig push the phone into his pocket and cross the road.

When he reached the car, he swung himself into the driver's seat. There was no sign of the handkerchief or any blood. His lips were pressed tight together and his eyes avoided mine. I pretended not to notice.

'Right, we can get going now.' His voice was nasal and slightly breathless. 'Thanks for waiting. Sorry it took a bit longer than expected.'

He made no effort to explain what he'd been doing.

We drove in silence, Craig wrapped in thought, me bursting with curiosity, my hands gripping each other under the blanket.

What had that been all about? This wasn't the Craig I knew. Was he alright? I didn't dare ask, I didn't know what to think. Perhaps Craig had challenged Angus about his treatment of me, but that wouldn't have led to a punch-up, surely? The idea should have made me smile, except it didn't.

No, this was about something else – but what?

Back home, I unlocked the front door. I looked up at the sky. The clouds had drifted away to leave a cooler, sharper night. The stars were clearly visible, white pinpricks against the midnight blue. The moon shed a silver glow across the fields as bright as any village hall floodlight and I heard the flutter of wings in the trees behind me.

I touched Craig's arm.

'Look!' I said.

I pointed toward the top field.

A single tree stood in the middle, skeletal against the horizon. The moon filtered through its branches casting a deep shadow across the turf. As we both raised our heads, the tree moved in the wind, swinging gently from side to side. It took on the shape of a human scarecrow, exaggerated in height, long arms reaching out with spindly fingers, wriggling against the field. A sudden gust caught it from the side and an arm swung up, seemingly punching the sky.

I slipped a hand around Craig's arm, leaning close, the proximity of his body chasing away my wariness. I wanted to bring him back to me again, to say something that would make us both laugh.

'Look,' I said again. 'It's the Apple Tree Man!'

I thought he would smile, use the moment as an excuse to kiss me. But he did neither. His body was tense. He was upset from the fight, of course he was, who wouldn't be? But now there was a distance between us.

Why? I felt myself withdraw. I didn't know what to do. It was as if I wished I was back in the anonymity of London, shutters down, avoiding all contact with anyone who might hurt me.

Safe.

Was that what I really wanted?

CHAPTER 32

Craig didn't stay that night and I was relieved. The next day, I scurried round doing jobs, reaching deep into cupboards, piling up stuff in the dining room, firing off emails about bills to the lawyer. Anything to distract me. Finally I closed the laptop lid and started to make myself some dinner. It was whilst the meal was cooking, steam filling the kitchen, that the house phone rang.

I was surprised; it was the first call on Elizabeth's phone I'd had since my arrival.

'Hello?' I said.

'Is that Caro?'

I recognised the voice.

'Mary Beth! Is that you?' I felt pleasure at the call, the first gesture of friendship from someone local. Well, apart from Craig, of course. 'How did you get my number?'

'It wasn't difficult. Elizabeth was a parish councillor, she's still on the contact list. I hope you don't mind?'

'Not at all. How can I help you?'

'Oh, there's nothing really, I was wondering if you'd like to meet up for a cup of tea some time? Isn't that what you folks do in England?'

I laughed tentatively, cautious in spite of myself. 'I'd like that.'

'Fabulous. How about this coming Thursday at about eleven?'

'Okay, that would be lovely.'

I felt a flare of pleasure. The New Year had brought a fresh start, or maybe it was Craig's strategy to socialise me actually paying off.

The snow had gone, but fog and mist had descended on the county. As I approached Mary Beth's house, it snuggled low in the street like a child resting between its siblings: the quintessential Derbyshire worker's cottage, a Georgian terrace built of sandstone. It had been partially modernised, with a walk-in sitting room/kitchen/diner and what I guessed were two bedrooms and a tiny bathroom tucked under the eaves. A wrap-around garden was neatly laid out with flower borders, a vegetable plot and a large wooden shed. It was all a bit neglected-looking at the moment but I could tell it would be a riot of colour in the summer.

Mary Beth's taste was eclectic to say the least. Inside, I gawped at the oversized bright yellow dream catcher dangling from the central ceiling lamp. Feathered and beaded, like a replica spider's web, it was hard to avoid as I passed underneath. I perched on a pink velvet sofa overlaid with a patchwork crocheted blanket. I didn't think you could buy pink velvet sofas in Derbyshire.

Mary Beth's crockery was impressive too. There was a quirky brown teapot in the shape of a dormouse, one paw acting as the spout. I couldn't resist lifting it up to see a pair of sleepy eyes painted under the lid. Next to it on the tray was a pair of mismatched china cups and saucers featuring Beatrix Potter characters. There was one of the kittens from *The Tale of Tom Kitten* and Jeremy Fisher in his black ballet pumps, one foot in the water, a fish about to nibble on his toes. Oversized chocolate chip cookies, evidently homemade, sat on a plate shaped like the handsome head of a black horse. Black Beauty, nobility personified. It couldn't help but bring a smile to your face.

'Oh, I love your teapot!' I said.

And I did. I adored *Alice in Wonderland*. The illustrations were as brilliant as the text, with its Cheshire Cat grinning from a branch and the Mad Hatter's hat, its owner pontificating, jauntily bedecked with a selling price of ten shillings and sixpence. When I'd thought of Mary Beth's pottery business, I'd imagined earthy brown hues and chunky ethnic mugs, not this colourful nod to classic British children's books.

'Are these yours?' By which I meant had she made them herself.

'The teapot is,' she said, bobbing in pride at my admiration. 'I love all that cosy, quirky, nostalgic charm, the period characters and references to nature. You Brits do it so well.'

'Have you been in England long?' I asked.

'Oh, years. I was in Yorkshire before this – had a partner there, but she and I split up and I thought I'd start again, up here in the Peak District.'

'Well, you and I have something in common,' I said. 'I illustrate children's fiction.'

We chatted happily for over an hour, munching on biscuits and sipping tea, until at last I asked her about her plans for the kitchen.

'Did you find someone to do your kitchen?'

In the corner of the room was a slightly dated-looking collection of 1980s flat-pack cupboards in yellow pine and a square of black and white chequered linoleum.

'Oh yes, your lovely Craig has agreed to come and build me something more in keeping with the house.'

'Oh, I'm pleased. I'm sure he'll do a good job for you,' I replied.

'Much better than that awful Angus McCready.'

'Angus McCready?' I asked.

'That builder guy we were talking about, remember?'

'Oh, the Wassail. With the tan.'

'And the teeth!'

We both laughed, me a little uneasily. Mary Beth, it seemed, had known all along who Angus McCready was. I brought out my hand as I coughed over my tea, flapping my palm in apology to Mary Beth.

'You know he's got your Craig in trouble, don't you?' Mary Beth leaned forward, her expression suddenly serious.

My teacup jittered on its saucer. I struggled to know what to say next, but I was desperate to ask.

'I . . . that is, Craig and Angus . . .'

'Well, of course you know all about it. Most of the village do too. I mean, it's a lot of money!'

What had she said?

'I don't want to do business with a guy like that, it's not fair.'

'I'm sorry, I don't understand.'

Mary Beth threw me a quizzical look. 'You don't know?'

I shook my head.

'Ah.' She paused as if to consider what exactly she should say next. But then what had been said could not be unsaid. She sighed.

'I was asking my neighbour, Josie, for recommendations – for the kitchen, you understand. She warned me about Angus. You see, Craig did a great deal of work for Angus last year, some classy development on the edge of Derby. He was subcontracted to Angus, but Angus hasn't paid him a dime! I do hope it comes out alright, my dear, and that Craig gets paid. It's a lot of money, twenty thousand pounds.'

CHAPTER 33

The fight in the village hall car park made sense now – I'd been right, it had absolutely nothing to do with me. But this? Why hadn't Craig mentioned it?

As I drove home, the violence of that confrontation replayed in my head. It still shocked me, Angus head-butting Craig, Craig punching back. But Mary Beth's story, didn't it explain everything? Shouldn't I feel relieved that now I understood what was between them?

When I got to the house, I headed for the kitchen and poured out a small glass of whisky. Not too much this time. I grimaced when I thought of how much I'd been drinking since coming to this place. Paul had read the riot act if I'd so much as had a thimble-full.

I moved to the sitting room, reaching up to the window, one hand pressed against the glass pane as I sipped the drink, waiting for the kick of alcohol in my stomach, the heat to spread through my limbs, the sense of floating indifference to calm my nerves and assuage my thoughts.

Why hadn't Craig said something to me? Shame? Had he worried that I wouldn't like him any more if I thought he was struggling for money? Was that what he thought of me? I contemplated the view over the hills.

I thought of all that had happened here, how unwelcome I'd felt in the village, the scratch on my car, the rat in my bed. Steph's revelations about Danny, her obvious distress and the pear drum still in the attic waiting for me to open it. I felt more and more confused. Poor Craig – he had as much reason to hate Angus as I. So why had he seemed so friendly with him at the Wassail? I couldn't figure it out. Perhaps Craig thought he should stay on good terms with Angus, until later, in private, they'd argued over the money. Even the best of friends could fall out over money. I sipped the whisky and let my other hand drop to my side.

I stood there listening to the hum of the pipes in the wall, a bluster of wind slapping against the windows and rattling the wooden frames, smelling the scent of furniture wax and an unexpected drift of lavender, watching the chintz curtains swaying gently as if Elizabeth was still standing beside me. Enjoying my distress.

The fog lifted, burnt off by the morning sun. Lunchtime came and went but I had no desire to eat. I decided on another walk. No reservoir this time, just down the lane from the house – away from the cottage. I couldn't come to any harm this time, I could still see the house.

The cat followed me. Her tail was held high, curled at the tip, like a lemur trotting along the road. She seemed to sense my sour mood as she kept pace behind me. The lane wound its way to the main road at the bottom, where the sudden rumble of a truck going by made the cat finally give up, jumping through a hedge.

I didn't want to go into the village. I climbed a stile in the corner of a field and walked alongside the hedgerow. It led to a copse and a stream – it was only a trickle of brown water, winding between the trees under small overhanging banks of soil. After a while it disappeared underground and I passed into another field. A pheasant hurtled out across the stubble, a burst of red flying low over the ground, clattering in alarm. A group of wind turbines rose from the brow of the hill, great white blades revolving slowly, catching the afternoon sun.

I remembered this hill. Alton Heights. It was the one my sister used to drag me to when she was babysitting me but wanted to see her boyfriend. I'd hated being forced to watch the two of them snogging on a bench. Elizabeth would have been livid if she'd known. Was that why Steph had left home so young? An argument over boyfriends? Elizabeth had never said and I'd never asked. It occurred to me I could ask Steph myself now, not that it was really any of my business. I turned my face into the breeze, closing my eyes, feeling the weak rays of the winter sun.

They say that siblings feel a connection, even if they're far apart. Even though we hadn't spoken for twenty years, I realised Steph had always been in my mind. But you can't force a person to respond if they don't want to. It had been her choice to lose contact. It had left me with an emptiness, a regret for a loss over which I had no control. Was this how she felt about Danny? He'd been our half-brother, but the connection must have been there. She hadn't said much about how she felt, but it was in her voice. Why was it not the same for me? Because I'd been so young? Or was something wrong with me?

I opened my eyes. Yes, I remembered this hill, watching Steph with her boyfriend. She hadn't seemed to care that I was there, the child in me repulsed and curious both at the same time. The turbines drew my eyes, their steady movement was hypnotic. It was on the way home, sort of.

I climbed the hill, finding a narrow road that zig-zagged to the top. I was out of breath when I got there, high up overlooking the valley and the hills beyond – they swept out across the horizon, three hundred and sixty degrees of rolling banks of dusty blue, pitched against a clear sky. The light had begun to fade, a haze of pink silk highlighting the turbines behind me. They stood on the heathland right on the brow of the hill, caged off behind a wire fence. A white sign pronounced 'East Midlands Power Distribution Plc. Trespassers will be prosecuted'. It was the car park I remembered. Abandoned cigarette ends and takeaway packaging rolled in the wind and a bench faced the view, a single motorbike leaning on its side. My heart gave a small leap. I looked about but the car park was empty. There must be another walker nearby, perhaps a couple, but I could see no one.

I sat on the bench, swivelling in my seat to identify the different landmarks. In one direction were the six cooling towers of the power station south of Nottingham. In another were the cliffs of Matlock and the beginnings of the Peak District. To the west were the grey hills of Staffordshire. I spotted an opening in the land on the far side of the car park. It looked as if the ground had collapsed, but I knew it was an old quarry. I stood up and walked across.

I peered over the edge. It was a steep drop, with no fencing, no warning. I felt my stomach lurch. A narrow path led down either side, forming a horseshoe shape, the sandy grass peppered with rabbit droppings. At the bottom, I knew, was another bench. This was where Steph had used to meet her boyfriend.

I couldn't resist. I followed the path down, loose stones rolling under my feet. As I got close to the bottom, a vague smell drifted up, a whiff of stagnant water and rotting vegetation. The cliffs rose like a sheer wall, hacked away to leave a circular pit gouged in the rock. Water pooled in the cracks and craters left behind and a number of large boulders were strewn across the quarry floor like abandoned pieces on a chess board. In the middle was the bench.

The sun couldn't reach down here. The cold made me shiver, the smell made me gag. Why would anyone want to sit here? Privacy, I realised. I made to leave, but something caught my eye: a cluster of beer cans, a half-eaten burger and a pile of charred wood. People had been here before, of course they had, young kids no doubt. But there was something else. Beside another giant rock a motorbike helmet lay on the ground.

The visor was closed. It glinted black and iridescent. I cast around for its owner. I wasn't happy that someone else might be here with me, a man (why did I assume it was a man?), perhaps the rider from the bike in the car park overhead. I had no phone and was suddenly aware of my own vulnerability. I felt angry, it wasn't rational, the shadows were playing tricks on me. I couldn't see clearly, my eyes drifting out of focus. I swallowed and lifted one hand to my face; that smell. Helmets were expensive, it was an odd place to find a thing like that, apparently discarded. I took a step closer.

I sucked in my breath. The helmet hadn't been discarded. It was still attached to its owner. A body lay prone upon the ground. A man, hidden behind the rock. He wore a leather jacket and trousers, his feet facing the wrong way, his arms splayed awkwardly against the ground, his face hidden behind the visor. He was lying quite still.

My stomach heaved. I hovered in an agony of indecision. Was this some kind of a trap? Surely not, from the look of him. I stood rooted to the spot. I didn't want to touch him. But this was a human being, I couldn't *not* do anything. I looked up at the car park – had he fallen?

'He . . . hello?'

It seemed a daft thing to say. I reached down and touched him lightly on the arm.

'Hello!' I said again.

There was no response, his body stiff and cold. I snatched my hand away. I felt a jolt of shock and a sickening sense of knowledge. A wave of nausea made me turn away. The man was dead, wasn't he?

How long had he been lying there? I dropped to my knees, still unsure. Something hard dug into my skin, a key. The shape of it was familiar and it had a yellow tag – my house key. It must have fallen out of my pocket. The pain of it spurred me into action and, panicking, I reached out again.

My fingers shook. It was as if I was waiting for someone to give me permission, to take over and save the day. But it was just me here in this lonely spot. If I didn't look and he was still alive, then it would be my fault, if there was something I could do.

My fingers gripped the visor, feeling the edge of the plastic,

251

all the time terrified he would wake up, yet terrified he would not. Slowly I pushed the visor up and over the helmet.

He was definitely dead. The face was grey and swollen, completely distorted, the cheeks pressed out against the padding of the helmet. His lips were bloodied and split and his tongue hung fat and grey between his teeth, like a cow's tongue, oversized for its mouth. My heart pounded like a drum. The hair was blond and damp against his cheek.

I scrambled to my feet, turning to run. But at the last minute, I swung back. I wasn't sure. I took another look.

That face, that hair. The size of him.

It was Angus McCready.

CHAPTER 34

It took me twenty minutes to scramble up the slope and find the nearest house, a cottage rooted in the hillside like an obstinate goat. The woman who answered the door must have seen from my face that something was wrong.

The words tumbled from my lips and she drew me in, guiding me to her sitting room before reaching for the phone. My skin was clammy, I felt tired, a numbing, empty kind of tired as I stood blankly by the window. It was that same view, the hills now steeped in shadow. I watched a cloud of starlings twist and turn in the wind, one large amorphous black shape against a purple bruised sky.

She handed me the phone and I told the police where he was. They asked to meet me there. The woman locked up her house and came with me and we stood, buffeted by the wind, in the car park overlooking the pit, the orange street lamps of the villages twinkling on their hills.

Eventually, two police cars swung in off the road, one after the other, lights spinning, blue and yellow squares plastered to their doors, like two angry mutant bees. The men disappeared down the slope, bands of torchlight flickering across the scrub. Another policeman stood next to me, wittering on about the view. He was guarding me, I realised. What did they think I was going to do?

More cars arrived and a van. Suddenly the place was buzzing, lights, tents, people in white suits. He – Angus – was someone else's problem now.

It was so late by the time they'd retrieved the body, they'd told me to go home and get some sleep. I had to go to the police station in the morning to make a full statement. The woman from the cottage had stayed with me till I was free to leave and she very kindly drove me home.

I moved like a robot around the house, locking the doors and climbing the stairs and getting ready for bed.

Finally, I closed my eyes and slept.

I awoke to hear the sound of him breathing. A rasping breath, rattling through nostrils bloody and wet.

I lay frozen in my bed, eyes held shut.

I could still see it, the body of Angus McCready, the strange angle of his limbs, the grey colour of his skin, his tongue rolling outside his mouth.

But all I could think of was another dead body. Images flashed beneath my eyes. That of a young boy. His face was obscured, his hands curled into small fists, his chest curved in towards his legs. His clothes were soaked in fresh blood. Beneath the blood, I recognised the garments – Power Rangers red.

I wanted to open my eyes, but they were glued shut, my body pinned to the bed. With each sound of his breath, it was like a strobe light firing off in my head, each flare a new close-up of the same scene. The boy corpse crumpled on the ground. The head facing the wrong way. His eyes staring at me in shock. His bubbling and bloodied mouth accusing me.

I tried to move, to will each limb to lift, my legs, my hands, my fingers. I felt that should I move one inch, then all the evil spirits in the world would find me, would come crashing down on me, fluttering at my side, pushing and shoving, each of them clamouring for a piece of me, a chunk of my flesh, a lump of my hips, my hand, my big fat tongue . . .

When my eyes did open, the impenetrable dark of the room was the same as the suffocating blackness in my head and I opened my mouth to scream.

The dream had gone by the morning, the way that dreams do. There one minute, gone the next. The details had dissolved into the night, but the feel of it hovered on the fringes of my memory, teasing me with an echo of the terror I'd felt, my body charged with adrenalin, my skin slick with sweat.

After breakfast, I drove to Chester Green in Derby. The police station looked like any other corporate office – a large brick building surrounded by car parks, a reception desk with a glass screen and a bank of blue plastic seating. I sat down and waited.

'Miss Crowther?' A uniformed officer scanned the room.

'Yes?' I stood up.

'This way please.'

I followed the man down a white, characterless corridor and he indicated a door on the left.

'In here, Miss Crowther. Can I get you a cup of tea or coffee?'

'No thanks.' I stepped inside.

The room had one table and three chairs, economical in its furnishing. A single window ran the full length of the wall, but the glass was frosted with only a blurry hint of grey roofs and white cloud beyond. Two officers were already sitting down and I felt a wave of dizziness – this was beginning to feel worse than finding McCready's body. I swallowed and took the remaining seat.

'Miss Crowther, thank you for coming in. I'm Sergeant Mansfield. This is my colleague Susan Nowak. We'd like to run through exactly what happened yesterday. Any little detail can be really helpful.'

I began by describing my walk, the weather, the time of day, arriving at the hill. They asked me why I decided to go up there. Just because, I said. It's a nice view. I didn't want to go into my memories of the past. It wasn't relevant. When I got to the moment I saw McCready's helmet, I had to stop. My eyes dropped to my hands. I found myself clutching and unclutching them like a small child in the headmaster's office.

'I'm sorry, it was just so . . .'

There had been something almost inhuman about that helmet, the way it hid the face, the visor glinting rainbow colours.

'It's alright, Miss Crowther. Take your time. We know this isn't easy.'

Nowak had leaned forward and touched me on the arm. I looked up. Her eyes were soft and sympathetic.

'I didn't know what to do. I thought he might still be alive. What if I could have helped him? What if I made things worse?'

'He was dead long before you arrived, Miss Crowther. Few

256

people ever experience what you've seen, you did exactly what anyone else would have done. You did nothing wrong.'

I didn't reply. The sergeant nodded in agreement.

'Tell me, Miss Crowther, is there anything else you remember about the site, anything you noticed, any other objects or clothing or whatever, even rubbish?'

I tried to think – there was the litter in the car park, the motorbike tipped on its side, the debris down in the quarry. Nothing out of the ordinary. I described them all, then shook my head.

'I'm sorry, I can't think of anything else.'

'And you say you recognised the deceased?'

'Yes. Angus McCready. He's a builder. I didn't know him, but he's known in the village and I met him once in Ashbourne. I bumped into him outside a shop. No twice, I think – he was there at the Wassail last week, but I didn't speak to him.'

Not then at least. I told myself it wasn't a lie, I just hadn't told them the full details of exactly what had happened in Ashbourne.

Fucking bitch . . . the words resonated in my head.

I'd answered every question truthfully, hadn't I? They hadn't asked me about Ashbourne or Craig, or if I knew anything else. Why would they? I needed time to think.

'I see. Thank you, Miss Crowther.'

As I left the police station, guiding the car back into the traffic, I chewed on my thumb. I hadn't told them about McCready being rude to me, or the scratch on my car, the latter was entirely my supposition. And I hadn't told them about McCready knowing Craig or the fight at the village hall. Or the money Mary Beth said Angus owed Craig. I couldn't put Craig under suspicion.

But there were so many questions in my head. I couldn't forget that fight, Craig and Angus squaring off, Angus's head shooting forward onto Craig's, Craig's anger and aggression, the unexpected power behind his punch.

I didn't see Craig for the rest of that day, or the next. Didn't he know what had happened? Wouldn't a boyfriend have rushed to my side? Had something happened to him? I tried to ring but there was no reply. I didn't want to leave a message; how would that look?

Besides, what would I say to him: *Did you have anything at all to do with Angus McCready's death?*

CHAPTER 35

On the Monday, I phoned Mary Beth. I didn't know who else to ring. I didn't tell her about the nightmares or what I was thinking – no, fearing – about Craig. But she got the gist that I was upset. My voice was tremulous and even to my own ears I sounded a wreck.

'Oh, you poor dear, let me come over.'

She already knew about Angus; the village grapevine was well ahead of me. Everyone, it seemed, knew it was me who'd found his body.

'I'll cook us some lunch and you can talk to me, tell me all about it.'

She didn't wait for my reply.

I replaced the phone on its cradle feeling only marginally better.

I went to the sink in the downstairs cloakroom to splash water on my tearstained cheeks. I stared at my reflection in the mirror. I pulled the hood of my old jersey top over my head. But it didn't hide the shadows under my eyes, the haggard expression on my face, the pale skin and the built-in scowl that pushed my lips downwards.

I tugged the hood back down again. Had I always looked like that?

'I'd love to see your paintings, if you'll let me?' Mary Beth's cheeriness filled the hall.

She seemed to understand. That I couldn't launch straight into what had happened, and how protective I would be of my work.

'Sure,' I said.

The word stuck in my throat. At the sight of her kind face, I didn't trust myself. I led her to the kitchen and gestured awkwardly to a large folder on the table.

'What's your current project, if I'm allowed to ask?' Mary Beth had already divested herself of her oversized coat and a fringed shawl.

'It's a collection of fairy tales. All traditional stuff, not made up. You know, Brothers Grimm, the *Pentamerone* . . .'

'Now Grimm I know about, but what's the *Pentamerone*?'

'Oh, sorry, it's a collection of Italian folk tales from the seventeenth century, tales within tales,' I said. 'A bit like the *Arabian Nights*.'

I perked up, smiling. Mary Beth knew how to make me feel at ease.

'They're great stories,' I continued, 'if a bit gruesome in places. People wrongly assume that fairy tales are for children. Many of them are far too grown up. You know, abusive parents, incest, cannibalism – it's all in there!'

The darker, the better, from a visual point of view.

'They're all connected, the same stories told again and again all over the world, growing like Chinese whispers. The Grimm brothers based a lot of their stories on the *Pentamerone*.'

I paused, thinking that was probably enough detail.

Mary Beth leafed through the pictures: the black-winged deformity of my swan prince, the stubborn child pleading from his grave, the singing bones from *The Juniper Tree*.

'These are amazing! You have a very distinctive style.'

Was she being genuine or diplomatic? Mary Beth had laid the sheets out side by side. I stood beside her. I could see what she meant. This particular collection had a consistency and morbidity beyond my usual fashion – bold lines slashed across the page, the faces angular and haunted. The colours too were of a limited palette, variations on perylene green and black with the odd splash of purple and cadmium red, each picture crawling with insect detail, like a decaying corpse, exoskeletal bodies, iridescent armour, a multitude of eyes blazing out from the peacock dead. I blushed, wondering what Mary Beth made of it all.

'Thank you.'

'No, really. I love this. It's so raw.' She gave me a fleeting look. 'Like you've been there. You're very talented, Caro.'

She smiled, reaching towards her bag on the table.

'I've brought us some lunch.'

She began to unpack, salad, pastrami, bagels and home-made soup. Craig would have approved. She busied herself in the kitchen heating up the soup in the microwave and setting out two plates with the food. Did everyone think I needed feeding up?

We sat down to eat. She tapped her fingers against her

261

bowl, 'mmm'ing as she swallowed the hot liquid. When she next spoke, her voice was quieter.

'So, my dear. Are you alright?'

I was not.

'I haven't slept very well.' My voice faded away.

'I'm not surprised. Most of us see dead animals at some point in our lives, but a dead person? That's quite another thing.' Mary Beth closed her eyes momentarily as if imagining it for herself.

'I keep seeing his face, his . . .' My voice wobbled.

I was in imminent danger of bursting into tears. Already the image was there again in my head – Angus McCready's body, the helmet. I dipped my head, hot tears pricking at the corner of my eyes.

'It's alright, love, you don't need to tell me, not unless you want to.'

'No, it's okay, the police have been asking me too.'

I shook my head, pressing my eyelids shut. Oh God, the police. What if they found out Craig had reason to hate Angus? What if the police asked me to go back in, asked me if I knew of anyone who had a grudge against him? Would I tell them I'd seen Angus and Craig in a fight last week? I swallowed.

'I don't suppose they get many dead bodies around here,' said Mary Beth. 'It's a nasty drop on that hill. I've seen the place, fabulous views, but dangerous. He could so easily have slipped, there's nothing to stop you going over. Perhaps now they'll put up some kind of safety barrier.'

I pushed my hand into my pocket, feeling with my fingers. How could I tell her? How could I explain how uncomfortable I felt, as if wherever I went, I was always followed by grief and death and tragedy.

* * *

262

Later, when Mary Beth had gone, I sat down in the kitchen, reaching into my pocket. I was checking that it was still there, my house key.

It had fallen out of my pocket when I'd found Angus. Or so I'd thought. Like all the other keys at Larkstone Farm, it was carefully identified by its yellow plastic tab. Except this wasn't *my* house key.

It fit the house, sure enough – the front door. But my key was still on my key ring, along with the car keys, clean and safe on the hall table. This one was covered with mud, the little tag window wet beneath. It must have been a spare.

Why would it have been at Alton Heights, lying next to Angus McCready's body? Could Angus have had a key to Elizabeth's house?

CHAPTER 36

Tuesday morning and Larkstone Farm had a dreary post-holiday feel about it. There wasn't even any snow left to make it feel cosier. The sky was grey, the lane was grey and the dark hedgerows and bare trees just seemed to accentuate the grey by their contrast.

As I trailed through the house, I began to notice all the little frayed corners on the sofas and chairs, the tattered hems on the curtains, the once smart fabrics that had faded in the sun. Only the sitting room and Elizabeth's bedroom had been kept relatively smart. It was as if the neglect of the house reflected my own childhood and Elizabeth's treatment of me. More likely Elizabeth had been reluctant to spend money on a house I now knew she hadn't owned. How she must have resented me on so many counts. Wouldn't I myself have felt like that? I tried but failed to shake the thoughts from my head. I didn't want to understand Elizabeth, to admit that she'd been human.

After Steph had left, that day when I was nine, Elizabeth changed. In subtle ways she was different. She still told me the story of the pear drum, she still taunted me with those words, making me stand for hours in the study. But it was as if there was something missing – a detachment, a hollowness to her words, a lack of satisfaction in the punishment. She wanted me to suffer, but she no longer *felt* anything. Perhaps her loneliness, the passing of time, growing older, had dulled her senses. I didn't understand. Only later did I realise that her feelings had simply been driven even deeper.

As the years progressed, things changed. I grew into a young woman, too old for stories, so it was a different game that we played. Now it was all about control. The household jobs that I did were never good enough – I had to re-do them the 'right' way. I couldn't use the phone, I couldn't go out, I had no money. Everything to restrict my contact with people. Even my clothes isolated me – dated and ill-fitting, she bought them without me being present, the minimum required to dress me. Secondary school was ten times worse than the village primary. They laughed at me and my clothes with the viciousness of a pack of hyenas and at home I hid from any visitors.

Only once had I tried to leave. At fourteen, I'd sneaked out of the back door in the early hours of the morning and walked to the village. The houses on the street surrounded me, each door closed, each window blank and brooding. At that time in the night even the orange lights from the lampposts were switched off. I was overwhelmed by the dark and the cold. I had nowhere to go, no money and no home. I knew what happened to girls with no home.

So I went back. I slipped into the house and up the stairs

to my room and I went back to bed as if nothing had happened. If Elizabeth knew that I'd left for a while, she never said. I felt a failure. Except this time, I knew I had to wait. Till I was old enough.

I studied even harder and painted whenever I could. It seemed I had a talent of sorts. My first prize-winning picture was of the lamppost in the village, the old-fashioned glass lamp near the Co-op, partially obscured by rolling mist. The glass was cracked and the lamp infested with beetles, like the ones in the summerhouse. The teacher had looked at me with astonishment in her eyes.

Then, when I was sixteen, I plucked up the courage to defy Elizabeth. She'd told me to clean the downstairs cloakroom. I had scrubbed and mopped but the toilet had an old rusty stain in the bowl and, no matter how hard I rubbed at it, it wouldn't budge. She came to inspect as I left the room.

'Caroline! Come back.'

She was standing by the toilet, staring down at the stain. I knew what was coming next. I placed the bucket and mop on the floor and turned back towards her. I planted my feet firmly apart and looked at her straight. Her eyes had narrowed and her face looked pinched, I could see she was working up to another dressing-down. Before she could open her mouth, I launched in there first.

'No! I won't do it again! It's rust and it won't come off. Perhaps you could have a go?' I felt my heart thudding in my chest, heat rising up my neck as the temerity of my words dawned on me.

Fury flooded her face and I could see her hand itching to slap me as she had when I was younger. I was already taller than her and the last time she'd tried it I'd ducked and run away. She wasn't going to let me get away with that this time.

'How dare you speak to me like that,' she said.

'How dare you speak to *me* like that!' I flung back.

She took a step forward.

'Careful, Caroline! You know, the school have told me that you have a talent for art, that you're hoping to go to college after your A levels. Would that be so?'

'Yes.'

Manchester University, that was where I wanted to go – I'd heard they had a vibrant Art department and I couldn't wait. Just two more years, that's what I kept telling myself. I swallowed. Where was she going with this?

'And how do you think you're going to pay for it?'

'I . . . I don't understand.'

'The fees are three times as much as they used to be. And where are you going to live, how are you going to eat – how are you going to pay for all that?'

'There are student loans for the fees and I'll get a maintenance loan.'

'But it's not enough. Believe me, accommodation and subsistence in Manchester is expensive.'

She knew about my ambition to go to Manchester? My art teacher must have been talking. I felt betrayed.

'Then I'll get a job,' I said.

'You and a thousand other students – it's not so easy out there on your own with no money.'

'I'll find one! Even if it's cleaning loos!'

She laughed then, a shrill, decadent laugh that pierced my ears.

'Well, you'll have to get a lot better at it then! There's a bit of money your father set aside for your education, did you know that?'

It was a shock to hear her say that.

'What? I . . . How much?'

'Oh, I can't remember the exact sum, not a lot, but it's under my control. I have to sign if you're to get a penny of it, so I suggest you mind your manners, young woman, and do exactly as you're told!'

'Why do you hate me?' My voice had dropped. I heard a pathetic plea creep into my words. 'Ever since I can remember, you've always hated me!'

I thought I saw her hesitate. As if her emotions were so strong they had momentarily overwhelmed her. She hated me that much. Her eyes slid to the study door, and I felt the familiar leap of apprehension. She smiled.

'You don't belong in my house!' she hissed.

My house. That's what she'd said. It reminded me of Steph's words, all those years ago. I felt even more alienated.

I turned back to the toilet with my scrubber and my rubber gloves, and I started cleaning it again. I felt my shame. I'd never been very good at rebellion. I was conditioned to respond exactly as she wanted. And perhaps, even then, I had still wanted to mend things, to somehow fix the relationship between us. Who else did I have?

In a weird sort of way, money aside, I thought I needed her.

So I waited. And with the grudging help of the school, I applied for funding and got myself to uni. The money Elizabeth had promised me was never forthcoming. And by then I didn't want it, it was tainted and I wouldn't give her the satisfaction of asking for it. I was an adult now: I didn't need Elizabeth.

Instead, I got myself a job in a bar, serving customers too drunk to know better, mopping floors slick with vomit and cleaning toilets.

That night my dreams were even more intense. Angus McCready lying at the bottom of the cliff, Elizabeth sprawled at the base of the stairs, the Power Rangers boy in his red suit soaked in blood. I thrashed in the bed, I could hear moaning, like a wild animal. I awoke realising that was me, my heart pumping in my chest, my eyes wide open in the dark.

I lay there trying to focus on the ceiling, to relax. Before coming here, I hadn't had these dreams for a long time, the night terrors that beset me as a child. It must have been seeing McCready like that, stirring up childhood fears. I tried to block it out. I thought of the key instead. I'd picked it up without thinking, assuming it was mine. Such an innocent thing. But now I realised I'd unintentionally taken evidence from the scene. I rolled onto my side, drawing my knees in, hugging myself. I could hardly admit to it now, could I?

But I couldn't stop thinking about Angus. Had he fallen or jumped? Suicide – was it suicide? It lingered in my head, the unnatural pose of his limbs, the stillness of his body, the helmet . . . That helmet troubled me, somehow it made him into something else, inhuman, an inanimate object. Not a person, not a living, breathing, flesh and blood person. Just a body, dead. Slowly, I drifted back to sleep.

When I woke again it was daylight. I was calm, but my head was full of images. Were they real? Were they memories from behind my blank wall?

I rolled to my feet. I had to paint before they dissipated

into the day. Always it was the way with me when I was upset, I became obsessed with the need to get them out of my head. But this was something else.

I ran to the kitchen still in my pyjamas. With a sweep of my arm, I cleared the table, laying out the largest sheet of paper I could find. The pads of my fingers felt its surface, the rise and fall of the fibres, like a blind person reading Braille.

Outside, on the lane below the house, I heard the clip clop of a horse's hooves, the regular motion of a trot, the rise and fall getting louder then moving away. But the sound was distant, detached, something somewhere else.

I was driven, oblivious to the living world. I rinsed the paintbrush in water, there was no need to sketch it first, I knew exactly what to do. I squeezed the watercolours from their tubes, dipping the brush into the paint, mixing and folding the colours until I was satisfied. Rinsing, mixing, rinsing, mixing. Then I trailed the brush across the paper.

I worked fast, slashing lines across the sheet, dabbing, flicking, leaning over the table until my back ached and my neck was pulled tight. The image grew. It showed the summer-house as it was now, the panes of glass broken, all sharp edges and jagged spikes. Leaves had been blown into piles across the floor, heaped against the walls where multiple trails of ivy wriggled upwards. The colours were brown and green and russet red, spiders clinging to the roof struts, beetles clustered on the ground. There was a whole mound of insects, worms and maggots writhing one against another, their segmented bodies clearly defined with additional pen and ink. A heaving, breathing shape hidden under the leaves, except for one small delicate hand, peeping out like a little white mouse.

I paused to evaluate the scene. Something was missing.

Something was not quite right. I dipped my brush back into the paint. Carefully, I added it in beside the hand. At first, it was only a little, a small pool touching the fingers. Then a bit more, spilling out across the floor.

There – that was it. *Stop right there.*

Red. Bright vermillion red. *It's enough.*

I stood back to look at the picture. Why had I drawn it that way?

Something hovered out of frame, a growing feeling of fearful recognition. I reached out for another sheet, pulling it up so that it aligned with the first. I taped it top and bottom so that it was fixed to the kitchen table. Picking up my brush I began to paint again.

This was a different summerhouse. Cleaner, newer, the one from years ago but still neglected. This half of my picture merged seamlessly with the first, window frames and sky fitting perfectly together. A figure kneeled on the ground.

I stopped. My hands were covered in paint, my hair escaping round my face. I rubbed my fingers together as if to clean something that wasn't there. My ribs felt like bands of iron squeezing my lungs and heart, my breath came short and fast, my eyes darting from the red paint on the paper to the red stain on my hands. Slowly, I stood up.

I moved like an automaton across the kitchen. I went out into the garden, heading across the lawn towards the summerhouse. A spray of rain fell from the branches overhead, scattering over my clothes. I hadn't bothered with a coat, nor a jumper. I was barefoot. The cold sank into my flesh, numbing my feet, my face and arms as if the Snow Queen herself blew upon my skin. I stopped at the entrance to the summerhouse.

I watched the wind teasing at the dead leaves on the floor.

Like the ones in my painting. Even now there were shards of broken glass scattered on the ground. The summerhouse hadn't changed for over twenty years, abandoned to the elements and a mother's grief. Steph had said it was an accident. In the garden . . . In the summerhouse, she meant.

I was drowning in memory, the sound of breaking glass, the impact of a thousand pieces falling to the floor, my own voice screaming, Elizabeth's voice telling me that story, malice dripping from her tongue, the pear drum throbbing in the distance.

Have you been bad enough, Caroline?

Finally, I remembered.

CHAPTER 37

It was autumn, a few months after the birthday party, the one where Elizabeth's friend, had locked me in my bedroom. I'd been playing with a ball. My brother had snatched it from me as he often did. Another trick to taunt me with.

Danny ran off into the summerhouse and I chased after him. The group of trees surrounding it leaned overhead, their branches overwhelming the building. It was steeped in shadow and the glass and wood that should have made the summerhouse a thing of beauty were covered in moss and green algae from damp and lack of daylight. This time I was determined to fight back.

It was dusk already, the dying light playing tricks on me. For a moment I couldn't see Danny. The wind rattled the too-thin window panes and the branches of the trees scraped against the glass. It had never been a pleasant place, the summerhouse, used more for storage by the gardener than its original purpose of pleasure.

'*Where are you Danny? I want it back!*'

I moved into the shadows. I saw the rows of empty flower pots, chipped and cracked and leaning against the wall. I saw the bags of compost, piled high, the top bag split open where a knife had cut it corner to corner, the black innards spilling out. I saw a fork, some spades, a bucket full of dead and dying weeds tangled in their roots. I saw the dry leaves that had blown through the door, spiralling up against the corner where the draught played out, the spiders on their webs hunkered down against the weather.

A figure stepped out from behind me.

I spun around, surrounded by the six walls of glass. Like the eyes of a fly. My heart was pumping, my head full of indignation at the theft.

'Give it to me, Danny,' I cried. 'Give me my ball. Give me my ball!'

'*Caroline, limpy, lumpy Caroline!*'

Danny darted this way and that, like a basketball player throwing the ball from one hand to another.

'I want my ball back!'

He didn't reply.

My head was filled with pain, as if a knife had gouged out the middle of my forehead. I was so angry, a rage of red flooding across my eyes.

'You give me my ball back! I want my ball back, Danny! Now, Danny! *Now!*'

But he only danced some more.

'*Scaredy cat, scaredy cat, come and take your ball back!*'

I reached down towards the flower pots, grabbing the nearest thing. When I stood up, I saw myself reflected in the glass. A metal spike was in my hand, one of a collection of

274

spikes bought for the gazebo in the garden. It was the length of a ruler, brand new and unused, its weight heavy in my hand, the point of it as sharp as a kitchen knife. I held it out in front of me.

'Leave me alone!' I cried. 'Fuck you, Danny Crowther! Fuck you!'

My six-year-old self didn't understand the words, but I knew their potency, Danny had taught me that. I waved my spike and the figure retreated.

Danny was backed up against the glass, his face brilliantly aware. He wasn't bullying me now. He had a hand up as if to hold me off. He looked afraid. For the first time, *he* was afraid of *me*!

'Steph!' he screamed.

He was calling for his big sister now, like the snivelling boy that he was. How quickly he had changed. I was emboldened.

'*Steph!*' His voice was thin and whining. He was properly frightened now.

I felt the power, the satisfaction of a reversal in roles. He was feeling it, how I had felt it, small and weak and vulnerable. My metal spike beat his hands. It beat his stick and his words too.

His feet kicked out but I dodged clear. He tried again, his leg catching on a roll of barbed wire. He panicked, screeching and throwing his arms about. One arm caught me from the side and I reacted. Head down, I pushed. He was thrust backwards against the summerhouse. In that split second the windows shattered, chunks and slivers of glass slicing down all around us like a sudden summer squall. His body pitched forwards towards me as he tried to escape the glass. He was bigger than me so that my own body was sheltered under his, my face, my shoulders, my back protected from the onslaught. I felt my other hand tighten around the spike. I didn't see the blood until it was too late. I lifted my head. Danny had slumped against me, his body sliding to the ground. Steph was standing in the doorway, horror on her face. I looked down. I saw the blood on Danny's hands, the red stain blossoming on his chest, warm, scarlet, gleaming blood pumping from his body, seeping down towards the floor, running along the cracks between the concrete slabs, the metal spike buried between his ribs.

CHAPTER 38

They blamed me. Of course they did.

Wasn't that why they despised me in the village, even after all these years?

'*How does she put up with it?*'

'*How can she even bear to keep that child in the same house?*'

That was what they'd said.

They all knew.

I hadn't meant to do it, I really hadn't. It all happened so fast. One minute I was standing there, shouting for my ball, the next minute there was glass everywhere and Danny was in front of me, blood pouring from his body.

Oh God, so much blood. I'd never seen blood like that.

Have you been bad enough, Caroline?

It was like a devil had taken hold of me. I staggered to my feet, my body launching towards the house. I burst into the kitchen and through the hall. I ran up the stairs, one floor, two floors, to the upper hallway and the door that led to the attic. The key almost fell from my hand as I unlocked it. I climbed the steps, not bothering to switch on the light. I found what I was looking for. The crate. The pear drum.

It was after Danny's funeral that Elizabeth had started telling me the story – just me, not Steph. It had been her way of punishing me.

Have you been bad enough, Caroline?

She never spoke about what happened. Not once. I lived in a vacuum, nothing, no one touched me, spoke to me, even acknowledged me, in those first few days. I had a vague memory of being dragged into somebody's office, later, the smell of lilies in reception, the perfume of the lady behind the desk, the depth of the carpet under my feet. But I couldn't remember anything else.

I had nowhere else to go. I was Elizabeth's daughter, at least in the eyes of the law. She'd never liked me before, me, her predecessor's daughter. She'd tolerated my presence for the sake of my father. But later, after . . . ? Perhaps it would have been too easy to send me away. To palm me off on the authorities or some relative on my father's side, if they'd have had me. To never see me again. To never have the opportunity to do what she wanted to do. To punish me.

No, she'd found another way to torment me, with *that story*.

I flung open the lid to the crate and lifted out the pear drum. I cradled it in my arms, hating it, dreading what was to come.

I placed it on the attic floor, kneeling in the dust.

It was a beautiful thing. The wood had been shaped with

278

the eye of a perfectionist, its curves smoothed and polished to a rich mahogany brown. The main body, the pear-shaped bit, was painted like a Greek urn, birds and animals decorating the top. On the side were figures, a trail of eager musicians cavorting one behind the other, arms akimbo, wild-eyed and whirling, their clothes flying out in bright colours. The colours of blood and war paint. The colours of the devils in the medieval paintings of hell, writhing in ecstasy to the sound of Satan's music.

I traced the strings that lay taut along its frame, across the wheel that rotated with the handle to where they disappeared inside the box – the one the story spoke of, long and thin, it housed the little people, the mechanism that made the notes. I'd never opened it. I'd never dared. I didn't want to admit that I'd been bad – that bad.

'If you open the pear drum,' Elizabeth had said, 'and the little people are hiding, then when you get home there will be a new mother with a wooden tail and glass eyes . . .'

She'd been my new mother long before I'd ever seen the pear drum.

I held the handle with my shaking fingers and turned.

A noise began to grow, like the slow heat of pleasure from a lover's touch. The handle was S-shaped, twisting backwards as it moved, an optical illusion that had fascinated me as a child. I wound it with one hand, the other fingering the keys on the side of the box. I had no real knowledge of how to play it, but I hit the keys anyway in whatever order I wished. Clack, clack, clack, the drone hissing through the box. Clack, clack, clack.

I saw Elizabeth.

Elizabeth sitting on the sofa in the sitting room holding

the pear drum. Elizabeth sneering at me as the drone began to hum. Elizabeth closing her eyes as the noise filled the room, a heavy vibration causing the curtains to shake, the decorative figurines on the mantelpiece to jump. Elizabeth opening her eyes again, fixing her gaze on me, smiling in that cold, speculative way that she had.

'Have you been bad enough yet, Caroline?'

She spoke quietly over the sound of the pear drum.

Had I? Been bad enough?

I let my fingers slide to the catch on the side of the drum, still turning the handle with my other hand. I could hardly touch it, my fingers falling clumsily away, but I forced myself to reach up, to push it again. The music hung on one note and it felt as if I would explode, fear, panic, excitement pulsing through my body, my thoughts racing, darting from one thing to another like a drug shooting through my veins.

I could see the trees in the orchards of Larkstone village, bedecked with lanterns blowing wild in the wind, their branches writhing against the sky. I could see the house, Larkstone Farm, its huge shape stark against the horizon, its empty windows blazing in the glowing sunset, like the day when I'd arrived. I could see Elizabeth's grave, the gown of the vicar standing overhead, his clean brown hands, his pristine white skirts dragging in the dirt, stained with black.

I could see Craig. His naked body lying by the fire in the sitting room, red and yellow flames reflected in the damp beads on his skin. My body remembered his touch, the scent of his hair, the taste of his skin, the dark hairs that coiled down his chest, his breath feathering my cheek. He was rolling me over, smiling, holding me secure until I lay on top of him, looking down upon his face. I blinked.

I could see Angus at the base of Alton Heights, his finger-nails scratched and torn, his motorbike helmet bulbous like the giant head of an insect. But now he was lying somewhere else. On a bed of leaves in the summerhouse. Dead and dying leaves, the colour of mahogany. I could see the leaves scattered beneath his head, the trails of ivy that climbed the walls behind us. As he lay there, he began to wake. Slowly he began to move, one hand grasping for my skirt. His knuckles clenched the fabric tight, one hand after another, dragging himself up. His breathing wheezed and curdled in his throat. I pushed back, shoving him as hard as I could. I heard the glass crushing beneath his weight. I saw his eyes flutter in alarm, the blood seeping from beneath his body, trickling between the leaves, one line joining another, pooling, growing, flooding the floor, one large pear-like pool of shining scarlet blood.

Have you been bad enough, Caroline?

My head swayed with the weight of the images in my head. The present and the past blurring into one.

I understood now what Elizabeth wanted. She wanted me to remember.

But why hadn't she just told me? The truth that I'd been hiding from myself all this time. It was as if with each image layered one over the other, I sought to block out the one I dreaded most, the horror of it rising in my throat.

Danny dying at my feet.

I gripped the handle in my hand, turning it still.

'*Have you been bad enough?*' she hissed.

Yes. I had been bad enough.

I let go of the handle. The wavering drone stopped.

I opened the pear drum.

CHAPTER 39

The house stood in silence, the only sound the clock ticking slowly in the hall below.

The little people weren't hiding. Inside the box, the keys were lying neatly lined up. Each was a straight wooden peg, one for every note. There were twelve in all. I pressed upon a key and saw the corresponding peg lift to meet the strings. I moved the handle again and it changed the whining tone of the drum. I pressed another key and another, listening and watching with growing fascination. It was such a simple instrument, the handle turning the wheel, the keys pressing against the strings, like the fingers on the neck of a violin, playing each note.

Why had I been terror-stricken by this thing for so long? It was just a *thing*. I rested back on my heels to peer inside the pear drum. I thought of all those years when I'd lived in dread of it, wondering what awful thing could be within.

Elizabeth had simply used it to torment me, to control me. Why had I let her do that? I knew the answer now – my own buried guilt.

I saw something inside the box, a glimpse of yellowed white against the wood. I leaned forward – there was something trapped beneath the pegs.

I tried to push my fingers in between, but the pegs were too close together. I lifted up the box, tipping it so that what-ever it was could slide down the length of the box to where the pegs were further apart. A thin package. My fingers waggled and pushed, pinching and grasping until I could pull it up between the pegs. At last, I had it.

It was a sheaf of papers, flattened and smooth where they'd lain under the pegs. Why would someone have placed them there? How long had they been hidden? Apprehension held me back. I smoothed the papers on my lap, delaying the moment. It was only a small bundle, one or two sheets and a handful of photographs.

The first one was small and well thumbed. It showed a brown-haired baby, his eyes puffy and closed, lips pursed and a tiny fist folded against his mouth, the kind of picture they take from ward trolleys peddling bedside mementos of new-born babies.

I looked at the next three photographs: a toddler, head thrown back, grinning to camera; a small boy standing on a beach, wrapped in a sodden, sandy towel; an older boy, maybe seven or eight years old. He was brown-haired too, his locks too long. His pose was defiant, clutching a bright yellow plastic machine gun. It was the boy I'd seen in the bedroom, the one with the pear drum. Danny.

I didn't believe in ghosts. There was always a rational

explanation for everything. What I'd seen in that room was a warped memory, stimulated by my return, by all the stuff that had been going on, my manic, frantic state of mind.

It came to me clearly, all the times he'd bullied me, his face pushing into mine, snatching toys, pinching me in the back seat of the car until I shrieked and Elizabeth told *me* off – for pinching *him*. That moment at the campsite, when he'd placed a rat in my bed, glorying in my horror and humiliation. He'd boasted about it to Steph afterwards, relishing every word. The Wassail and the apple-bobbing when he'd gone too far and almost drowned me. How I'd *hated* him – I'd had good reason to hate him.

I unfolded the papers. It was a two-page letter, headed with an official-looking black typeface. *Bannerman and Friedland, Child Psychiatry.* It was dated 30th October 1997.

Dear Mrs Crowther,

Thank you for bringing your daughter, Caroline, to me on Tuesday 24th October. We spent a very productive couple of hours together and I was able to observe her in play and conversation. She is a very creative child with a vivid, highly visual imagination, and she responds well to artistic activities as well as the more generic ones that do not challenge her own sense of security. But I regret to say that we have made no progress on her memory. Your daughter is suffering from severe memory loss relating to all episodes prior to your son Daniel's accident a year ago.

Her short-term memory is fine and she has settled remarkably well back at school, as you know, albeit unusually subdued and quiet – but in all fairness, this is to be expected. I can reassure you that I have found no evidence of developmental conditions. It is simply that she cannot recollect anything prior to last October.

My conclusion is that this is a form of post-traumatic stress disorder, a condition that typically affects adults experiencing severe trauma or life experiences that induce shock and emotional shut-down. All events prior to and including the triggering event have been blocked from her memory. It's a condition that occurs less often in children but in the case of your daughter is explained, I fear, by the tragic events that took place on 18th October last year.

I'm so very sorry for your loss. Losing your son like that – I can't begin to express how you must feel. I understand your concerns regarding your daughter's poor relationship with her brother, but with no other witnesses, we will not be able to prove one way or another exactly what happened that day. Nor indeed would Caroline have been old enough to understand the consequences of her actions, deliberate or otherwise. At such a young age, she cannot be held legally responsible. Indeed, her memory loss is quite likely an instinctive response to her severe stress at what she experienced, and to her inner distress at what happened. It's her body's way of protecting her. As such, I cannot recommend any treatment that will cure the condition. And I must reiterate, as I have told you before, you must not tell her directly what happened. It will only make things worse. Memory is a delicate thing and she is in a very fragile state. For the moment, and perhaps permanently, she is best left alone and allowed to live a normal life, under your care, love and supervision.

I have now prepared my report for the courts, and I am happy to say that I will be recommending that she

285

remains with you. At only seven years old, I am confident the courts will agree to leave her in your care, so long as she remains under psychiatric supervision, at least for the next two years when I am sure it will be reassessed.

I am prescribing your daughter a mild sedative to help her with the night terrors and generally getting off to sleep. I would expect that over time these problems will reduce and eventually her memory may return, at least in part. But that must happen at her own pace. Whether or not she recovers all her memory, and in particular that of the triggering event, is at this point unknown.

I must warn you that it may even affect new memories being laid down, anything that might remind her of what happened before. We can't control that. I can only say that the more positive memories you can give her the better that will be. Anything negative and linked in some way to what happened will only disturb her further and may be suppressed.

In many ways, she will be happier as she is now, ignorant of the past. With her family's love, care and devotion, it will do her no long-term harm.

If you have any questions, do please ring my office and I will do my very best to call you back and help in any way that I can.

Yours sincerely,

Edward Bannerman,

Consultant Child and Adolescent Psychiatrist, FRCPsych MBBS LLM

I dropped the letter on the floor, my head spinning. The letter said my memory had been severely impacted. It explained why all these years I couldn't remember anything about Danny. It explained too why other memories, later in my childhood, were so unpredictable. And the nightmares that I'd suffered from all my life.

But it didn't absolve me of any blame for Danny's death.

'*We will not be able to prove one way or another . . .*' he'd written.

What had he really thought, this psychiatrist?

I closed my eyes. For a second, I wished I'd never read that letter. But what had been found could not be unfound. I could not un-read the words still jangling in my head. Had I been protecting myself all this time, like he'd said? From a memory too devastating to accept? I tried to rewind the moment in my head, the crack of falling glass, the expression on Danny's face, the bloodied spike in my hand. What had I really felt in that moment? Horror? Fear? Intention? To get back at him for all the things he'd done? Yes. To stop him? Yes. To make him feel the same pain that I had felt? Oh God, yes.

In that split second, had I not *wanted* him dead?

I knew the answer to that. I felt my fingers tighten as if still holding that spike. I'd hated him with a passion. Not just for his cruelty towards me, the taunts and bullying. But because he was all that I was not, loved and adored. His mother's pride and joy. In that single moment, had I *meant* to kill him? Could I believe that?

'*With her family's love, care and devotion . . .*'

Family. It was a word I couldn't bear to repeat. I had committed the worst of sins. I had knowingly, deliberately killed my own brother.

The thought was too much to bear. I'd been a child, a very young child. Hadn't the psychiatrist said that? I wasn't culpable. But Elizabeth had thought I was, she'd asked the question, the letter made that clear.

Tears dropped from my face, splashing on the paper in my hand, soaking through until the ink ran and the paper became transparent. Were these tears of self-pity? Tears of shame? I was mocking myself. I didn't deserve pity, let alone my own. Now I knew what I really was, what I was really capable of. No wonder everybody hated me, even now. Elizabeth had known. Hadn't they all known? Elizabeth's friends, the people in the village, the kids at school. Wasn't that why they'd all treated me like they had?

No, how could they know? How could anyone know what had been in my head in that split second? Even the psychiatrist acknowledged that. It had just been an accident. As far as everyone knew. Except me.

But somebody had kept those papers and stored them in the one place I feared most. Because it was the last place I would ever look, or because it was the *very* place I would look? Eventually. Who would think like that? It must have been Elizabeth. Was that why she'd carried on telling me that story and said those words. '*Have you been bad enough, Caroline?*' Did she think that eventually I'd be so overwhelmed by curiosity – and guilt – that I would indeed one day open the pear drum? Even after she was dead?

That I would see for myself what I had done?

CHAPTER 40

I'd found the mirror, the one my sister had given to me all those years ago. I had kept it, in spite of everything, my last connection with Steph, folded between a cloth and tucked into the corner of a box filled with other bits and pieces.

As I looked at my own face, I saw skin too pale, a nose too big, cheekbones that were neither prominent nor flat. I'd never been overly feminine in my looks. An ordinary person with ordinary features, the kind that didn't photograph well, that disappeared in a crowd. Insignificant.

That was how I felt, insignificant. A piece of flesh that served no purpose. Unloved and unloving. What difference had I ever made to the world, even to one person? What difference could I ever make? I'd never had the knack of making friends, or boyfriends, no more than I'd ever even deserved the love of my family. Looking back, I could see now that Paul had homed in on that. He'd enjoyed reminding me that I was estranged from my family.

And Craig, what if he found out, what if he knew what I had done? Would he still want me?

My head felt heavy, there was a pain behind my eyes that would not shift. I wanted to sleep, to never wake up, to drift away and never be. To be forgotten by everyone around me. It was too easy, too seductive, that sleep. The nixie in my head was smiling. She had returned to watch and she was happy, this time she would win. Her eyes were slanted green, her head twisted at an angle, her curiosity melting into jubilant satisfaction. I felt her malice and let it wash over me. It was no more than I deserved.

I looked at the plastic bag on the bed, the one with all Elizabeth's pills and medicines ready for disposal at the pharmacist. I'd pulled them out, boxes and blister packs strewn across the counterpane. Mostly they were prescription morphine derivatives and opiates designed for serious pain relief. I'd looked some of them up on the internet, to be sure of what they were. Elizabeth had been taking them daily in her last few months. I'd already swallowed what I thought were sedatives. A handful more of those and I would sleep and never wake up. Next to the bed was a new bottle of whisky, enough to wash down every pill.

I unscrewed the bottle, tipping the liquid down my throat. The pain hammered in my head. With each glug, the fire spread, the pain belched, until my body burned in hell exactly as the maker of the pear drum intended.

My eyes fluttered open and my hand fell from the side of the bed. The whisky bottle lay rolling on the floor and I lay pliant on the covers. Early morning sun streaked across the room stabbing at my eyes.

I was still alive. I tried moving, a small shift of my head. A spasm shot across my forehead. I felt a surge in my belly, jack-knifing to my feet and stumbling across the room towards the bathroom. I emptied my stomach into the sink and sank to the floor to lean my forehead against the cool ceramic surface of the pedestal, feeling the blood coursing through my veins, the hard texture of the tiles beneath my knees, the sour wetness of the vomit still clinging to my cheeks.

Every touch and taste was a reminder of the sensuality of my existence. Whatever crimes I could commit, my own death was not one of them. I was not as brave as Angus, I couldn't kill myself, if that was what he'd done. Poor Angus. I had sinned far more than he. No, I was too in love with the vibrancy of life, the colours that I painted, the faces and expressions of my characters, the landscapes brooding on the page. And Craig. He was the one good thing in all of this. I should believe in him. Did I not have a chance with him?

I hauled myself to my feet. I could not, after all, pay that price. Whatever I had done then, when I was six, I'd been a child. Who knew what that child had really felt. Was my memory even reliable? Skewed by time and guilt? How could I know what really happened all that time ago? I was different now. I was grown up. I had to *live* with what I'd done. Surely for the first time in my life, I had a chance to make a future for myself, with Craig.

Steph's face was smiling on the screen. A small round circular image. Her ice-blue eyes, her perfect hair, her flawless skin.

Her glossy painted lips. The familiar sound of a Skype call had woken me from my daze and I clicked reluctantly on the picture.

'Caro? Are you there?'

'Yes, I'm here.'

'How are you? We haven't spoken for ages.'

The image wobbled, her face dancing on the screen, struggling to regain the internet connection. I schooled my voice.

'I'm great.' My voice belied the apparent cheeriness of my words.

'I'm sorry I've not been in touch for a while – it's been party season, you know what it's like.'

'Sure, don't worry.'

'So, how are you doing with that commission of yours? You never said – what's the book called?'

I felt the blood drain from my face.

'*The Pear Drum and Other Dark Tales from the Nursery.*' I spoke the words slowly and carefully, to make sure no emotion came through.

'*The Pear Drum*? Isn't that the story Elizabeth used to tell you when we were little?'

I didn't reply.

'Didn't she have one – a pear drum? It used to give me the creeps. Have you found it yet?'

What could I say? I clenched my eyes shut and prayed she'd just stop speaking.

'Caro? Caro, are you there?'

'Yes, I'm here. I don't know anything about a pear drum, Steph.'

'Oh, but you must remember it; Elizabeth was always on about it with you – it was her little pet joke!'

Joke? That wasn't how I remembered it.

'I . . . I . . .' I felt the anger rising up inside me.

'It was in the study, I'm sure it was, for a long time. In the corner, in a crate. Weird thing. Don't know where she got it from, she never said. It was rather beautiful in its way. Has it not turned up?'

Why did she keep banging on about it – couldn't she tell I didn't want to talk about it? She didn't want to talk about Danny, I didn't want to talk about the pear drum. Couldn't she let it alone?

'What was it she used to say, after she finished telling you the story – it would really wind you up! *Have you been . . .*'

Steph laughed. She was actually laughing, like it was some kind of benign family prank.

'*. . . bad enough?*'

'For fuck's sake, Steph – SHUT UP!!'

I reached out with my hand and smashed it down on the keyboard, and Steph's face exploded into pixelated shrapnel.

I sat there gasping, tears rolling down my face. I'd ruined it. I'd been trying so hard – I thought she had too – at our reconciliation, and now it was all gone to pot. Because of my temper, my stupid emotions getting the better of me, because of that hideous story. Because of the pear drum.

I couldn't stop crying, hot salty tears streaming down my face. I'd wanted my relationship with Steph to work, I really had. I laid my head on the table, resting against my hands. For a moment I stayed like that, partially comforted by the cool of my own skin, yet ashamed of my very existence.

Then I sat upright, exhausted from the strength of my own emotions. My eyes were prickly dry and a headache stabbed above my eyes. How could I explain it to her? My unwilling-ness to tell the truth, about the pear drum, the psychiatrist's letter, the memories flooding back after all these years. What would she say – how much did she even know? I couldn't tell her any of this, let alone about my near escape at Carsington Water, or finding Angus dead at the base of Alton Heights. This was the old me, shutters down, unwilling to trust or share. Now it was back to how it used to be, just like when we were kids, and I couldn't bear it. She was all the family that I had left, wasn't she?

I stood up. I snatched my car keys into my hand and marched out to the car. I drove down the lane to the village way too fast, screeching to a halt outside the Co-op. Two middle-aged ladies gawped as I almost collided with them as I strode into the shop. I didn't care about the whispered words down by the milk and dairy cabinet, the stares from the queue, the assistant not even speaking a single word as I slammed a bottle of whisky and a ready-made turkey dinner onto the counter. I paid for it in cash and glared at her defiantly.

'What the fuck are you staring at!' I said.

The woman behind me looked aghast. But I simply ignored her, ploughing through the queue, back out of the shop, jumping into my car and revving up the lane.

Damn the lot of them. Let them rot in hell. Let them think whatever they wanted to think, it was none of their business.

There was a message for me when I got back, flashing on the screen of my laptop.

Dear Caro, I'm so sorry – I should have thought. I'd forgotten what Elizabeth was like about that pear drum.

I guess I thought it was all a bit of a joke, the way she used to tease you, but you took it so seriously, even then. I'd forgot – I'm so sorry! Can you forgive me, dearest Caro? Can we be friends again?

My heart gave a leap, was it all okay, after all?

You were asking about Danny – I have my weakness too and I still can't bring myself to talk about him. I was older than you when it all happened, you don't understand . . .

I swallowed – she sounded as much in pain as I was, my heart went out to her.

. . . but why don't you go and see Sarah Chandler. She used to be Elizabeth's best friend. She was at the funeral, you'll recognise her. I'm sure she still lives in the village, somebody will know her address. Try asking at the shop.

Like I was going to ask anyone at the shop!

There's something you need to know about Danny. I'd tell you if I were there, but I'm not and it needs to be said face to face. I don't think it can wait until we see Briscoe together. It's – oh Caro, I wish I were in the UK and we could talk properly. But Sarah can explain – she's not as fierce as she might seem. Why don't you go and see her? She'll remember it so much more clearly than me. She'll be able to explain it so much better than me.
Steph xx

I didn't understand – *something about Danny*, she'd said. About how he died? Why would it be better coming from Sarah Chandler, who clearly hated me, rather than my own sister?

CHAPTER 41

Now that my knowledge of Danny had returned, the snatches of memory from those early years grew, little things that sneaked up on me as I continued to clear the house, triggered by objects or a fleeting sense of déjà vu.

Like the bucket I found under the stairs, stuffed with dusting cloths and a bar of soap. I had a flash of Elizabeth watching me as I played outside with a man – my father I presumed. He was laughing as I threw water at his face from a small bucket. Elizabeth snatched the bucket from my hands and told me off.

'Oh, let her be,' said my father. 'She's only little.' He swept me off my feet and threw me in the air. I whooped with glee as he caught me, swinging me round so that my chubby legs flew out and I whooped again.

It was only a brief memory but it meant the world to me, that one small insight into my father.

I found a photograph of Elizabeth and her friend, Sarah. On holiday, I thought, quaffing wine in some European street café. I didn't have to try very hard to remember Sarah Chandler. She'd been a part of my life for far longer than my dad. She was the woman at the Wassail, the posh lady who'd also been at Elizabeth's funeral with her tame umbrella-bearing husband. Older, greyer, but I knew her now as Elizabeth's closest friend.

When I thought of her role in my childhood, it made sense, the antagonism. She'd often stepped in for Elizabeth, 'dealing' with me when Elizabeth could bear no more, that's how it must have seemed to Sarah. Disgust ran through me.

I didn't want to call on her. She'd snubbed me completely at the funeral and had been little better at the Wassail. But Steph had told me to visit her, that I would learn something about Danny. What else was there to know?

I didn't have her address. I couldn't ask Craig, even as an excuse to call him. I'd left him a message after all, but he still hadn't been in touch. It had been a week since finding Angus McCready's body at Alton Heights and there hadn't been one word from Craig. I knew he was fine – there was smoke coming from his workshop chimney. But I was anxious and angry. Didn't he care how I was feeling? It felt like neglect after we'd been so close, even though it was only a week. At the very least he could have called. I was confused.

No, I wasn't going to ring Craig, or walk across to him. I was determined to leave him be, for now at least. I would ask Mary Beth. She seemed to know everyone in the village already. She could surely tell me how to find Sarah Chandler.

* * *

I rang Mary Beth first thing the next morning. She was kind and concerned – had the village gossips done the rounds already? More irrational swearing from 'the nutcase'. I felt guilty lashing out at that poor woman in the Co-op like that – it made me no better than Angus. I kept it short and a little while later I was driving through Larkstone. There was no point ringing Sarah Chandler for an appointment first, it would surely be a no.

It was wet, the rain gleaming on the kerbside and the stone walls of the buildings looking browner and darker than normal. The houses glowered at me like monastic priests ripe with disapproval. Marsh Lane was off the lower end of the High Street, leading down towards a brook. One large house stood at the end, with a wide frontage. It was exactly as Mary Beth had described it – another Georgian creation with multi-paned windows in original glass, heritage-green paint and a glossy black front door. Two bay tree planters had been placed one on either side of the entrance like it was primed for a photo shoot with *Country Homes & Interiors*. I rapped on the door.

After a few minutes, a woman opened the door. It was her, in white slacks, blue heels and a blue and white striped jumper. I remembered her clearly now, not just from the funeral or the Wassail. My hands clenched behind my back.

'Hello?' Her voice was piercing and instructive at the same time. I felt as if I'd been dismissed already.

'Er, is it Mrs Chandler? I'm sorry to disturb you. We met at the Wassail. I'm Elizabeth's stepdaughter, Caro,' I said.

She looked at me for a moment.

'What do you want?'

No pretence at friendliness, then.

'I'd really like to talk to you, if you could spare me five minutes? I know you were her friend and, well, I . . . I've got something which I'm hoping you can help me with. I'm trying to settle her affairs.'

I couldn't exactly come straight out with it: what can you tell me about Danny?

She considered me for a moment, then nodded. She stepped back to let me in. The hall was as beautiful as the front of the house, with original stone flooring and a wide sweeping staircase. It reminded me of Larkstone Farm, but better cared for. She pushed open a door and we passed through into an elegant Farrow & Ball sitting room, all white chandeliers and discreet grey tartan sofas. She nodded her head and I sat down.

'Is there some kind of problem?' she said.

Oh God, I thought, how do I even start this?

'The estate includes a cottage next door,' I said, improvising.

Sarah nodded. 'That would be Lavender Cottage.'

I nodded back. 'I hadn't realised, you see. But it's occupied.'

'Craig Atherton, yes. He rented it from Elizabeth.'

'Erm . . . He, that is . . .' I hadn't a clue what I was saying, anything to get her talking. 'He has her dog?' That hadn't come out quite as I'd intended.

Sarah blinked once, slowly.

'I couldn't take Patsy – a dog in this house . . .' She waved her hand. 'I'm not a dog person, and Craig was more than happy to take her in. He knew Elizabeth well. I'd say Elizabeth was genuinely fond of him, and besides . . .'

There was a pause. She appeared to assess me, as if working out what, if anything, I knew. My heart skipped a beat. Or remembered? I really didn't want to go there. She spoke again, her voice clipped . . .

'In many ways, Craig was like a son to Elizabeth.'

The words hung in the air between us.

She looked at me speculatively, as if deciding what to say next.

'Why do you ask, Miss Crowther? About Craig and Lavender Cottage?'

She couldn't bring herself to call me by my first name. I could see the revulsion in her face at the very idea.

'I wanted to know how close they were as we have to make some decisions about what to do with the cottage. I didn't like to ask him direct. I'd like to do the right thing. You know.' I waved a hand.

Sarah was smiling now, as if something had dawned on her and it pleased her. I couldn't for the life of me think why.

'Craig has lived in the cottage for several years. It's his workplace as well as his home. If you insist on selling, you could perhaps at least give him first refusal,' she said.

I nodded again. 'Yes, that would be kind, of course, I can see that.'

'Was there anything else?'

I pushed my hands over the knees of my trousers, an old habit. I was getting nowhere with this.

'Steph said . . .' I was stammering now, unable to formulate a question that made any sense. Danny was the one thing I didn't want to mention to this woman.

'Elizabeth hated me!' I spoke in a rush. It was almost a confession.

Now we'd got to the heart of the matter. Sarah observed me, like a heron staring into a pool of water, its long beak ready to stab.

'You took away her son, her only son. She loved that boy!

Then she had to look after you, foisted upon her by her husband, philandering bastard that he was.'

I lowered my eyes, trying not to think of Danny cold and unconscious on the floor, me standing beside him, crying, my tiny hands covered in blood. *Wake up, Danny, wake up!* How could I blame this woman for how she felt?

I lifted my head.

'What do you mean, *philandering*? What about Elizabeth? She must have known he was married. It was *her* who had an affair with *him*, whilst he was still married to my mother!'

'Who told you that?'

'My sister.'

'Your sister . . . Stephanie? She told you what exactly?'

'That Elizabeth married my father after our mother died, bringing Danny with her, the son from their affair together.'

'Really? Is that what she said?'

Sarah leaned forward in sudden intensity.

'I think you need to check your facts, Miss Crowther. Elizabeth had always been married to your father, long before you or Danny or Stephanie were born.'

'I don't understand.'

'Elizabeth and John had Stephanie and Daniel during those years and very happy they all were too, until your mother arrived on the scene.'

'My mother?'

'Yes, your whore of a mother!'

I flinched.

'She kept following your father around at work, like a besotted teenager, Elizabeth said. She couldn't take her eyes off your father. He was won over, had an affair – well, what man wouldn't be bowled over by some nubile teen offering themselves up to him? Only she got pregnant didn't she, ended up having *you*.'

Sarah scarcely paused for breath, almost spitting the words that followed.

'Then she died. Post-natal haemorrhage. Left Elizabeth with a right problem. What she did for her husband, for you! Taking you in, giving you a home and a name! It's outrageous that you should inherit a bean! It should have gone to Elizabeth outright, and then *her* children – Stephanie, Daniel!'

What was she saying? That it was *my* mother with whom my father had had the affair, not Elizabeth? That *I* was the bastard child, not Danny? That it was *me* who was the cuckoo in the nest?

Then the penny dropped. Danny was my half-brother, as before, but Steph . . . I leaned forward onto my knees, bringing my hands up to cover my eyes. Steph was my *half*-sister. Was that what Steph had wanted me to learn? That she couldn't bring herself to tell me? Why?

I left after that, stumbling down the front steps. Sarah couldn't wait to get rid of me. Yet she lingered at the front door. I swung the car out and did a three-point turn, painfully aware of her observation, my agitation making me clumsy. When finally I drove past, she was still there, a look of smug satisfaction plastered on her face.

CHAPTER 42

I looked it up when I got back. I didn't know what to believe so I was determined to check. I signed up to one of those family tree websites and plugged in the details. I scanned the death records first. It took a while, but then I found it.

Daniel Martin Crowther, died 18th October 1996.

Parents listed as *John and Elizabeth Crowther*. Both of them, Crowther.

Then I checked the birth records:

Stephanie born 1983. Daniel born 1987.

Again, parents listed as John and Elizabeth Crowther.

Next, I searched the marriage records. When it appeared on screen, I could hardly take it in. 1980. Sarah had told the truth; Elizabeth and my father had been married long before my birth. It was I who was illegitimate, just as Sarah had said.

I checked my own birth record.

Caroline Crowther, born 1990, mother Louise Wilkinson,
father John Crowther.

I realised that I'd scarcely even looked at my own birth certificate. I'd never realised the significance of that one small detail it revealed – Louise *Wilkinson*.

I was still confused. And I wanted to be sure. My next call was to the lawyer.

'Briscoe, Williams and Patterson,' came the familiar voice.

'Hello, could you put me through to Gareth Briscoe?'

There was the usual tuneful burst of Vivaldi's *Four Seasons*.

'Good morning Miss Crowther.'

I winced at the 'Crowther'; I felt I was no longer entitled to that name.

'Mr Briscoe,' I struggled to speak the words. 'I . . . I need to ask you a question.' I took a breath, rushing when I finally spoke. 'Until recently I . . . I didn't realise that I wasn't a legitimate daughter of my father. It's a long story but I was the result of an affair and my father and his wife took me in when my mother died.'

'Yes, I know, Miss Crowther.' He sounded patient.

He'd known? Before me? Of course he knew, he was a lawyer. He'd been handling probate. It was probably the first thing they did, check out the family tree.

'You knew? Then why didn't you tell me? Why has no one ever told me?'

I thought of my stepmother, her hatred of me – wouldn't she have enjoyed telling me that I didn't belong?

'I don't know what Elizabeth told you, Miss Crowther – I never interfere with personal family matters, it's not my place. I can only say that perhaps everyone wanted to be discreet

– people often do with these matters.' Briscoe's voice was gruff, apologetic.

'But surely that means my name should be Wilkinson, my mother's name?'

'Not at all, Miss Crowther. Your mother died in childbirth, as you say. Your father immediately took you in. It was he who registered the birth, and he was adamant you should have his name.'

'So Crowther *is* my name!'

'Of course it is. I handled all your family's affairs. Your father was very keen that the paperwork was properly done, that everything was watertight.'

That everything was watertight . . . what did he mean by that?

'Elizabeth would not agree to an adoption, so John set up the trust instead.'

Ah – now things were making sense.

'As to your inheritance . . .'

Briscoe thought I was worried about my inheritance, I hadn't even thought about that.

'. . . you are the named beneficiary of his will, as I explained before. Your father was very careful to ensure the trust clearly named you as an equal beneficiary. But he also ensured Elizabeth could live in the house and was properly provided for as long as she wished until her death. On condition she looked after you till you were eighteen.'

'And Elizabeth knew this?'

'Of course, she had to agree to it. If you were taken into care, she would lose the financial benefits of the trust. It was discussed at the time and again when her husband died.'

'I see. Thank you, Mr Briscoe. Have a nice day.'

How had Elizabeth felt about that? A child from an affair foisted upon her from babyhood. Clearly, she'd not been willing to accept me completely – I'd always known her as my stepmother. Now I understood why Elizabeth had never sent me away. She'd effectively been tied in to looking after me. How she must have hated that, even before Danny's death.

I found it difficult to concentrate on anything after that. I paced the kitchen, made a cup of tea, sat down and stood up again, walking to the window overlooking the garden.

Perhaps Elizabeth had felt humiliated by my father's affair. Perhaps she'd ordered Steph never to say anything, to let people think we were one happy family.

My fingers gripped the cup too hard. I'd learnt everything I knew from Steph, my big sister. It had been *she* who'd eventually told me the story of Elizabeth's marriage to our dad.

It had been the day before she left home. Her parting gift.

'Caro, sit down a moment.'

She'd been all smiles, patting a space beside her on the garden bench. I sat down, wariness on my face.

'You're old enough to know, now.'

I was nine, yes, I thought, whatever it was I was old enough. I straightened my back to listen to her.

'You know your mother died when you were little?'

'Yes.'

'*Our* mother.'

The subtle change was lost on me. Why didn't she get to the point?

'She died in childbirth, when you were born. Bled to death.'

She watched me as I winced. I always freaked out around blood.

'It happens, you know,' she continued. 'If the baby has been difficult.'

Difficult? What did she mean by that? Had I been difficult?

'Bleeding doesn't stop after the baby comes out, there's lots and lots of blood, and the mother dies – that's what happened.'

My eyes widened in horror. An image of the blood had immediately jumped into my head. A flood of scarlet liquid seeping out from between her legs. I had a vague idea at that point about childbirth. What was Steph saying, that it had been my fault?

Steph smiled at me and gave me a hug. 'After she died, Dad married Elizabeth – she's your stepmother. You know about stepmothers, don't you?'

I nodded. Yes, I did – from the stories, all my favourite stories.

'Well, what you perhaps didn't know is that Elizabeth had an affair.' I looked puzzled at that. 'She had sex with Dad whilst he was still married to our mother. Before.'

Sex – it was a word rarely used, one of those forbidden words like *fuck* or *shit* or . . . the words I'd heard in the playground. I knew it was something bad. I looked at her blankly.

'She made babies with Dad, you numbskull!' She hugged me again, in a sisterly, friendly kind of way. So many hugs, she wasn't normally like that.

'That's how Danny came about. You remember Danny?'

I didn't. What was she talking about now? Steph was smiling still.

'Oh, never mind. You'll remember one day, just you see. I thought you should know.'

She was grinning happily as she stood up.

Steph – why had she lied to me about Elizabeth? What

possible reason would she have for such a bizarre misrepresentation of the truth? But no one had ever explained it afterwards, certainly not Elizabeth, if she ever even knew what Steph had told me.

Whenever I remembered Steph's words after that, as I grew up, the word Danny had gone from my mind, but the reference to sex stayed. Elizabeth was this evil stepmother who had had sex with my father whilst my mother was alive, had betrayed my mother, had stolen my father, who hated me, abused me – it was just like all those stories.

My fear and hatred of Elizabeth grew.

CHAPTER 43

I'd gone out to empty the bins that evening when I saw the jeep navigating the drive to the house. My heart leapt uncomfortably in my chest. It was late, the night broken by the small lights set into the low walls that surrounded the front drive, flaring out over the gravel to give the effect of miniature monastic cloisters. The car headlamps swept across. Patsy was on the front seat. She barked as the car came to a halt.

I didn't say a word. Craig stepped from the jeep and waited for the dog to jump out. I opened the front door, moving around to block them from coming in. Craig looked down at me, his eyes narrowing. He'd recently shaved and in the evening chill he smelt of soap, fresh pine and wood smoke. I wanted to reach up and touch his jaw, to kiss him, but I held back, blocking his further movement into the hall.

'Caro, can I come in? We need to talk.'

To my fragile mind, he sounded distant, business-like. The

last time we'd met, we'd been lovers, and now we were strangers.

'Where have you been? I haven't seen or heard from you for almost a week!'

It came out from nowhere, the last thing I wanted to say.

'Caro . . . let me in. I've missed you. Please, I'm so sorry. I'll try to explain.' His voice was deep and husky.

Was that supposed to convince me? Like hell. But I stepped aside and let him pass.

'We need to talk, Caro.' He took my hand. His touch sent a warm pulse firing up my arm. 'Can we sit down?'

I bit my lip. I'd been so wrapped up in my own thoughts all day with everything that I'd learned that I'd almost forgotten about Craig. And Angus. Craig was anxious, I could see it in his eyes. You have to learn to trust, a voice said in my head, to have any relationship you have to learn to trust . . .

We went into the sitting room. I snapped on the lights and perched on the arm of the sofa whilst he sat down on a chair. I thought he looked tired, his face a little older and his skin a little grey.

'I take it you know about my business with Angus McCready?' he said.

I nodded, not sure that I did but it seemed the right way to encourage him to talk.

'Mary Beth told me she'd mentioned it to you. She's already got a soft spot for you, Caro.'

I didn't reply.

'I'm sorry I didn't come round after you found him at the quarry.' Craig eyed me carefully. 'Or ring. It must have been awful for you. It's just . . . well, it's been difficult. I wanted to, but I couldn't.'

'Why not?'

He looked at me, his demeanour different.

'How are you, Caro?'

I was furious – he'd ignored me. What was going on? This was crap and he knew it. What could have stopped him? Weren't we together? Didn't I matter to him? He'd come to me after Carsington. Why not now? God knows I'd needed him over these last few days.

He sighed.

'Angus and I worked together. He took over his father's building firm when he retired. The business did well. I ended up working for Angus several times, as I did for his father, we became friends. Then he bought some land on the edge of Derby. He had this plan for a small estate of high-end new builds. They needed a quality finish. But he'd overstretched himself financially. He asked me to do the kitchens and I agreed. I should have known better but I hadn't realised how far in debt he was. I did three kitchens for him then stopped because he wouldn't pay me for any of them, not even my materials. He wasn't happy after I refused to do another. One minute he was Mr Nice Guy, the next, Mr Nasty. It wasn't like him and I knew he was under a whole heap of pressure. We argued on the night of the Wassail. He'd been trying to persuade me to work for him again and I said no, not until I was paid. That's why I kept you waiting in the car, he rang me and insisted we have it out.'

This bit I knew. It wasn't a conversation to have in public.

'He got physical and hit me.' There was a pause. Craig's hand lifted up to his nose, touching the top as if he was remembering. 'Someone must have seen us, or maybe Angus told a friend afterwards that I'd punched him, but anyway, after his body was found, the police called me in. They're not convinced his fall was an accident. They've had me in for questioning several times.'

He raked his hand through his hair. I watched the way it sprang up again, longing to reach out and smooth it.

'God, it's been awful. You feel like you're guilty even when you're not! I didn't kill him, Caro. I have no reason to. Now he's dead, his creditors will all be clamouring. I won't see a penny of that money he owed me. It was over twenty thousand pounds.'

He shook his head.

'That's a big dent in my finances. But I don't have an alibi and the police won't let it go. I'm sorry, Caro, that's why I didn't come to you, or ring you. I was worried they might think I was trying to influence you or that we were connected in some way. Since it was you who found the body, they might even have thought that you were somehow involved. I was trying to protect you. But I couldn't stay away from you any longer.'

He was apologising – for *not* staying away from me. I slid off the sofa arm and sat properly on the cushions, facing him.

'But that's crazy. And if you didn't do it, they won't be able to prove a thing.'

'No, but they'll try. They want answers.'

'Why do they even think his death was suspicious? How can they be sure it wasn't an accident, or suicide?' I swallowed.

'Well, firstly, they found bruising on his face. I did punch him, you see, that night. After he hit me. And secondly, they found evidence of Elizabeth's car in the car park.'

'What!'

Craig had lowered his head, pulling his long legs in towards his chair.

'There are time-lapse cameras by the wind turbines apparently and one of them caught pictures of her car parked up by the fence. They must have tracked the ownership down via the number plate.'

'How can Elizabeth's car have been there?' I said. 'I mean, I haven't seen her car since I got here.'

But I'd found paperwork for it, service receipts. It had been on my list to ring the garage, but I hadn't got around to it yet. You couldn't live out in the country without a car and there was nothing parked up in the outbuildings; the car had to be somewhere, stranded perhaps.

'What's the car got to do with you?' I said.

'Elizabeth asked me to take a look at it for her, the day before she died. It wasn't starting right and I said I'd charge up the battery. It was in my garage for a while, after the funeral. I didn't know what to do with it. Then it got stolen.'

'Stolen?' I asked, my voice rising.

'Yeah, it went missing one night.'

'You never once mentioned a car to me. Why? And how do you expect the police to believe a story like that? Is that what you told them?'

'Yes, no. Not exactly. They were more interested in my business with Angus. What else could I do? It wasn't me! And I know I should have told you about the car, after we met, but I've been so distracted by what was going on with Angus that it just wasn't on my radar.'

And now the car had turned up at the hilltop car park where McCready's body had been found. And someone had reported Craig for hitting Angus. You could hardly blame the police for asking questions.

I searched his eyes, looking for some sense of the truth. I

thought it was evident in the lines across his forehead, his eyes hungrily chasing after mine. Our eyes met. This time I couldn't resist. I didn't want to wait any longer. I stood up and stepped towards him. He met me half way, his hands dropping around my waist.

'Caro . . .' He nuzzled my cheek. 'Your si—'

I moved my head and kissed him. I wasn't listening. Whatever he was about to say was no longer important.

CHAPTER 44

The morning was shrouded in mist, a cold wall of white whispering against the windows. The world beyond was hidden except for the one tree that stood closest to the house. Its branches rubbed up against the glass, the individual twigs twisted back upon themselves like arthritic hands curled in pain. My fingers itched to paint.

Silence brooded upon the valley, no birds or cars nor any sign of life beyond our walls, just us, bewitched within the mist. I looked at Craig, still asleep in my bed, his breathing slow and even.

My life had been incomplete, until now. Paul had been a massive mistake. The jibes, the arguments, the slow erosion of what little confidence I had; he'd played me with such expertise until I'd almost believed him. That I was a failure, that his world was everything.

The sex had become an act of submission, not love.

'Give it up, Caro,' he'd growled that last evening. 'You'll never make it as an artist. Haven't you realised that by now?'

Paul's hand moved around my neck, his thumb pressing against my throat, his hips crushing into mine. With each thrust of his body I felt his will defeating mine.

'Say it, Caro!'

I couldn't breathe.

'No more painting, no more commissions.' His voice was thick with hate.

My head began to spin. His body ground into mine and his eyes rolled back as if he was no longer aware of what he did. Then he snapped back to himself and his hand eased its grip, enough for me to speak.

'Say it, Caro,' he hissed. His eyes bored into mine.

'Please . . .' I gasped.

His grip tightened.

'Yes!' I cried.

'Yes, what?'

'Yes, I'll give it up. No more painting. I promise!'

Oh God, what had I said?

I'd rung Harriet the next day, after Paul had gone to work. She heard it in my voice. She came round straight away and saw the state of me, the tears upon my face, the bruises on my neck.

'You have to leave, Caro. Do you really want this?'

I shook my head.

'Then let me help.'

For the first time I did. I let someone help. We packed up all my stuff there and then and she bundled me into a cab. Paul didn't know where she lived. He screamed down the phone at me but I just cut him off. There was nothing he could do. But I lived in fear of him discovering me, tracking me down to one of the galleries, following me back to Harriet's home, forcing me . . .

Larkstone Farm, the inheritance, it couldn't have come at a better time.

I turned to look at Craig, his face relaxed in sleep. I wanted this so much – Craig. The way he was with me, it was so different from Paul; I felt it with a conviction I'd never had before. At some point, I had to forgive and forget. Paul, my family, myself.

Watching Craig over my shoulder, I slid from under the sheets, catching up a blanket that had fallen to the floor and dragging it around my body. I crept from the room, barefoot down the stairs, to stand upon the stairwell half way down and look out from the tall window that faced the garden. The mist pressed against the glass and I felt a chill breeze pushing through the gaps in the old wooden frame. It tugged at the tendrils of my hair about my face. I felt my eyes dry from sleep, my lips full from kissing. I yearned for acceptance, for belief, like the ghost of Cathy Earnshaw scratching at the window.

The tears seeped out from beneath my eyelids, unbidden and fast. It was different from before, a release I hadn't allowed myself. For so many years this house had been Elizabeth's home, her space, her refuge. Had she stood in this very spot, looking out of the window, beyond which the roof of the summerhouse lay brooding in the mist? Always reminded of her loss? She could have had it razed to the ground, to destroy the memory of Danny's death. But it was his monument too, a wound she could never let heal because it meant so much to her – the place he last breathed. She was the mother who could not love me, who did not see or value the love I had to give, who'd never given me a chance. Who could blame her?

I thought of Steph, the sister – no, half-sister – who'd stayed away from me all those years. I had longed for her affection, her friendship, to make some sense of our sisterhood. Her distance was explained now. She and Elizabeth both had made their choices. These had been opportunities for love that had been lost, gifts that had been rejected, for I knew then that I could have loved them both, if they'd let me, and my love would have been worth having.

The pointlessness of it all sank into my mind. I'd always craved an understanding, reasons I could accept. Steph's words, firmly placing the blame for my mother's death on me, repeated in my head. I was a grown woman now, I knew there was no fault. Nature had taken my mother from me, not I. Steph had said that deliberately to hurt me. Her story about Elizabeth too had been to hurt me. Or was it to hurt Elizabeth, both of us, to plant a seed that would foul our relationship even further? Why would she do that? Elizabeth was Steph's mother, as I now knew. What had gone on between them?

As I stood there at the window, my father's love meant more to me than anything else. Not in the amount of the inheritance, but the fact that he'd given me his name, had provided for me and recognised me with an *equal* share. Perhaps he'd loved my mother too and this had been his way of making it up to her, to us, for her lost life. I'd never known my parents, but I knew they'd loved me. That gave me faith.

And what of Danny?

I saw the little boy that had teased and tormented me,

gloating in my submission. But he'd been a child, too young to understand the damage he did, too young to have died like that, to lose the life that stretched out in front of him. I had carried the guilt for his death locked inside since I was six years old. It *had* been an accident. A terrible, heart-rending tragic accident. Whatever had happened in that split second as the glass shattered around us, as he fell towards me and the spike in my hand, whatever I did, whatever I had *felt* in that moment, I'd been a child, a very young child who couldn't understand.

I cried for Danny then. For Elizabeth and Steph too. And for me. Pity, self-pity, warm and comforting, held me standing naked in my blanket.

CHAPTER 45

Craig stayed with me that day and overnight again. Early on the Monday morning, once the mist had lifted, the two of us took Patsy for a walk. It was as we were heading back up the drive to the house that we heard a car pulling in behind us. We both stopped by the front door. It was a police car.

Patsy barked and Craig called to her, reaching down to hold her collar as he hooked on the lead. I could tell from his expression that he wasn't happy with our visitors. Patsy sat down on the gravel, tongue hanging from her mouth, her tail wagging in pleasure, quite indifferent to the antagonism in Craig's face. We both watched as two policemen and a policewoman got out of the vehicle.

'Mr Atherton, we were due to visit you next, so I'm glad you're here. And you would be Miss Crowther?'

The first of the policemen held out a hand to me, his voice

level and appeasing. I nodded and took his hand reluctantly.

'My name is DI Oliver Harding. This is Sergeant Mansfield and Constable Jones.'

I didn't recall a DI Harding, but I recognised the sergeant as the officer who'd interviewed me at Chester Green. He smiled at me reassuringly and I saw DI Harding look from me to Craig before reaching down to pet the dog. Patsy snuffled obligingly forward, earning a quick tug on the lead from Craig.

DI Harding stood up.

'Do you think we could come in for a chat?'

I nodded and led them inside, gesturing to the front room.

'I'm very sorry, Miss Crowther, that you had to see what you saw. Finding a dead body is always very distressing, even for those of us who have seen them before. If you would like to speak to anyone about it, I can refer you to our support services?'

'I'm okay,' I said. 'But thank you. How can we help?'

DI Harding turned towards Craig first.

'Mr Atherton, I know you've already been helping us down at the station, and we do appreciate your assistance. I hate to keep taking up your time, but we have to get to the truth, to gather as much information as we can and track things from every perspective. I hope you understand?' There was a veiled hint of steely instruction to the detective's words.

'Our enquiries have expanded a little and I'm currently trying to trace Elizabeth Crowther's car. Miss Crowther, I'm here to ask if you have any idea where it might be?'

I realised then that the policewoman hadn't come into the house with us. I looked out of the window and there she was,

322

heading in the direction of the barns. The detective followed my gaze.

'My colleague has gone to check the buildings on your property, I hope you don't mind?'

If I did mind, it was already too late, I thought. The police weren't supposed to do that without a warrant, were they? But hadn't I just given them my tacit permission? I felt myself stiffen, wariness creeping into my back. But there was no car in the barns, I knew that, so why should I worry?

'I'm aware that Elizabeth did have a car,' I said. 'I found the service record amongst her papers. But the car hasn't been on the property since I got here.'

'And how long have you been here, Miss Crowther?'

'Since early December.'

'It was parked up at my house for a while,' Craig said.

I looked at him in surprise. I hadn't thought he would have wanted to disclose this. He shrugged at me.

'Elizabeth was my neighbour. She'd asked me to look at the battery the day before she died last October. So it was in my garage at that point.'

'Why didn't you mention this before?' Harding leaned in closer.

'I wasn't asked.'

DI Harding looked annoyed at this, flashing a glance at Sergeant Mansfield, who shifted uncomfortably in his seat.

'And have you driven it since then?'

'No. I charged up the battery and then I heard Elizabeth had died. There seemed no point in doing anything with it whilst the house was empty, waiting to be cleared, so it stayed in my garage, until it went missing.'

'Missing? When? Can you be more specific?' said Harding.

Patsy had jumped up onto the sofa beside me and I reached out to give her a hug. Craig passed me the lead. Missing, Craig had said *missing*. But he'd said *stolen* to me earlier.

'It went missing, like I said. One day it was there, the next day it was gone.' Craig's voice was firm, his jaw pushed slightly out of sync. 'It would have been about mid-November.'

Mid-November: that would have been shortly after Elizabeth's funeral.

'Did you report it as stolen, Mr Atherton?' The DI was politely insistent.

'No, I did not.'

We could both see the sergeant busily scribbling in a note-book.

'Can I ask why? Surely, you'd want to recover it? Or at least register it as stolen for insurance purposes.'

'I believe Elizabeth's other daughter took it.'

I looked up from the dog, rigid with shock.

'And why did you think that?' the DI asked.

'Well, it was her mother's car, and she, along with Caro, has inherited everything that Elizabeth had. Steph had visited me earlier . . .'

Steph had visited him? I opened my mouth to speak but Craig was already talking again.

'. . . and I noticed that the car keys were missing off the rack, so I guessed she must have helped herself and taken the car. I didn't report it because technically she's entitled to it.'

'She visited you? When was this?' Harding's expression was cool.

My eyes were pinned on Craig.

'Mid-November, like I said. I can't remember the exact

date. Not long after Elizabeth's funeral.' The repetition clearly annoyed Craig.

'I see. So you think . . . sorry, can you remind me of her name?'

'Steph, Steph Crowther.'

'Thank you, so Steph Crowther . . .'

Sergeant Mansfield at the far end of the room looked up from his notebook expectantly.

'. . . took the car without telling you?' Harding continued.

'Yes, that's right.'

'But you didn't actually see her take the car?'

'No. But I'm sure it was her.'

The detective turned to me, the sergeant still scribbling. 'Miss Crowther, were you aware of this? Has your sister said anything to you?'

'No, I wasn't aware of this and she hasn't mentioned it.'

I bit my lip, debating in my head what to say – I'd gone back to London after the funeral. I thought Steph had too, on her eventual way to New York. We'd even had dinner one night. What had she been doing up here? Why would Steph want a car when she was about to go home to New York? Why hadn't Craig, or Steph for that matter, mentioned it before?

And who was driving that car now?

'Where exactly is your sister?'

'In New York,' I said. 'She's been back there for several weeks.'

I heard the front door open and someone stamping on the door mat, presumably the constable returning from her investigation of my stepmother's outbuildings. The woman hovered at the sitting room door and Mansfield stood up to go speak to her, their voices too low to make out the words. I swivelled to face the detective.

'I don't understand, why—' I asked.

'Do you have a contact number for your sister?' Harding said, ignoring me.

I looked at Craig. He raised his eyebrows.

I nodded to the detective, then shook my head. 'I did, but it was in my phone and I lost it two weeks ago at Carsington Water.'

'Ah, Carsington,' drawled the detective. There was an expression of amusement in his eyes. 'Yes, we heard about that.'

I squirmed in my seat. I felt embarrassed now, as if I was some foolhardy woman who'd strayed from the path, like one of those stupid woolly sheep.

'I do have a Skype address though.' I spelt it out for them. More scribbling.

'Thank you, we'll try that.'

'Is there anything else?' Craig was leaning forward, about to get up.

DI Harding sat back and observed him, making it clear he wasn't ready to go anywhere yet.

'Yes, we've found evidence of three substantial payments recently coming into Angus McCready's personal bank account. Would you have any knowledge of these?'

Craig exchanged another look with me, his eyes widening.

'Why would I have any knowledge of that? Angus owed me twenty grand for work I'd done for him, kitchen installations, as I've already told you. If I'd known he had the money, I would have been very interested.'

'This wasn't in his business account. I know you've already

mentioned that sum to my colleagues. No, this money arrived in three different batches during December, from a private account to his *personal* account. We're still trying to trace it.'

'I'm sorry, but I've no idea where that's come from. Is there anything else?'

Craig stood up, clearly indicating the meeting was over.

'Hmmm.' DI Harding paused. 'Yes, one more thing. Am I right in believing that you and Stephanie Crowther are married, Mr Atherton?'

Shock riveted through my body. I felt the blood rush to my head and I couldn't see. The shape of the policeman shimmered in and out of focus. My head swung towards Craig as if in slow motion and I saw him look from me to the detective. For a moment Craig's face was one of unbridled fury, then it changed to one of schooled restraint.

Craig nodded. 'Yes, that's correct.' Each word was bitingly precise.

My eyes were caught by Craig's. I felt as if I was drowning. I could scarcely take in what came next.

'But she didn't take your name when you married?' Harding was watching me now, not Craig.

'No, no she didn't.' I could hear the anger rising in Craig's voice.

'Thank you, Mr Atherton, Miss Crowther.' Harding nodded at me and finally stood up. 'I think we've covered everything for now. Once again, thank you for your cooperation.'

The sergeant snapped his notebook shut and stood up too. DI Harding reached down to pet Patsy.

'You have a lovely dog, there, Miss Crowther.'

'She was Elizabeth's.' My voice was scarcely audible.

'Ah, of course. You have inherited her too.' Harding smiled.

He looked directly at me then. Our eyes met briefly. My body swayed and I hugged my arms. I didn't know what to make of his expression.

Was it pity, or something else?

CHAPTER 46

I was standing up, facing Craig in the hall. He was between me and the front door.

'You and Steph are *married*?' The raw pain in my voice almost frightened me.

'Caro.' His voice was soft, his eyes holding mine. 'It's not what you think.'

'Not what I think? I want you to leave, right now!'

'I'm not going anywhere, Caro. We need to talk. You need to listen to me.'

I took a step backwards. My world was crashing down around me and he was about to try and talk me out of it?

'Get out!' My voice was louder – more confident. 'Get OUT!'

I was thinking of Paul. Craig was no better than Paul – maybe worse. Humiliation and searing pain rained down on me. He stared at me then, as if working out what to say, holding his hands in front of him.

'I will go, Caro. I promise. But first you have to listen to me.'

He'd gone. I was calmer now, sitting on the edge of the armchair in the sitting room. There was still an indent in the cushions on the sofa where Craig had sat.

He'd told me how they were separated, in the process of getting a divorce. How they'd met after he'd moved back to Larkstone. She'd started visiting her mother again, he'd said, and I'd winced – when had Steph started seeing Elizabeth? She'd been ill, keen to reconnect with her daughter, and Craig and Steph had started dating. Steph moved in with him, they married. But after a while, their differences had begun to emerge. Steph missed her career and it turned out they couldn't have children; the strain tore them apart. And Steph kept falling out with Elizabeth. That bit sounded familiar. Steph left him, returning to London.

London? I didn't understand – she'd been Skyping me from New York, hadn't she? She'd lived there for six years. No, Craig said. She'd always been in London.

So many lies, one piling up after another, the way that lies do.

'I don't believe you! You've been lying to me all along!' I'd said. 'I saw you fighting with Angus at the village hall – after the Wassail. Why didn't you tell me about that then?'

My voice had risen to a tone of desperation. As if I still wanted him to deny it all, to have a plausible explanation for everything.

'I . . . I couldn't,' Craig replied. He seemed temporarily confused, as if he was taken aback to realise I'd seen him and Angus fighting.

'She *was* in London. At least up until the funeral. Then Angus told me otherwise, that night at the Wassail.'

Angus – what had Angus got to do with Steph? Craig had sighed, as if finally giving way to the truth.

'She's been here in Derbyshire since then, more or less. That night at the car park, Angus told me he'd been sleeping with her. She can do whatever she likes, I don't love her any more. She's free and the divorce is almost done. But Angus threatened to tell you about me and Steph.'

Slowly, I was beginning to understand. The fight with Angus, why Craig had kept it quiet. Why all that time, when he knew that Steph was in the UK, he'd never told me. He couldn't let on without revealing their relationship. And she had colluded with him – why? I remembered that Skype call on Christmas Day, she'd been so off with me, scowling when she saw Craig at my side. She must have been consumed by jealousy. Did she still have feelings for him?

'I still don't get why you didn't tell me you had Elizabeth's car when we first met.'

'I'm sorry, but it's like I said, it just didn't occur to me. Steph had every right to take the car, so I didn't question it. And then you and I got together. My relationship with Steph wasn't something I wanted to go in to. Not yet.'

'But earlier you told me it was stolen.'

'I know. I did try to tell you about Steph, but by then, well, you distracted me.' He'd tried a smile, but I wasn't buying it.

Why tell me she was in New York? Had she and Angus really been lovers? Suddenly the car thing made sense – and the key. Hadn't that hill been one of Steph's old romantic haunts? Had she driven Elizabeth's car to Alton Heights to meet with Angus? I'd assumed the key had fallen from Angus's

331

pocket. But what if Steph had had a key to her mother's house? Wouldn't that make more sense? I felt the questions swamp me.

And all the time, Craig's demeanour had been so sincere, like he expected me to believe him.

'You and me,' he'd said. 'This is real, Caro!'

He *hoped* I would believe him. I felt shame wash over me as I recognised my own desire to be convinced, the way I remembered his body, the way I wanted this to all be okay. In spite of everything I'd experienced with Paul.

Craig had gone. Promising to let me be. Promising to talk again later. But warning me to stay away from Steph.

'I don't know why she's told you she's in New York. And I don't know why she's still here in Derbyshire or what's been going on with her and Angus. But I don't want you anywhere near her, you understand me? Don't contact her!'

He was already acting as if it had all been forgotten, his complete failure to tell me he was married. To my sister.

CHAPTER 47

'Hi Steph, it's Caro.'

She could see me on the screen, but I still said my name as if we were on the phone. *Don't contact Steph*, Craig had said as he left. What right did he have to tell me what to do? It had taken a couple of goes to get hold of her.

'Hiya, Sis!'

She sounded cheerful and apparently unaware of the tension in my face, or the hands that were clenched to my side. I held myself back, hoping this meant my features were out of focus.

'Listen, aren't we due to meet up with the lawyer this week?' I said.

'Oh yes, of course, I've got a flight booked for tomorrow. I hadn't forgotten!'

How easily she lied, the words as smooth as her perfect air hostess make-up. I clocked the clear, flawless skin and the delicate line of Steph's lips. Now I thought about it, I could see Elizabeth in those lips, her cheekbones, even her hands, the way they moved and the immaculate nails. My nails were always chewed to bits. When I was little, I think I had secretly envied her sense of style, her ability to do hair and make-up and look good. *Just like Elizabeth.*

'So, when will you be in Derby?' I tracked her face, watching her eyes flash with empty charm.

'Oh, I should think by Wednesday afternoon; I'll be knackered though. The appointment's on Thursday at eleven am, isn't it?'

'Yes.'

'That's okay then. I've booked a hotel in the city centre.'

'Don't you want to come and stay at the house with me?'

Could I even contemplate that? But I knew what her reply would be.

'Oh, I don't need to do that . . .'

That seemed an odd way of phrasing it.

'. . . I'll just want to crash out that first night. My hotel's opposite the solicitors so I can roll out of bed and get there without any bother.'

'Okay, if that's what you want.'

'But I'd love to come to the house for lunch, see the old place and have a chat, if that's okay? After the papers have all been signed.'

'Of course it is,' I said. I swallowed. I knew I had to do this. 'It would be good to talk. I'm looking forward to seeing you again. I'll drive you, so don't worry about a car.'

It was hard keeping the irony from my voice.

I'd been peering at the picture, looking for clues as to where she might be. I'd thought her kitchen, with its country wood panels and muted colour, was a nod to her Derbyshire roots, but now I realised with a jolt, it *was* a Derbyshire kitchen – all oak cabinets and iron handles. Now I was looking for it, it was obvious. How could I have been that naïve?

'Listen, Caro, you were asking about Danny and I suggested you go to see Sarah Chandler, last time we spoke, remember?'

My twisted enjoyment began to fade. I let the bitterness wash over me.

'Yes?' I replied.

'Did you –' her voice was saccharine-sweet '– speak to her?'

'I'm not sure what you mean?' I said, playing for time.

'Oh, come on, Caro, I think you do!' Her voice shifted a gear.

'Yes,' I said.

'Good.' She gave a strange kind of laugh. 'I look forward to seeing you again very soon!'

After she had gone, I sat there motionless. I could scarcely believe the lies of the last few months, the sheer hypocrisy of Steph's words, her pretence – to what end? I had a feeling that on Thursday I would find out.

I knew the painting I would do for her – the Christmas gift for my sister. The idea had come to me in that call with her. I knew too that I couldn't resolve this thing between me and Steph via Skype, or in some meeting in front of a lawyer. It would have to be face to face. Just her and me. Here at this house.

Steph – all these weeks and I'd been so blind.

Didn't I know, as an artist, that we see what we want to see, not what is actually there?

CHAPTER 48

It was the afternoon and I was in the Co-op, having just paid for a bottle of milk. Mary Beth tapped me on the shoulder.

'Caro! How lovely to see you. How are you feeling?'

She was wearing a tweed jacket, pinched in at the waist, and a pair of well-rounded jeans topped by a yellow jumper under her jacket. She looked a bit like a miniature egg timer. I drew a breath, very aware of the people around us.

'Hi, Mary Beth. I'm fine, thank you. And you? Getting settled in at the house?'

'Oh, I've been settled in for a while. Got the plans drawn up for the kitchen and been thinking about how to install a kiln in the back garden.' Mary Beth's eyes lit up.

'Ah yes, of course.' This was a safe topic. 'Where do you get one of those from?'

'The internet, my dear, you can get almost anything over the internet.'

She made it sound like an illicit black-market item, pottery kilns on the dark web. I smiled half-heartedly.

'I'll need a builder to install it properly,' she continued. 'It's going in that shed but there are adjustments to make first. I can't wait to get started on my pots again!'

She chatted on. I must have seemed distracted because Mary Beth was frowning as I left. But the truth was I felt as if someone had just thumped me in the chest.

I'll need a builder . . . I'd been so stupid!

When I got home, I threw the milk onto the table and retrieved the key I'd found beside Angus's body. I had no real justification for thinking it was Steph's. It could have been Angus's after all. Elizabeth had recently employed a builder – that brand new en suite of hers with its fresh mastic and unfinished tiling. Then there were Angus's money troubles. Had he taken to his old work as a jobbing builder to breach the gap in his finances? Was that the money the police had spoken of? Extra work, bypassing his business to avoid his creditors. Had Angus been working for *Elizabeth*?

I could imagine her lady-of-the-manor voice.

'You might as well have a house key, Angus. Then you can come and go as you please when I'm out and about. Get the job done more quickly.'

It was easy to check. I jumped up and rummaged in the box of papers I'd left in the hallway, stuff from Elizabeth's bureau. It was still there, her diary. I thumbed the dates searching for the week of Elizabeth's death. The date jumped out at me: 18th October.

I hadn't twigged when I was researching the family's birth and death details on the internet – that the date of Elizabeth's death was the very same as Danny's.

And yes, there it was, an elegant spider scrawl in blue ink, an arrow marking up the entire week: *McCready Builders – bathroom.* Angus *had* been there. In that exact week, the very same week at the end of which Elizabeth had died.

These dates – they couldn't just be coincidence.

First Elizabeth and now Angus McCready. Two funerals within three months of each other.

I hung back as the funeral cortege arrived, watching the family gathered round the coffin. The police liaison officer had rung me to check if I wanted to go. After all, I had found his body.

The family filled the front two rows of the village church, a solemn group in black and grey. The vicar took his place at the front. Virtually the whole village had turned up and we sat down to a hushed chorus of shuffling feet and discreet coughs. I looked but there was no sign of Craig. I'd refused to see or speak to him since that day I'd discovered he was married.

But Mary Beth was there. She rustled in to the seat beside me, wearing an outlandish black taffeta blouse and tapered trousers. Her short hair was spiked up with a black fascinator perched on the top. She looked like something out of a 1980s pop video.

'Thanks for saving me a seat, hun,' she whispered.

I nodded, unwilling to admit that the space was more due to the fact no one else had wanted to sit next to me. An expectant silence fell.

As the service began, I looked at the plain oak coffin, the modest flowers and the grieving family. I watched as they stood in prayer. Perhaps they thought it *was* suicide, their beloved son suffering depression. How much had the police told them? Only the presence of that car possibly indicated otherwise; and the key, the one I'd unwittingly removed from the investigation. I felt doubly guilty. That key bothered me even more now.

The organ began, a subdued grandeur of sound that filled the church. It jolted me, its drone like that of the pear drum. It thrummed with a sombre vibrancy, each note held a milli-second longer than necessary. We all had to stand for the first hymn.

I twisted round to watch the organist, his arms spread wide as he plucked the stops, slowly stamping on the pedal board with black shiny-clad feet, his fingers holding the notes of each chord as he closed his eyes in concentration. I willed myself to be distracted by the architecture of the church, the brilliant blues of the stained-glass windows and the soaring height of the roof struts overhead. The music halted, leaving only the background hiss of the organ, waiting to launch into the next musical phrase.

Someone walked up to the lectern.

I listened to the words of the reading but they didn't go in. I didn't believe it was suicide. When I'd seen Angus at the Wassail, he hadn't looked like a man suffering from depression – he'd been drinking with friends, enjoying himself. He'd struck me as a vigorous, ugly man, gloating in the pain of others, not weighed down by his own. It must have been an accident, then. Like Elizabeth. Both of them falling to their deaths . . .

No, I had a sudden conviction that was wrong. Angus had been there at the house, the day Elizabeth died. She'd died some time in the morning, that's what Briscoe had said, the coroner had confirmed it. So why hadn't Angus told anyone? Had he been somehow involved? Had he hurt her, killed her? That didn't make sense either, why would he do that?

The groaning music of the organ began again. The congregation stood up. I rose to my feet, opening my hymn book but not actually singing. I surreptitiously looked at the people around me, their heads lifted in song, faces inevitably drawn towards the coffin. Mary Beth belted out the words, quite oblivious to the subdued voices of the family in front of us.

Then it came to me, my heart racing. I felt short of air, the breath sucking from my throat. What if neither death had been an accident?

The book in my hand fell crashing to the floor. The music of the organ rose to a crescendo, then silence fell upon the church.

What if Angus *had* seen something he shouldn't have? The sole witness to Elizabeth's death. Would he have been threatened by the killer and kept silent in fear for his life? Until . . . Panic crippled my thoughts and I gave a strangled moan. I didn't care that there were people all around me, that Mary Beth was watching me horrified. The church, the funeral, the mourners, they all faded from my consciousness. Was *that* why Angus had ended up dead at the bottom of Alton Heights?

I fumbled for my coat, pushing past Mary Beth and the other people on the row. I finally escaped the tangle of their arms and feet and dived towards the back of the church. The great wooden door crashed open, as, gasping, I reached the fresh air, wind whipping through the church banners hanging down the aisle behind me.

CHAPTER 49

The lawyer's offices were on Friar Gate in the city centre of Derby. It was a wide road, of once elegant Victorian residences, but student high-rise housing and a new ring road had left them marooned on an island surrounded on three sides by traffic. I could hear the cars zooming by and the windows shaking as I entered Briscoe's office. It was an old-fashioned room with oak panelling, a solid-looking antique desk at one end and a fireplace at the other.

'Welcome, Miss Crowther, it's lovely to meet you at last.'

Gareth Briscoe extended a firm hand. His waistcoat didn't quite meet under his suit jacket and its broad girth matched the image I'd had of a man in his middle years who enjoyed a few too many long business lunches. I'd clocked the row of trendy wine bars and chic restaurants further down the street.

My eyes were drawn to Steph, in a dark burgundy trouser suit and matching lipstick. She was already settled on a leather

341

sofa beside the fireplace, her heels neatly crossed. She stood up to greet me, reaching out with one arm and planting a delicate kiss on my cheek before sitting down again. I could barely keep myself from leaping back and rubbing her touch from my face.

'Lovely to see you, Caro,' she said, all smiles and sisterly devotion.

Briscoe took the armchair, so I was forced to sit next to Steph.

'Can I offer you a cup of tea, Miss Crowther?'

Briscoe waved at a tray set out on the coffee table between us. A pile of chocolate digestives had started to melt where they were too close to the teapot.

'Thank you, but I'm okay.'

I inched a little forward on the sofa to lean towards Briscoe.

'Can I just say again how very sorry I am for your loss.' Briscoe smiled hesitantly.

'Thank you,' I said, jumping in before Steph. 'I meant to ask before, who was it that found Elizabeth's body?'

I felt Steph's weight shifting on the sofa beside me.

'It was a local farmer, I believe,' replied Briscoe. 'Pete . . . I'm sorry I can't remember his surname. He'd gone to the front door and saw her through the window.'

'Oh.'

I felt my hands clench at my side. I knew exactly who that was: the sheep farmer from over the road. Briscoe straightened his back.

'Now then, I called this meeting as there are some documents you both need to sign. But I do have some news for you too.' Briscoe was looking pleased with himself.

'Oh?' It was Steph.

Briscoe poured a cup of tea with a surprising flourish and passed it to her.

'Indeed. Probate has been granted.'

My sister leaned back on the sofa, silently drinking her tea, her fingers elegantly curved around the cup.

'Which means I'm now free to distribute the estate!'

Steph placed her cup on the table and folded her hands on her lap.

'However, the last time we spoke, Miss Crowther,' Briscoe addressed Steph, 'you indicated that you wished to refuse your share of the inheritance?'

'I did, but I've changed my mind.'

My head whipped round to face her.

'I don't understand,' I said.

Her eyes didn't quite meet mine. 'My circumstances have changed.' She picked up her tea again and the cup rattled on its saucer.

What the . . . ?

Briscoe sat forward in his seat, looking a little flustered. He carried on.

'Well, that's absolutely your prerogative and as your advisor I wouldn't have recommended that you sacrifice your share, anyway.'

He looked from me to Steph and me again.

'It was, after all, what your father intended. That the two of you should benefit jointly from the estate. The house and cottage will have to go up for sale, I'm afraid. Unless one of you buys the other out, or the two of you choose to live there together?'

He looked at each of us once more, but both Steph and I refused to respond.

'In the meantime, after you've both signed these forms, I can arrange for the funds in your father's investments to be liquidated. They are very considerable, as you know, and it's a complicated process. I'd like to get it started.'

It was then that I noticed the thick file on the coffee table between us.

'Very considerable? I don't understand.' I looked back at Steph.

I knew there had been some investments, but neither Briscoe nor Steph had given me to believe they were 'very considerable'.

Steph's face was deadpan. I felt a wave of nausea wash over me. Another lie? Albeit one by omission. Presumably it hadn't occurred to Briscoe I didn't know, that Steph hadn't shared that bit of information with me. He looked uncertain, turning to face me.

'My apologies, Miss Crowther, I thought we had spoken about it. Your father was a wealthy man and a careful investor, he left several capital investment funds which have done extremely well over the years, the income of which was taken by your stepmother whilst she was alive. But now the capital passes to the estate. That, together with the value of the house, land and Lavender Cottage, all comes to a very large sum.'

'How much?' asked Steph.

The two of us looked at Briscoe. He lifted up the file with a calculator tucked inside, pushing a pair of glasses onto his nose.

'Let me see, after all debts, fees and expenses . . .'

His fingers tapped on the calculator. He rifled through the papers before giving a sigh and reading out the number.

'Two million, six hundred and seventy-six thousand and ninety-eight pounds and thirty-two pence.'

He peered over his glasses.

'Each.'

We drove in silence through the countryside. Steph was looking out of the car window and my hands gripped the steering wheel with an intensity that hurt. I tried hard to focus on the road, but all I could think of was that number.

£2,676,098. And thirty-two pence.

I shook my head, still unable to process that we were talking about that amount of money each.

No wonder Steph had decided not to give it up after all. Had she known already? Before the meeting? If she'd been in Derbyshire all this time, had she also been in the house, before I'd arrived, at the same time as she'd been to see Craig? Had she gone through the papers and taken away anything about investments? I hadn't found anything about any investments. When Briscoe mentioned them to me in his first call after I'd arrived at the house, I hadn't thought to ask much more about them.

I felt the same stab of betrayal I'd felt at Briscoe's offices as she'd announced her change of heart. What else had she kept from me? A part of me, I realised, had hoped that all my suspicions were wrong, even knowing what I now knew about Steph.

My circumstances have changed, she'd said. I threw her another glance, but she was still looking out of the window.

We approached Ashbourne along the dual carriageway to a large roundabout where the road veered off to wind through the town.

'Did you know?' I said.

'Not exactly, but I had an idea.'

She sounded empty, emotionless. Perhaps the exact number had shocked her too. I braked at a set of traffic lights and we waited for them to change.

'But you knew it was a large sum?'

She nodded.

'Why didn't you tell me? Why did you say you were going to give it up? What did you mean by that?'

'You can have the house if you want. You can buy me out with your share of the cash from the investments.'

She tossed me a glance, almost a sneer, as if recalling Briscoe's brief suggestion that we live together. Then she seemed to remember herself and turned to look out of the window once more.

'I'm looking forward to our lunch,' she said. 'And seeing the old house.' Her voice was once more all sweetness and light.

My head was bursting with questions, accusations, fury, but as I drove, hands gripping the wheel, trying to control my feelings, I didn't dare start that conversation – not yet. It needed a private space, and not when I was driving.

The car was moving again. I negotiated the narrow roads through the centre of Ashbourne, along the cobbled section and past the market square where I was able to speed up. I accelerated up the hill out into the countryside and onto the road to Larkstone.

The fields were green and damp, the sky bright with sunlight reflecting on the road, making it difficult to see. I had to raise my hand, holding it against my eyes as the sun blinded me. The car swerved, then I had it back under control and I fell silent as I concentrated on the road. Briscoe's answer to my question as to who found Elizabeth's body also rumbled in my head. Not Angus. What did that mean?

We drove through the village of Larkstone, slowing down as we passed along the High Street, with the Co-op on one side and the butcher's and the pub on the other. It was quiet inside the butcher's. A fresh brace of pheasant hung in the window, their beaks dully open, their wings partly extended, sad pathetic things despite their glorious feathers.

I had to stop at the corner by the church, where someone had started to cross the road. Steph and I were ignoring each other. It was a few seconds before I realised the pedestrian was Mary Beth, in her favourite long coat and another of her exotic hats. She wasn't a fast walker, and I saw Steph grit her teeth as we waited.

Mary Beth had followed me from the church, after I'd run out at the funeral. We'd sat on a bench and she'd held me gently, one arm across my shoulder.

'Do you want to tell me about it?' She'd said, her voice quiet, but earnest.

For a moment I'd thought she'd known, about everything. It was as if I hoped she knew, for then it would all be so much easier. My guilt, the truth – whatever it was – out there for all to see. Everything resolved, forgiven. My tongue had cleaved to the roof of my mouth and I looked at her almost begging her to understand, then shook my head. She'd patted my hand.

'It's okay,' she'd said. 'I'm there if you need me, Caro, just remember that.'

The words repeated in my head as I watched her cross the road. As she reached the other side, she turned around, suddenly recognising me in the car. She smiled and waved at me cheerfully. I didn't respond. She looked surprised. Offended maybe? I didn't care, I was too preoccupied. She frowned as I accelerated off and away down the street. I pulled my eyes from the rear-view mirror and quashed another pang of guilt.

I parked outside the house in my usual spot, swinging my body out of the car to open the front door. A car door slammed shut and I felt Steph walking behind me. I'd moved into the hall, Steph beside me, when I heard footsteps on the gravel outside.

'Hi, Steph.'

It was Craig. His frame filled the entrance.

I looked at him in surprise. We hadn't spoken since that day of the police visit and I hadn't been expecting him. Seeing him here with Steph was a shock. I felt a stab of latent jealousy. Had they talked? Had he known she would be here? I looked for Patsy behind him but she wasn't there.

Steph ran up to Craig, flinging her arms about his neck.

'It's over five million!'

She was grinning. My stomach gave a sickening lurch. She was embracing him as if she had the right. And Craig was letting her.

Five million was the total for both of us. Why would she be telling Craig that? I looked at them, a sweep of hatred for Steph engulfing me. Craig reached up to peel her hands from his neck, the pair of them turning to face me. Steph was still beaming; Craig's own face was like stone.

'Dear Caro,' Steph said. 'Did you really believe him? Did you really think he was yours, even after he told you about our marriage?'

I looked from Steph to Craig again.

'I don't understand. I thought . . .'

'You thought we had separated?' There was a laugh in Steph's voice.

I stared at Craig. At the new coldness in his eyes.

I stared again at Steph. Her skin was shining in the dim light of the hall, her eyes like narrow slits, her tongue running briefly across her lips.

She laughed at me then, that same nasty, foul kind of laugh I knew from before, a look of triumph spreading on her face.

The old Steph. The true Steph.

Who had never really been my sister.

CHAPTER 50

The blood must have drained from my face. I felt faint, a fist of nausea welling in my stomach.

'I . . . I don't understand. What's going on?'

Dawning washed over me, like a freezing blade of steel had slipped into my chest to lodge between my ribs, its glacial fragments splintering throughout my body.

Steph stood in front of me in her designer trouser suit, dark red lips flashing.

'Did you open it, Caro? Did you open the pear drum?'

My hands felt for the car keys in my pocket and I turned to leave. But Craig reached out, grasping my arm and holding me firm.

'Where are you going, Caro?' His voice was hard, his eyes warning me.

I tried to pull away but his fingers tightened and he moved to block the door. I jerked my arm upward, trying to break

350

free from Craig, but his other hand reached out, holding me fast so that I was facing Steph.

'Do you really think I've been to all this trouble just to let you walk out?' Steph's eyes narrowed, she seemed taller than I remembered.

I struggled to free my arms but Craig was too strong. I tipped back to gaze at him, desperation and uncertainty clouding my eyes.

'Craig . . . what's going on? Are you . . . are you with *her*?' I could scarcely speak.

He didn't reply. He gripped my arm tighter. Another warning?

'Of course we're still together!' Steph's voice rose. 'We've always been together. I needed him to help you remember. And you're no better than your mother, fucking someone else's husband!'

I looked up at Craig, but he didn't meet my eyes.

'This is the end of the road, Caro.' Steph spoke again. 'You took my brother's life. You made my mother hate me. You ruined my life! Now it's my turn – to make you suffer as I did, to take your life from you!'

I could scarcely believe what she was saying.

Except she was right, wasn't she? I had killed our brother – *her* brother – and if Elizabeth had hated her, wasn't that my fault, just like she'd said?

Five million pounds, she'd told Craig – double her share.

'That was her money, not yours.' Steph knew what I was thinking. She meant Elizabeth of course. 'You were nothing more than a bastard child, foisted upon our family.'

'If you want the money, the house – you can have it! I never expected a thing!'

'Do you think I care about the money?' Steph spat the words. 'It's about so much more than *money*, Caro.'

Her face was contorted, pure rage twisting her features into a parody of her face.

'Oh, I'll take the money – all of the money. Because it's *mine*. I'm entitled to it. But you be sure now, Caro, to understand that this is not about the money!' Her voice deepened. 'So tell me, did you open the pear drum?'

She didn't wait for my reply.

'Elizabeth was very clever, wasn't she! She couldn't hurt you, she couldn't punish you, not properly, after Danny died. There were too many people watching us, the family, the psychiatrist, the social workers, the village even. And we were forbidden to remind you exactly what you'd done in case *you were even more traumatised*!'

Her voice shook with virulent scorn.

'*Hah!* She had to be clever. So she told you that story, worked on your conscience, building an image of your wickedness for all to see! And you soaked it all up like a sponge, didn't you – you loved your stories! But she took it out on me too. She never forgave me. I was supposed to be babysitting you both, but I was on the phone, talking to my boyfriend. When I got to the summerhouse, it was too late. She hated me after that.'

Steph's voice faltered. I saw her pain. It was true: the day Danny died, Steph's life had fallen apart. Because Elizabeth had blamed Steph every bit as much as she did me.

'I've waited a very long time for this – for you to remember,' Steph continued. 'Where do you think your latest commission came from?'

What was she talking about now? *The Pear Drum and Other*

Dark Tales from the Nursery? Cuillin Books – was that *her?* *Steph* had commissioned my illustrations for the book?

'Got it yet, have you? I chose the stories – with *The Pear Drum* at the top, of course. Elizabeth had you round her little finger with *The Pear Drum*. It used to make me laugh, to see how scared of it you were. Did you open it, Caro, did you finally open the pear drum? I knew it would work.'

My realisation grew. She'd planned it all right from the start. The commission, persuading me to return home to Larkstone, then somehow planting the clues, the tricks, the clacking window and strange noises, the rat in the attic and on my bed, moving the pear drum downstairs – whatever it took to freak me out, to soften me up, to make me remember. The photo of Danny in the garden, the one ripped in half – had she arranged for me to 'find' that too? In amongst the photos of my mum, hidden in Dad's old study? She would have known they'd be hard to resist. Had she found them when she moved the crate with the pear drum to the attic?

And the stories – each of them carefully chosen to prod my memory, mirroring my family circumstances, unravelling my buried sense of guilt until I opened the pear drum. Had she known what was inside? Had she put the letter there herself?

All the time Steph had said she was in New York, she'd been in Derbyshire, watching me, pulling the strings, pressing my buttons . . .

My eyes flew to Craig, my face a mute plea for help, a way to understand what was going on. But his fingers around my arms gripped like steel and his features were expressionless.

'Don't think that he's going to help you!' Steph nodded

towards Craig. 'It was never real, you and him. He was using you, just like I was.'

What did she mean? But I knew what she meant – that he'd been a means to report back, to manipulate my reactions, to torment me on my journey to remembering. Steph was watching me with glee, loving every moment of my doubt. Her cruelty took my breath away. I'd lost my sister again, and now I'd lost Craig too. I felt the truth of it shoot through me.

I struggled against Craig's hold. I tried to kick and bite, but he swung me up against the hall table, the glass bowl sliding off the edge. Pain crunched into my body and I saw the bowl crash onto the ground, splintering into three jagged pieces. I screamed. Suddenly my night terrors were coming back to life, the falling glass in the summerhouse, my nostrils filled with the earthy stench of Danny's blood, the taste of bile fresh in my mouth, Danny's eyes flaring as they flew from the spike in his chest to my empty hand, my fingers splayed and shaking, my mouth wide open.

'You killed my brother!' Steph screamed. 'Now it's your turn!'

'No! Steph, no!' I could scarcely take in what she was saying. 'You're not a murderer! You couldn't kill me!'

'You think not? Think about it, Caro. Carsington.'

Carsington? What did she know about Carsington? I tried to picture it. There had been no one, just me and my own stupidity . . . and the runner beckoning in the fog. I'd thought it was to help me. My head flew up. Steph was grinning now, enjoying my confusion.

The runner had been Steph, pointing to the lake, sending me in the wrong direction. Had Craig told her where I was?

And she'd decided to follow me. Why? Because she was obsessed? What had been her plan? Had she even had a plan?

'Penny dropped yet, *sister*?'

Then the fog had descended upon us and she'd seen her opportunity, to send me to my death in the lake. Had she really meant for me to die?

'I've waited a very long time for this, believe me. I almost messed up that day. It was too tempting, you were such a fool!' Steph's voice was ice cold now.

I had lived. Craig had called for help and I'd lived. My head swung back to Craig. Why had he done that? His face was impassive, his fingers digging into my arms.

'But why – why now? If you were going to kill me, why not earlier? Months ago? Years ago, even?'

I urgently racked my brain. Had my memory loss protected me in more ways than one? Or had Elizabeth's death somehow been the trigger? I didn't understand. I couldn't believe what was happening.

Then my eyes swung back to Steph. Elizabeth. Suddenly I knew, from the gleam in Steph's eye to the excited pout of her lips. It had been *her*. Steph had killed Elizabeth!

She'd seen my recognition. She looked up at the stairwell over our heads.

'People don't just fall over a banister, do they? Not without a little help!'

Oh God, what was she saying?

'She was standing right there, by the rail.' She nodded. 'All it took was one little push.'

'The police said it was an accident.' I willed my voice to be steady. Perhaps I could talk her out of this.

'No,' replied Steph. 'It was no more an accident than your *accident* with Danny!'

She seemed to want me to know what she was capable of.

'I went to see Elizabeth that morning. She'd been ill a long time – did you know that? I'd thought, why don't we talk properly, the two of us, on our own? I wanted to tell her how I felt, how much I'd loved Danny too, and her. She never seemed to understand that. It was always about him, her son.'

I could hear the anguish in Steph's voice.

'But it all went wrong. She'd been remembering, drinking, drowning her grief. Instead of welcoming me, she screamed abuse from the stairs outside her room. *You killed him too*, she kept saying. *You killed him too!* I loved her – I swear, I loved her. After I married Craig, I thought maybe she'd start to love me again. She had a soft spot for Craig. But she turned her back on me. She chose Danny, her dead child, over me, her living one. She deserved to die.'

She sucked in her breath and lowered her voice.

'There was a toolbox left at the bottom of the stairs in the hallway. I picked up a spanner and threw it at her head. It missed. There was a hammer too but she swayed backwards and it bounced off the banister.'

The splinter in the wood – was that how it happened? Horror at her own act seemed to momentarily flit across Steph's face. Then she was herself again, fury spitting out the words.

'I raced up to her. She was still shrieking. Then I realised how easy it would be, she was so close to the rail. One push, one solid shove and she fell. The sound of her body broke my heart.'

Those last words were laced with sarcasm.

'That's when I decided. I must have fantasised about it a thousand times over the years, killing you. I just had to wait a little longer, for you to remember, for you to suffer the same torment that I went through, for you to understand *why*.'

CHAPTER 51

Craig dragged me up the stairs, along the landing and up the next flight of stairs, hauling me kicking and yelling but there was no one else to hear – only Steph, following us right to the top. The door to the attic juddered open and Craig thrust me tumbling inside.

'Craig, what are you doing? Please . . .'

'If you have any sense, Caro, shut up.'

The door slammed to and the key cranked in the lock.

I lay sprawled on the steps. My head was numb and I reached up to feel the stickiness of blood on my forehead. I stared at the strip of light under the door, bewilderment flooding me. Had Craig been helping Steph in her plan to make me remember Danny? And her plans to punish me for what I'd done? And now . . . to do *what*?

Angus. All I could think of was that Angus was dead. He *had* been there.

Had he been in the barn, cutting up fitments for the bathroom, or on a break, his van off the drive and out of sight? Had Steph not realised till after she'd killed Elizabeth? He must have seen or heard something. A witness. But he hadn't reported it. Why? And now Angus was dead.

Steph's face loomed large in my head, the venom burning in her eyes. Why had they locked me in here? What were they waiting for? Steph's words rang in my ears. I knew they'd been no idle threat.

I tried to dredge up every memory of Steph that I could think of. To make sense of what I now saw. As I pulled myself up from the floor and crouched against the wall, there was one that bubbled up, a memory I realised was so traumatic, I'd always tried to forget, like the repressed memories of Danny. Hadn't the psychiatrist said that could happen?

Except this one was different, it *had* stayed with me, not as a specific event, but as an overwhelming sense of horror, a strength of emotion that I'd never quite understood, attached to every time Elizabeth had said those words; *Have you been bad enough?*

Jolted by my new awareness of the truth, it came bursting into my head.

I'd told Steph the story of the pear drum. She'd seen Elizabeth taking me to one side that first day, when I was six, in our father's study. It was after Danny's funeral, I knew that now. Steph must have been listening at the door and couldn't pick it all up. So she'd waited till after Elizabeth had finished, until later when I was in my bedroom. She'd asked me what the story was about. She'd laughed when I got to the end.

'Shall we be naughty then, Caro? You and me? Come on!'

There was a gleam in her eye, a flash of something I didn't recognise.

She caught my hand and dragged me down the stairs and out the house, crossing the courtyard towards the two barns. She was twice the size of me, thirteen to my six years, I couldn't fight her. She pushed open the door of the first barn and the smell of sweet stagnant hay assailed me. Bales were piled up in great stacks. The floor of the barn was strewn with more hay and on one side lay an old Belfast sink, brown and thick with grime. On the other side was a stone circular wall, denoting a well. I knew about the well. It was forbidden. A wire grille had been screwed tightly to the top.

Steph let go of my hand and I staggered to a halt. In a corner by the lowest hay bale, there was a pile of sacking. It was moving, small black objects crawling one over the other. I gave a cry of joy and ran over to it.

'Kittens! Is that Tabitha's kittens?'

I stepped towards them, excitement illuminating my face. Tabitha was the farm cat.

'Can I pick one up?'

'Course you can,' said Steph.

She leaned forward, scooping up one small wriggling bundle. She dropped it into my lap. The little thing was still blind, its ears folded back, a small white mark on its front paw. It gave a series of scrawny mews, mouth opening and closing as it sought to be reunited with its mother.

Steph had another one in her hand, its legs dangling beneath, its short damp fur wrinkled under her grasp. She lifted it level with her face, grinning at it and then me.

'Isn't it cute, Caro!'

She waggled the kitten so that its back legs waved back and forth. It mewled painfully.

'Do you remember the story, Caro?'

I looked at her in confusion.

'Turkey and Blue-eyes and the pear drum.'

I nodded.

'What did they do? Do you remember?'

I blinked and nodded again.

'What? Tell me, Caro.'

'They put salt in the stew.'

'And . . . ?'

I hesitated. 'Broke the furniture.'

Steph sighed exaggeratedly, 'Oh come on, Caro, what else?'

I looked at the kitten in her hand.

'They killed the chicken.'

'*And* . . . ?'

'And the kitten.' I lowered my eyes to the floor.

'Come on then.'

She turned away from the sacking, moving across the barn towards the well.

'We don't have to do it like in the story,' she said.

My shoulders slumped in relief.

'But look!' she said, her free hand clasping the metal grille on the well.

Her fingers curled around the thick wires and she jiggled it. The grille held firm. She turned back towards me.

'What do you reckon, Caro, do you think the kitten will pass through the gap?'

The gap in the grille, she meant. Dawning spread over me like a storm cloud rising over the valley.

'Have you been bad enough, Caroline?' She mimicked my stepmother's voice.

I could feel Steph's spite, her hatred – for me or her mother? She wanted to get me into trouble.

'Have you been bad enough, Caro?' she repeated.

Had I been bad enough?

'No!' I said.

I dropped the kitten in my hand back onto the floor. It landed clumsily on its feet and I shooed it away with my palms. It sniffed the air and staggered slowly back towards the sacking. I followed it, shielding it from Steph with my body.

'Oh, come on, why not?' Steph reached out to haul me back.

I started to struggle, pulling this way and that, but Steph's grip was too strong. She forced me round to face the well. She plucked my hand from my chest, thrusting her kitten into my fingers. Her hand closed around mine, holding the kitten in place as she guided it towards the grille.

'How does it go? Let me think . . . *Ding, dong, bell, Pussy's in the well.*'

The kitten began to squirm furiously.

'*Who put her in? Little Johnny Flynn.*'

I screeched, pulling my head away, sobbing against Steph's arm.

'*Who pulled her out? Little Tommy Stout.*'

The kitten's head was between the wire grille, paws scrabbling in thin air. I looked back at Steph, she was teasing me, she wouldn't really . . .

'*What a naughty boy was that, to try to drown poor pussy cat, who never did him any harm but killed all the mice in the farmer's barn.*'

The kitten's body passed through the grille, my hand cold against the updraught.

'You have to let go, Caro. Now, Caro,' Steph hissed in my ear.

I gave a sob, and Steph shook my hand. My little fingers were too small, the kitten too wriggly. My fingers opened.

'What do you think, Caro? Have you been bad enough?'

CHAPTER 52

This was the Steph I knew. The one whose voice instilled me with fear.

Have you been bad enough? That's what my stepmother would say.

But it hadn't just been her. Later, after my stepmother had left me alone, Steph would repeat the very same words, watching my reaction.

Have you been bad enough, Caroline? Followed by that strange kind of laugh.

She'd set me up, with that incident with the kitten. To make sure that Elizabeth's words struck home. Because even though my conscious mind had tried to forget it, my hands would remember, the feeling of the little kitten slipping from my grasp. My lips would quiver, unable to speak, and the tears would come.

Have you been bad enough?

My sister's sweet good-girl voice.

Have you been bad enough, Caro? CARO!

This was the real Steph.

At last I understood the way my own memory had deceived me, like the leaves of an old book, some pages half torn, some re-written with the passage of time, others completely missing. Open to poor interpretation, the reader unable to see the truth behind the words.

I scrambled to my feet, rushing to the door, pulling on it to no effect. I hammered uselessly at the panels, then felt for the light switch. I flicked it on but nothing happened. I tried again, off, on, off, on, but still it failed to work. I hadn't replaced the bulb.

I climbed the steps, surveying the space. It was cold. Empty of all its clutter, there wasn't even a sheet or a blanket to keep me warm. I still had my coat and I pulled it tight about my chest, wrapping my arms around myself.

The dust flew up beneath my feet, flecks dancing in the narrow shafts of afternoon sun, boards creaking in a weird accompaniment to my footsteps. I checked the window. Thanks to my efforts earlier it was jammed shut. It was too high up, anyway, I couldn't possibly climb down and escape that way. Now I found myself facing the only object left in the attic – the crate with the pear drum.

I ran down the steps again, grasping the handle and rattling the door. I thumped it, once, twice, but there was no response. I took a couple of steps back, as much as the space would allow and threw my shoulder against the door. It bloody hurt. I tried again. The door wouldn't budge. My hand opened and closed in anger against the wood but to no avail and I slid back to the ground, dipping my head and nursing my shoulder.

Craig. I understood Steph's motive, at least I thought I did, but Craig – why would he do this? I remembered his loving touch, his gentle kiss, the meaning behind his words. *This is real, Caro.* Just words, to seduce me further. Oh God, I'd been so naïve, falling for my own fairy tale. He'd been the perfect storybook lover, hadn't he? What was he after in all this?

Revenge? No. Love? Why didn't I believe that? Money? Maybe. If he was still married to Steph, he stood to benefit too, just as much as she. Perhaps there was a half-truth in there, about his relationship with Steph, that he'd never loved her either, that she too was a means to an end. His face had been inscrutable in all the time that Steph had been relishing in my defeat. I felt woozy, my head beginning to spin. I couldn't believe any of this.

I must have stayed like that for a few moments, on the floor in the gloom of the steps beyond where the daylight could reach. I could hear noises from downstairs, voices, a door opening and closing. What were they doing?

I thought of Steph's lies about New York. Where *had* she been living? Somewhere nearby for sure. I groaned. Had she been staying with Craig the whole time? Was that why I'd never seen inside his cottage, not once? He'd always come to me, sleeping with me here in *this* house. When Patsy, the dog, had stayed behind at the cottage, had she been with Steph?

I heard a door open downstairs, voices louder and fading away.

'The big one, by the summerhouse . . .' It was Steph, almost hissing.

A door slammed. Were they talking about how they would

kill me? It had to be some way that would seem like an acci-dent, a tragic accident. I felt the blood pounding at my temples, sweat breaking out on my skin. I closed my eyes, unable to process it all. My head sank against the wall. I watched the strip of light under the door, dreading a movement of shadow, footsteps on the stairs, voices getting louder. Craig and Steph coming back for me.

What were they waiting for?

But no, they weren't coming up the stairs. There was the bang of the front door and silence. I rushed to the attic window, peering round as far as I could. Were they leaving? No, they were walking towards the barns. They disappeared inside only to emerge a short while later, now heading towards the back of the house and the garden. Steph was carrying a coil of rope, Craig walking beside her, the two of them deep in conversation.

I froze – the trees, the ones that surrounded the summer-house, the big one that used to have a swing. I watched in disbelief as they disappeared from sight. The rope Steph was carrying had a noose. Oh God, was that their plan to get rid of me? Not an accident but suicide. I thought of the picture I'd painted before Christmas, of myself hanging from a tree. If the police found that, and my body . . . Panic overwhelmed me and I leapt for the door again, rattling at the handle, screaming for help, hammering with my fists until the blood seeped from my skin and I leant my head against the door, sobbing. Who wouldn't believe it after all that I'd done . . .

The flashy one or the *nutcase*.

CHAPTER 53

They were back. I could hear voices once more, drifting up the stairs from the hall far below. My head swayed, the ground heaving beneath my feet. I clutched at the door, trying to hear, struggling to stay calm.

I looked across to the attic window. There must be some way out. The first burst of a crimson sunset bloomed like some exotic cocktail, orange and red quivering over an aqua-blue horizon. I pushed myself onto my feet, moving towards it. My fingers clawed at the window catch but it was no good. I contemplated breaking the glass, but the frame was too small for me to climb through, and to what purpose? To leap from the roof and make their plans for suicide real?

I spun around, my eyes darting from wall to beam to ceiling. There must be another way out. This room didn't cover the whole roof, only the highest section. Most attics were inter-connected. If there was a hatch to the rest of it, if I could

368

escape through some other opening, then maybe I could find a way into the main house. My old bedroom on the floor below had an attic trapdoor.

I'd wasted too much time, brooding on my sister and Craig's betrayal.

I began to feel the walls, groping the rafters with shaking fingers, beneath the tiles, in the corners and behind the beams where the light didn't quite reach. Yes, there *was* a hatch, screwed into place above the floor. I flicked my eyes toward the steps, listening. It was quiet.

I looked at my thumb. It was my longest nail and I slotted it into the first screw. It was a really crap way to undo a screw – even though it wasn't tight, I had to press down hard to get it to move. It was so painful and kept slipping, my thumb bleeding. But eventually it shifted and the screw dropped to the ground. Using the head of the first screw, I freed the next one and a third. They were tighter, the skin on my knuckles shredding, but I carried on. The fourth screw fell into my hand. I licked my lips as the hatch door lifted smoothly away. Propping it up against the wall, I peered into the hole.

Carefully I climbed into the void. I'd thought it would be pitch black but the roof wasn't felted and through the gaps in the tiles came tiny chinks of dying sunlight, like scarlet pinpricks over my head. I inched across the joists, razor-sharp beams of fiery red moving across my body, my arms and legs. I heard something scuttling in the distance and swallowed. The wood was rough, splinters caught in my hands and knees, I was terrified of my weight crashing through the ceiling. Slowly I progressed, exploring with painful fingers for another hatch. At least on the second floor, the rooms below were empty. I couldn't be heard.

Dusk began to fall. My pinprick lights were fading. I hadn't found a thing except an old plastic bottle, a crisp packet and some loose wiring, left behind by a previous builder no doubt. Then I felt a cold draught, a change in depth, a square shape emerging beneath my touch. Excitement bubbled. I traced the edges: no screws this time, thank God, but loose planks of wood resting on a frame. I peeled them off, one by one. Relief flooded my body. I felt the rush of fresh air. One of the planks slipped, I caught it just in time and held my breath, my heart thudding as I waited for a reaction. But there was none. My head hung over the hole, my eyes blinking from the dust as I tried to figure out where I was. Yes! It *was* my old room!

I pulled myself back into the roof. What was I going to do? I had some half-baked idea that I could sneak across the landing and down the stairs, all without either Craig or Steph noticing. Really? I held a hand against my chest, willing my heart to slow its beat, so loud I was sure it could be heard two floors below. The house had a front door and a back door but that was it. Either I got across the main hall and out the front or ducked into the kitchen and round the back. I felt my coat pocket, I still had my car keys. But it seemed so completely impossible either way.

Then I heard something – a car outside revving up the drive, skidding on the gravel. A visitor?

I hesitated – did I drop down now? Into my old room where the window faced the garden? Whoever it was could be in as much danger as me. How did I warn them? Or did I go back to the attic where the window overlooked the drive, where I could see who it was, get their attention, call for help? I wavered in an agony of indecision. Who was it?

I clambered back across the joists as far as I could, through the hatch into the attic. I scrambled to my feet and ran to the window. In the far west, the sky was blazing red, the horizon alive with colour. I gasped. The figure climbing out of the car was Mary Beth.

My hands splayed against the window. She was tugging a woollen hat further over her ears, fishing out her bag, locking the car door. She couldn't see me. Was she a part of this? No, I didn't believe it. That time on the bench outside the church after the funeral, she'd spoken like a true friend, for all that we hadn't known each other long.

I swore as the fear gripped me. She was in danger, interrupting Steph and Craig's plans. Another witness was the last thing they wanted. I hammered on the window, shouting and screaming. But outside she couldn't hear me. Downstairs, Steph and Craig were still ignoring me. Did they know yet about our visitor? Mary Beth moved out of sight and then the doorbell rang.

I flew down the steps to the door to the attic and hammered again.

'Mary Beth! Mary BETH!'

'Caro? Are you there? Are you alright?'

She'd heard me! Her voice sounded distant and confused.

'Get out of there!' I screamed through the door, hammering still. 'Go!'

'Caro?'

Mary Beth's husky voice was followed by a yelp and the crashing of some kind of a struggle.

'NO!' I cried.

I rattled and hammered at the door with all my strength, determined to break through but it held fast. I heard the sound of furniture smashing, the splinter of breaking glass.

Mary Beth screeched in alarm. My heart thudded in my chest, what were they doing to her? What could I do? Anything to distract them, to get one of them to come up here.

My eyes flew to the crate with the pear drum and then to the hatch into the roof void. Maybe?

I ran to the crate and lifted up the lid. I grabbed the pear drum. I dropped to my knees, grasping the handle on the pear drum. It was stiff at first, but then it began to move, sliding round as the fingers of my other hand fumbled with the keys.

I pressed on the first note and a melodic drone began to thrum.

CHAPTER 54

The sound of the pear drum filled the house. Perhaps it was the tension in me that gave it a strange underlying beat, like a real drum, my own heartbeat echoing the tone of the notes.

I kept winding the handle. The volume rose and fell until my chest felt tight and my grip on the handle loosed. I paused to listen below.

The noise in the hall had stopped.

I wound the handle again. The music growing once more. I held my breath, ready to leap the moment I heard footsteps on the stairs. The music mesmerised, a haunting tangle of notes over which I had no control, dust clouding beneath one last flare of crimson daylight. I stopped again.

I stretched my other hand flat against the wooden floorboards. The sun had gone and I was plunged into darkness, the attic lit only by a narrow beam of pale moonlight, the exact same shape as the small window behind me.

The silence was more unnerving than the sound of violence. Was that the scraping of feet? Then I heard another screech of alarm from Mary Beth. Heavy footsteps pounded up the stairs.

Now!

I jumped from the floor, dropping the pear drum with a crash, darting for the open hatchway. I slipped through, only just managing to pull the cover in place behind me as the key jangled in the lock.

I didn't stop to listen. I clung to the joists like a rat on a ship's rope, crawling on my hands and knees. Every second stretched out. The light from the roof holes had gone and I was sure I wouldn't find it, my heart in overdrive as I scrambled to locate the bedroom hatch. There it was, a grey box of light. I swung my legs down into the hole. They were bleeding, the fabric of my trousers torn to shreds. My hands grasped the opening and I fell tumbling to the floor below. I'd planned to roll in my attempt to land safely but my body seemed to crash like a whale into the sea. The pain rocketed up my limbs but I held myself to the floor, listening.

I could hear Craig in the attic. He was calling my name, vibration in his voice. I sprang forward, the bedroom door swinging open as I plunged towards the attic door. The key was still in the lock. Craig was at the top of the wooden steps, his face turning just in time to see me slam the door shut. I cranked the key. I heard his feet thundering down the steps but it was too late. He was locked in.

I spun around.

Steph was at the top of the stairs. She had Mary Beth in front of her. Mary Beth's neck was pulled back and Steph held a chunk of glass to her throat – a piece of the broken bowl.

Mary Beth looked so small, her eyes wide open, leaping towards mine as her feet stumbled on the stairs. Her hands clutched at my sister's arm, scrabbling to loosen her grip. I could hear Craig hammering on the door behind me then a loud thud as he threw his body against it. It held, but only just.

'Let her go, Steph!' I staggered towards her, then stopped. My voice was far more confident than I felt.

My hands waved uselessly as I flung my head around trying to find something to grab hold of. The hall was bereft of any furniture, not even a painting. I felt as if I was back in the summerhouse, reaching out for something to defend myself with. Only this time there was nothing.

'Climb over, Caro!' Steph gestured to the balustrade.

Mary Beth squeaked as Steph adjusted her hold, the glass blade pressing into her skin. Mary Beth stood rigid against her arm.

I held out a hand, rasping as I caught my breath.

'No, please!' I cried. Mary Beth – she hardly knew me yet had been so compassionate.

'Climb over the banister, Caro. Now!' Steph's voice was ragged and wild. When I didn't move, she pushed the glass again, up against Mary Beth's chin. Mary Beth mewed in terror.

I took a step towards the railing.

'Please, Steph, this is crazy. Don't do this.' I was hoarse, snatching great lungfuls of air. 'You don't have to do this. Think of the consequences!'

There was another crash against the attic door. Steph blinked but didn't answer.

There was yet another crash. I heard the attic door splinter at its hinges. Steph had pushed Mary Beth round so that they were both looking down over the railing to the hall below.

'Go on, Caro, climb the banister!'

My feet edged backwards.

'Don't hurt her,' I cried. My eyes swung from Mary Beth to Steph. 'Think of Elizabeth – she *did* love you, I know she did. Don't do this again!'

Mary Beth gasped, her eyes rolling back to try to see Steph, her hand reaching along to grasp at Steph's. They struggled but Steph was stronger. I saw a bead of blood on Mary Beth's neck.

'Just as you loved Danny? You're the murderer here, Caro!'

I saw Mary Beth's eyes switch to mine. There was confusion on her face. I felt a stab as if Steph had taken her blade to me. I closed my eyes momentarily, unwilling to meet the look of incredulity on Mary Beth's face.

This time the crash behind me made the walls shake, the attic door peeling off its frame. Craig was standing there, his face red with effort, his shirt stained with streaks of black dust and blood.

In that moment, Mary Beth twisted her body free. Steph jerked the blade down. There was a sharp squeal from Mary Beth, then nothing. Just a hissing. I swung round to see Mary Beth's eyes wide and staring, her body folding to the floor. And Steph stepping towards me, the bloodied glass in her hand inches from my chest.

Craig grabbed me from behind. I felt his weight throwing me to one side, away from Steph.

He lunged towards Steph. They struggled and she crashed against the handrail. I screamed. Staggering to my feet I dived forward, only to be flung against the wall. Steph reached out for my hair, dragging me up. Craig fought to separate us. But Steph hung onto me and we both grappled against the railing. It shuddered against our bodies. All I could see was the blood pouring from Mary Beth's side, her eyes dull and fading.

I heard an almighty crack. I felt the railings give. My arms flew out against thin air. I was falling. Steph too. Our hands, our fingers snatching in vain. Both of us reaching out for Craig.

CHAPTER 55

I am floating between two worlds, the living and the dead. As I lie here in my hospital bed, the faces shimmer above. I can hear their speech, the machines, the clicks and beeps that mark each breath. They've no idea that I'm awake, that I can hear. My eyes are open but I cannot move. Even my eyes are fixed in one direction. Someone else is lying on this bed, not me.

My sister, my lover, they think that I am dead. Except I am not dead.

I drift in and out of consciousness. Most days I can see the window so I know that time is passing, the sun blazing in my eyes, the stars pricking the midnight blue. I watch the clouds, the speed at which they cruise the sky, their shapes constantly changing, each one a new story to distract me – the black swans flying in a dark line, the handless girl weeping for her lost innocence, the hare hugging the lover she cannot have. I am haunted by my own creations.

Slowly the stories fade. My memory returns, voices familiar and repugnant. My sister, my lover, they are both at my side. The hospital staff are like white ghosts hovering on the fringes of my sight. Always I hear the machines, the constant whirring and clicking of my heartbeat and lungs, like a slow steam train rolling down the track. That's me, I realise, this cyber patient hooked up to keep me alive. This is to be my punishment.

'I'm sorry, Miss Crowther, there's no sign of consciousness. Sometimes there are signs of life, awareness. And a very small hope of recovery. But in your sister's case, there is none.'

They are wrong, but I can't tell them. The voice is kind, the consultant. He's different when my husband and sister aren't there, clipped and efficient. Now he's almost hesitant. For a moment the words don't go in.

'There are some basic brain stem reflexes but no higher function. She has sustained a severe brain injury. Several bones were broken in the fall, including her neck, but the trauma to her head is what we're dealing with. We can keep her alive, as you see, observe a little longer, but we've reached a point where really a decision has to be made.'

A decision. Isn't he going to spell it out? He sounds sympathetic, a man who regrets this information. He knows the outcome. I feel detached; this isn't me they're talking about.

'Caro?' The voice is my husband's.

I feel my heartbeat falter. The machine beside me gives a skip. Craig. I can't think of him without rage fizzing in my head. When we both tipped over the banister, he saved *Caro*, not me.

The fucking bastard saved *her*!

I want to spit in his face, to tear the skin from his cheeks.

The noise of the machine skips again, rattling like drums in a carnival. I imagine the doctor frowning, reaching out to adjust the equipment, the monitor returns to a steady beat.

'Yes.' Caro speaks.

She moves slowly across the room with her wild hair like a cloud about her face. She never did look after herself. But she's fine, absolutely, bloody fine.

Craig leans down and I feel his hand against my cheek. Like he *cares*.

'We have to decide,' he says.

His words are like the touch of ice against my ear.

How dare he? He's my husband! And her – Caro. She isn't my sister. Look at her standing there on the fringes of my sight, pretending to be my devoted loyal sister. I won't have her as my sister. She was the cuckoo in our nest. She doesn't have the right.

Caro doesn't reply.

'I'll leave you both for a little while.' The consultant makes to leave.

'How long?' It's Caro, rushing in. 'How long does it take, after . . .'

The consultant hesitates as if deciding how honest to be. 'It depends, Miss Crowther. Steph's on breathing support and medication to maintain her blood pressure. We will of course give her drugs to ensure there's no pain.' His voice softens. 'Usually it's almost immediate. As soon as the respirator is switched off.'

'Will she wake up?'

'No. I'm sorry,' he says. He misunderstands.

'Thank you,' says Caro.

'We'll be outside, if you have any questions.'

There are footsteps, a door closing and he's gone.

'Sit down, Caro.' It's Craig, pulling out a chair. I hear it drag along the floor.

'I still can't believe what she's done . . .'

Caro's voice. How it grates on me.

It's snowing outside. Small white flakes driven by the wind, darting in different directions. Not big enough to settle, like gnats buzzing under a tree on a summer's evening.

'I know,' Craig says. 'But the police are sure. They have forensic evidence from Angus's body, a clump of her hair in his hand. Enough to know what Steph did. He was blackmailing her.'

Craig's voice is almost a growl. I can hear his derision.

'They've tracked the funds in his bank account back to Steph. She'd been paying him to keep quiet. Perhaps he got greedy.'

Ha, yes, Angus helped. He hated Caro almost as much as I – he and Danny had been best mates at school, the two of them always up to mischief. Angus never forgot. And besides that, I told him he had to help us – he owed us a huge sum of money. Until Angus decided *he* would blackmail *me*. I wasn't having that.

But Craig helped so much more! It took a while to persuade him, especially after he found out I'd killed Elizabeth. Too risky, he said. Then I showed him the investment papers. Once he twigged about the inheritance, he was all for it.

'I still don't understand. I really thought that you wanted to kill me, you and Steph both.' Caro's voice is almost tearful.

It gives me some satisfaction at least to hear her pain.

'I told you. I knew she wasn't in New York, but I had no

381

idea what she was really up to. That she and Angus were using Elizabeth's key to access the house and do those things. In all the time I've known Steph and Elizabeth, neither of them ever talked about Danny. Caro, you have to believe me when I say that Steph deceived me too. She was my wife – imagine how I feel about that! I'm so very sorry I didn't tell you about our relationship. I didn't know how to. I fell in love with you so fast, it became impossible to tell you about Steph.'

Lies, so many lies.

'When I realised what was going on,' says Craig. 'I had to play along with it, to delay things till I could figure out how to protect you!'

I would laugh if I could. Oh, Caro! He's lying, can you still not tell?

Craig helped me from the start. He knew exactly where I was – with him at the cottage. He had the spare key Elizabeth gave him – he always was a charmer. He shifted the crate into the attic for me and moved the pear drum that night to freak her out. *He* put the rat in her bed. He even took her to the Wassail so she'd see the apple-bobbing – that one worked a treat. We did it together, Craig and me. We were a team. How convenient it is for him to blame Angus – he can hardly defend himself, can he!

'It wasn't me.' Craig sounds tired.

I can feel the tension. But Caro wants to believe, I can hear it in her voice. I saw the shock on her face when Craig pushed her out of the way, tried to stop us fighting. And then he saved *her*! Like he did at Carsington! I feel my hatred boil over – he kept that quiet, he must have had a backup plan all along. So now she believes him.

'I know how it must have looked when I put you in the

attic. I was terrified for you. She rang me that morning, demanding I come to the house. She was unhinged, I'd never seen her like that. I'd no idea that she'd killed Elizabeth, or Angus. Or that she planned to kill you – until I got there. I had to think on my feet, convince her I was loyal until I figured out what to do. There was no phone signal, I thought you'd be safe in the attic till I could get help. Look what she did to Mary Beth! She was a lunatic! Thank God Mary Beth survived. She was in intensive care for weeks, she was almost killed – that could have been you!'

Oh, he's so convincing! But then, don't we believe what we want to believe? Caro's so in love with him, even now.

I can hear her crying, sobbing her little heart out. Poor Caro. He's holding her, murmuring in her ear, playing it to the hilt. He's very good! He's still after the money. *All* the money. That's what it's been about for him, ever since I showed him the investments. He found a better tactic, dump me and take her. All those visits. He slept with her and *liked* it. I should never have allowed it! He preferred *her*. I should have seen it coming!

It was my own fault. I joked about it before Christmas. Why don't you fuck her? Go all the way? Then she'll follow you around like a lamb and you can do anything you want, make sure she *does* remember. I was getting worried. After all, she'd kept her memories buried so long, there was never any guarantee our plan would work. When he *did* sleep with her, it spiced things up, turned us both on. He said it meant nothing.

He was playing us both!

But Mary Beth? That was my real mistake. He was already rethinking his plans after the police got involved. I see that now. When I stabbed her, he had to choose, to side with me and risk being arrested, or side with Caro and place all the blame on me. I made a huge mistake attacking Mary Beth. How could we possibly explain that? I lost control!

The snow is slowing down, the flakes larger, fatter, clinging to the branches of the tree beyond the window. I feel so cold.

I don't need to kill Caro now – he'll do it for me. When he's ready. Craig knows how to kill. *He* killed Angus, not me. He took Elizabeth's car and pushed Angus over the edge when he wasn't expecting it. Craig must have planted my hair on the corpse just in case. I should have realised he'd have a plan B, he always was a calculating bastard, that's why I loved him. He doesn't have to stick with her once they're married. He can still engineer her 'suicide' or some kind of an accident.

He'll still get her money, *all* the money.

'It doesn't matter any more, Caro. She's gone. Look at her.' Craig touches me again.

Doesn't he remember he loved me once, that he's still my husband?

Caro's chair scrapes on the floor, moving closer. She's stopped crying now. She picks up my hand, holding it as if she cares. Now she's reaching for my head, positioning it to face them both, gazing into my eyes as if searching, hoping that I'm still inside.

Does she know? Has she guessed that I'm still there, that I can hear every word? I know what Caro is capable of. I saw it in her eyes that day at the summerhouse. She's a killer. It's all about losing your inhibition.

Now she's watching me, as I watched her at Elizabeth's funeral.

* * *

I can't see the snowflakes any more. But I can hear them, soft smudges thudding against the window pane, like moths fluttering to their death. I can hear them, even though no one else can. They're filling the glass, each flake merging with another, a wall of thick white snow like the fog that day at Carsington Water.

It's been, what, half an hour? They've been thinking about it, talking about it. Craig's all over Caro, hands touching her shoulders, so caring, so supportive. Not exactly the grieving husband. He's already made his decision. But what about her? What will Caro decide?

'Shall I call them?' Craig says.

Caro nods, still watching me.

He leaves the room and comes back. There are voices. The doors open, a nurse wheels in a trolley. They'd been waiting, as if they all knew which way it would go. There are loads of them now, doctors, nurses. They're muttering, conferring. More people. They're taking notes, readings from the machines, adjusting the drip. Is that how they do these things? Craig holds Caro's hand. She leans back into him. Her gaze on me hasn't wavered once.

Someone pushes the bedside cabinet, placing it closer to me so they can pass. There's not much on it. Just a picture in a frame. Caro gave it to me for Christmas. She must have put it there, an apparent gesture of affection. For the benefit of the staff. It's an odd sort of Christmas present, I heard one of the nurses say. It's a painting. One of *hers*. I can see it now.

For the first time, I feel real fear.

It shows an old, flat gravestone beneath a juniper tree. It's from the story I wrote for Caro. Ivy clings to it like in the summerhouse, fingers crawling into the tree. A boy sits on

385

the grave. He's only young. He holds a pear drum. Is it a boy? Or a girl? As I look at the painting I can hear the music. It grows and fades, grows and fades with each rotation of the handle.

That drone, the vibration, it cuts through the very heart of me, almost sucking me in as it gets louder and louder . . .

'Are you ready, Miss Crowther?'

Caro looks at Craig. He looks at me.

And she speaks.

'*Yes.*'

Author Note

The Pear Drum story is loosely based on 'The New Mother' by Lucy Clifford, a children's story published in her 1882 collection, *The Anyhow Stories, Moral and Otherwise*. This brilliant but disturbing tale has inspired several different literary interpretations and offshoots, and is also popularly retold by oral storytellers. But it caught my imagination because of its description of the pear drum – a colloquial term for a sort of mechanical violin called an *organistrum* (an early medieval musical instrument later reinvented as a *hurdy gurdy*). You can see a wonderfully surreal depiction of a pear drum in the third panel of *The Garden of Earthly Delights*, a late 15th century painting by Hieronymus Bosch. I can't say whether or not Lucy Clifford was familiar with that painting, but Bosch's inclusion of mischievous and devilish 'little people', both tortured by and delighting in the various musical instruments of Hell, could well be connected to the 'little people' referred to in the story. And they do say that the devil has all the best music . . .

Acknowledgements

One autumn, just after moving house to a renovated farm up in the hills of Derbyshire, I woke to mists rolling up against the windows and a pile of unopened packing cases. The place wasn't yet home, and with the boys back at school and no neighbours for at least two fields in all directions, I felt a bit lost and alone. So I dug out my computer, lit the stove and started to write a story. It's such a daunting task writing a book, I don't think I quite realised what I had taken on. But it's been a joyous journey, not least for all the support and help of the following:

Beta readers and fellow writers: Gemma Allen, Fay Saxton, Glenda Gee and Carl McGarrigle. Fellow Doomsbury Group writers: Roz Watkins, Jo Jakeman, Fran Dorricott and Louise Trevatt. Each of you has been amazing, patient, funny and very kind. Artists: Iain McKay and Jenna Catton, for invaluable feedback on the characterisation of Caro.

Coleen Coxon, a colleague and valued friend who read the book in its final stages one snowy weekend and made so many useful and astute observations. Mark Henderson, whose early support and championing of both my writing and oral storytelling has been tremendously encouraging. Giles Abbott – an oral storyteller with a rich, vibrant voice – for generously sharing with me the story of Eostre. Sue and Mark Tyrer for reading, chatting, walks, BBQs and patient ongoing support and encouragement.

Writers/tutors: Alex Davis and Stephen Booth and the teams at Writing East Midlands, Winchester Writers Conference and the York Festival of Writing (who selected my book extract for the Friday Night Live 2017). And in particular all the agents, editors and experts I met over the last few years who gave advice and expressed an interest in my writing – there are some very kind and generous people out there in the publishing industry and writing community.

Special thanks go to the team and judges at the Bath Novel Award 2017, especially Caroline Ambrose (chief organiser), Laura Williams (head judge and now my agent . . .) and Joanna Barnard (who very kindly gave the book a 'golden ticket' for which I'm still very grateful!). This competition was a major turning point on my journey to publication.

Ronald and Irene Draper, who have followed my literary exploits with equal thrill and excitement. Rob Snell, for being a critical sounding board and consistent support throughout the process, even when I had abandoned all pretence at doing my share of the housework, meals and school runs . . . and for chopping wood to stoke my study fire and keep me and the cats warm. Likewise, Ben, Jamie and Jasper, for putting up with my distractions and bringing such warmth and light into my life. Love you all so very, very much.

A special thanks to the team at Avon: my editor Rachel Faulkner-Willcocks, who nudged several new scenes out of me that I now love, publicist Sabah Khan and everyone else who has given me such a warm welcome on my first steps to publication.

And in particular to my agent Laura Williams, her colleagues at Peters, Fraser & Dunlop, and her new colleagues at Greene & Heaton. Laura has been the most patient, editorially incisive, intellectually brilliant and hard-working agent. Thank you so much.

Finally, to all my friends and colleagues in the fabulous oral storytelling community, who help keep all those amazing folk tales, songs and snippets alive, told and retold to each new generation, finding new audiences in an age of multi-media storytelling. I love stories in all their forms!